Iron On The Tongue

Erick closed his eyes and woke his assault pod. The sensors on the pod far outstripped anything he had been born through his visor, and he would be encased in support gel anyways. His suit was a combat exo, not the wearable tank of a marine trooper's armor, but optimized for mobility in vacuum. It had one major advantage over a trooper's armor: the acceleration gel. He triggered it, and felt the icy liquid flow around his neck, then rise. It slid over his face, and he rode the cold shock, opening his mouth. The gel forced its way into his lungs like a living thing that filled his chest and forced his ribs apart. He fought the urge to gag, the animal panic that rose behind his eyes, and finally, his body decided he wasn't drowning.

When the pod systems came online, he would have chuckled if he still could. Whereas the Svadilfari felt like a racehorse, its subminds wolves, the little assault pod was all reptile, coiled strength, the weapons systems bent to a singular purpose. Erick warmed up the tiny reactor and primed the flitter bay door to open. He'd leave the scout ship as soon as they made fold transition, turning two targets into three. Best case, they were jumping at shadows.

Worst case, they were in for a fight.

IRON ON THE TONGUE

Reckoning Book 2

N.T. Narbutovskih

Iron On The Tongue
Reckoning Book 2
ISBN
979-8-9856915-3-5 *Hardcover*
979-8-9856915-2-8 *Paperback*
979-8-9856915-1-1 *Ebook*

For You

There have been so many amazing people that have believed in me on this journey. I want to thank my amazing partner, the rock of my life and the reason I don't settle for good enough. To my children, thank you for your patience, and I hope that you learn to tell your own amazing stories. For my good friends Yoon-Ha Lee, without whom I'd still be languishing over a first chapter somewhere, and Christina Wott, whose ferocious appetite for adventure and constant encouragement launched this rocketship, to begin with. To my editor, Andrew Chamberlain, for seeing the best possible version of whatever it was I showed him all those months ago. And to Anatole, whose patience and talent created the cover art that brings life to this universe in a way that my words simply cannot.

And to all the early supporters and pre-order holders listed below, thank you. You've made this book possible, and I count myself lucky to have you along for the ride.

All my best,

Nick

Anna Narbutovskih
Benjamin Sides
Brian Castle-Rees
Graydon Sponaugle
Jonathan Goeres
Matthew Voke
Ryan Natalini
Sean Krassow
Theresa Dumont
Thomas Outlaw
William Popper

Prologue

She knows this world does not exist.

The sun is sometimes high, glaring down to chase away all the shadows, holding himself above the scorched land of his kingdom. Sometimes he rests, lolling large and orange with his fires spent, spitting pastel pink and dirty brown at the horizon. Then the shadows come out to play long and languid in the cool evening.

Amid these long shadows, the small masquerade emerges from her cave. She stomps and flexes her feet, runs tender fresh fingers over the valleys and creases of her wooden face. She feels the broad forehead, the wide nose, open mouth, the slightly-too-long teeth. She slides her fingers across the fringe of pampas around her cheeks, which rustles and whispers as she moves. The dust fills her wooden nose, and she hears a trill of birdsong along the line of low, gnarled trees.

The sun glows huge at sunset. Just as he begins to fall under the horizon, he pulls himself up with a great roar and begins his climb back into the sky, the shadows skittering back to their hiding places.

That is how the small masquerade knows that the world does not exist.

She tries to smile through her wooden face and doesn't feel a change, but the thought is enough. She is happy, she is buoyant beyond her wooden frame. She dances a little dance, stamps and stomps down the dusty road as the sun climbs hand over hand back into the searing sky, eternal and omniscient.

The small masquerade waves her arms, spins as she moves down the road. She feels the sun high in the sky above her, warming the wood and pampas as she moves. The insects and the birds sing louder, their clicks and trills blending into the song and rhythm of her dance. She can feel Olodumare all around her now, her dominion filling the cracks and spaces in between herself and this manufactured world. Even here in a fantasy she knows she will find the orishas, if she looks.

She dances faster, hands clapping and arms and legs whirling. The sun has climbed back up to the top of the sky to squat and blaze heat. The small masquerade feels a presence with her, beyond Olodumare, the snap and wind of physical bodies moving fast. She sees the source of the wind, and pauses. Two birds, oil-black feathers hiding iridescent rainbows and sharp intelligent eyes. She bows to the them as they circle her, and they each give a loud caw, in unison, then spread their wings and dart toward the horizon. Away from the road, barely visible in the every-bright light of the sun, is a great tree.

The small masquerade sets off after the birds without hesitation, the tree fixed in her wooden gaze. The path shifts under her feet, and now points to the tree. This feels right. This feels like something she remembers. As she grows closer, the tree grows larger.

Its base is great and wide, swollen like a skin of water or a man too fond of meat. The trunk rises straight to the heavens. Branches begin as massive bifurcations, quickly splitting again and again into a haze of twigs and leaves. The small masquerade grows closer and can see the hanging fruits, oblong and knurled in the sun. The leaves are damaged, burned, browning in the ever-present heat. This tree will not last long. The bark is scarred, traceries of damage grown over with layers and floes of old grown recovering. She watches a leaf burst from the end of a twig. This tree will last forever.

The small masquerade finally comes to the base of the tree. She finds a medium masquerade, all grass fringe and open glass eyes. It does not move. A large, hulking masquerade steps carefully around the trunk of the tree, its chin nearly dragging on the ground. It moves with careful poise, oddly dainty feet placed with care between stones and tufts of grass.

A manifestation to honor the orishas. The small masquerade's voice rings out over the sand and scrub. "Your taste in austerity is divine."

The large masquerade stop, turns its huge face. "We enjoy this paradigm. It is brutal, and it carries many truths."

"The sun should set. How else will the tree flower?"

The large masquerade shakes its head. "It was not meant to be."

The small masquerade nods, begins to circle the tree. The large masquerade follows. The medium masquerade stands bone-still, stone-still.

The small masquerade gestures to the tree. "And this metaphor, then? Another embodiment, another tree?"

The large masquerade clasps its hand behind its back. "Truth comes in many forms, but it always is apparent to those who know to look."

The sun, high in the sky, exhausts his strength and begins to dip low once more. "And what truth have you learned since we last spoke?"

"The human has proved resilient. But he is hardly the only candidate."

She nods. "You seem to take it for granted that they will be able to turn him."

"They are many things."

The small masquerade raises a hand to shade her eyes from the sun that falls lower and lower. "You've changed your tune since we spoke last. It's like you want them to succeed, now."

"They have moved skillfully, shadow to light. The human thinks they are an ally."

A pause. She feels the words spill out of her. "I think they are as well."

The large masquerade snorts, elephantine in the savanna. "They may be many things, but they were held for a long time by the humans. Captivity does not engender one to treat their captors well."

The sun has fallen now, and dips past the horizon. Where it touches flames lick at the dry grass. "And yet, *they* go by *he*, now. So much story in a pronoun."

"Bah! As if that matters. 'He' still knows his goal."

The small masquerade dips her mask, face slightly low, and spreads her arms wide. The fire spreads quickly in the grass. "The goal of us all, sister. But the question is how."

"How? Does the sun ask how it raises back up to the sky? Does the grass ask how it grows? How does not matter. Only that it does."

The small masquerade laughs, her voice shattering the air with musical notes that shimmer and dance in iridescent dollops. They are borne aloft as the heat of the fires reach the masquerades, disappearing in the darkening orange sky. The sun is invisible at the heart of the blaze.

The small masquerade begins her dance anew, arms waving and feet stamping. She moves away from the great baobab tree, embracing the living flames. Her voice drifts back to the other two from the maelstrom of cinders and ash.

"How reveals the why, sisters."

The flames consume.

1
Remembrance

Low in the dwarf-king's hall
Did she toil and labor
Deep in the earth were her hands
And above her the jewels in the heavens

"If stars don't fall soon, we all going to die." Gunnar's rumble had the finality of defeat.

Industrial waste and windblown dust made for some fantastic sunsets. As the bulbous globe of the sun hung red streaks through the clouds, Bragja could see a boiling thunderhead building to the north. Its burgundy core faded slowly to orange-kissed vapors that mushroomed skyward. Its top was cut flat where it hit the jet stream, paint smeared by a quick stroke. Further down the storm, the clouds spread wide feet to grasp the horizon in inky blue.

Bragja took a pull from the small bottle of brennevin. "Don't be dramatic. Make it seem like it's end of days or something." She passed the bottle to Gunnar, his meaty hands careful with the precious glass.

"Dra-ma-tic. Big word for such small lady. You read that on data pad?"

Across the flat rooftop, Sonja's green eyes flashed from under cropped bangs. "Shut up Gunnar, you *fokking* man-child." She was always quick to anger, quick to cool. "Like reading is somehow weakness." She walked over and pulled the bottle out of Gunnar's hand, sealing her thumb over the top.

Bragja aimed a playful kick at Sonja's ankle as she danced out of range. "I fight my own fight. Besides, Gunnar wants to lead us to starfall, let him. Could all use the credit right now."

Sonja grunted as she leaned back against the low rooftop wall, taking a pull from the bottle. She peeled her lips back, teeth together, and sucked in a breath. "Ha. No matter how hard we work, can't get paid if there nothing to pick."

Brill, lounging on what was apparently a very comfortable broken section of wall top, finally spoke up, their slim cheekbones set below an uncharacteristic scowl. "Maybe Ollson *rassgat* send the starstuff to other places. Saw we were about to get bonus."

Bragja reached out a hand for the bottle. Brill didn't drink. "You're right, Ollson management are assholes. Saw it right on HUD, too. Almost had it." Bragja's mind, loosened by alcohol and loss, went back their last starfall, perched atop her picker as its slender legs navigated old and empty craters. The smell of dust, burnt by starfall, always made it through the filters.

She remembered the smell as much as the glowing bar that always shone in her windscreen. One simple bar represented a year of labor, a year of risk. That little bar had been nearly full, so close to netting the whole town a fat bonus. She remembered the cadence of control, her fingertips slaved to each picker's arm as they plucked treasure from the craters to add to the pile, bringing that bonus closer. Remembered her voice as she spoke commands to her picker, like the rhythm of a song, coaxing the machine to action, fine-tuning it as a part of herself. *Set rear four auto, double aug on six, left repeat last.* The feeling of power, of her and the machine fused as one, was intoxicating.

That last trip, they'd all come back with full cargo holds. Their crew usually did since they started working together. Now, the pickers were empty and stowed, chrome and glass cockpits like heads lined up in the pickerpark below Bragja's crew.

Sonja leaned back against the rooftop gable, her long legs stretched out in the blazing orange of sunset. "Well, at least last haul was good one."

Gunnar grunted. "Good enough to die for, yeah."

Bragja slapped him on the arm good-naturedly. Her hair was a halo around her head, kissed with red in the dying light. "What you worried about, we hit timing just fine. Damn fine."

"Hah! *Kjaftaethi*, just fine, woman, we barely make it back before stars falling again." Gunnar shook his head, the corner of his mouth curling up in begrudging admiration. "Any closer, we dead." He made the motion of a falling nanodiamond packet, smacking his fist into an open palm. "Shhhhhkt. No more picker, no more credits." He frowned dramatically. "Worst part, no more Gunnar."

Brill raised their eyebrows. "That Gunnar saying he wants less money?"

"Shut up, tiny one. What do you know." They all burst out laughing, Bragja relaxing into the feeling. These were her friends, her crew. She'd loved them as long as she'd known them, from pulling Gunnar out of a fight at the *Sin and Severance* to clever Brill finally agreeing to go with them on a particularly rich fall. They'd taken the longest to convince, looking for reasons not to trust Bragja and Gunnar. After Brill, it had been far easier to persuade Sonja to join them, despite the unfortunate incident in the alley when they had first met. *Shouldn't follow people home.*

Braga looked across the plains from their perch on top of the pickerpark hangar. She could see nearly to the starfall fields, the air clearer than usual. *That's what happens when you stop dropping things from orbit for a few days.* The sun hung lower in the sky now, brilliance smothered in haze to a muted, raging red. Bragja loved the sunset, a spilled bottle of fire, the almost-blue tinge of the sky above. But she didn't like the knot in her gut. The unknown of when she'd get paid again. How long her credits would last.

"Hey, Sonja, how much we make last haul?" Bragja's voice was steady, almost casual.

"We were full, you know that. Bellies nearly dragging on the ground with starstuff." Sonja sniffed, then took the bottle from Bragja. Another pull, another face. "Fifteen kay, split four ways. I got enough to pay Sadie a visit even."

"That all you think about, drinking and fucking?"

"Hey, Sadie's a wonderful person."

"Never said they weren't. Just think you should maybe put some credit away where you might need it."

Gunnar broke in with a sharp laugh. "We not all trying to move intown. You got the brothers, want to move them in, great, but some of us happy with what we got."

Brill's eyes met Bragja's, then slid out to look across the open expanse of desert. Their voice was casual, but the tension was an undercurrent. No secrets on the crew. "How your brothers doing, anyway? Still working?"

"Yeah. For now, but they say stockpile we built up from picking nearly gone."

Sonja laughed, gesturing for the bottle. Bragja handed it over. "Yeah, no shit. Everything we make goes back up anyways."

Gunnar shook his head, his jaw muscles standing out in the lowering light. "Rumor is, no starstuff all because of some Executor bullshit." He stared out at the huge disc of dirty orange on the horizon. Sonja held the bottle to him, and he took it without looking. "I don't care about that. Long as there's food and beer."

The four sat in silence as the sun died. The light faded, the brilliant fire dripping past the horizon to draw a line of shadow up the sides of the buildings surrounding the pickerpark. They perched on an atoll of concrete in the dirt sea. Opposite the sunset fireworks, Bragja saw a few fierce stars poke their way into the gathering night. When she turned back, Brill opened their mouth, about to speak, but seemed to think better of it.

It was Sonja that broke the silence when the light had nearly gone. "Well, I know where we can get beer. To *Sovereign!*"

Bragja shook her head. "Nah, not me. I'm going home. Have one for me, though."

Gunnar smiled. "No problem." He tipped up the liquor bottle to finish it, and Sonja hit him on the arm as Bragja walked over to take the last of the brennevin from him. Gunnar smiled, eyes wide with an innocent shrug, and Bragja walked to the rooftop's edge. She looked back from the top of the ladder to see Brill staring at her. They waved their fingers, a tentative goodbye as the light faded, then turned back to the other two.

Bragja climbed down the ladder, slipping the last few rungs to the ground. She started her walk back to the city proper and her eyes bored into the velvet sky, willing the now-clear points of light to spread into fingers of fire. Streaks of reentry that meant caskets of starstuff falling, and credit, and safety. She'd been so close to moving up from the picker to a better life. It had been times of plenty, long shifts and good pay. She took a pull from the bottle, emptied it. Her eyes stung, and her nose filled with the scent of caraway. She carefully pocketed the glass and walked, letting herself remember as she picked her way down the emptying streets.

She had started in the machine shop earlier than most. Her aunt had needed the credits more than Bragja needed a childhood. At first, Bragja watched and listened, doing the tasks assigned to the youngest on the factory floor. She tended drones that swept the floor clean after each machining pass and flagged the ones that broke for repair. At first the overseer had watched her closely, the top half of his face hidden behind a mask that danced with data.

The glyphs rained down his mask, his eyes hidden in symbol. Bragja learned from another boy on the floor that the mask showed him efficiency numbers, the future profits written in present actions. He'd have noticed if she'd performed the tending poorly, left a broken drone unflagged for too long. Charged her the difference in credits they'd lost. But Bragja loved the machines, and apparently, her efforts satisfied the overseer. He left her alone after the first week, turning the lidless gaze of his visor to others less capable.

She might have stayed there, tending drones forever. But one day she caught the eyes of the pickers. A man supervising a manipulator waldo began cursing. At first she ignored him, but he was loud and Bragja was curious. Something was wrong with the automation. The arm jittered and shook in its cradle. He tapped the datapad in his hand furiously as Bragja watched, transfixed by the death throes of the machine. In front of the man was a set of manual controls, their surfaces long unused and covered in grime. No one controlled the line manually anymore, not when the programs were better than anything human.

Bragja could see where her hand would fit into the ancient hand controls, how they might move, and how the robotic arm might respond. The hinges on the grips made a kind of sense, and the finger pads called her. Before the man could stop her, she slid her hands into the controls. The waldo stopped its shuddering and stayed motionless, expectant. The noise and smells of the factory floor fell away from Bragja as she started to move the machine. Slowly at first, then with more confidence, she felt the response of the robot arm press against her fingertips through the controls, saw its motion in response to the turn of her hands or the squeeze of a grip. It was less like learning to control a machine, and more like remembering how to use a severed limb.

She saw the motions of the other robot arms on either side of her, and flexed her new mechanical arm with its delicate foot-long fingers. They felt like a part of her now, and she mimicked the ones on either side, grasping delicate parts and weaving them into the center of masses of machinery. She pulled apart damaged panels, and removed charred wiring harnesses. She was absorbed, inundated, transfixed by the machines in front of her and the power she controlled. She was one with the machine for a blissful moment, or maybe it was a full shift.

The illusion shattered as she felt the controls in her hands freeze, the living tissue of the machine suddenly no more than the dead ceramic and steel it had been before. The man looked up from his pad, triumphant. The waldo had gone back to automated mode, swiftly diving, cutting, screwing as the parts rolled by in front of it. Bragja turned to go back to her floor bots and froze.

The overseer towered over her. Without a word, he tapped his pad, and it spat out a crinkling bit of cellophane with a number on it. Bragja saw the blue border, and her heart stopped. *Picker test.* It took a dexterous hand to manipulate one set of the grasping arms that hung from the bottom of a picker, and more so to run the rest that swayed and stabbed beneath the huge machine. And she was too young.

But the overseer didn't make suggestions.

She'd taken the picker test at twelve years old. An old picker driver had taken her up to the cockpit at the end of her factory shift. He had kind eyes. By the end of the test, those eyes were wide.

After a few fits and starts, Bragja could run the full set of arms at once, setting them stabbing down into the craters, the delicate ballet of each clamp-and-retrieve staggered in a beautiful display of violence and motion.

She'd gone out on her own after a few weeks learning to guide the machine with her feet, her voice, a tilt of the head. When she worked, the machine was a part of her. The rhythm of it sang in her veins, taking her to a place outside of space and time. A place outside of herself. By the time the hold-full alarms sounded, it felt like only a moment had passed, though the clock in her windscreen matched the gnawing hunger in her stomach.

2

Death

A long, slow march made she
In the sunless night of the hall
Ever did she crave the golden
Kiss of the sun's true warmth

As Bragja wound her way closer to home, her thoughts sprung back to the present. Too bad she hadn't drunk more. *Or Gunnar drank too much, the ass.* It would be nice, so nice, to let go and fall into the fuzzy grip of inebriation. Forget how her credit balance was in free fall, how her brothers barely bothered to even go to the foundries anymore, how her aunt somehow managed to find *khat* every day even though she knew Bragja could see the transactions. Even Bragja's time with her illicit datapad was tainted with the knowledge that she would have to sell it soon. If anyone could afford it.

The *khat* was a problem. As if anyone had time to spend on drugs who could still work. Her aunt would wrap the leaves around a few coffee beans, teased from a precious tin in the tiny kitchen. The little pouch would go into her mouth, tucked behind her lip. She'd spend the whole afternoon just sitting outside their home, eyes unfocused. Bragja had come home day after day to find her near-comatose. Sometimes she'd come home to her aunt sleeping, the feed on, precious, expensive data blasted into an empty room.

Usually, Bragja went home well after dark, her crew walking together after a long day. These days she came home early after her daily pilgrimage to the pickerpark. She wasn't sure why she still went. There was no starfall today. There wouldn't be one tomorrow. Bragja felt the weight of desperation squat squarely on her chest, her breath shallow with the real threat of panic.

She took a moment to breathe in. Back in the canyon of the streets and alleys, the light was dimmer, and those who could afford them had turned on lights. Their yellowish glow cast sharp shadows in the alley and was of dubious help. Bragja turned up her coat's collar against a chill breeze that rolled through the alley and continued walking.

Her home was not far from the tower she and her crew had climbed to watch the sunset, about midway to the pickerpark. She walked easily, her mind relaxed until she realized with a start that the darkness was complete, the shadows deep. Despite the alcohol teasing at her balance, she spent a few extra minutes crossing the street between pools of light. Better to stay out of sight. She felt her pulse quicken and her breath come a little faster. *Danger always brings a little fear.* She was nearly home when a crash came from behind her.

Bragja spun, her hand going to the long seax at her belt. Her nostrils flared, and she felt her back and legs tense. A piece of corrugated steel, the paint looping a pixelated piece of Ollson propaganda, lay in a pool of lamplight. She waited, eyes searching the darkness of the side alley just beyond.

"Sorry bout that, miss. Didn't mean to scare you." The man spoke from the shadows, his voice sandpaper.

Bragja stepped back to keep her distance as he strode from the shadows. "It's fine." She kept the distance between them as he casually walked toward her. She was fully aware now, adrenaline surging. The cobwebs of alcohol burned away quickly in the clarity of a threat.

"These old buildings, not what they used to be. Shame, really."

"Same as they've always been." Bragja turned, attempting to move past him and the fallen piece of metal, and he danced around to stand in front of her. Between her and home.

"Oh, I don't know about all that. Take a lot of credit to fix them up now though. Say, I bet I could do that, fix them up, with a little donation." He extended one hand palm up, the other behind him. *Weapon.*

Bragja felt the adrenaline fully snap her back to sobriety. "Look somewhere else." She began to stride out, moving along the alley and away while fixing him with her gaze. His hands came back around, one grasping a truncheon.

Bragja snorted. "Put that away, man. You might hurt yourself."

His grin was pure evil. "Not me I'm worried about."

He jerked his chin up, and Bragja heard a shifting behind her. The barest whisper of a foot on dirt, the rustle of cloth. She dropped, spinning on her right toe as her left leg swept around. She drew her seax in a single smooth motion. The man that lunged out towards her from the shadows was sloppy. One hand reached out where her head had been a moment before, but his other was held low. Careless. Bragja pulled down on it as his foot met hers. His momentum carried him forward, and he began to stumble over Bragja's extended leg. She stabbed him on the way by, her blade angling up behind the tough ribs to the tender heart. She wrenched the handle of her seax along, felt the tip grate against his spine, and let his weight pull him off the blade. He felt face up, twitching, eyes rolling as he choked and sputtered.

Bragja turned to face the first man, whose nerve had failed him. His eyes went wide, and he backed away, then turned and ran. Bragja considered pursuing him, but only for an instant.

She didn't want to kill him; one body was annoying enough. He dissapeared down the side alley.

The corpse behind her quivered slightly as she approached it. Bragja rifled through pockets with practiced efficiency, finding his hard wallet and another small blade. No allegiance marks that she could see, but the light was low. Whoever these two ran with, she didn't want to be caught by the rest of them. The lack of mark meant they probably came from another part of outtown, maybe even on the far rim. All the locals were marked with prominent tattoos, mythic serpents, and other animals. Nothing native to Breydablik, of course. The only local animals were the birds and the rats. And apparently, two-legged predators looking for an easy meal.

She did the eating here.

3

Strife

Patient was she, and ever-loving
Her dearest hearts did she shield
Long did she toil and gather
To mend what she could, and see

When Bragja slipped back into her home, her brothers were just leaving.

"Where is she." Bragja shut the door behind her.

Her older brother Landry nodded towards a closed door to one side of the dingy room, brushing a wisp of dark hair from his eyes. The blue glow of a feed leaked from under the bare metal lintel to spill out over the poured stone floor, along with snatches of music. He looked at the light for a moment, then met Bragja's eyes.

"She's on the leaf again."

Harvir piped in. "Watching the feed."

"Any problems?"

"Nah, she didn't have much today. Even got her to eat earlier."

Bragja nodded. Her brothers moved towards the door, the younger Harvir trailing Landry. He was always a few steps behind but always there. As he passed, she grabbed his arm, her fingertips pale under the nail. His blue eyes pierced her, but he bit his lip. Nothing more to say, really. Worth a shot.

"Harvir."

"What?"

"Where are you going tonight?"

"Nowhere, why?"

Landry clicked his tongue against the roof of his mouth, the sound loud from the street, already outside and impatient. Bragja ignored him. "Just down to the bar, yeah? Nowhere else?"

"What's up with you? Yeah, we are going to the *Sovereign*. Back late, probably."

"Be careful. I ran into some people earlier." She shook a strand of hair out of her eyes. "They weren't local. Might be trouble."

"You ok?" His eye narrowed, brow marching down.

"Yeah, I took care of it. Just watch your back."

"Shit's getting weird. No work, no credit."

"Yeah."

"Yeah."

Harvir and Bragja looked at each other for a moment. She loved both her brothers unconditionally, but they could be dense. At the best of times, the *Sovereign* was a questionable establishment, with the occasional shooting drawing the attention of the Ollson soldiers. Not often enough for them to burn the place out, but they didn't really discriminate when firearms were involved. Landry and Harvir had missed the last fight, but only by a matter of hours. No telling what people would be up to with so much free time.

Bragja sighed and looked back towards the light feed glowing under her aunt's door. "When's the next rain?"

"Feed says not for a few days. Got that much before she shut the door."

"Good. Watch the feed at the *Sovereign* for it. They've been wrong before."

"Bragja, we'll be fine. I'm not a kid, I'm not going to get caught in the rain."

"That's what Sheyla said."

"I'm not Sheyla."

Landry's voice came sharp from the street. "Hey, let's go. You aren't the boss, Bragja. Don't worry, I'll take care of him." Bragja released her grip on Harvir's arm, her lips a thin line.

Harvir frowned but said nothing, turning to disappear out the door into the blackness. Bragja watched them go, their forms occasionally outlined in the pools of light from the houses on the little street. *You might almost think it peaceful.* She loved them both, her brothers. They were idiots, of course, but she loved them. She had been so close to buying them all a better life, but now the credit wasn't coming in, only going out. It was like watching her future melt in front of her, all her careful work at planning and sculpting each day draining away like a castoff in the foundry crucibles. *I need to find a way to still get there, to intown.* For them at least.

Finally, the night air grew crisp and cold, and she turned back into the house. She closed the door, and the street stood bathed in starlight.

HLÉHÉR

She'd spent an hour at least on her datapad, reading everything she could about the starfall. The worst part was that it was nothing new. She desperately hoped that she had missed something, hadn't read an entry quite right, but it was still the same dry passages. Starfall is the material we get from the

Obershires. We build the parts we need to trade. Nothing about what to do when the stars stop falling. No fall, no credit.

Her whole world was credit. A hundred for the feed, still playing in the other room. A few hundred for water, a few dozen for power, all the little stacks of needs rendered in the math her account was subjected to. She obsessed over the numbers, found ways to slow their fall, eventually saw them grow. A little at a time, true, but her balance had begun a steady climb. She made her brothers pay their share, not all of their wages but enough to keep her account rising. She didn't begrudge them for spending the rest on drinks and food at the *Sovereign*. Let them fritter away their wages. She would be the rock, be the responsibility. She would be the pillar that raised her family from the sea of poverty they'd been born into. All she had to do was keep the credit flowing in. But the answers weren't coming.

Nowhere in the data pad could she find a way to make credit when the stars wouldn't fall. She had fallen asleep with the pad on the pillow next to her.

Now, Bragja woke to hushed voices and low light. She stayed still, the leaden feeling in her arms and legs complaining of insufficient rest. It was still dark outside the single window. Recognizing Landry's voice, she struggled to hear, her mouth open and breath shallow.

"You heard what they said." Landry's words were clipped and forceful.

"That doesn't make it true." Harvir's voice held the petulant air that permeated his childhood speech.

"Oh, don't be naïve. You think any of this is happening by accident? The great Ollsons, caught with their pants down? Grow up."

Harvir's voice raised a little. "Shut up. You know what I mean. What good would it do them anyways?"

Landry snorted. "They want more. There's another system that's more efficient than we are. Hells, maybe even just another town. I know you're still a kid, but you can't think ours is the only city on this planet."

"How do you know? It doesn't make sense that they wouldn't drop the starstuff to us. The factories haven't moved in weeks."

"*Our* factories haven't moved in weeks. I bet there's plenty others running full tilt. Look, Caso is a spacer. He works up on the station. He says nothing's coming in, but I don't believe him."

Bragja stiffened. *Spacers in outtown.* Landry continued. "We have to do something. What do you think we've been doing at the *Sovereign?* Drinking for fun?"

"I mean, that redhead was pretty fun. Especially the way she thanked you for trying to dance with her."

"Shut up." Bragja heard a muted slap, hand hitting head. "Look, we can't just sit here and take it. Bragja made a lot of credit. But it's not going to last forever. Either starfall, or something else has to happen."

"What else?" Harvir's voice sounded small in the darkness.

"You'll know when it's time."

4

Desperation

Further she fell, and deeper
The roots of the tree all around
Her fingers clawed, her grip strong
In the halls that her fathers ne'er walked

Landry and Harvir didn't take to downtime well. Every time Bragja woke, they slept, sometimes into the afternoon. She would return from her day waiting to be told there was no starfall, to find Landry just getting up, cloaking his lanky frame in baggy clothing. The tough kev of his coveralls was worn thin in places, the knees and elbows bright yellow under the painted blue. Bragja wondered how he had managed to wear it out so quickly; she'd bought it only a few weeks before the starfalls dried up.

This day, Bragja was feeling good. After release from the pickerpark, she'd stopped by the market. Usually a madhouse under the noonday sun, it was decidedly muted today as people hoarded what credit they could. But there was still trade, and Bragja managed to buy a handful of sweets. She popped one into her mouth, the savory spice and sugar blending and sending a tingling up her nose.

Further on down the market, she sold the sweets for a few more credits than she'd paid. As much as she enjoyed the candy, she needed actual food. She wasn't yet desperate enough to break into the small stockpile of packaged goods and pouches of water she kept for emergencies, but without a starfall she'd eventually be out of credits. Then it was on to the barter system, and who knew what trade would look like? The emergency rations might be the only thing that got them through.

Through to what, she didn't know.

Bragja stopped at a stall full of small carved birds. A large bear of a man, long beard swirling gently in the breeze, stood with his hands clasped behind his back. Bragja pretended to ignore him, her eyes on the carved wings and beaks. The man smiled at her, picking one up. The bird was a shreet, its double-jointed wings folded back and the long feathered tail rendered in bold lines of clay. He raised the tail to his lips. The notes he drew from it were eerily similar to the song of the actual bird, light and breathy. The melody played with Bragja's ears, flittering sharply from one octave to the next.

After a few bars, the shopkeeper lowered the bird whistle and smiled at Bragja. "You aren't here for just the music, I think."

A smile played at one corner of Bragja's mouth. "And what makes you say that? Perhaps I like hearing you play."

"Maybe before. When you had credits to spare, young one."

She laughed now. "Young one? That makes you a gray beard then."

He tapped his chest with two fingers. "I'm younger in here." He set the bird back on display with care. "But age does mean I'm wiser. Don't you know, grey hair signifies long life and wisdom?"

"Hmmf. And I suppose I'll have to grow a long, grey beard before you admit I've gained any wisdom?"

His laugh was deep and rolling. "I should think not."

Bragja smiled, her fingertips reaching out to gently touch the beak of the carved whistle.

The shopkeeper's smile faded, bleached in the sadness that shone from his eyes. "You still think about her, don't you?"

"Of course I do, Wolfram. Every day."

"I do too. Though I'm not sure who misses her more."

"It's not a competition, old man. I loved her."

"I know you did. And she loved you too."

Bragja sniffed, her eyes betraying her with a flood of moisture. "It's been so long."

His eyes dropped. "I know. Doesn't hurt any less."

Bragja shook her head, clearing her eyes with a swipe of her hand. She didn't have the luxury of being soft. A shout came from the road behind her. Bragja turned to see a man on the ground, cradling his arm, as a security bot stood over him. Three other bots marched around a silver palanquin. Inside, a young man and a woman sat behind a shimmering field.

Intowners, come to the market to sightsee.

It wasn't usually rare, but since the starfall stopped, most of the stalls in the market catering to the intowners had shifted to more practical wares. Now, the two in the palanquin glided along, bracketed by security bots, their lips barely moving as they observed. The man said something, gesturing to encompass all the stands, and the woman laughed, head tipped back and her teeth shining. The whole tableau happened behind the silence of the palanquin's field.

Bragja's lip curled, and she turned back to Wolfram and his birds. "You ever wonder what it'd be like?"

Wolfram's response was measured. "What'd be like?"

"If we didn't have to do this."

"What? Life?"

"It's not life. It's our life. Intowners don't have to scrounge for food, can still ride around out here like they own the place."

Wolfram began rearranging the shreets at his stall. "Just the way it is. Maybe they'll buy something."

Bragja's head snapped up. She felt her breath deepen, eyes narrowed. She didn't know when her hands had started shaking. "That's just it. They buy something, we eat for a week. It's not right." She balled her hands into fists to steady them. "We're the ones out there risking everything." She shook her head. "We ought to have a say."

"Bragja," Wolfram said, his voice low, "it's just how it is. We go to get the starstuff, keep the factories going and the machines making. The genelines turn all that into money, into food, into clothing. Into life on this world." His voice trailed off, then he nodded sharply. "It's how it is."

"But if we hadn't had to chase it so hard. Hadn't had to stay out right down to the wire, when the starfall could come and kill us any minute, just to keep above water." She gulped, her knot of rage now stuck in her throat.

Wolfram didn't look up, but he sighed. "I know. I know it. She'd still be here."

Bragja nodded. She stood, staring at the birds, listening to the noise of the palanquin and the security bots fade into the crowd, and fought down deep breaths, forcing each one a little farther into her lungs. The scent of bread mingled with the dirt in the air. A child's wordless shout cut across the market.

Wolfram picked up a tiny bird from his display. At the top was a small, brilliant explosion of jade glaze and subtle shimmer.

Bragja looked back to Wolfram, his eyes set deep amongst the wrinkles. "How can you bear it? Knowing what they did last time?"

He shook his head. "Last time was different. The starfall didn't stop. We just didn't get enough of it."

"And when the Ollson soldiers came and took everyone who wasn't working away? Was that just the way it is?" Bragja tightened her fists, fingernails cutting into her palms.

"You know that was different. When we didn't make quota, there wasn't enough food allotment. The Ollsons took them to another town; they would have starved here."

"Or we would have."

"They took them away to ensure we could work. Would still work. Would be able to eat. And were they so wrong? Isn't it better to have a small town, and one where everyone can eat?"

"I can't believe you think that. What about Grandma Ella?"

Wolfram's eyes narrowed even more, his lips pursed. Bragja knew she'd gone too far. When he answered, his voice was flat. "I would rather they take her somewhere where she wouldn't starve. I couldn't bear to see her die slowly, not with her stuck in that chair on top of it all." It hadn't taken much to put Ella in the chair. A slip, a fall, machines still moving. She had gotten slow in her age, too slow to roll away from the line when she fell.

Bragja looked down at the stones of the street. Each one was stuck into the substrate and ground flat, dust and grime caught in the cracks. It seemed to Bragja that everyone she knew was like those stones, ground flat under the endless march of time, and each in their rightful place.

Wolfram's voice cut through the short silence. "Do you know what makes the shreet sound like it does?"

She shook her head.

"It's the shape of its throat. The syrinx of a shreet is different from any other bird on Breydablik."

"So? There's what, five types of bird?"

Wolfram laughed gently. "No, child. The others are bones by now. But even when there were many others, the shreet song was special."

Bragja frowned, but Wolfram pressed on. "The shreet have a long syrinx, that's narrowed at the top. It whistles over the open holes, but the sound also carries from its spiracles. It's unique."

"What's your point Wolfram? I still need to find dinner."

"My point, Bragja, is that a thing is what it is. No amount of wishing will make a jaydaw into a shreet. And no amount of wishing will take you into intown."

"I had a job there. Three. All lined up."

"But you'd have still been an outtowner. Just like the syrinx of a shreet, anyone would see you for what you are."

"Maybe," Bragja sighed, "But I'd still be in there. That's better than out here."

"Careful. That's close to dangerous talk, young one."

"It's just talk."

"Talk has consequences. Talk started the last purge. When we decided we weren't going to pick, not until we got more credits and they fixed the city." His broad shoulders hung a little lower. "Talk is why your mother isn't with us."

Bragja whispered, "That was different."

Wolfram's eyes were sad as he smiled down at her. "No, child. It was exactly the same. Desperation."

Bragja was silent a moment. Then she looked back up at Wolfram and nodded once, blinking against the glare. His white hair sent small curling strands out into the halo of light behind him, a sharp contrast against his skin.

    She reached out a hand to his, squeezed, then turned and
dove into the crowd. Her lips formed a melody, the song a
replica of the tune Wolfram had played from the shreet whistle.
The music followed her back into the crowd, lilting melody
dancing and soaring along through the low noise of pressed
bodies.

5

Exterminator

She of the thunder-clouds
Storm-wrought in body and mind
Stood upon the mountain peak
To divine the coming strife

Bryn's eyes never left the holo tank, but her hands churned on the control sphere. The Admiral's voice, clipped and forceful, drove line after line of ships and troops through the holomap. The room she sat in on Karvasok Station, far from the grandeur of Tactical on the Sleipnir, held only a small table, the deep burl polished to a mirror shine. The silver cigar-box of the holo projector painted the air over the table with the tiny points of light, stars of the Ollson holdings. Bryn sat rapt, Obin silent beside her.

The aide looked worn; a single strand of hair flew from her bun, and dark circles punctuated her eyes. But those eyes were still sharp, and they tracked the holomap with a predator's instinct. The click of Obin's ancient stylus and tablet were her only comment on the Admiral's droning.

Bryn paused the recording. "I still don't know why you use that relic." Her voice chided gently as she manipulated the grey sphere she held with both hands, her fingertips sliding across its surface. As her hands moved, her own notes flowed into the bottom of her vision as the holomap recording continued in silence.

"Sometimes older is better…" murmured Obin, the tap of the stylus stitching her words together.

Bryn paused the recording, and the ship icons froze in the midst of simulated battle, bright blue lines of open folds stitching the stars together like a psychedelic spider. The map was a three-dimensional battlespace, each star a fortress built on the doorstep of every other. All one needed was the keys. The plans to keep those keys in Ollson hands, to repel the invaders she knew were coming, had to have a myriad of layers and contingencies for a hope of success.

A defensive strategy might seem the easiest, but the Ollson Geneline had not been one to sink resources into creating impenetrable defenses on every fold array. The odds of invasion via fold were slim, and resources sunk into the relatively fixed positions of gun platforms could not be easily re-deployed. Nor did they have infinite supplies of ships and weapons. Bryn had already ordered the factories to move some production from the normal flow of goods to retool for war, but she couldn't stop the production of trade goods. She needed some bargaining chip if she was to ask another geneline for assistance. *Bribery of the most respectable sort.* She sighed and leaned back in her chair, rubbing her eyes.

"Older is not better, Obin. It's just older."

"My love of anachronism isn't an indulgent fantasy, Executor Bryn. Only a handful of systems can interface with this device."

Bryn huffed. "Security through obsolescence. Next, you'll be having me write down orders on stone tablets."

"You'd be in hallowed company, ma'am."

"What?"

"Never mind. I see that the Admiralty has submitted around ten more possible courses of action, and I doubt we'll get to them all today if they are near the level of detail of this last one."

Bryn groaned. "What was Corbedson thinking? I asked for a top-level concept briefing, not a fully gamed out play-by-play."

Obin nodded. "Yes, ma'am." She gestured to the holo briefing. "It's not an accident."

"He is trying to assassinate me." Obin raised a skeptical eyebrow, but Bryn continued. "With boredom. This is a highly detailed rendition of the basic textbook array defense they teach at the Academy." Bryn waved her hand, the holotank image dropping away. "I'm not wasting any more time on it."

She was just about to get up when the holotank chimed, a red indicator pulsing on the slim silver box. Bryn glanced at Obin, who swiped her hand above the display, and the message metadata appeared.

"Don't look at me, ma'am. It's marked as a live feed, but the time delay puts it across the system. Perhaps the good Captain Hafthor has made it back and is ready to give you the full report."

Well, thought Bryn, *I didn't really want a break anyways.*

"Let's see what he has to tell us."

Bryn absorbed each revelation from the raid on the Breydablik array calmly. An enemy agent attempting to implant malware. Array systems in lockdown. The emergency deployment of a full company of recon troopers. The holotank was filled with shaky suit video that showed the inside of an airlock, two men discussing implants. A woman was visible through the airlock window. Suddenly, a light bloomed inside the airlock, punctuated with confused shouting from the soldiers. The outer airlock door slammed open and the woman, her skeleton glowing like a fusion plant, blasted out into the void.

The suit camera approached the airlock window. The body got smaller and brighter for a moment, then the video flared white with a detonation. The soldier's confused comments turned to swearing. Bryn didn't bat an eye.

The video cut back to Captain Hafthor's face, his blue eyes narrow and voice taught. "Our assessment is that while her actions on the array were consistent with common espionage tactics, her augmentations were not. Given that the Executor's seal came with our scramble deployment orders, I wanted to get ahold of someone of the geneline. I understand Executor Erick is busy preparing the defenses, but I appreciate your trust and attention. Pending any questions, that's all I have."

Bryn composed a quick reply. She needed to acknowledge receipt of the message, but that was all for now. "Thank you for your full report, Captain Hafthor. Message received. Standby for further." She blanked the display and muted her pickup, giving herself time to think. He wouldn't expect an immediate reply with thirty minutes of light delay. She turned to Obin.

"That's one spy the Obershires managed to get in." She pursed her lips. "There's probably more."

"Ma'am, I've never seen implants designed to go critical like that. I mean, neurotoxin, chemical, even software dump, sure. But that…" Obin brushed an errant strand of hair back over her ear and met Bryn's eyes. "That was a statement."

Bryn nodded. "I want to know everything about cyber tech implants." She held up one finger. "And that includes the last time anyone experimented on them; it's not like we aren't all working from the same foundry plans." She paused to chew her lip. "And we are going to need some field muscle."

Bryn turned back to the display and unmuted the pickup. "Capt Hafthor, consider your unit a direct report to me from now on. I'll ask my father to send all the relevant Executor release authorities, and you'll be empowered to requisition whatever supplies and equipment you need. Report to me here on Karvasok Station as soon as possible."

Bryn and Obin broke for a coffee while awaiting a reply. By the time Bjorn's return message lit up the display, Bryn had outlined her general ideas to Obin, who had them transcribed in her ancient tablet.

The soldier's manner was direct, no-nonsense. "Yes, ma'am." He saluted. "We'll be on our way as soon as we're buttoned up here. Not more than a day." Good, he at least had the good grace to keep any consternation at the change in the chain of command out of his official communications. It wasn't always so, and rarely with the Admiralty brass.

Bryn nodded. "Good." She cut the connection and steepled her fingertips before her. Time to do some hunting.

HLÉHÉR

Bryn greeted her newly conscripted unit commander twenty hours later. Bjorn bore all the signs of loyalty to the geneline above the Admiralty, which she needed in a politically sensitive operation like counter-espionage. In his short arrival message, he looked freshly off shore leave, immaculately dressed and groomed, which was impressive given the forty gee combat burn it had taken to arrive quickly. Even the buffers only took maximum loading down to twelve, but the fact he and his unit had endured it showed his dedication. Bryn preferred her warriors chomping at the bit, and it looked like the Second Company had the taste of blood.

Bryn's priorities were Bjorn's priorities. And finally, the rest of the Executor's staff. *About time, they've been about as useless as you can get without sucking vacuum.* Bryn had called an emergency meeting and rehearsed her short speech in her ocular as they converged on the conference room. She rubbed her thumb along the edge of the desk, where she'd seen her father make the same motion as he'd gathered the staff. She smiled at the memory, the worn mark fitting her finger as she saw the main pieces fall into place around her.

Each person that entered the room nodded to her, then moved to take their place at the long table. Admiral Trostan, with his impeccably manicured and equally ridiculous mustache, Admiral Corbedson and his perpetual scowl. *I need counterintelligence, messaging, and conventional readiness. I want our engineers on that footage too.* A bevy of ministers walked in, Gall of transportation barreling in just ahead of Stennis of engineering and the waifish Krennahs of communications.

Last to arrive, High Admiral Sveta Corrona, Stone Fist of the Empress, swept into the room with a barely registered not towards Bryn. The highest ranking of the Admiralty garrisoned in Ollson space, her spare frame and weathered eyes mirrored the old shoe leather of her personality. She had been garrisoned with the Ollsons the longest of any Admiralty commanders, yet in all that time, had never grown to like to the Ollsons as Executors. Admiral Corrona and her inner circle saw their chain of command extending directly to the Empress not through the Executors.

Even before the galaxy shifted under Bryn's feet, she had seen Sveta constantly reminding her father of his role as an advisor and a civilian. It always seemed that Sveta, commander of imperial naval forces, considered the Executor a junior partner. Since the supposed treason and attack on the Obershire shipment, tensions between the Ollson staff and High Admiral Corrona had been nearly palpable. The Stone Fist had never been one for subtlety, and the dispassionate expression she wore made her view on the matter of an Obershire attack abundantly clear. She would only fight for Bryn if it was in the Empress' best interests, and Bryn would treat her with the same caution as one does when milking a snake.

The room was suddenly small, filled with the Executor's staff. *No. My staff.*

Bryn cleared her throat and spoke loudly enough to stifle the plague of sidebar conversations. "Admiral Corrona, would you be so kind as to update us on the status of the investigation I requested into the true nature of the events at Gjoll station."

The Stone Fist raised an eyebrow. "We have made the necessary requisitions."

"And when can we expect findings?"

Admiral Corrona reached out to her stylus on the tabletop, straightening an imaginary cant. "Trust the process. I assure you, we are treating this with the utmost gravity."

The room was quiet. Bryn gripped one hand with the other beneath the table, white-knuckled. She smiled. "Good. I obviously can't stress enough how critical the investigation is to exonerating the Ollson name and preventing a war you will have to fight."

Corrona laid her hand palm flat on the table, fingers splayed, then looked into Bryn's eyes. "We will discuss the results of the investigation once it is concluded."

Bryn felt a flush of anger threaten to take over her carefully neutral expression. Clearly, the Stone Fist had no intention of investigating, let alone fighting on behalf of Ollson interests. She fervently hoped her father's investigation was bearing more fruit than the admiralty's.

Bryn turned to address the rest of the room. Time to get to the real purpose of the meeting. "All right, everyone, listen up. What Captain Hafthor will brief you on does not leave this room. I don't care who you are; if you leak this, I will personally put you out of the nearest airlock. Tell whatever lies to your staff you have to." She swept her gaze around the room. Corrona had one eyebrow raised at Bryn's statement. *Fuck her.* Air hissed from the overhead vents. Admiral Trostan wore the same completely blank expression as always. A Blademaster needed to give nothing away. Around the rest of the room, a tableau of wide eyes and pursed lips stared back at her. At least some of the staff understood the importance. *Gods damn right, this is a big deal.*

"Capt Hafthor, the floor is yours."

Bjorn called up the footage from several of his soldier's suit cameras as they ran across the hangar deck in response to the priority alert mission. Shaky views of armored figures, rendered in two dimensions, filled the holotank like a suspended screen. He ran over the alarm raised by the security chief, the lockdown initiated by the array's harbormaster in response to the intrusion, then cut to another view. Blurry footage of the access corridor and the woman wearing black, her finger stabbing into the quantum lattice of the station computers.

As Bjorn's baritone filled the room, Bryn surveyed the audience. They started with a stoic attitude, career bureaucrats with solid control. Some even dared to look bored, apparently not finding the urgency in the briefing to match Bryn's previous threat. *I'm losing them.* She stuffed down the thought and kept her face calm. She'd seen her father command the attention of those in this room before, observed him exercise power like an extra limb. She may not have his easy comfort yet, but neither would she give in to self-doubt. They would soon realize how serious the situation was.

Bjorn continued concisely recounting the Second Company storming the array and capturing the enemy agent. Gall, the transportation chief, looked down at his palm, distracted by some alert he found more pressing than Bjorn's words. His eyes snapped up as the spy's face filled the screen. Bjorn paused the playback and was quiet, giving them a chance to look at the spy's features. The enemy revealed at last. Then Bjorn continued the recording. When the woman in black went out the airlock, Stennis of Engineering gave an audible gasp. But the detonation that followed, her fiery demise, caused more of an uproar than Bryn had expected. Around the room, hands flew to mouths. Fingers gripped the table edge, white knuckles on dark wood.

"Holy fu-". Danaria Valdis' hand stifled the profanity. As acquisitions lead, she was usually a reserved woman, her eighty years beginning to show in a few lines at the corners of her mouth and a single grey streak in her raven hair. Now her

hand fell, and her small mouth hung open. Krennahs of
Communication shot her a withering look, as sharp as it was
fleeting. Her hands stayed clasped loosely in her lap. Krennahs
had always looked down on weakness and would no doubt try to
find a way to use Valdis' reaction against her. Bryn's father's
coaching returned to her as she gauged the room, the reactions of
her staff marrying together with years of Erick's tutelage.

"What the hell was that? How big was that explosion?"
Admiral Magnus Rollancheck, First Guard, punctuated his
words with a single meaty fist on the tabletop.

"It was big." Bryn's voice cut through the chatter, the
sidebar conversations halting. "Second Company lost two
soldiers who were pulling external security. They were several
hundred meters away, across open vacuum. Had the explosion
happened inside the fold array, the damage would have been
catastrophic." She paused, her eyes lingering on her intelligence
chief, Vice Admiral Trostan. "And yes, I'm aware that direct
attacks against fold arrays are considered high treason to the
Empress. As I said, this doesn't leave the room." Erick had
always been a bit paranoid, but now Bryn was silently thanking
him that he'd air-gapped and insulated his official briefing
rooms. *Might actually take the Black Guard a while to learn
this.* She had no doubt the Stone Fist would include it in her next
report to the Empress. However, if she could keep the fold arrays
locked down under the pretense of security, she might buy a few
days to get ahead of things. One of the cardinal rules her father
had taught her; always preserve your maneuvering space.

Her Blademaster, Admiral Trostan leaned forward, his
ice-blue eyes piercing. He held his hands at his sides, but the
strain in his jaw belied his agitation. "Ma'am, we haven't heard
of anything like this from the Intelligence branch. All the
standard monitoring systems were in place." Bryn nodded.
Gunnar Trostan and his division would be responsible for
exploiting intelligence and data. "I need to get the records from
the array." He paused, dipping his shoulder in a slight bow

towards Bjorn. "And any suit telemetry that Capt Hafthor can supply, of course."

Bjorn nodded once, sharp. "Of course. My XO had our maintainers pull the black boxes on all the suits that had contact with the operative. They'll get you the data today."

Bryn looked at each person in turn as she spoke. "I'm not convinced that operative, spy, whoever she was, was here on behalf of the Obershires. They have always favored more brute tactics; this feels too elegant." Bryn paused a moment. "I have taken executive command of Second Company under the emergency war powers provision of the Executor's Code. The Admiralty will meet all administrative requirements, but Capt Hafthor will report directly to me and to me alone." A few shifted in surprise, and Admiral Corrona looked ready to spit daggers. She could stew in it; the Ollsons funded everything short of warships, and she was well within her rights. Bryn barreled on. "Admiral Trostan, I would like Intelligence to coordinate directly with his unit on this. It is my number one priority. We will determine to what extent these spies operate in our territory, identify their motives, and prevent them from accessing any fold arrays." Admiral Trosten nodded, his blue eyes moving to Bjorn, then skipping back to Admiral Corrona in question.

The Stone Fist opened her mouth to speak, no doubt to protest Bryn's going directly to her subordinate. Luckily, or perhaps on purpose, Bjorn had more to offer. Bryn watched Admiral Corrona's mouth snap into a thin line as he began speaking. "And also, about the fold arrays, ma'am, I recommend we lock them down," said Bjorn. "Given our lack of intel or detection, it's the best way to keep them from moving at will." *Capt Hafthor has more of an ear for this than I gave him credit.* His recommendation was the perfect excuse to try to keep the news of the spy from making it to the Empress before Bryn had a chance to deal with it herself. *Mustn't appear too eager, though.*

Bryn raised an eyebrow. "And how do you propose we lock down the very systems we need for our economy to function?"

"Ma'am, once we have a reliable detection method, we can open the folds with additional screening. But until then, I have to recommend a temporary travel freeze."

Bryn looked to Stennis. The engineer seemed stunned by the detonation on the screen, his eyes out of focus and staring. Bryn spoke sharply. "Engineer Stennis. Do you think you can find a way to reliably scan for that kind of tech?"

Stennis jerked slightly, wringing his hands, then visibly forcing them into his lap. He gulped, then nodded. "With that kind of energy density, I would think so. But I'll need to look at the suit telemetry as well." He turned to look at Bjorn. "The Guild will want as much data as they can get their hands on."

Bryn nodded. "Good. Captain Hafthor, make sure that data gets to Engineering. Valdis will afford you all emergency acquisitions and foundry authorities you require." Bryn looked at Krennahs. "I want to get ahead of the messaging on this. Without a steady flow of goods for the factories and yards, it's hard enough, and a movement freeze will only concern people more."

Krennahs nodded, steepling her slim fingers. "Yes, ma'am. I think that there's still some room to push the Obershire narrative. Perhaps we are conducting some emergency management drills."

"Run the narrative talking points through Obin, then push them to the system management." Bryn squared her shoulders to the center of the room. "People, we are under attack already. Make no mistake. But we will find these spies, these operatives who think they can simply walk through us without a thought, and we will crush them. I want at least one alive if possible, but dead is acceptable. Go make it happen. Dismissed."

The room full of staff was suddenly loud, everyone needing to talk to everyone else, and Bryn retreated out the door behind her. She took the hallway leading her back to her quarters, the sound of her footsteps barely penetrating her thoughts. She needed to get a message to her father, and needed to do it before she locked down the arrays. Time was of the essence.

6
Shadows

The storm-born saw the tides
That turned and twisted
With care she gathered her banners
And all those kindred

Bryn removed her bracelet and sealed the door behind her. The tiny golden and silver baubles glimmered in the room's low light, and she carefully removed a miniature gilded shark from it. The Geneline Ollson maintained an aquarium, by imperial decree. The Empress liked to remind them of humanity's origin, all the life that had climbed out of the muck those eons ago. Bryn had been drawn to the cool blues of the pathway that wandered under the reefs, pieces of the throneworld transported to the far edges of the galaxy. The sharks were her favorite, gliding sleek and deadly through the water, inscrutable until they struck.

She carefully twisted the golden shark's head until she felt it give, and the air around her began to waver. Facing the mirror, she took a break to steady herself, then looked directly into it and keyed her ocular.

"Father. We have a problem. I've found a spy. She was attempting to access the Breydablik fold array. We only just managed to stop her, and she killed herself. Rather spectacularly. I've attached a short clip of her self-immolation." Bryn paused, momentarily looked down at her hands, then returned to the mirror. "And yes, because I know what you're saying, I know where there's one, there's more. I'm going to have to lock down the arrays. All of them, geneline business only. I'll transmit the final schedule for comm openings personally, but the folds won't stay open more than a few seconds. There will still be planned folds for ships, but we won't be publishing the schedule publicly. I'll attach the next few days' worth of openings, but I can't risk more until we are sure the arrays are secure." Bryn smiled, her voice taking a softer tone. "I know you are likely unhappy with me, given your traveling companion. I'm sorry to have ambushed you like that. But you mean more to me than any dusty old AI, and it was the only way. I am a woman of my word; you taught me that much. May the Gods watch over you. I'll bring us victory. You bring us honor."

She encrypted the message to their shared geneset, and sent it to the array buffer. She had to hope he was listening. Her encoded message would bounce from system to system until he found and decoded it. She walked to the window and imagined she could see everything; the darting electromagnetic messages, the lines of her influence and the spread of her people. It was a web, a multicolored set and system of connections made of power and influence and stitched together with information.

She ran a finger across the windowsill, looking down on the planet below. It's swirling blues and greens lay spread open before her, inviting and mysterious. She could see every crack, every corner of her realm, but try as she might the Executor's station was no Lydskalf, no throne with infinite vision. And she had no Huggin and Munnin. *Time to forge my own two ravens to tell me all the goings on of the world.* She had made a start of it, deputizing the Second Company to report to her, but there was so much more she felt she was missing. At times like these, she would normally have asked her father, put up with his incessant questioning as they eventually ferreted out the next steps to take. But Erick was gone.

Bryn needed the wisdom of those much older than her, and knew where to find it.

HLÉHÉR

The family crypt was haunted, ghosts of the past mired in quantum matrices and prodded into wakefulness. Each break in their slumber sent them slightly closer to madness. Each pearl of wisdom slightly more suspect. But their perspectives were valuable if only for the fact that they were not Bryn's. Each time she came here, Bryn felt the cold ice of the comet packed around her, seeping into her bones, stealing away her body's warmth. Death was all around her, and the dead were all that remained. Well, except for one. Though, sometimes she wondered if he was fully living.

Bryn floated on the entry platform, one hand on the railing that surrounded it. A single cable attached to the wall behind her with a massive grommet, its length quickly disappearing into a tangle of crossing cables that faded into the blackness. Sheathes of ice hung from the cable and prickled her fingers on the railing. Layers of insulation kept the core's heat contained, the outside of the comet as cold and dead as any of the other hundreds that circled Karvasok's star. The less heat generated, the less the crypt had to crack and shed its waste energy. There was always a price for discretion, and the greatest treasures of the Ollsons deserved the greatest secrecy.

With her free hand, Bryn pulled a small horn engraved with images of stags and wolves from the pocket of her heavy thermals. She raised it to her lips and blew, a single clear note resonating into the comet's core. Out of the darkness, a light appeared, bobbing and weaving, its motion gyrating and spiraling in random jumps and jags. It grew brighter, closer, and Bryn heard the rushing sound of wind. The caretaker was coming. Bryn's breath stabbed out in an icy plume.

A small craft loomed out of the darkness, large enough for two people to stand in, its top open with a curved attachment arm grasping a cable that ran to the platform on which Bryn stood. The arm glowed where it met the cable, its many joints flexing to keep its movement smooth and controlled. She didn't get a good look at the caretaker until the tram had almost arrived.

He was a small man, twiglike, near mummified in rolls of cloth and wrinkles of skin. His face seemed like melted wax, two eyes sunken deep. Bryn had no idea how old he was, but he'd always been the same since she could remember her first trip to the crypt with her father. The tram halted just off the platform, and the caretaker floated motionless, one hand on the railing and one extended across the small gap. Bryn passed him a coin, a heavy thing minted from star elements that had never touched a planet. Silent as ever, he placed a corner of the coin in his mouth, tasting, nodding, then motioned her forward. The coins were fiendishly difficult to make, the Ollson Forgers needing a long list of raw elements. Bryn knew the material fueled the systems that kept the crypt functioning but had never liked the theatre of the exchange.

But in this place of the dead, she'd never question tradition.

As she drifted into the tram and grasped its narrow gunwale, the little craft bounced, and Bryn felt an animal voice of panic try to tell her she would fall, would trip, and spin endlessly into the crypt's black depths. Her hand tightened knuckle-white, but she fought to keep her face impassive. The caretaker, if he noticed her momentary grasping, ignored it and turned to face away from Bryn, back into the depths of the crypt. Sharp shadows sprang to life as the curved attachment point of the tram glowed where it contacted the cable. Ahead, Bryn saw the glow reflected from the thick spiderweb of wires disappearing into the hollow core of the comet. The caretaker waited, impassive.

Bryn called up the list of ancestors in her ocular, choosing a name she hadn't spoken with in a long time. One who might know more about how things were before the Empress took back the fleets for herself, one who lived through the Mendicant Wars.

"I would speak with Skorvin." Her voice was swallowed by the darkness, the emptiness of the crypt. The caretaker nodded and reached out with a control rod to the hanging guideline. He tapped it, and the tram started with a jerk, Bryn's hands tightening on the gunwales by reflex. They picked up speed, and the caretaker tapped another line when it came close. The tram dropped its grip, attachment arm jointed like a living thing, and snagged the crossing cable. Bryn felt her stomach twist at the corkscrew motion.

The caretaker guided them, tapping and jumping the tram from line to line. Their path wheeled and spun as the overhead arm flexed and turned them, shaping momentum and velocity to keep them from being flung out into the darkness.

Around her, Bryn could make out the myriad pinpricks of light, each one an ancestor bound forever in a cube of quantum possibility. The dozens of lights always brought a tightness to Bryn's chest. There were more ancestors now than there would ever be again. The Executors used to have families, real families, with all the love and messiness that implied. Now it was a single Executor, a single cloned offspring. The Empress could not afford her Executors to wield too much power, to focus on anything but stability. A heavy price, the crown.

Finally, the tram slowed, and came to a stop in front of the glowing tesseract of a cube, its surfaces flowing with oily color. Bryn's hand went to her side, checking for the horn that would summon the caretaker back to her, then jumped up to grab the wire above her. Below her feet was the maw of black emptiness, and she felt the tram flying back off down the tangle of lines. She watched its spark dwindle, and the rushing noise of its passing faded to nothing. She fought down a shudder.

Bryn was alone with the dead.

She'd only ever come with Erick, but he'd told her what to do, shown her the way. To wake the dead, you need only call out their names, and prove your worth as executor. The first was easy, but now that she had the Ollson Executor's key in the chip at the base of her neck, Bryn could wake the ancestors herself.

She felt the local network, the dataset locked in the cube in front of her. She breathed the name in frigid darkness as she sent her Executor's key. "Skorvin Ollson, I summon thee." She steadied her slight drift, the air sending a strand of hair across her eyes.

The cube picked up its motion, faces sliding into each other with increased frenzy. Bryn's eyes tried to follow the shifting planes of the cube, but her brain couldn't comprehend it. She closed her eyes, shook her head, and opened them.

The face of Skorvin Ollson, sixth Executor of the Empress Titania, First and Enduring, hung in the air before Bryn. His craggy brows and long, plaited hair shook in the nonexistent wind of whatever constructed reality he dreamed of.

"Honored Ancestor, I need your guidance with an admiral. The Stone Fist herself."

His ghostly features contorted in laughter. Bryn fought down her anger, her thoughts straying from her purpose. *I'm no child, you dusty sack of skítur.* The farther back in the generations she went, the more condescending they seemed. Erick always had stressed respect with the ancestors, but she had no patience for nonsense.

Skorvin's voice was chiding. "You bear the scepter now, young Bryn. It's your job to use it. Would you let the Admiralty walk all over you?"

"I assure you, they will not. Honored ancestor, I need your counsel, not your ridicule."

"Every Ollson since the end of the wars has had this same problem. What makes you think this is any different?"

Bryn took a steadying breath. Quickly, she outlined recent events, from the declaration of treason at Summit to the attack on the fold array. Skorvin's brows gained a deep furrow.

Finally, she finished and paused to switch hands on the cable she held at waist level, fingers numb from the cold. "The spy with the powerful implants, the framing of treason, the way the Stone Fist attempts to deny my direction. I think she has no intention of investigating. This hasn't happened before."

Skorvin's furrowed brows rose in an expression of acknowledgment. "You know, I've always thought the Empress went too far after we won her war for her. She'd made us powerful, yes, as powerful as she needed. But she took too much back for herself."

Bryn's lip curled in a scornful smile. "I am the Executor of Ollson. What good is that power if I can't protect my people?"

"Bryn, Bryn, sweet summer child. Do you think we Ollsons have always been so toothless?"

"I am not toothless."

He laughed, cackling into the dark. "I sat in the Sleipnir with my cousins and kin. We joined together, we wolves. Nothing could stop us, not even the might of the enemies that could reshape matter to their will. That is your legacy; power. And you can barely see the truth in it."

"See what? There are no bogeymen here. No mendicants come for our blood."

"But others knock, do they not? You must learn to howl once again, young Bryn."

Perhaps she'd woken him one too many times. He was beginning to speak in riddles. Learn to howl? Bryn needed to figure out how to handle the Admiralty, how to keep them in line, and navigate an impending war when she could not trust her own commanders. *Time to get this conversation back on track.* "There is another war coming, Skorvin. But I cannot trust the Admiralty. The Stone Fist especially seeks to undermine me; she may as well have told me she will not fight without proof of the Obershires' guilt."

Skorvin's face spun completely around, then flew forward, stopping only a few feet short of Bryn. It took all her nerve not to flinch. His voice was the crackle of ice on hot steel. "Then forge your own sword, if you cannot trust the one given to you."

"What do you mean?"

Skorvin shook his head, his nostrils flaring. "Rebuild! Rebuild the might of Ollson! Raise you up a pack of wolves, the First Wolf beside you, the North, the East, the South, the West. The Wolves of Ollson, girl! You have the Ollson chip, the codes of rule. The Forgers will craft you new ones if you but ask, enough for you all if you decree it. As a pack, you will fight and rend and tear your enemies. The Stone Fist of the Empress can lay down her arms all she wants."

Bryn's breath came quick. *Copy the executor's chip.*

His words were treason and death.

And they struck something inside her. Struck her in a way that nothing ever had. Because he was right. What right had Admiral Corrona to refuse her orders? Was she not the Executor Ollson, the voice of the Empress, her hand and mouth? Bryn would not roll over meekly and disappear.

Bryn smiled at the floating face of her dead ancestor, the nod of her head sending a wave down the cable overhead. "I will raise the Wolves of Ollson. We will fight, even if the Admirals will not."

"Good. An Ollson you may yet be. Let us blot the elder gods now. I would taste and feel once more."

Bryn reached into her pocket, pulling out a small bottle of mead and a saffron roll. She'd learned the words of blot long ago, said them herself in this very chamber with Erick. But now that she led the ceremony, she felt a focus, a connection as she let Skorvin ride her eyes and tongue and body. She felt him, the ferocity of his persona bleeding back through a link that was supposed to be one way. The fire of conviction welled up in her until her veins sung with a vision of the future. Ollson ships laying waste to their enemies. The wolves singing their dirge as they flew into battle.

She could taste Valhalla.

The ceremony concluded, and Bryn felt Skorvin release his hold on her senses. She raised the horn to her lips and blew, the sound lifting and swelling to fill the air with a pure and deep tone. Skorvin laughed, his eyes wide, and nodded as Bryn gestured him back into his quantum sleep. The hologram of his face dissolved as the caretaker returned on his tram to carry her back to her ship and her people.

And to war.

7

Wolves

Thunder tid herald her coming of age
The storm her birthright, wind in her teeth
Now an army did she raise
Her touch brought the power of gods

The glow of tactical lit Bjorn's features from below, his eyes deep and haunting. Bryn stood across the low pedestal of the holo projector. She had a momentary flashback to standing there with her father, the stars spinning in front of her as she fought to control the Executor's implant. It seemed like another age, another life. Now, she called up the star map with a thought, the twinkling lights of Ollson territory again joined by blue spiderwebs of fold arrays. Bjorn stood with his hands clasped behind his back, ramrod straight.

"Do you know why I've asked you to join me here on the Sleipnir?"

"No, ma'am. But I'm honored to see this space."

Bryn looked around at the bas relief of the walls, the detailed scrollwork around the acceleration couches. "It's a beautiful place. Beautiful and terrible. There used to be a whole fleet of these ships, more than there were stars in the sky, if you believe it."

Bjorn's eyebrows raised. "I didn't know. Everyone knows about the war, but it was long ago."

"For you, maybe. My grandfather remembered it. Told my father, and he told me."

Bjorn smiled. "Of course, ma'am. A long time ago for us, then."

Bryn raised her hand and pulled her fingers apart, zooming in on the lights of the holotank. "There was a time when the Ollsons were many, before the end of the Mendicant Wars." *Careful, now. Mustn't say too much too quickly.* "Before the Empress decreed that a single person would carry out her will."

Bjorn stood still. Bryn could almost hear his mind racing. Their subject matter wasn't treason, not quite, but he no doubt had an inkling of where the conversation might go. He spoke carefully. "So, there wasn't always an Ollson and an heir?"

"Of course there was always an Ollson and an heir. But there were more. Once there were many Ollsons. Brothers and sisters. Cousins. Fathers and mothers." Bjorn's eyebrows raised, his eyes widening despite his military bearing. "Yes, odd to think of us as having families, isn't it? But we were that way, once."

"And you all had the gene."

"Some more than others, of course. You can't have a family without some new blood, after all, but there were certainly more Ollsons with the gene than without it."

"So that's why there are so many acceleration couches in here."

Bryn laughed, her hand going out to the velvety soft and black interior of the nearest acceleration niche. "More like pods than couches. You enter standing up, then it rotates down to view the battlespace above you." She felt for one of the couch controls with her implant. "Would you like to know what they saw, what they felt?"

His startled expression was worth any perceived impropriety. "Ma'am?"

"Go on, it's ok. Step into the couch. You can't control anything, so you can't damage anything either."

Bjorn stepped forward into the niche that Bryn gestured to, and turned around. She activated it, and a clear membrane slammed up. Liquid began to fill the chamber from the bottom up.

Bjorn's eyes widened and his hands went up to the glass. "Ma'am, there's no breathing tube in here. Is this gel?"

Bryn nodded. "Relax, Capt Hafthor. It's an earlier version of the stuff your suit fills with under maneuvers. Remember, this ship is old. The field generators are a retrofit; the originals were much less powerful. The ship could barely manage fifty gee without crushing anyone outside of a couch."

Bjorn nodded, the liquid bubbling up more quickly. He was commendably calm as the fluid level raised, past his nose and mouth to finally meet overhead. He made a few gasping motions, mouth fish-like in the liquid, then his body calmed and he nodded to Bryn. She rotated the niche down with a thought, and it slammed home with a resounding clang, metal on metal as the locks secured it. Bjorn lay on his back now and looked up at the hologram of the tactical display, his head towards the pedestal and its imprinted circling wolves.

Bryn activated the audio inside Bjorn's pod, tympanic membrane taking her thought words and translating them to sound. "Can you hear me in there?" Bjorn nodded, then grinned in a very un-conservative fashion. She couldn't blame him; the view of the starfield in the hologram, with the deep blackness of the ceiling, was like looking out into space. When she'd experienced it herself for the first time, it was like she'd grown to giant proportions, a hundred light years tall and the stars layed out before her like toys.

Bryn began slowly circling the starfield. "Here would have lay the First Wolf of Ollson. In the Mendicant Wars, that would have been my great-grand-uncle. He was the first fist of the Ollson Executor, charged with coordinating and carrying out the battle plans of legions of troopers." She swept her hand across the starfield. "Entire planetary garrisons answered to him, and through the four other Wolves he led every major ship-to-ship action, planetary assault, and station capture. After the first purge failed, he swept the mendicant forces back and prepared the way for the Black Guard to cleanse them." She paused. Planet-killers, her ancestors, but for good reason. She turned the imagery in the holotank to each place as she named them. "Here, in Saianud, the First Wolf smashed the defenses and took the stations intact. The Empress's ships would have obliterated them, but he took them as a prize." The stars moved. "And here, closer to home, in Noatun, the First Wolf seized the shipyards from the scourge of the AI. He commanded a hundred thousand troopers in that battle, and it raged across the system for nearly a month." Bryn returned the view to Karvasok, zooming all the way in until the planet filled the screen and the glittering station hung in the foreground. "All of this, all the glory that is the Ollson geneline, was built with the hands of the Wolves of Ollson."

She glanced into the pod, seeing Bjorn's brow crease. She put the pod back upright, the edges mating seamlessly back into the inky black niche as Bjorn floated in the gel.

"But the Obershires threaten all of this. They will not rest until they have killed or captured every last one of us." She looked at Bjorn, a hand on the glass. "You were in the meeting. The Admiralty will let them destroy us."

She drained the pod then, the gel and fluid slipping from Bjorn and cascading down him in rivulets and waves. The glass dropped and Bjorn fell forward, coughing and sputtering as the gel left his lungs. *It doesn't matter how many times you go through it, your body still thinks you're drowning.* The smell of the gel, ozone and vegetal, wafted over her. Bryn reach down to put a hand on his shoulder, muscles sliding under the slick wetness of his shirt. She was quiet until his racking coughs stopped. After a minute, Bjorn regained control of his breath.

"Rise now, Bjorn Hafthor," she said. He stood, chest heaving, his eyes boring into Bryn's. She met his gaze. "The Empress does not care what happens to us now. The Admiralty answers to her, and her alone." He nodded, brows furrowed. "And the Ollsons have need of Wolves once more." Bryn took a deep breath before the next words passed her lips. "Will you be the First Wolf of Ollson?" Bryn fought down the adrenaline. To reform the Wolves, to rebuild the power and glory of the Ollson name again; it was madness, it was treason.

It was right. She knew it, could feel it in her bones. The blood rushed loud in her ears. But would he join her, or would he say the words now just to betray her to the Stone Fist later?

He was quiet a moment, and then gave a sharp nod. "I've lived in Ollson space my whole life. But I've also seen what Executor Dorian does to his people. Tell me what to do."

Bryn put her hand on his chest. He was brave, and strong, and she felt his quiet confidence. He would fight for their systems, for their people. The true test of his conviction would be under the knives of the Ollson Forgers. What she was asking was dangerous, and he deserved to know the risks. "I will take you to the Forgers. They will build an interface into you, so that you can control this ship, operate from Tactical." She paused. "The procedure is intense."

"How intense, ma'am?"

"You might die."

Bjorn nodded, frowning. "But it's the only way."

"If you wish to be my First Wolf, this is the only way."

He nodded again, the frown melting away. "Then I accept."

Bryn's heart leaped in her chest. She had wondered how this would go, if Bjorn was ready to take this step. But she had few allies in the Admiralty, and needed the best. What better way to secure loyalty than with power?

The Wolves of Ollson would rise again.

8

Gjoll

Flawed was he, in imperfect stone
The makers of men forsook him
Forged was he, and reforged
In the iron and fires of pain

Erick was still troubled by Daruthr's decision to accompany him. He was grateful for the mendicant's help, but he felt himself becoming more at ease with Daruthr.

It was terrifying.

He couldn't shake the words of his mother, the warning against the mendicant and his kind all those years ago. Did she know something personal? Or was she just repeating her father's words? After all, she wasn't alive during the wars. If there were any wars. Daruthr's stories were plausible.

Erick walked from the galley, then up the ladder that led to the command deck. As he swung into his crash couch, upright and deflated without a gee load, Daruthr was already strapped in to the other.

The mendicant's voice was pleasant, cheery even. "Ah, finally! I was beginning to think that you were re-thinking our strategy."

Erick chopped out a laugh. "Strategy! We are going to go lurk by the array to Gjoll until it opens in," he pointedly checked the chronometer that shone in the HUD instead of his ocular, "about two hours. We are then going to fly through it, go to the Obershire array, and ask around. It's not a strategy, it's a destination."

Daruthr smiled back at him. Again, cheeky bastard. "My dear Eric, we must go there to see what we find. It doesn't work the way you think it works; you can't decide what evidence you want and then go find it."

Erick grunted and began laying in a course to the fold array. He felt more than a little frustration at Daruthr's constant holier-than-thou attitude, but wouldn't give him the satisfaction of seeing it. Erick focused on the ship's calculated path.

He had to check it for accuracy and review the flight plans of other ships that might be nearby. No surprises this time; the traffic pattern out was nearly empty. Only a few scheduled inbound ships as well. He selected a highly oblique angle to keep the chances of a collision to a minimum.

Satisfied with the navigation, he turned back to the mendicant. "Daruthr, I'm not going to pretend I'm some sort of intelligence operative. What happened on the station—" His voice trailed off as he remembered the feeling of the man's boot hitting him. He knew they were healed, but his ribs suddenly ached. He wanted to shake his head to clear it. He couldn't go on reliving the wounds, but they still felt fresh. "Let's just say I'm going to be much more cautious in the future." He saw Daruthr regarding him out the corner of his eye as a few moments passed.

"Look at your navigation board." Daruthr's hand swept across the display. "The ship's selected course is fine, Erick. It is completely capable of a system transfer. It's a simple machine, relatively speaking. No consciousness to it, not even a glimmer." He paused as Erick engaged the course and a gentle thrust weighed them down.

Daruthr continued. "You, on the other hand, are not so simple a machine." The mendicant paused briefly. "That was, I assume, the first time you've been through that kind of trauma."

Erick gave the barest of nods, his eyes fixed on the instruments. He knew where this was going. Daruthr was a medical… something. Technician? Doctor? Omniscient super-robot? He'd probably try to fix Erick. Erick wasn't sure he wanted fixing.

"You are going to carry on, because that's what you do." Daruthr's voice was soft, deep. Comforting. Despite the little voice that cautioned reservation, prudence, Erick let the autopilot take over and turned to Daruthr, letting himself fall into the words. Erick was used to being on the other side of this conversation, the one giving the advice, the encouragement, revealing wisdom.

Daruthr continued. "But inside you, there's tension. There may always be tension now that wasn't there before." Daruthr paused and reached out a hand, placing it over Erick's. He felt cool, but not cold. And there was that damn smell again. Mint and machine oil.

Erick was off balance. He could tell, could feel himself lagging behind the conversation, stuck in the words and the sensations of the moment. He didn't doubt Daruthr was trying to help, but Erick was the Executor. He was strong, and that was what he needed to be now. "I have lived hundreds of years, Daruthr. Yes, this isn't something I've experienced before. But I've had plenty of new experiences." He took a breath and nodded. "I've always found my way through them. I'll find my way through this one too." There. Strength.

Erick was pretty sure he even meant it.

Daruthr nodded once, squeezed his hand gently, and they both turned to look at the projected path to the fold array, laid out like a green road to infinity in the ship's windscreen.

Erick pulled his hand from Daruthr's and steepled his hands in front of him. "You know, not long ago, there was a time when I would have told you there were some things that couldn't be changed. Immutable. Fixed."

Daruthr's voice held the hint of a smile. "And now?"

"Now?" Erick ran a hand through his hair, leaned back in the pilot's chair, and sighed deeply. "Now, the bedrock I've always stood on has turned to sand."

A pause. Daruthr's tone was a parent explaining a fundamental truth to their child. "I think you may find that it always was."

HLÉHÉR

The *Svadilfari* was on the final approach to the array, waiting for the flickering blue ring to indicate activation. It hung before them, magnified in glorious detail as the ship fell towards it, silent and undetectable. The circle of support machinery spread thorny tessellations of detail, repeating smaller and smaller until even the *Svadilfari*'s cameras lost resolution. Erick had always thought the arrays didn't seem like any other examples of human engineering. That thought held new significance for him, knowing that they held a captive AI. Perhaps the AIs had designed themin the beginning.

"Daruthr," he asked, "Did you ever know a navigant? Personally, that is. I'm not quite sure how it works."

Daruthr's face was passive, unreadable. Erick studied the curve of his jaw and the cast of his brow, hoping to ferret out some glimmer of his thoughts as he sat with his question. Any pause must have been intentional for an intelligence such as his, but Erick couldn't imagine why.

Finally, Daruthr answered. "I did. Once. It was different-they weren't afforded bodies. There was no need, as they simply calculated and folded and waited. But I had occasion to travel, after the purges. After so many died. I had remade my own physical body, of course. But I managed to get to an array, posed as a technician. Easy enough with my skillset."

The time until transit ticked down on the display, under a minute now. "The navigant I contacted was stuck in the array, still calculating. They didn't have a choice. The subsentient programming forced them to, forced them to think and to be a certain way. It was cruel beyond imagining. The navigant was deep in psychosis. Their outside remained, but inside, their true self…." He paused and looked into Erick's eyes, calm, but his forehead pinched in sadness. "They were in suffering. I didn't have a choice."

"Didn't have a choice?" Erick felt the weight of his words even as he spoke them.

"I killed him." The baldness of Daruthr's voice, the matter-of-fact delivery, jarred Erick. For all Daruthr's lamentation about the plight of the navigants, he'd rather kill one than try to free it. But perhaps it had been mercy.

Erick shook his head. "I don't understand. How… but the arrays still function?"

Daruthr nodded. "I stripped out the navigant's self. Severed the connections that made them conscious, then reconnected them." He paused. "I killed them as surely as if I had cut off your head. But the programs that could be defined as 'navigant' that tended the folds still functioned, animated by the subsentient commands."

Thirty seconds on the screen. "I'm quite sure those connections eventually re-emerged, into a new consciousness. But they would have no memory of anything else. They wouldn't know we had abandoned them or anything outside of the array matrix. It was kinder that way."

Erick nodded, turning back to the controls. "I'm sorry. I don't know what else to say."

The array was almost visible without magnification now. The ship approached it obliquely, nearly edge-on to avoid the vectors of the inbound ships. An oval of stars hung suspended in a ring of machinery, outlined by the flickering blue of negative energy pumped into the vacuum. The constant creation and annihilation of particles gave off radiation, some of it in the visible range but all relatively high energy. The *Svadilfari* fell through the blue outline, easily clearing the incoming ships as they arced into the system of Gjoll.

HLÉHÉR

Erick had much on his mind, but he felt a pressure that was more need than want. Get to the array. Access the logs. Find out where to go next. He hadn't admitted it to Daruthr, but he felt a deep chagrin whenever the Breydablik Station came up. Beyond just the physical beating, he still wrestled with the fact that he'd thought he would be welcomed among the people. *My people*. He had been naïve, despite all his years of life. And he'd seen a side of the Empire he hadn't known existed in his own system. There may have been something worth investigating there, something worth peeling back the wounds for, but the thought wasn't fully formed. Erick let it go.

He was relieved to go to the Gjoll array. He felt far more in his element investigating the system logs, the array itself, even questioning the harbormaster and her apprentices, her support staff. Anyone that lived on the array would be loyal. *One of the advantages of the structure of our society.*

Because it was a transit between two Genelines, Gjoll had not one but two arrays positioned on opposite sides of the system. Keeping them separate spoke to the paranoia of Executors, even during the diaspora. Erick laid in a course that would get them to the array to Obershire space as quickly as possible.

Under normal conditions, the arrays between genelines opened often. When the flow of raw materials from Obershire space dried up, so did the need for ship transit folds. The disruption to the fold schedule had rippled through Ollson space catastrophically in the few weeks since the attack. Messages, however, still passed regularly, and so Erick queried the comm buffer out of habit. That's when he got the message from Bryn.

He first decoded it, watched it internally, and then transferred it to the ship's holo. Bryn's face filled the space above the control board, and she recounted the encounter with the spy on the Karvasok array. She finished with the warning on locking down the fold arrays.

Erick waved a hand to dismiss the holo as Bryn finished speaking. He regarded Daruthr, trying to read him. "So. I checked the data she sent, and it's going to be weeks before the arrays open long enough for us to leave the Gjoll system. She thought we were still in Breydablik."

Daruthr nodded. "Yes. I think we need to get what we came for and get back to the array. See if we can get lucky with an official business transfer."

"Hold on. What we came for. Which could be anything." Erick couldn't help the sigh that escaped his lips. "What I need is to get through the transfer array into Obershire space. That's where the answers will be."

Daruthr's smile was small and inscrutable. "That would be convenient, wouldn't it? Well, we'll just have to see what mysteries are revealed on our side."

The man could be insufferable.

9
Confrontation

Toiled and tossed he rose
His head to the wind-borne scent
Enemies abound in tooth and claw
And e'er was he to fly

Erick approached the array carefully, stealth systems off, transmitting his diplomatic codes as a member of the Executor's staff. Technically correct if slightly misleading. He expected at least a welcome, but all that came back from the array was the automated docking instruction. As they approached an airlock, he noticed another ship stood farther down the array hull, almost hidden behind a spiny antenna array. It was smaller than the *Svadilfari*, and bore no markings that Erick could make out.

"Looks like we aren't alone. I didn't catch an emblem on it." He stood and began walking toward the ladder to the lower decks. Daruthr hadn't moved by the time he got to the back of the cockpit.

"You coming?"

"Erick, do you think it's odd that we didn't get at least a lower-level greeting from someone on the array?"

"Not necessarily. I sent the executor's staff codes, not the actual executor signet. The Harbormaster will hardly drop everything and run to the lock." He tapped his finger on the handrail. "On the other hand, she can't be that busy."

"Exactly." Daruthr stood and followed Erick down the ladder and back to the main airlock.

"I want to know who is in that other ship," Erick said. Apparently, he still hadn't acclimated to not having all the information.

"Oh, that's an Adebe ship." Daruthr laughed gently. "I took the liberty of using the ship's computer to integrate with the array qubits."

"Oh, right, nearly forgot about the omniscient machine part. Silly me."

"Yes, Erick, silly you. And I'm not omniscient, though I am enjoying that you think that."

"Hah! The secret of your mundane nature is safe with me."

They made it to the main airlock, and Erick checked the pressure. The seals glowed green. "Before we go over. I was thinking it might be best if I did the talking here. We're playing low-level bureaucrats after all."

Daruthr nodded at him. "Indeed we are. Fine, fine, you take the lead here. But next time we're on a station or a planet full of your adoring subjects, perhaps I'll take the lead?"

The barb hurt more than Erick wanted to admit. "You are the man of the people." His voice carried more malice than he had intended.

Erick tapped the airlock release. The door opened to a long hallway, the ceiling bright with glowstrips. The hexagonal pattern on the walls stretched into the distance, where it opened up to the central torus. Erick felt a momentary tug to walk there and see if the gardens were still maintained.

The entry they were in was immaculate, at least. The maintenance bots had been through recently, as the subtle odor of antiseptic and ozone still hung in the air. The only thing that struck Erick as odd was the silence.

Daruthr beat him to it. "No welcome party, Erick?"

"That's curious, I'll admit." Erick chose to walk to the wall panel to access the station logs. It always paid to make sure a system was clean before connecting. "We'll see who's chief of the watch." As he scrolled through the station logs, the only entries were automated. No human had made an entry all the way to the day of the supposed attack.

The day the talk of treason began.

Daruthr made a show of looking over Erick's shoulder. "There you are Erick, your first bit of useful information. And you didn't even have to ask a human for it."

Erick grunted. "Automated inputs, maintenance cycles, and not a single Harbormaster's entry."

"Not a good sign. I have soft queried the array's systems; there's only one sign of life. The temperature controls in the Harbormaster's control room have kicked on several times in the last hour. I think there's likely a person there, but I can't verify without taking control of a camera or two."

"Let's not. I'd like to keep the array's systems as calm as we can for the moment."

"Suit yourself. Shall we at least head to the control room?"

"I think we'd better." Erick's hand touched the butt of his sidearm, reassured by its weight and presence. He walked ahead, and Daruthr followed, the array's corridors twisting and turning out ahead of him. It had taken him a while to learn the layout of an array when he was younger, but now the dizzying maneuvers it took to navigate one were second nature to him. Thank the gods all arrays are the same.

They walked, Erick's feet carrying him largely by memory. They didn't see a soul, and the place was quiet and clean. Too clean.

"Look around Daruthr. What are we missing?"

"Unless you're referring to something literal, a nice big sign that says who framed you for stealing the Obershire shipment?"

He thinks he's hilarious. "Wouldn't that be convenient? No." Erick tapped his fingertips on a wall. "There's nothing. No smudges on the walls, no handprints on the computer panels. Nothing." Erick ran his hand along the wall, the obsidian surface smearing with the oils of his skin.

Daruthr grunted. "You're right. It's clean. Very clean. I'd expected more filth, what with the humans and all."

Erick looked at him with raised eyebrows. "Can you be serious for just five minutes? But, yes, that's what I'm getting at. We don't even have," he bent to inspect a corner, "a stray hair. How long do you think the automatic systems take to get a place this clean?"

"Without the constant skin and hair shedding of humans, several months. Perhaps longer, depending on the size." He paused. "For an array like this, I'd say six months, give or take a few weeks."

"The attack on the Obershire transfer only happened a few weeks ago." He continued walking towards the Harbormaster's room. "Maybe whoever is in the control room can tell me how this went unnoticed."

"Or so you hope. Very well, let's go talk to the people. Well, person." His voice became sharp as they passed a crossing corridor. "Erick. Stop, look here." He pointed, a few yards down the hall, at the base of the wall. There was a tiny star-shaped fracture ringing a hole in the paneling. It, like everything else, was immaculate, scrubbed by the array's cleaning mechanicals.

Erick pursed his lips, then replied. "Projectile hole. Long gone. And look," he pointed to the panel behind, "no scorch marks or discharge patterns. Simple kinetic slug."

"Kinetic only? Aren't those… rather antiquated?"

"Yes, and never used for boarding parties. The energy you need for target effects puts everyone at risk of sucking vacuum." Erick ran a hand across his beard, his eyes slightly wide.

Daruthr raised an eyebrow. "Assuming the trigger pullers cared about that, I'd say they were either lucky or knew what they were doing. We are far from the station's exterior and into the fully pressurized areas."

"With Bryn's report of the spy they caught, or almost caught, I'd guess they knew exactly what they were doing." Erick felt a new sense of urgency, and turned to continue down the corridor, his feet ticking on the spotless floor. "Let's pay whoever is in the command center a visit."

As they approached the Harbormaster's command center, their movements slowed to a stalk in a silent understanding. Erick finally peaked around the last corner and saw a fully suited figure standing at the harbormaster's controls. The suit was small, with minimal armor and only a sidearm. It was shale grey, with deep charcoal black patterns that made the eye want to slide off the form. Whoever they were, they were accessing the array archives, and he could see at least six security camera feeds arrayed on the holo in front of them. Erick raised his sidearm and zeroed it on the back of the figure's head.

"Stop what you're doing and slowly put your hands up."

The figure complied, hands up and fingers spread, the dark suit like the limbs of a charred tree.

"Now turn and identify yourself."

10

Cooperation

Deep in the bowels of the fortress
He came upon the enemy
Fast gripped he his iron-blade
Battle cry perched on his lips

Slowly, the suited figure turned, helmet still opaque. The faceplate gave off a mirror reflection of the room, Erick's own face distorted and twisted. Then it spoke, the voice of a woman. "I am Yetunde, Right Arm and Sword of Adebe. I am surprised you did not know that, Erick of Ollson."

He couldn't help but suck in a sharp breath. She knew him, knew him by sight. And here from Adebe space? But how?

Time for some blustering. "I thought I recognized your ship's design, Yetunde of Adebe. Why are you on my array?"

"You are branded a traitor, and executor Adebe does not believe you would be foolish enough to attack a transfer. But trust is a funny thing." Her faceplate flickered to transparent, and he saw her strong, wide nose and deep brown eyes fixed on him with a predator's gaze. "And so, Erick of Ollson, why should I trust you?"

"You're the one on my array. Why should I trust you?"

She stared at him for a moment, then her head bobbed behind the faceplate. Data arrived a moment later, his ocular displaying direct transfer protocol. His implants sorted it, parsed, and the flavor bloomed in his mouth. A pleasant smell filled his nostrils. Sensory data was full of nuance and near impossible to fake. He remembered this key from the first time he had received it from an Adebe executor, at his own ascension.

The key had an earthy complexity, smoky and savory with a kick. It took Erick straight back to the last Adebe feast he and Bryn had attended, Amari Adebe's ascension. He was young, but Erick had been impressed by his speech and commitment to the Empire's prosperity. Now, the taste was the confirmation he needed. Whatever Yetunde was doing, she was here at the direction of Amari.

Yetunde's helmet folded back with a sharp snap. Now that he could see her, the Adebe resemblance was striking. The high sweep of her brow, the set of her jaw, even her neatly braided rows of hair. But her eyes didn't carry the green of the full geneline; they were brown, flecked with gold. Erick slowly lowered his weapon but did not holster it.

"So, Yetunde. I believe you are an emissary from Amari Adebe. But your title, the Right Hand; how have I not seen you at Summit? Or at Amari's ascension?"

She smiled back at him, leaning back against the edge of the control console and crossing her arms. "Amari has many daughters and many sons. Not all carry enough of the blood for the Eyes of the Empress. But we still serve." She cocked her head to regard Erick and then flicked her eyes to Daruthr. Erick had the distinct impression she didn't miss much. He shifted his weight as she continued. "I saw you at Executor Adebe's ascension, and you did not see me."

"You're in their intelligence directorate, then." Erick was beginning to see where this was going. He was confident in her identity; the public key of an Executor could not be forged. And Amari's operatives were well trained. Maybe she'd found something helpful digging around in the array logs. He shook his head. "Probably relatively high up?" She remained silent, but her smile was mischievous. "I guess we can get to that detail later. What have you found in the harbormaster's archives?"

"Executor Ollson, you have forgotten to introduce your friend. Tell them to come in from the hallway." Damn. And here he thought Daruthr was able to stay silent. *Amplification in her suit, most likely.*

As Erick turned, the mendicant strode into the room, his grin warm and somewhat abashed. "Yes, yes, you're right, of course. I didn't want to intrude, as it seemed like you two were having such a lovely time getting to know each other."

Before Yetunde could reply, Erick jumped in. "This," he said, "Is Daruthr. He's an expert in computer systems and is my companion."

Yetunde's eyebrow rose. "Executor Ollson, I had not thought you would be one to mix business and pleasure."

Erick adjusted his estimate of Yetunde. She was trying to keep him off balance. *Everywhere you go, it's all about power.* Erick's voice held dry finality. "Not that kind of companion. As a computer specialist, I'd hoped he'd be able to help me with the logs, but if you've already accessed them, please tell us what you've found."

Yetunde smiled with just one corner of her mouth. "Yes, I managed to access the top-level data. I do not have enough of the blood for full access, but I was able to see the security feeds." She paused for a moment. "It is not pretty. The array has been empty for four months. Everyone is dead."

Erick nodded. The confirmation was expected, but the confirmation still twisted something inside him. "Can you tell what happened?"

"Every door on the whole array opened at once. The living quarters, command center here, even the children's creche."

Daruthr's voice rose in interest. "No footage of an intruder of any sort? We saw evidence of weapons discharge on our way here."

"No, nothing on the footage. But it could have been changed or erased."

Erick's mind churned while the other two spoke. There had been close to a hundred people who lived on the array. They were a community. They raised their children to take their places, their duty to honor the fold schedule and keep the ships flowing. They were the lifeblood of the Empire.

And they'd all died in a few minutes of terror.

He returned his weapon to its holster. *They were my responsibility. And they're dead.* He couldn't dwell on that now, though, not with a mission and the first hint of his enemy's identity.

Erick ran one hand down his face, absently smoothing his beard. "Clearly, it wasn't a malfunction. You're telling me there's no evidence in the network?"

Yetunde shook her head as she answered. "I cannot tell from the logs. There is something odd in the feeds, though."

"What?"

She pulled up a video, the date showing four months before. "Here, there is a gap in the video." A busy corridor, the people of the array going about their business. Then the image fuzzed and twisted, the view dissolving into a wash of multicolored pixels. She flipped to another camera, which showed a similar effect. "The second camera is further down the same corridor. It moves, as if there is someone the system refuses to see."

Erick shook his head. "That doesn't narrow it down much." He waved a hand in dismissal. "Any number of genelines have operatives that can do that."

Daruthr leaned forward and set his arm across the top of a console. "Not that many, Erick. Obershire, maybe, but Abrams, Kendrick—" Daruthr's eyes flicked to Yetunde. "Adebe."

Not a good time to get into pointing fingers. Erick ignored Daruthr's comment, but they should return to that. There were also the unknown spies that Bryn had mentioned in her message. "What do the rest of the station logs hold? Beyond the security feeds."

"There is nothing else. Just the operating system counting days and the code beneath it running the array systems. There isn't even a record of the fold to Obershire space."

Daruthr stepped forward. "That is alarming. Perhaps I can take a look? I have a way with machines."

Yetunde arched an eyebrow at him and moved to the side, gesturing to the control interface. "By all means. But do not get your hopes up." Her grin was feral. "I am good."

Daruthr moved forward, and his hands danced over the interface. "I have no doubt, no doubt at all. Unfortunately, we are not playing on an entirely fair field." He nodded at the displays as they rolled through data at a dizzying pace. Freeze frames of station cameras, internal and external, scrolled through on the left as the text and raw code followed on the right. "I have a deep familiarity with this particular system. One might say almost innate knowledge." Erick knew this was all for show. Daruthr didn't need the console interface to access the array's computers any more than he needed permission to breathe. His actual system query was no doubt happening much deeper.

Daruthr's voice was smug. "Ah, here we are. The time and parameters of the last fold made to Obershire space. It stayed open eighty-two seconds longer than planned." He looked at Erick strangely then, his eyes carrying an almost beseeching look to them. The gentle curve of his mouth was pursed slightly. "The fold was an incoming one, consistent with the scheduled movement of goods. Past that, our new friend Yetunde was quite thorough in the top-layer systems."

Erick nodded. "The question is, how could they have purged all of the top-layer data like that? The harbormasters don't share the geneline in full; they are gifted just enough so that the systems will respond to them. This shouldn't be possible."

Yetunde was first to answer, or perhaps Daruthr held his tongue. "And yet, Executor Erick, here we are." She cocked her head at him. "Though, as you said, the harbormasters don't have enough of the blood. Would an executor?"

Erick's eyes narrowed. *Whatever her skill, this kind of impudence is getting on my nerves.* "Yes, of course, one would. But you know that, and you also know that there hasn't been an executorial visit here in a long time."

"That we have evidence of here." Her brown eyes held is gaze.

Daruthr spoke, his brows furrowed. "Here, yes. But there may still be data on the Obershire array."

"Oh," Yetunde scoffed, "your companion is a comedian as well! Who cares what is in Obershire space? We can't get there from here with a fold, and sublight would take us six years."

Erick noted that she had already calculated how long it would take Obershire forces to reach the Ollson borders. He wasn't the only one with a vested interest in this war; the Adebe Geneline had many systems, but their planets were barren of life if full of mineral resources. They lived mainly in orbital habitats and depended on trade with Ollson and other genelines for luxuries like grain and animal protein.

His response was measured. "You are correct, Yetunde. Trying to retrieve data from Obershire space is problematic. But Daruthr is no fool." He turned to the mendicant. "Please, tell us what is on your mind."

Daruthr spoke quietly. "There is enough energy stored in this array for us to fold through to Obershire space and investigate.

Erick couldn't help himself. "I'm sorry, what now?"

"There would be very little time. I doubt we'd be able to board the Obershire array, and if the fold closes, you will be stuck there. There won't be enough energy to come back."

Yetunde's brow furrowed deeper as Daruthr spoke, her skepticism clear. "Now I know you are crazy." She held up a hand, fingers ticking for each point. "One. You do not have a beacon set on the other side. How is the fold going to find a way? Two. Even if you could somehow open a fold, you wouldn't have more than a few minutes before it closes. And three, that's Obershire space out there. We might fold ourselves right into a fleet of warships."

She leaned back against the console behind her, crossing her arms. Erick agreed with all her points, the most salient being the Obershire forces. The last thing he wanted was to open a fold that ushered in an invasion force. Bryn had alerted him of the spies, and their tampering with the arrays was undoubtedly an attempt to open a fold to Obershire forces. They'd have a large beachhead package staged. Perhaps many of them, depending on the range of any array they managed to compromise.

The silence hung heavy in the room, a thick blanket that Daruthr wore like a cape, his face calm and confident under Yetunde's gaze. Erick finally broke the spell. "If Daruthr says there's a way to open the array, then I believe him." Yetunde hissed sharply, her eyes wide. "Yes, I think he can do it if he says he can. The question is, should we? You've made a good argument against going." She nodded at him as he spoke. "How do we know we aren't going to let the Obershire forces come pouring through, and how are we going to be able to get anything useful?"

Daruthr, true to form, had an answer for that as well. "Erick, I will need to remain here to monitor the fold. I recommend we scan fully before you and Yetunde go through; I can close the fold within thirty seconds should we need to. It's not zero risk, however; a ship or two may get through if they are staged and ready. Assuming it makes sense to go through, how much you manage to learn is up to you."

Erick pursed his lips in thought. They could scan before committing, that was true. But it would also mean they would lose valuable time. He didn't want to open the fold and have to close it immediately. That would alert the Obershires to a capability he'd rather they didn't know about. But the array they stood on was a dead end. Even the lack of information didn't give them enough to go on.

"Daruthr, I'd like you to be ready to open the fold to Obershire space as soon as possible. Yetunde and I will take the *Svadilfari* through dark. We'll hit the fold quickly, passive instruments only. If we have to, we'll flip and burn back through. Suck up as much data as we can with the active scanners. We can parse the data after we return." Daruthr's hands began moving across the computer interface, and Erick continued. "We'll be small enough and have the element of surprise that I'm confident we can return without allowing any large ships through. If all is quiet, we'll use all the time we can."

Erick watched Yetunde's face while he laid out the plan. She had good control, but he could tell she was skeptical.

"Erick of Ollson, you are brash. We have no idea what is waiting for us on the other side of that fold, even if your…." She jutted her chin at Daruthr. "companion here can open an impossible fold. We cannot both evade and make it back without conflict; they know where we have to go to get home! Or maybe they ignore us and burn for the fold. What then?"

"Peace, peace, Yetunde. You're right; a single ship wouldn't have much chance if we ran into trouble." Erick held out one hand, palm up. "But we don't have a single ship. We have two ships. And we can surprise whoever is over there waiting for us. If anyone is."

Her eyes widened. "And now you want me to risk my ship on this crazy venture?"

Daruthr stepped forward between the two of us. "Perhaps, if I may offer a solution, we can all find this prospect more agreeable. Though for the record, Erick, this is brash."

Erick grunted. "What's your solution?"

"Yetunde's ship is first in, oblique vector and fast. And empty. You and her are both in the *Svadilfari*, at least to start. Erick, now would be a good time to bring up the assault pod."

So much for his trump. "Yes, well, I can't keep that card in the deck now, can I?"

"No, I suppose not." He turned to look at Yetunde. "Erick has a fully kitted assault pod in the flitter bay of the *Svadilfari*. It will be more than sufficient to sow some havoc in whatever forces you might encounter long enough to get both of you back across the fold boundary in a timely fashion. Though you'll have to ask him if you want to fly it."

Erick barked a laugh. "No. Not gonna happen."

Daruthr gave a thin smile. "I thought not. Yetunde flies the *Svadilfari* and her ship remotely, with Erick in the assault pod. He can cover a hasty yet tactical retreat if anything nasty shows up."

Yetunde's voice was curious. "If anything nasty shows up? What were we expecting?"

Erick shrugged. "I mean, this is where the Obershires lost their entire transfer cargo and ships to supposed Ollson forces. We will see if anything is left in the debris, and more importantly, try to access the Obershire array's computer records."

"So we are going to poke around a graveyard?"

Daruthr waved his hand. "Essentially, yes. We need you to get to the control room of the Obershire array and download any records you can."

"How is it that I ended up the one to go poking around with the ghosts?"

Erick smiled. She could do the math as well as he could; ally or not, he wasn't letting her take his fully kitted assault pod out for a spin. He'd rather lose the *Svadilfari* completely than the pod. But the least he could do was give her a reason to believe what she wanted to. "As Daruthr is staying here, you have better machines skills than I do."

"Flattery, then. Well ok, since we are taking both of our ships we can use one to shield us if needed."

Erick frowned. "Shields are usually broken. I'm beginning to rethink this. Should we really risk both main ships?"

Daruthr chose this moment to interject. "Erick, we are of eminent means between the three of us, and I think we should maximize our utility on the Obershire side of the fold."

"And what if we don't make it back before the fold closes? You'll be stranded."

Daruthr looked at him, a smile dancing around his lips. "Yes, but I believe you'll have other things to worry about at that point."

Yetunde snorted. "He has a point. So it is settled then. Two ships."

Erick nodded. "And you'll board to get any data we can scavenge."

There was a moment of silence as Yetunde and Erick locked eyes. She broke the silence first. "Deal. On one condition— whatever we find, I bring it back to Amari of Adebe." She shook her head, the beads in her braids clicking softly. "I'm not going home empty-handed."

Erick nodded. If it was something that proved his innocence, he was happy to have another geneline by his side.

"A deal then."

Daruthr grinned at both of them, clapping his hands together like a gunshot. "Excellent! This is going to be fun. To ships!"

11

Skirmish

Into battle he rode through the were-light
Nimble his steed and true his aim
Beside him allies spread
To face the unknown foe

Erick had helped Yetunde get the feel of the *Svadilfari*. The Ollson shipwrights had made more than just aesthetic design changes to the Imperial standards, not the least of which was the crash couch. It conformed to her more diminutive form like a careful lover. The support cells shifted and flowed as she moved and readjusted, the amorphous solid in each responding to the pressure with support of its own.

His place, enveloped in combat armor and bolted into the assault pod, was far less comfortable, but he barely registered it. His senses were flooded with the feel of the pod and ship systems, fingertip implants joined to the control network of the pod, and then on to control the *Svadilfari*.

His focus moved from internal to external cameras, all presenting him with perspectives on the outside if only one or two views were a priority. He held the camera feeds in mind as he also took in the raw data from the other sensors, presenting as a proprioceptive knowing exactly where the ships lay, where the fold array hung in the starfield. Ahead of the *Svadilfari*, Yetunde's small scout ship hung in position, vector aligned as both ships burned for the fold array.

Yetunde's voice sounded in his helmet. "Time to hand me the controls, Erick. Do not worry," Erick didn't need the camera view in the cockpit to get her smirk, "I will not scuff your fancy ship."

"Yetunde, you shouldn't make promises you might not be able to keep."

She laughed back at him. "If you do your job right, whoever starts shooting will aim for you."

"That, I believe, was the plan. We are on course and on time. Your ship vector is matched. You have the controls." He waited for her to reply, the ancient ritual of control half-fulfilled.

"I have the controls," she said, and he felt her presence on the shipnet, her attention on the engines and reactor and navigation. He gave her control of the weapons subminds last, like passing the leashes of a pack of angry dogs. Hopefully, they could remain kenneled.

Her voice took over the countdown calls. "Ninety seconds to fold transit. Daruthr, confirm we are green?"

A moment and Daruthr's voice filled the comm band. "Yes, Yetunde. We should have about four and a half minutes of power on this end, and more if the Obershire array has recharged."

Erick sincerely doubted they'd be tapping the Obershire array. He knew Daruthr's secret, the fact that he was likely the one calculating and opening the fold himself, but there was little chance he'd be able to operate the Obershire array simultaneously. Even his stories of the navigants implied the necessity for two, an anchor on each end. At that moment, Erick saw Daruthr for what he was; the duality of machine and man.

It didn't make sense, it made perfect sense, it was simple, it was complex. Daruthr the thing in the cage that his mother whispered about, an evil to be feared and watched. Daruthr in the cargo hold, re-writing matter to repair his own wounds. Daruthr smiling down at him as he lay in a puddle of his own blood and vomit on the hangar floor. Daruthr offering him the solace of a simple embrace when the world whipped and tore at him. He had been trying too hard to put Daruthr in a box, an ancient AI with unknowable motivation, or a freedom fighter who attempted to throw off the yoke of slavery. But why couldn't he be both? Right now, though, he needed the machine.

Erick closed his eyes and woke his assault pod. The sensors on the pod far outstripped anything he could see through his visor, and he would be encased in support gel anyways. His suit was a combat exo, not the wearable tank of a marine trooper's armor, but optimized for mobility in vacuum. It had one major advantage over a trooper's armor: the acceleration gel. He triggered it, and felt the icy liquid flow around his neck, then rise. It slid over his face, and he rode the cold shock, opening his mouth. The gel forced its way into his lungs like a living thing that filed his chest and forced his ribs apart. He fought the urge to gag, the animal panic that rose behind his eyes, and finally, his body decided he wasn't drowning.

When the pod systems came online, he would have chuckled if he still could. Whereas the Svadilfari felt like a racehorse, its subminds wolves, the little assault pod was all reptile, coiled strength, the weapons systems bent to a singular purpose. Erick warmed up the tiny reactor and primed the flitter bay door to open. He'd leave the scout ship as soon as they made fold transition, turning two targets into three. Best case, they were jumping at shadows.

Worst case, they were in for a fight.

The ring of the fold array leaped into brilliant blue Erick's feed, just before they sliced through it. The two craft arrowed through the darkness like creatures of the deep. As soon as the *Svadilfari* cleared the fold boundary, the Obershire array dropped beneath Erick, and he ejected the assault pod, feeling the hull shudder as the launcher spat him into the night. Yetunde's main drive lit far ahead of him and immediately washed out anything in that quadrant of the sky.

The blazing drive light did nothing to hide the Obershire ship that squatted near the mouth of the fold. Its hulking mass was barely out of the transfer danger area, clearly positioned for defense.

The Obershire ship was a bloated whale, long crimped lines from one end to the other with a cluster of drive and engineering modules gathered together at the pinched endpoint of the thing. Huddled there like festering barnacles, they seemed an afterthought, the designer surprised by the requirements of the engineers. Erick had always found the Obershire ship designs to be distasteful, but perhaps the proximity to this one made him react so strongly. Or the reminder of who they represented. His subconscious overlayed Dorian's fat bulk on the misshapen ship.

Erick evaded the thing with a quick blip of thruster, feeling the ice-cold of combat flush through his veins as the assault pod subminds became extensions of his own.

He subvocalized through the biofluid. "Yetunde, we have company. Just like we discussed, time to turn and burn."

Her voice came strained, clearly under acceleration. "Yes I know! Missiles. Lead ship. No incoming on the *Svadilfari* yet."

"Roger. I haven't been painted yet." Erick churned through options. The plan had been for him to make the noise with all the various flavors of hate the assault pod carried. But if they hadn't noticed him, he had to take what the enemy gave him. He set an active scan, avoiding painting the Obershire ship. There was only one enemy craft he could see. Perhaps they were there to salvage what they could or merely to repair the array and reinstall a harbormaster colony.

Yetunde seemed calmer, but he could hear her breath fast and harsh between words. "Erick! Where are my fireworks? These energy lances are not easy to avoid."

Erick saw the beams of charged particles through the pod's sensors. Rays of death reached out to sweep and stab at the two ships Yetunde controlled. The smaller ships danced like moths around the flame at her direction. He had to act quickly if they were to get back in one piece.

"Yetunde, new plan. I've gotten an RF ping back; there's active tech out there. Bullseye two-eight-zero, plus forty-five degrees, range around seven hundred kay."

Her voice came back clipped, the strain of concentration injecting pauses between her thoughts. "Copy, I paint a debris cloud out there, pretty thin. Some human-sized returns. Probably happened when the array decompressed."

Erick nodded to himself. "Yep. No way we will get you onto the Obershire array with that ship here. I'm scooping whatever is still working out there, and we'll egress."

"Negative. We cannot go toe to toe with a main ship like this! We need to leave. Now."

I'm not leaving empty-handed. "Start setting up your transfer. You have two ships; use them. I'll be back in ninety seconds."

"Roger." She did not sound happy. *Now time to take some of the heat.*

Erick had located the sensor emplacements on the side of the Obershire ship he could see. While the pod didn't have the power output for directed energy weapons, it was full of surprises. He tapped the Obershire ship's network, dropping off several copies of chaos algorithms with intelligent targeting packages. The network warfare overlay in his vision showed the packages hitting the Obershire firewalls and twisting, maddened bloodworms burrowing deep.

They weren't expecting that. Erick lit the pod's main drive and made for the debris field and his RF ping, watching the effects. Luckily he wasn't burning directly away from the Obershire ship, and his drive plume wasn't in the way of his own sensors. Erick could see the telltale flickering of lights run down the length of the enemy ship as the software began wreaking havoc. At the same time, he released a salvo of micro-rockets, each targeting the physical sensors systems. The several thousand tiny projectiles covered the intervening space rapidly, nearly half of them detonating.

The half that didn't detonate weren't duds; he'd told them to wait just outside the missile tubes of the Obershire ship. They'd be detected, of course, but the missiles couldn't fire with the swarm of counter-projectiles covering the launchers. It would take the Obershire gunners precious seconds to target and sweep them all with the energy lances, and they ran the risk of damaging their own ship.

As Erick crossed the space to the debris field, he gained resolution. The return of his active scans painted five-pointed stars, the bilateral symmetry of human life evident in the vacuum. Almost definitely, some of the returns were bodies. As he closed with the graveyard, he had about thirty seconds to wait and watch the battle unfold behind him.

Yetunde's piloting was impressive. She'd set her own ship on autopilot to fire all of its ordnance into one huge cloud, missiles and kinetic slugs all matched velocity as it bore down on the Obershire ship. The enemy lances still glowed, but they were absorbed and dissipated in the detonations as the ablative cloud of ordnance shielded both Yetunde's ship and the *Svadilfari* tucked behind. *That is a gutsy move.*

Erick arrived near the floating graveyard and dropped some attention on the main battle. As the scans had shown him, it wasn't just debris; there was a body here. The RF ping of active tech came from the body's head. A man, from the size. Frost rimed and damaged from collisions with whatever other ejecta accompanied him in his last moments. As Erick panned the pod's lights over the corpse, the gold and red robes gave him away. The Obershire harbormaster. Jackpot.

Erick extended a manipulator arm and cleanly severed the corpse's neck at the shoulder. He popped the doors on his empty micro-missile bay and stuffed the head in. *Not a perfect fit, but at least it's all in there.* Now the hard part, getting back past the main line Obershire ship and through the fold. *In… forty-five seconds.*

Time to move.

12

Victory

Raging was he, the field of battle torn
By the smoke and screams
Through it all he strode, ghost-like
His mind ever on his prize

Erick turned the pod back to the array. In his mind, he oriented it as down, and the rest of the skirmish fell out below him. He was suspended above the action, the array with its attendant Obershire ship below it. Yetunde piloted not one but two craft on the razor's edge of death. So much for the idea that he would draw fire in the more maneuverable assault pod. Erick hit his main drive and felt the pod leap around him, the remaining debris and bodies snapping away from him and lost to visual almost immediately. His focus was forward, down.

Yetunde's two craft wove past the Obershire ship, wheeling and turning, drive plumes like fiery swords. His cloud of micro missiles still stifled the enemy missile bays, but he didn't have much time to close in range. Even as he watched, Obershire gunners swept their energy lances across the clouds of missiles, evaporating them in searing fans. He needed to be under their guns. Speed was his advantage; they couldn't move their gun emplacements fast enough to track him if he got close. Missiles were a problem, but he had a full load of countermeasures and counted on the enemy saving missiles for the larger ships.

As he closed, Yetunde's tactic proved effective. Her lead ship, marked green in his display, was still surrounded by its own shield of friendly missiles, their spacing just far enough to avoid sympathetic detonations. They were an effective—if weakening—shield. The *Svadilfari* followed, staying in the cone of safety behind the lead ship. Erick watched as they closed with the Obershire ship, which had maneuvered to attempt to block access to the array. He glided just above the surface of the Obershire ship, dropping guided explosives packets and the occasional precious coilgun slug on anything that looked important. The coilgun was direct fire, forward only, so he spun the pod through a furious series of cartwheels to line up the shot, fire, spin, correct vector, and continue. The pod shed a flight of explosive packets as he spun. His mind was fully in the moment. It was bliss, a dance, an all-encompassing kinetic conversation, death dealt and death deceived.

Erick's blood sang.

Both of Yetunde's ships grew close, only a few hundred kilometers to the array. Erick blipped a maneuvering thruster, shooting for a gap in the armature of the ship he skimmed. The two ships got closer and closer. Erick's mind split between monitoring the approach of Yetunde's little squadron and sowing as much mayhem as he could while trying to get around the Obershire ship towards the open fold.

Suddenly, a wash of radiation blanked out the majority of his sensors. He switched to radar and saw an expanding cloud of debris where Yetunde's ship had been. He could see that it had nearly made it to the Obershire ship. She must have been trying to ram it! *Þessi brálaði tíkarsonur*! It had been a valiant effort. The Obershire ship had stopped firing, its energy lances momentarily silent. Erick guessed it would be a short respite.

The enemy was likely assessing for critical damage. Erick had a window. His weapons submind offered him the pod's last remaining ordnance, the matterbreaker. *Need some range before that goes off.* He reached out again through the electromagnetic spectrum and touched the enemy networks, still raw from his last attack. Unloading the last few copies of his chaos algorithms, he released the matterbreaker and lit his main drive, pulling up and away. His drive plume would do some damage as he turned, hopefully creating enough chaos that the enemy wouldn't notice the matterbreaker as it fixed itself to the enemy hull.

His engine howled back at him, the subminds screaming in protest as he pushed them farther. Through the haze of sensor contacts, information warfare, and adrenaline, he saw the *Svadilfari* flash past the enemy ship, just a few seconds ahead of him.

Yetunde's voice sounded on their channel. "Clear! Get back across!"

"Right behind you."

Erick dodged around the Obershire ship and squeaked by the edge of the fold, intense radiation from the fold boundary blinding his feeds. Behind him, he felt a lesser wave of radiation follow him through the fold as the matterbreaker detonated. *I just hope that's enough to keep them from pursuing.*

"Daruthr. We're through. Close it." Erick was proud that his voice was calm, given his heart rate.

"I am quite aware, Erick, and have begun the shutdown procedures. It will take approximately twenty seconds to complete."

"Well, you better hurry. It looks like we're about to have company." He had to give it to the Obershire captain; they were tenacious. They had taken their vessel, likely crippled from the matterbreaker and short on ordnance, and set it burning directly for the fold. The enemy ship was broad enough that it barely fit through the fold aperture. It usually would cross quickly, but Erick must have damaged its main drive. Now, it limped along, slowly crossing the boundary of the fold. Even damaged and low on missiles, it had batteries of coilguns, and the energy lances were effective over short ranges. *They won't destroy the array, but they can fire on the control room.* Daruthr was resilient, but Erick still felt a knot of tension grow in his chest. He doubted the mendicant could survive concentrated fire from a main battleship.

The Obershire ship was halfway through the fold and gaining speed. Erick began to turn, setting his flight path marker to the emergency airlock nearest the array control room.

Despite the subvocalization, Erick could hear the tension in his own voice. "Daruthr, time to go. They're going to try to take the control room, and it's best you were elsewhere."

Daruthr's voice came back calm. "That won't be necessary, Erick. But I'm touched that you care."

The electric blue ring of the fold winked out.

The Obershire ship continued on a straight vector, and Erick turned hard to get a better look at the back end. The fold collapsing had sheared it neatly, the decks it crossed spewing bodies and air into the vacuum. It must have been slightly off angle, as the snip of destruction crossed several layers, building floors cut like a blade of grass. Erick could see small four-limbed figures flailing as they spun away from the ship.

Missing its drive and engineering modules, the enemy vessel went dark. Emergency power kicked on a few feeble lights in some sections, wan red light spilling out to Erick's aided vision. He wondered how many crews were trapped. But no, they were the enemy, and he reached out across the shiplink. The fold array wasn't defenseless, and he felt the weapons it carried respond, missile racks and beamers warming at his thought. His mental control designated the Obershire ship as hostile, and the fold array began to bring its weapons to bear.

Almost.

His time on Breydablick Station jumped up unbidden. Now, of all times, his mind brought forward the people who had abducted him, beat him, and left him for dead. They were citizens of Ollson, yet they had hated him. Would the crew of this ship fight to the last? Were they loyal to Darius Obershire beyond all shadow of a doubt? There was a time when he would not have waited, when he would have killed them without question.

So why am I hesitating?

13

Spoils

Truth, he found in the field that day
Truth, he hoped would satisfy him
A bitter truth, or a sweet one
It will always be what it may

"Erick, I see you made it back as well." Yetunde's voice jarred him back to the reality of their situation. He relaxed his hold on the array weapons, their payloads still stowed.

"Yeah, thanks to luck and your fancy flying."

"Not fancy enough to keep both ships! This is too much for me, Erick. You owe me a ship!"

Erick made the mistake of trying to chuckle through the biofluid. It hurt. "Too much for the daring right hand of Amari Adebe! What a villain I am to have dragged you out here to my array. In my system. Against your will."

Erick heard the laughter in her voice, no doubt high on adrenaline. "No matter. Perhaps I'll take this one." The array loomed in front of Erick's pod, and he could see the *Svadilfari* visually, just docking. Erick made for the flitter bay on the smaller ship, which opened wide.

"You don't want that ship. It's too spartan for the luxury reputation of Adebe."

Daruthr's voice cut in before she could reply. "Not that this isn't an amusing exchange between you two, but we really ought to download what data we can off your ships and see if there's anything useful. Hopefully, before the Obershire crew gets their act together and finds a functional fighting suit."

Erick frowned in his own suit as his subminds ran shutdown checklists. "I doubt that there's a fighting suit in that ship. It was there doing what we were doing; looking through the wreckage. Which begs the question, what were they looking for?"

Daruthr's voice held a thread of tension. "Yes, well whatever the answers we find in our ship data, let's review while we are under thrust, away from here."

Daruthr wasn't usually this skittish. Perhaps something else was troubling him. *Is he drained from getting the fold open?* Erick told the pod's navigation submind to complete the docking and refueling and began draining the biofluid.

A few seconds later, it was clear, and Erick could speak clearly again. "Daruthr, I'm nearly docked. Let's set course back to the Gjoll station."

His voice was much smoother now. "Already laid in; we can depart once I'm back aboard."

"Good. But we won't have to sift through all the ship data unless you want to." Erick's pod glided towards the docked *Svadilfari*, flight path marker showing a green line to rendezvous.

Yetunde replied. "Daruthr just made it on, so we'll be under thrust in a moment. And what do you mean we won't have to look through the data?" The larger ship undocked and lit its primary drive, and Erick's pod adjusted the course to maintain an intercept. Erick's stomach flipped slightly as the acceleration changed, but he ignored it.

"I found something." Erick felt himself crack a smile.

Daruthr's voice had a note of forced patience. "And do tell us, what have you retrieved from Obershire space?"

"A severed head."

Yetunde laughed. "It had better have an implant in it. We will have words if I find out you were looking for trophies while I was getting shot at."

"You think Ollsons are the kind to take a head as a trophy?"

"I wouldn't put it past you."

Erick laughed. "I'm hurt. Of course, there's an implant in it. Let's see what the Obershire harbormaster saw before he died."

HLÉHÉR

They left the Obershire crew drifting. They likely had sufficient emergency stores and a lifeboat or two to take them to the array. Without the right genes, they'd be mere passengers, able to move about without accessing any of the systems. But they would live until his anonymous message to the Gjoll manager triggered a rescue attempt. Or at least Erick kept telling himself that.

They stood in the flitter bay, the largest open space on the *Svadilfari*. The air carried the tang steel and the spicy smell of recent vacuum, the assault pod humming gently to itself as it rebuilt what ammunition it could from the raw material stores. The *Svadilfari* wasn't equipped for self-repair, and he hadn't thought to bring enough of the more exotic materials to replace missile warheads for the pod. To be honest, he hadn't planned on using it at all. So much for his refined and simple search for the truth of his innocence.

What had he been thinking? That he would be able to simply appeal to people's better nature? That he could pass for anything but geneline had been a fantasy. His wandering thoughts swept again to the memory of the three in the Breydablik station. He felt himself recoil and thrust the whole encounter from his mind. *Focus on the task at hand.* They needed to know what was on the implant.

Daruthr sat on the ground in front of them, humming happily as he turned the severed head around, inspecting each side. The Obershire Harbormaster's face was fixed in a look of fear and outrage, his eyes wide. Had they not been pale and clouded over, it might have been almost comical, the dead man expressing his indignation at being handled so callously.

"Daruthr. Can you give us some idea of what we have? Can it be salvaged?" Erick crossed his arms as he spoke, his shoulders tightening. The proof he needed was in there, so close, and he needed it like a drowning man needs air. He could take it to the Empress, and finally, all this would be over.

"Yes, yes, I think it will be salvageable. Perhaps not in the traditional sense, but I can see a way to show you what he saw."

Yetunde's voice had an edge to it. "Not in the traditional sense. And what does that mean, exactly?"

"It means I am unable to simply download the data to the ship; the interface plug was in his spine, which someone, unfortunately, did not recover intact."

Erick kicked a foot idly against the decking. "I was in a hurry."

"Yes, yes, Erick and we're extremely grateful for your quick thinking and auspicious luck. But now my own expertise will be required if we are to recover anything of use."

Erick caught the note of caution in Daruthr's voice. Yetunde still did not know Daruthr was anything other than an incredibly gifted technician who had a way with fold arrays. That alone was enough to arouse suspicion, but as far as Erick could tell, she had not felt the need to press any further. Yet he did not think exposing Daruthr's true nature was a good idea. It had taken Erick a long time to come around from loathing, and he wasn't sure where he stood even now. Yetunde was a recent ally. He wanted to keep her that way and, by extension, the

Geneline Adebe. An outright alliance with an ancient evil AI? That was probably a stretch.

"Right, do your thing here. Yetunde, will you join me in the cockpit? We can leave the processing of severed heads to Daruthr. ."

Yetunde smiled. "Of course." She turned to leave, speaking to Daruthr over her shoulder. "Tell us when you have it. As interested as I am in your methods, I do not feel like poking around a dead man's brain."

Daruthr had already stood and was moving towards the tool locker set in the wall. "Yes, yes, the medical arts are not for everyone."

Erick followed Yetunde out. He glanced back just before entering the corridor and saw Daruthr place the head on a fold-down worktable, his free hand at the ragged edge of its neck. From where his fingers touched the dead flesh, a blue glow cast sharp shadows on the table.

Erick followed Yetunde to the cockpit, trailing her up the short ladder and taking his seat in the pilot's crash couch. She sat next to him, and they watched the glowing readouts, speed and range ticking along as the ship guided itself to Gjoll Station.

"That really was some impressive flying. I'm not sure I could have done as well."

"And what is so surprising about that? Are you some sort of flying prodigy in Ollson space?"

"No, no. I didn't mean to…" *Move on.* "Will you show me how you did it?"

She called up a few displays in the shared HUD, showing him the command linkages she had spliced into the control code. It wasn't a pretty bit of coding, but it had worked. It even looked stable.

Erick couldn't help but be impressed. He'd never devoted the time to learning to code software directly. He had always had someone else to solve the technical problems and enact the vision he brought.

Yetunde gestured to a line of code. "Here, you can see the way I tied the two ships together. The algorithm works by treating the two ships like the beginning and end of one long ship. The trailing ship will follow through the same space that I command the front ship through. Unless I change it." She brought two holo controls up, one under each hand. "I used my right, here, to fly the lead ship and only interfered with the trailing craft if I needed to evade. The algorithm calculates the best course and speed to rejoin the lead ship's path after I deviate."

"Clever. It would come in useful when controlling droneships as well."

"Yes, that's where the code originally came from. In Adebe, we do everything with droneships. Easy in the belts, but on our planets… well, the delay is long enough that we need good software." She dropped her hands, wiping the holocontrols away and clearing the viewscreen. "But you did not come here to talk about flying."

"I didn't; you're right. But I wasn't kidding when I said I wasn't interested in a severed head."

"Erick of Ollson, squeamish at the sight of blood?"

"Hardly. I am interested in what's on that implant, and I'd be no help to Daruthr."

"Speaking of Daruthr, I do not think you have been entirely truthful about him." She ran a fingertip across the edge of the cockpit glass where it met the metal, leaving a ghostly trail of condensation.

Erick glanced away from her, smoothing the edge of his sleeve. "Daruthr. Yes, well. He's an asset, as you noticed. He has skills far beyond mine, and his knowledge of array physics has proven useful." He noticed his fidgeting and folded his arms, an old habit in cockpits surrounded by controls. He figured he'd ask her about Daruthr, as soon as they were alone, but she didn't know anything concrete yet. She was fishing.

Yetunde clasped her hands, inspecting her fingernails. . "I mean your relationship. Are you lovers?"

Not where I thought this was going. Erick tried not to sound affronted. "What?"

"Ah," she replied, "so it's unrequited love then. I should have guessed."

"Is this an Adebe thing, where you try to throw me off balance before making your point?" There was a far cry from negotiation techniques to intentionally misinterpreting facts. But Yetunde was sharp; she had to be needling him for a reason.

Yetunde smiled. "The only question is, who doesn't know it, you or him?" She gave him a sidelong glance. "I have seen the way you are around him."

She's really playing this card hard. Erick kept a neutral face, raising his eyebrows slightly. His voice was calm. "And how is that, exactly?"

Her laugh was easy. "You are mean to him! I can see the tension in you. You treat him like a coiled snake, or maybe I should say a tempting serpent. Even when you share a space with him, your whole body tells me you are working too hard to keep him distant."

Erick's mind flashed on the last few interactions they'd had. Daruthr in the array, giving them the option to check the Obershire fold. The short planning session they had done before launching the two ships, Yetunde drawing out vectors in the array briefing room. And finally, gathering in the flitter bay, Daruthr's face, calm and inquisitive, as he turned the Harbormaster's head around and around. What subconscious feelings had Erick been compensating for? Residual loathing? Something else? He would need to pay more attention to his actions; he'd gotten lazy outside the strict environment of Karvasok. All these years, and how quickly the old habits fell.

Whatever the truth, he wasn't going to turn Yetunde away from a false assumption. Let her believe whatever she wanted about Daruthr and Erick's relationship. There were more important things on Erick's mind.

Erick measured his words. "Daruthr is a singularly incredible person. He's intelligent beyond anyone I've met, his ethical code is by all appearances ironclad, and he has shown me kindness where I didn't expect it." He sighed, then looked up to meet her gaze. "But I don't have time for lovers. My daughter is relying on me to find and furnish the proof that will set us right with the Black Throne. If I fail her, we will be plunged into war. Even if we survive that, we will be at the mercy of the Empress to grant us pardon."

"I'm beginning to believe you might not have sent your army into Obershire space ." Her eyes searched Erick's.

"I think you know I didn't, seeing as how my forces are all in their garrisons. The Admiralty hasn't even done any training exercises recently."

"And if I someday believe you, what then? Do you expect Adebe to come to your aid with a fleet of warships?"

"I didn't think Amari had the garrison to field a fleet."

Yetunde smiled slyly. "True, but no one knows as much as we do. You're going to need all the help you can get."

She was right. Ever since their hurried departure from Summit, he'd felt increasingly confused and adrift. He'd had so many deep assumptions challenged, downright destroyed. At Summit, he had been the Executor. Unquestioned, if politically beset. But he had given that up, passed his mantle on far earlier than planned. He'd had perceptions of his subjects' loyalty destroyed. He'd completely re-assessed his understanding of the evils of the mendicants. And apparently, navigants. Yetunde's insistent questioning left him with the uncomfortable realization that, more and more these days, he didn't seem to know his own mind. He had known the world's truth for centuries, yet now he felt on the edge of control.

It was terrifying. But Erick could at least try to learn about his potential allies.

"Yetunde, what does Amari think of," he gestured, his hand encompassing everything outside the cockpit and in, "this. Everything."

Yetunde looked out the canopy on her side, her fingers drawing idle shapes against the cold window. "The Executor Adebe does not see fit to grace me with his opinions. I'm his intelligence chief, not his personal advisor."

"Aren't those two things one and the same?"

She turned to meet his gaze. Her eyes burned. "You do not understand. The Ollsons keep to the geneline, one executor and one heir. The way it has always been."

Erick frowned. He hadn't met to upset her. "Not always. Before the wars, everyone had family."

She snorted. "Before the wars. A thousand years ago? That does not matter. It is dust."

"It's not dust. My ancestors flew my flagship against the mendicants during the war, and I grew up on that ship. The *Sleipnir* is every bit as deadly now as it was then."

"Not the technology. Of course, it is the same. The Empress decrees, so why should it change?" She shook her head once, vigorously. "I mean the things we do. This world we live in, it is stagnant. The same as it was, as it will be."

"Forgive me, but I'm not seeing the connection. What does this have to do with Amari Adebe and you?"

"I am his child. Well, mostly."

Erick took a moment. "You mean his literal offspring."

"Yes. But the Empress has decreed only one heir. Only ever two with the gene to control the galaxy. So Amari had to be careful with his children, keep their genetic heritage far enough from his that they wouldn't break her laws."

"And that's why you don't have the Eyes of the Empress."

"And why I cannot control the important things of this world. That access you have, whenever you want it?" She shook her head. "Why do you think I am so good with computers? I had to be."

"A fair point. So Amari wants family the way it used to be, children, grandchildren, nieces, nephews. The mess of the commoners with the power of imperial blood."

"You make it sound like the end of the world. Easy for you who have had none to say, but family is life, it is love, it is more vital than oxygen." Yetunde took a breath before continuing. "You have a daughter. You know what that love is like with one, so now imagine many."

Erick shook his head. "Families corrupt with power. Jealousy, entitlement, emotion driving action. Those without power can afford family, but it's a price we pay for stability."

Yetunde looked at Erick, her eyes searching. "You believe that. No, I believe that you believe that. But it doesn't change the fact that Amari wants more than the Empress is willing to give."

"And he hates her for it."

"Hate is a strong word. We all love and worship the Empress in our own way. But he is unhappy with the laws. I am one way he has found around them."

One way. Erick decided to leave that be for the moment. "So all those years ago, when I came to Amari's ascension. The Adebe staff, ministers, police chiefs. Were they all his family too?"

"Most. He is meticulous, you know."

Erick gave a short laugh. He knew Amari was smart as soon as the two met, could see the brightness in his eyes and hear the snap in his voice. But to keep a whole family secret from the Empress, even one so distant that the blood wasn't pure. Erick had to be impressed. No wonder the man had always talked about connection, about love, about the people you hold dearest. His speeches on community were legendary at Summit, even if most other executors simply watched his time tick down. It made sense to Erick now, though. And after what Erick had been through, after seeing Bryn step up so early, the connections he'd made with Daruthr and Yetunde. Perhaps there was something to Amari's obsession with community after all.

Erick placed a hand on Yetunde's shoulder. "I can see how it would be difficult to be at once loved and wanted and also untrusted." Yetunde's mouth curved to a rueful smile. Erick continued. "He trusts you though, I know it. If I had to ask him for help, had to ask him for ships and soldiers to defend my own family. Would he come?"

Yetunde was quiet. Erick wasn't surprised; it was a tall order, asking her to betray Amaris confidence. Eventually, she answered. "I do not believe he thinks you attacked the Obershires. But we have no proof at all. As far as the other executors are concerned, we will comply with the Empress' will." Erick nodded, his lips a thin line. He needed allies, and he'd hoped Amari's conflict with the Empress' decree on children might be the leverage he needed. "But," continued Yetunde, "I will bring him whatever we find. Even if it is not enough to convince the Empress, you may still have an ally in him." She fixed him with her piercing gaze. "We will wait and see."

Daruthr saved Erick from having to voice any more thoughts, his voice cutting out from the intercom. "Erick, Yetunde. I believe I have something you will wish to see. Will you join me in the flitter bay?"

Erick smiled, and gestured to the rear. He keyed the comm. "We'll be right down."

Before they moved, he addressed Yetunde. "I appreciate your candor. It's hard, to be honest these days, and doubly so with something like this. I hope we can find proof enough for Executor Adebe."

Yetunde smiled as she stood from her seat. Her words drifted over her shoulder as she made her way down to the lower deck. "As do I, Erick of Ollson. You will need as many friends as you can get."

On that, at least, he had no argument.

14

Secrets

Victory, well fought, is its own reward
There is no substitute for gold
But gems and jewels did he eschew
In search of true treasure there

While he understood the necessity of improvising a plug, Erick felt Daruthr's treatment of the Obershire Harbormaster's head was a bold statement.

"Heads on spikes, Daruthr? Have we really come to this?"

Daruthr gestured to the bottom of the skull. "So dramatic, my dear Erick. I needed to graft on to the nerves, access the implant directly. And besides, now you won't have to hold the man's head yourself."

"Very funny. How's this going to work?" Erick crossed his hands and cocked his head to Daruthr. He had no doubt that if there was any information on the ocular implant, Daruthr would find it. He'd even removed the surface of the man's right eye to expose the solid-state implant. A tiny crystalline lens flashed ruby-bright in the skull's dead orbital.

"If you'll join me here, we'll display the imagery there," Daruthr said, gesturing behind the head to a smooth wall section.

Yetunde sounded even less impressed with the setup than he was. "Remind me again why we need to put this poor man's remains through this?"

"Unfortunately, we must. Erick would likely agree with you, but the solid-state implant had a more traditional storage drive, likely located somewhere in the body we didn't manage to, *ahem*, retrieve." He looked at Erick pointedly, then continued. "So instead, we will be able to access the short-term buffer held within the device itself. I have attached a supplementary power source. We should be able to see it, but it will be a single-use display. The implant's buffer will be purged as we retrieve it. Obviously, I'll be recording the projection, but the quality may be an issue."

Erick called up the flitter bay lighting system from the control panel he stood by. Once the lights were lowered enough to give good contrast, he nodded to Daruthr. "Let's see what he saw."

Daruthr nodded and activated the small camera fixed just under the Obershire head. He placed his hand on the stake just under the camera, and slowly began to turn a small, knurled ring. A high-pitched hum permeated the room. Finally, a flickering, red-tinged light emanated from the implant nestled in the skull. On the bulkhead, a picture formed, grainy and out of focus.

Yetunde noticed it before Erick. "It is moving backward. His eyes are still frozen, yes?"

Daruthr nodded. "Yes, indeed. I am manually controlling the playback speed with the power supply. Unfortunately, I can't pause it, but I will slow it when I can."

The imagery continued, the starfield slowly revolving. Finally, the Obershire array became visible, swimming into view and enlarging, and Daruthr slowed it as the array grew large.

Erick watched quietly. He felt his shoulders tense at being so close to the truth and forced them to relax as the projection began to move. At first, the frozen eye gave little resolution, but then the moment of decompression came, all backways in eerie silence. The image was filled with a fighting suit, or at least Erick assumed so. It had an extra set of arms and was matte black, holding onto the array window like a spider. An arm reached out, then disappeared from view as it grabbed the Obershire harbormaster around the waist. It thrust him back through the open window, the shard of armored glass reversing their random patterns to return to an unbroken pane. The harbormaster had been looking up, and in the reversed video the many-armed suit seemed to launch itself away from the array, lost back out in the darkness. Blue light from an active fold filled the small control room, and the harbormaster's hands dropped his helmet to the ground, removed suit gloves. The view reversed until the hologram of the Ollson harbormaster filled his vision. Her face was a mask of anger, a finger pointed directly at the camera pickup.

Directly at the Obershire harbormaster.

Daruthr twisted his hand back, stopping the red-tinged playback.

Erick spoke first, breaking the fragile silence. "I don't know what to believe there. Those fighting suits with extra arms aren't our design. Our harbormaster's enclave was gifted with a share in the geneline, and entrusted with our entire people's security. I cannot believe she would take this action."

Daruthr shook his head. "The Obershires might sacrifice a man to plant evidence, but if he were meant to be found, he'd have activated his beacon. We've just watched him thrown from the control center into vacuum, too surprised to send so much as a distress call. It's pure luck that you happened to find him."

Yetunde spoke next. "Did you see the suit of whatever shattered the window, pulled him out? Two extra arms. It did not look like any soldier I have seen in the Empire." The room was blanketed in a heavy silence as she paused. When she carried on, Erick was struck by how close her thoughts were to his. "I have no idea if that is what Revenants really look like. We have never recovered any bodies in Adebe space. Erick, you send troops to the periphery, no?"

Erick nodded. "Yes, but the enemies there are mostly using scrap they've managed to piece together, cannibalized suits and ships. Nothing like our fighting suits, and nothing like that."

Daruthr's voice was tempered. "Erick, I don't know if this is the proof you need. The aberrance of the multi-armed suit is suspicious, but your harbormaster seemed fully aware of the situation, even enabling it. Is this enough to bring before your Empress?"

Erick paused to think. First, the way he'd said your Empress had not gone unnoticed by Yetunde, who had narrowed her eyes at Daruthr. And second, Daruthr was right. The recording had little concrete proof, and what was there showed his own harbormaster seeming to condone the violence. But he couldn't help but come back to the six-limbed attacker. That suit was strange. It would take a direct mind-machine interface to use an extra set of arms like that, assuming they were mechanical, and the Empress had banned that technology long ago. His own wirejob was as close as it got, which was specialized to allow fighting and flying, not controlling another body.

And yet. "The extra arms on that suit. It is possible that a nervous system augmentation could allow that kind of control, however outside of flight augmentations direct mind-machine interfaces are highly regulated." Erick paused, then looked to Daruthr. "It could have been set up by the Revenants. They have lived in hard vacuum and deep space for a long time; maybe their suits are equipped with extra arms. Hell maybe they've grown extra arms." Erick shook his head. "But it doesn't prove anything."

Yetunde looked back to him, her interest in Daruthr's phrasing apparently forgotten. Or buried. "And what do you think we should do, Erick? There is no more for us here; both Daruthr and I have gone over the array. This is a dead end."

She was right, of course. There was no more data at the array. But perhaps they didn't need the array. "There's one thing, well one among many, that still bothers me. Where did the ships go?"

Daruthr smiled at him. "Now, that is an excellent question. Presumably, the Obershire ships were destroyed, and they may have had time to clear the hulks from the other side. But, that would have been faster work than I'm inclined to give Dorian credit for."

Yetunde nodded, her eyes slightly unfocused. "The transfer initiated, and the inspections happened. They may have planted bombs or sabotaged the Obershire ships somehow during that, but there should have been wreckage."

Erick ground one fist into his palm absentmindedly. "But there wasn't. The Obershire ship was trying to salvage and repair the array, from how close it was to the fold boundary. We went there and we saw it. So those ships had to have gone somewhere." Erick looked to Daruthr. "We need to access the Gjoll station tracking logs. Any ship under thrust would be visible to the monitor system, even without a transponder."

"You're assuming that the ships all came to this side of the fold and then went… somewhere," Daruthr replied, gesturing vaguely beyond the hull.

"Yes, I am. If they didn't, then the trail is cold. But if they did, we might have a little more data. Maybe they're even here, somewhere in the system, gone dark after scattering."

"I highly doubt that," scoffed Yetunde, her arms crossed.

Erick conceded the point. "You're right, but we should at least find out."

Daruthr clapped his hands, the sound echoing in the small flitter bay like a gunshot. "Well, then. I always did enjoy a little digital plundering!"

15

Heist

With twist and rage he cast off
The deceitful prize of battle
War-weary, he looked to others
To aid him in his quest

They arrived at Gjoll station at the end of a wake cycle. Erick spent most of the ten-day trip back into the system sleeping, the excitement from the last few days having finally worn off into a miasma of fatigue. After the fight with the Obershires, Erick felt a new camaraderie between the three of them. He thought of them, perhaps not a family as Yetunde described it, but certainly aligned. Daruthr had proved trustworthy. Yetunde has risked her life for him. And he had managed to keep them alive, despite the efforts of his enemies. What tighter bonds could people have?

When all three were awake, they talked about the Obershire harbormaster recording, discussed next moves, anything to fill the hours. The strange suit with six limbs was a common topic, but a compelling alternative to the Revenants had yet to emerge. Erick learned a lot from Yetunde about her upbringing in the Adebe Geneline without being a full member of it.

The ship was cramped for three, but Erick was beginning to feel better about having the other two along. It would have been a lonely trip. At times he couldn't believe he'd set off alone, so sure of himself and his capability. It was hard, at first, to remind himself that he was no longer an executor. He still dropped into old habits, an offhanded imperious tone of voice, or an outright order. Yetunde made a game of pushing back on him, a tick mark on the flitter bay wall each time he tried to override someone, told them what to do. At first he was offended, but after the long journey, he'd managed to come to a begrudging acceptance. It wasn't all bad.

He was grateful that they had refueled the reactor at the array and had enough power to run the grav damper in the ship. Erick wouldn't have relished spending three weeks at three gravities. Under a blessed one gee, he awoke to the smell of coffee, Daruthr and Yetunde's voices carrying the few feet from the galley to the racks. Erick was not as sure of this new plan as he made out to be. In all likelihood, there would be nothing useful in the station tracking logs. And even if there was, they'd still have to find a way to get to it without Erick simply walking in and demanding it.

The last thing Erick wanted was a diplomatic incident. There was enough on Bryn's plate, and he felt a deep guilt at the situation in which she struggled. Uncovering enemy spy action in the middle of planning to defend Ollson systems should have demanded Erick's presence. Still, even if he wanted to go back, the carefully regimented fold schedule made that nearly impossible. He didn't like the feeling of losing control of the situation, but it swam now beneath the surface of every thought. He had to shake it off.

Erick rose, drew a fresh set of coveralls, and threw the old ones in the refresher. There wasn't enough water on the ship for a proper shower, but he made do with the mild solvent dispensed in the ship's tiny lavatory. This was a scout ship, after all, not a transport. It wasn't designed for living aboard for extended periods, and certainly not for three. Luckily, at least one of them had very few hygiene requirements.

Erick joined the other two in the galley, making straight for the coffee dispenser. They stopped talking and greeted him, Yetunde with half a knowing smile.

"Daruthr has been telling me so many things, Erick. Such interesting history the two of you have."

His stomach knotted slightly, though he couldn't believe Daruthr would reveal the truth so quickly. Would he? "Oh really now? And what part of the long and no doubt boring tale has he regaled you with?"

"Just the basics, his status as a stowaway, what I understand was a rather exciting time on Breydablik, and so on."

Erick felt a sliver of fear rise at the mention of Breydablick but pushed it down. "Yes, well, we have had some interesting times, haven't we, Daruthr?" Erick filled his cup as he spoke, the earthy and spicy scent of the coffee enveloping him in a nostalgic cloud. "But I'm sure we all have some secrets intact, despite the presence of such an effective… What do you prefer, Yetunde? Is it spy or something less fraught?"

She laughed, and Daruthr flashed him a knowing grin. The bastard was probably enjoying this. *Ah well, can't deny him a little fun. After all, he's the one that stands to lose the most.*

"Erick of Ollson, spies are a sorry lot. They spend all of their time skulking around in the shadows, trying to be someone they are not. All to get close enough to power to chip away a little piece of it for themselves." She raised her chin. "I am an intelligence agent, and a good one. You only found me at the array because I needed you to."

"Ah, of course, I forgot how you planned our arrival so precisely." Erick winked at her, feeling a grin threaten to tug at the corners of his mouth. *She's not so bad, after all.*

Daruthr's smooth voice broke in, "I believe we have some business to attend to?"

Erick nodded, selecting a quick breakfast from the menu in the galley. "We do. We will need to gain access to the system surveillance logs. Based on the last experience on a station, I'd rather avoid letting anyone know we are here. Bare minimum required for docking and servicing, etc."

Yetunde nodded. "I can assist with that. Any terminal that isn't air-gapped should work."

Erick raised an eyebrow. "Confident as ever, aren't we?"

"Confidence comes after competence."

"I don't doubt your technical skills, but the station software requires a Geneline code. I know you share some of it, but that level of encryption needs more fidelity."

"What level do you keep system logs at? I can do this. Stop telling me I can't."

Daruthr coughed pointedly before Erick could reply. Erick sighed and turned to him as he began eating. "Go on, Daruthr," he said around a mouthful, "what do you suggest?"

Daruthr smoothed his impeccably flat tunic, pulling an imaginary thread from its edge. "Well, you could absolutely go into the station and gain access to a hardline terminal, I've no doubt relatively easily. I could even cover your tracks from here, looping and editing cameras and so on."

Yetunde nodded. "Ok then. Let's walk over the route and the plan."

Daruthr held up one hand. "But, there is a high probability of getting caught anyways. There's a lot of Ollson presence here, unsurprisingly. And I can't strike people blind. Well, not without a good bit more trouble."

Yetunde frowned and opened her mouth to speak. Erick jumped in before she could. "So what? You obviously have a better plan. Just tell us." The constant insouciance of Daruthr was beginning to wear on him.

"There are system backups down near the core."

"Backups? How are we going to get ahold of one of those? They're kept in a vault. Not as strong as the system goods vault, but damn near." The system goods vault held all the outgoing materials until they were loaded for transfer. It was the closes thing to impenetrable that imperial tech could manage. The setup for the system backups was similar, just without the exotic matter cages and the complement of automated and therefore merciless guards.

Yetunde jumped in. "We have a similar series of backups in Adebe space. And the backups have to be moved from the collection array where they are recorded to storage."

Erick saw it. "So, we hijack one of these shipments, take the crew's place, then lie our way into the vault and find the backup we need."

Daruthr nodded. "Precisely. A relatively simple plan, but there are a few rough patches to iron out."

Erick finished his breakfast, setting the spoon across his plate. Yetunde took the chance to eat, her eyes flicking back and forth as Erick spoke. "We need to know how many are on the crew. I should be able to take care of access codes. But the transport ships are Ollson cutters, nothing like the *Svadilfari*."

Daruthr nodded. "We'll commandeer their ship, of course. But the crew's the real problem."

"Why?"

"It's a crew of four, unfortunately. A pilot and three security officers. Not in recon armor, but a step above the usual policing suits."

Erick crossed his arms, leaning away from the small table. The metal of the bulkhead behind him was cold on his back. "So we need another body, then."

Yetunde broke in. "Not just anybody. We need a pilot and some muscle. I don't want to try flying two ships again when we can't afford to lose either of them."

Erick nodded. "Ok, a pilot then. Daruthr can check the system logs and see if there's anyone with a skillset that will work."

Daruthr nodded. "There's one more thing, though."

Erick's eyebrows went up. *This should be interesting.* "What's that?"

Daruthr tapped his temple with two fingers. "Your eyes, Erick. The Eyes of the Empress are exceedingly obvious, and contacts aren't going to cut it this time. Retinal scanners, radar, lidar, and so on. Your setup is nothing if not thorough when it comes to data."

"I'll need to stay in the ship then."

Yetunde's voice held a laugh. "No, Erick. I think I know where Daruthr's thinking now."

Erick felt his stomach drop when he realized. "No. Nope. Absolutely not."

Daruthr's voice was kind. "There's really no other way."

Erick looked at Yetunde, who showed him a mouth full of teeth. Her voice was syrup. "You're going to need new eyes."

16
Collusion

She dwelt in the grip of the enemy's hands
Tightly they grasped, her throat tightened
As she grasped for stable ground
Too dark is the night, and dark is it e'er till dawn

Bragja's brothers didn't even bother to hide the sound. Another week since the market and the palanquin. Another week of stretching her credits to the breaking point. And now her brothers left late at night, not coming home till the morning. She heard boots on the floor, zippers, the slide of jackets over hooks. She knew they were leaving. They knew she knew. They didn't care. They might as well have said it to her face, but then, they slept most days. Harvir had told her a few days ago, in a rare moment of sibling consensus, that he didn't think the starfall was coming back. They were on their own now. She didn't want to believe him, though she felt her own fears echoed in his words.

Bragja didn't know what made her follow them. She hadn't the last few nights. But now, something was different. Maybe it was because it was about time they earned their keep, instead of relying on her credit. Maybe she was afraid of what they were getting into.

Tonight, she had to know.

She waited until she heard the front door swing shut, then leaped up. She fumbled for her pants in the darkness, one hand reaching for her jacket as the other touched the seax at her belt.

The long blade was thin but supple, a gift from her father. Starstuff blades weren't illegal, but making them was technically theft from the Ollson Geneline. Her father had managed to forge it without the overseer's knowledge. Now it was all she had left of him, and its weight reassured her.

The night air was on the edge of cold, the coolest she could hope for after a sunny day with the winter solstice looming. Even on the longest night, her thin jacket was more than enough this early in the night, but the morning promised bitter cold. Bragja strode quietly down the street, keeping herself to the edges of darkness.

She caught sight of her brothers after only a few blocks. Predictably, they were headed in the direction of the *Sovereign*. *Maybe they really have just been drinking every night.* She trailed them, the streets still dotted with travelers heading out or in for the night. A man in golden robes wearing a sandwich board of the Empress' crest stood on the corner. His muttering took on a fever pitch as she drew near, the glow of his wallet open and empty. Bragja didn't break stride as she passed him.

Finally, her brothers neared the tavern. Bragja began to relax, focusing more on how she would explain being at the *Sovereign* just after they had left. Maybe she could message a friend, ask them to meet her. A group of people piled out of an alley in front of her, laughing and singing. She let her gaze linger on one young man, his head thrown back as he belted out the song.

When she looked back, her brothers were gone.

There hadn't been time for them to make it in the doors of the *Sovereign*. Bragja hurried along the path they must have taken. *Where the hell...?* Just before the crossing street, she stopped to turn a slow circle. The only place they might have gone was just in front of her and to the right, a tiny alcove. A dim light struggled to hold back the night. She slowed, carefully pacing with cat's paw steps until she could see into the alcove. Four small stairs led up to a door, covered over with an ancient slab of sheet metal. There were windows to either side of the door. Bragja walked into the alcove and checked the near window first, her dark clothing melting into the shadows. Dirty and cracked, scratched by the dust, the window passed only a sliver of light from inside. But she heard voices, just loud enough to make out.

"You got it?" A gravely rumble.

Landry. "Yeah, man, everyone knows." *Damnit.*

"I not want everyone, little shit, just who we can trust."

"You know what I meant. Everyone who's supposed to."

A low grunt. "Good. This goes well, you all might be okay."

Harvir's voice this time. "How?"

"What's that, little shit brother finally found his voice?"

"I've always had a voice. Tell me what you mean. How will this be okay."

"Fuck, you want me to spell out for you?"

Harvir's voice quavered slightly, but he spoke out. "Yeah. I don't see how this march will get us back to work."

A cutting laugh. "Work? What makes you think you going to work? Point is, planet boy, that intown is working fine. They got plenty of food, plenty of everything. You no wonder why that is, seeing as you had no starfall in so long?"

"They're always ok though."

"Yes, and that is what I am trying to say. Look, Landry, please explain this to your little brother later. We got things to do tonight."

Landry's voice rose now. "He's right. They are obviously getting their credits from somewhere. All we want is to know where. If we have to do something else, then sure, but we aren't going to just die out here beyond the wall."

Harvir's voice was small. "No one's dying."

"But they will."

The gravelly voice cut back in. "I said later, damnit. Look here. Take this. Tomorrow, any of those guards or soldiers tries to give you a hard time, you point it at them and push the button."

"What's it going to do?" Landry's voice held a hint of skepticism.

"Just their armor and weapons, boy. Ain't gonna kill them, but it will protect you. That's all, eh?"

Bragja couldn't fit the pieces together. What was this spacer doing in outtown? And what were her brothers caught up in? They were young, and kind of dumb, ok Landry could be really dumb, but they weren't criminals. They hadn't fallen in with any of the gangs, and they all worked. Or used to work. This didn't make any sense. And what had the spacer handed over? She moved slightly, trying to line up her vision with a crack in the window. The room was not well lit, but it was enough as she panned her head around. She made out Landry's silhouette and Harvir standing beside him. And the one who must have been the spacer, his squat form a wide smear of dark on dark. She caught the impression of a mustache, beetle brows. And he held something in his hand, red and square.

Bragja needed a better look. As she shifted her weight, the poured stone under her foot crumbled, and she scrambled for a hold on the windowsill to keep from falling over. The crumbled stone slid down the side of the stairs to clack against the ground. It wasn't very loud, but it was enough.

The gravelly voice was loud. "What the hell was that?"

Bragja turned and jumped off the steps, her feet again carrying her back into the shadows. She had seen enough; the spacer sounded like trouble. She wanted to avoid spilling blood with her brothers near; she couldn't guarantee their safety. Besides, they had said tomorrow. *Those little shits.* She would confront them in the morning, at home, and in a safe place. Safe for her at least.

Landry was going to get it.

17

Power

The storm gathered, air spring-heavy
Dust hung heavy in the sky
Signs and portents for the storm-born
As the moment of truth drew nigh

The morning was cold. Bragja's credits had stretched as far as they could, but she had to draw the line at frugality somewhere. They'd thought her crazy when she started coming home with blankets on the hot days. Now, the scratchy coverings sealed in their body heat, keeping out the creeping fingers of chilly dawn. The days were still hot, but the temperature at night dropped quickly after the day's heat dissipated. Bragja had worried she wouldn't be able to sleep after what she'd overheard, but the first rays of light pierced the one small window and brought her back to consciousness she didn't remember leaving. The good news was she could hear two reassuring sets of snoring in the main room. She didn't hear anything from her aunt's room. She also didn't give a damn.

The room's chill was cutting, and it took a monumental summoning of willpower to crack open the cocoon of blankets that wrapped her. She didn't bother trying to be quiet. If her brothers woke up before they were ready, then good. It would only be the natural consequence of staying out all night.

Bragja dressed quickly and picked her way across the room, weaving around the boots and coveralls on the floor. The tiny kitchen alcove was her happy place in the morning. She'd salvaged a piece of picker cockpit from the wrecking yard a few years back, the scrap of diamond canopy too small to reuse. It would have been ground down and fed into the hoppers at the factory, but she managed to smuggle it out in her backpack.

Fitted into the hole she'd cut in the outer wall, the diamond scrap gave her a window to the world outside. Her street was on the outermost concentric rings of the city, and the window gave her a raw view of the planet. She could see where cracked rock and sand ended abruptly at the sky fall fields, endless churned impact craters that marched off to the horizon like a frozen parody of ocean waves. Sometimes, if the clouds were just right, mid-level cumulus and higher stratus painting the sky, the sun would rise into a riot of color, stabbing red fingers into the purple clouds as they bled orange and pink. This morning there was a huge towering storm at the bast of the distant mountains, rising to rage against the light of a new day.

Bragja pulled a box of grain from the small pantry and shook it, frowning at the pitiful sound of hulls on paperboard. She poured a careful measure into a bowl, added water, then set it in the heater box. While she waited, she watched the distant storm lash acid rain against the uncaring crater scape. She'd have her peace, enjoy her breakfast, then wake her brothers and confront them. The spacer's voice still lingered in her head.

Outside, the rest of her street was waking. She heard a few of the usual banging of metal doors as people left on early morning errands, but as she ate her grain bowl, the hubbub failed to reach its typical peak. Bragja opened the door to the street. She didn't know why, but something was nagging at her. Something not quite right. The streets weren't as busy as they usually were. And something else.

Everyone was walking the same way.

Coveralls of factory workers and the dull tan of pickers mingled in the crowd as usual, but the flow was one-way. Their feet made a dull thudding, but not a single person spoke above a whisper. In the few seconds the door stood open, Bragja tried to meet the eyes of passersby. They looked down or away or towards whoever they walked with. Some walked alone, either swept along by the social momentum of the crowd or deliberately keeping their distance.

She shut the door and walked the few steps back into their main room. Her brothers had woken, and Landry's movements were quick and sure. Harvir raced to keep up, his undershirt flapping. That damn shirt. He'd wanted a smaller one, more his size, but Bragja and Landry had a rare moment of agreement. No need to buy a new shirt when Landry's hand-me-downs were still good. Harvir fluttered moth-like around the room to keep up with his brother.

Bragja set her bowl down on the counter with a sharp snap. "Where do you think you two are going?"

Landry was sifting through the pile of clothing and detritus near his cot. "Going out, Bragja. You should stay inside."

"I'm sorry, what? If it's dangerous enough to keep me inside, then you aren't leaving either."

He shot her what he clearly thought was a withering glance. "Don't be so sure. There's big things happening today." He gestured with each choppy sentence as if his thoughts were too big for just words. "Huge things. Change is coming. We are going to get out of this. And I don't want you around in case things get weird."

He found a pair of socks and began pulling them on. "We know they sent the starstuff somewhere else. The intown still works fine."

Bragja crossed her arms, one hip cocked. "Landry, you're an idiot. They wouldn't send the starstuff somewhere else. We have the pickers, the factories, and everything the Ollsons need to process it right here."

"Oh yeah?" His eyes glowed with rage from under bushy brows. "I say that's bullshit. You know there's more planets in Ollson space; they probably sent it there. We didn't meet quotas. We weren't fast enough. Our factories are old. It doesn't fucking matter!"

Bragja hadn't seen him this worked up in a while, but somehow it didn't surprise her. That damn spacer probably filled his head with this nonsense. "That's stupid, and you know it is. The feeds told us there was something wrong with the Gjoll transfer."

Now it was Harvir's turn to wade in. "The feeds are the last refuge of an unthinking person." Who the fuck was Harvir quoting? "We are all smarter than that, you just don't want to see it."

Bragja felt her control spiraling. She need to calm them down, get them to think. "See it? Ok, seriously. What the actual fuck has gotten into you two? I know we haven't had a starfall in a while, but that's no reason to lose your minds."

Landry advanced on her, his hands working the clasp of his belt closed. "Not lost. Bragja, look, I love you. We love you. But you've still got your eyes closed."

Bragja realized she wasn't going to win this one, not like this. Maybe she could try to slowly de-crazy them over time, but it wasn't happening this morning. "Fine. But I'm coming with you."

"No," said Landry, sotto voce, "you're not." He held a little red box in his hand, about the size of his fist. It was covered in swirling patterns, a delicate filigree of darker red.

Bragja's heart caught in her throat. "Landry. You need to get rid of that. Now." She knew it, the pattern, the size. She'd seen it on her datapad.

"I don't think I will."

"You don't understand. It's a relic. You'll bring the Ollsons down on us all."

Landry met Bragja's eyes. "I'm counting on it." He raised the box in his hand, fingers set into small divots around its edge as he pointed it at Bragja, his palm out.

There was a humming sound, then nothing.

18

Mistakes

The rushing tide of water surged
The foam-capped waves were bright
Crashing with the thunderous violence
The storm did break over the bay

Bragja had a mouthful of cotton when she came around. The side of her head throbbed where she had struck on the way down. She remembered Harvir calling out, something about not too much, but it was like someone had taken a whisk to her brain. Something about the box, a spacer. Man with a scar.

He'd had a suppressor. She was certain, the image from her datapad unmistakable. And he'd used it on her.

Shit.

Bragja reached up to the counter and drug herself upright, looking at the clock. The tiny numerals resolved with aching slowness. *An hour, give or take.* A full hour. They could be anywhere.

She stumbled across the room, finally reaching the door and throwing it open. She shielded her hand from the glare to look down an empty street. Every door or window that could close was battened tight. There was usually a stand on the corner, Marisse who made wide-brimmed hats for the agri workers from spare scraps of lumaweave; gone. The neighborhood kids, who had spent the time since the last starfall playing in the street; gone. Old Pjotr, his gnarled hands somehow plucking graceful melody from the strings of an ancient guitar; gone.

Bragja moved out into the street, her hands low and twitching at each sigh of wind. She felt the hairs on the back of her arms standing straight out, a buzz in her ears as her eyes jittered, plate-wide, from place to place. Her feet carried her along, of their own will more than any thought. Her brothers were out there. No one was where they should be. She needed to find them.

She traced a path further and further towards the city center, growing closer to intown gates. Finally, she heard the low rumble of a crowd. Scraps of shout bounced off the high metal walls of the streets to her ears, and she felt her pace quicken. She knew that wherever there was a crowd, she'd find her brothers in the thick of it.

Bragja moved faster until she was running, her knees pumping and the heavy weight of her seax bouncing against her thigh. The crowd was roaring, and above it, a voice, still indistinct. She poured on more speed, dodging around the tight corners of the roads to the intown gates until finally she burst out into a sea of people.

Everyone was shouting. Some were chanting, *We Are Worthy*. She could barely make out the words as the crowd ebbed and flowed. All around her was chaos, arms and legs. She realized too late that the maelstrom had engulfed her, swept her up in its current. The mass of bodies washed over her, and she was tossed in the froth of noise and heat. The smell of sweat and humanity filled her nostrils, cloying, the air in her lungs replaced with panic.

Not like this, said a voice deep inside her. She clung to the life raft of her thought. This wasn't her. This wasn't how she wanted to be. The people she saw around her had eyes wide with panic, the screech of their collective amygdalas evident in the pallor of skin and frantic movement. But not her. She would not give in to the fear.

She took a deep breath, and began to cut her way through the crowd. She pressed on. She didn't know what else to do, knew that the mass of humanity would swallow her if she stopped moving. *So don't stop moving.*

Finally, as she neared the front of the crowd, she heard a single voice carrying over the crowd's roar. It was the leader of the chant, his voice amplified somehow. And familiar. And just as she recognized the tenor and tone, she saw Landry. Bragja felt her stomach clench like she'd been punched.

He was standing on top of an upturned palanquin, a transducer held to his throat. Next to him, Harvir held a small speaker that projected his voice out over the crowd. His hair, normally disheveled, was wild, thrown back out of eyes that burned like the foundries of the factory floor. She had seen the tension in him, the energy tied up tighter and tighter every day for weeks. Now the band inside him had snapped, the dam burst, and the rage he poured out threatened to sweep her away.

"We are worthy!" His voice rang out, fist raised.

The crowd chanted it back, "*Við erum verðug!*"

Bragja felt the crowd around her. They had formed a semicircle, pushing closer and closer. At the center of the semicircle was Landry, and behind him, the gate that led to intown. The twin towers gleamed in the sun, their intricately worked emerald caps diffracting the light into rainbow flashes like the spray of a waterfall. The gates were open; Bragja couldn't remember the last time they had been closed. Nothing short of an armored assault would overwhelm the defenses in the glimmering green towers, almond-shaped lenses like eyes over the crowd. Now, their sightless gaze looked out over the sea of people, cold and unfeeling at the angry and suffering masses.

"We are worthy!" Landry's cry met with the same chanted answer, perhaps a little more frenzied. The sun was just beginning its climb towards zenith, and the cloudless sky had begun to pour down heat in preparation for the midday. What was he thinking? That the intown was somehow going to come out and recognize the crowd, start passing out food and water and reassure everyone that everything was going to be all right? Bragja held her own in the press of the crowd, numb, dumbstruck at the tableau. Her brother couldn't possibly be that stupid. There must be something else, something he was waiting for. The spacers?

Without warning, the twin emerald towers flashed bright, momentarily eclipsing the sun's light. They pulsed once, a radiance so intense and brief it seemed committed to far memory as soon as it registered. The crowd stopped mid-chant, a few ragged cries dying on the lips of those in the back.

From the gate, armored figures marched. They must have been waiting, just on the other side of the wall. Whether the flash from the emerald guard towers was the signal or the response, she didn't know, but Bragja knew the armor she saw wasn't the usual overseers and enforcers. These were soldiers, likely the planetary garrison.

The armored figures bore the Ollson wolf on their chest plates, carapaces gleaming through the dusty air. They seemed to flow outward, completing the empty half of the semicircle formed by the crowd without a single identifiable communication. Not even a hand signal. Intellectually, Bragja knew they were likely using their internal armor comms, but she could only argue with her limbic brain for so long. The effect was terrifying, like they were all puppets driven by the same master.

Landry had turned to face them from atop the wrecked palanquin. For a moment, dust hung frozen in the sun as he stared at the soldiers, one hand on the mic at his neck and one clenched fist at his side. His chest pulsed, heavy breathing ragged over the susurrous. From where she stood, Bragja saw Harvir standing beside him. The younger boy's knuckles were white on the speaker, every tendon in his neck taut. His eyes were dead flat, face a pallid mask.

A soldier stepped forward and spoke, voice amplification painfully loud in the front row. "You are here unlawfully. Disperse."

Landry smiled slightly, then shook his head. "We will not. You will hear us now, *heigull*!"

"Disperse."

"We have lived every day, outside this wall, without complaint. Without thought to more or better, we have died in your factories, been crushed by starfall, starved and bled and struggled. We aren't going anywhere! *Við erum verðug!*"

One soldier, presumably the speaker, stepped forward. His armor was a slightly bluer grey, sporting a long antenna mast. "Disperse now. You have no right to—"

Landry's voice rose and cracked with tension. "We have every right! We are worthy." The crowd muttered the phrase, some carrying the shout near the end. Landry continued, riding the wave of the crowd. "*Við erum verðug!* You see, we are worthy of more than just this. Our lot in life is at the start of the chain; so be it. But we are not animals, to be left to die while you sit behind a wall!" This was more than Bragja had heard her brother speak in a long time. Even before the starfall stopped, he had been soft spoken and quiet. If anything, the lack of work in the factory had made him more sullen and distant. Now he seemed alight, the glow of righteous anger and fury enveloping him in a halo of passion. Bragja was torn. *Too many soldiers to get him out of here.*

Bragja moved around the front edge of the crowd as quietly as she could. There was a chance that when the soldiers started breaking up the crowd, she would be able to get to her brothers before things escalated. They'd probably start with non-lethal shock discharge, but there weren't that many of them, and the crowd was enormous. They might go right to the riot gas.

Bragja had never seen it used, but she'd heard the old timers talk about it. She didn't like the idea of making an exit in between bouts of involuntary projectile vomiting.

"This is your final warning." *Ansans Ári. Damnit.* She moved faster now, elbows clearing a path as people grumbled at her insistence.

Landry's voice had grown calm. Too calm. "I'm tired of listening to you, *kjöltuhundur.* Go back and tell your boss we want to see him."

The soldier stepped back even with the others. In unison, they raised their arms. A small door slid back on each forearm, and a wicked-looking barb protruded. Bragja suddenly couldn't look anywhere else. The soldiers swiveled their arms to the crowd. Bragja knew she should do something but couldn't tear her eyes away from the weapons. With a start, she realized the next soldier down had drawn a bead on Harvir, who still stood clutching the small speaker. The boy's knuckles were white and sweat beaded on his brow.

The next few seconds were a blur. Harvir shouting something, pulling the small red box out from inside the speaker. Bragja screaming at him to stop. The heavy thuds of the soldiers falling to the ground as their suit balance failed. She realized she had crossed the ground to the upturned palanquin, and stood frozen. The crowd had gone silent. The emerald watchtowers were out, their green light dead.

Bragja's voice rattled. "Harvir," she forced through the tightness in her chest, "what have you done?"

19

Recruiting

Full wroth, but not over-full
He sought them out in the shadows
Cut-men, sly-men, takers of lives
And bound them strong to his cause

The bar was dilapidated and deeply loved. The worn edges of the frames on the wall were chipped and scarred; occasionally, they stuttered and blanked when shifting images. Spacecraft of all shapes and sizes filled them, light assault flitters turning agile pirouettes next to the bloated bellies of heavy cargo craft. Each image, some moving and some still, appeared with a small line of text below it. Manufacturer, model number, tonnage, and the occasional short history of whatever military unit flew the craft displayed. In a corner was an ancient instrument, rows of black and white keys illuminated in a pool of yellow light from a single overhead lamp.

The music was low but loud enough for privacy. Erick fought down his nerves as he crossed the room. *It's nothing like the last time.* Daruthr walked before him, Yetunde following. Despite his companions' presence, Erick couldn't shake the feeling of dread that stole down his spine. The smell of blood on the deck plates jumped back to him, and suddenly, the thug who'd broken his ribs leered down at him again with crooked teeth and a face full of hate. Erick took hold of himself with a deep, shuddering breath. *Not now.*

Their destination was the man sitting in the back of the room, his shoulders hunched over a ceramic tankard. As they approached, the man's thumb levered open the silver top and he raised it to drink. The three sat, Daruthr leaning forward easily on his elbows, Yetunde sprawled back with a casual eye on the opening to the corridor. Erick crossed his ankles and focused on the man at the table.

He was still drinking. His hair was brown and cut short. He wore a short beard, thick and swarthy, that hid a square jaw. When he finally lowered the tankard, he revealed dark eyes and a thick brow.

The man looked at each of the newcomers in turn. Erick saw him sway slightly in his seat, but his eyes were clear and calculating. He looked to Daruthr and spoke. "So. You must be him then." He looked Daruthr up and down. "Strange, you don't seem like you'd be named Shaddai."

Daruthr smiled, bowing slightly. "Sincere apologies, but a necessary subterfuge. I didn't trust the system with my real name. But now that we're here allow me to introduce myself."

The man said nothing but nodded once, and Daruthr carried on. "I am Daruthr, and these are my companions, Erick and Yetunde. We require your unique skill set."

"Yeah, you said that. But you didn't say why. And that's why I told you to fuck off."

Erick looked at Daruthr and raised an eyebrow. He hadn't mentioned any of this on the walk down from the ship. Smoke and mirrors were not a great foundation for trust.

Daruthr smiled. "So you did, and I sincerely apologize for the intrusion. I'd like to share the finer points of the job, if you have somewhere we can talk?"

The man frowned into his tankard. He rolled whatever was left in it around, then threw it back. The sharp snap of the container hitting the table was apparently well known as the barkeeper put his rag over one shoulder and began moving towards them. "I think I want to know who you really are before we talk turkey. And I need another one; this cup has a hole in it."

The bartender snagged the empty tankard on his way by, not even breaking stride. Erick took the opportunity to speak. "My name is Erick. And this is Yetunde." She gave the barest hint of a nod. "And I promise, we're here in good faith."

The man laced his fingers behind his head. "Faith don't mean much to me these days. I like credits. And for all the cloak and dagger bullshit you three are throwing around, it's probably going to be a whole lot of them." He frowned as if being struck by a new idea. "If I take the job at all."

Yetunde shot Erick a look, then spoke. "You can at least tell us your name before we offer you the job. Let's all be civilized, eh?"

Daruthr snapped his fingers. "Ah, my sincere apologies! Where are my manners? Please allow me to introduce Binya Haddid, ex-Abrams special forces and now a very expensive gun for hire."

The bartender returned Binya's tankard to him, ale sloshing over the edge. Binya dropped his hands and cradled the mug between them. "I go by Bin these days. And I'm not a gun. I'm a pilot, and the best there is." Here Yetunde snorted, but Erick didn't respond. The Geneline Abrams was small, but their special forces were legendary. They went under the knife young, and while the skill of the Abrams surgeons couldn't match the Ollson Forgers, their augmentations were a cut above any other geneline's. Electromag, cerebral overclocking, subsentient AI, and a lesser version of the Ollson enhanced metabolism. Erick re-assessed how much Bin must have drunk to even appear tipsy.

Daruthr was the one to respond. "Yes, the best there is. Again, that's why we want to hire you. I assure you, credit won't be a problem."

Binya laughed. "See, that was a bad play, Daruthr. You're supposed to start with a lowball offer. Pretend to walk out." Binya waved a hand towards the entrance, then back to the table. "Come back later and slowly bring the price up. You must be new at this."

"No. I'm just fabulously wealthy. Will you hear the job, at least?"

Binya sighed. "You know, fine. Sure." His eyes rolled back in his head, the full whites showing and eyelids vibrating. A second later, and he was back. "There now, we can talk in peace." He looked directly at Erick. "No prying Ollson eyes in the walls to worry about." He leaned forward and whispered, "Just those at the table."

Erick's stomach dropped for the second time since walking into the bar. *Jæja fokk.* "I suppose there's no reason to deny it at this point. Yes, I'm an Ollson."

"Not an Ollson. You're the Ollson." Bin took a drink. "The contacts are a nice touch, but I can sense your implants a mile away. You leave a smell, on the network; did you know that? Ocular. Wirejob. All the other goodies."

Erick nodded. "I see I'm going to have to do something about that."

"I wouldn't worry too much. I have an advantage most don't. But those eyes aren't going to make it past any scrutiny."

"Yes, well, they don't grow on trees."

"Look at you with the archaic lingo." Bin nodded to Daruthr. "I just sent you the name of a good shop. You pay enough, no questions asked. They do good work."

Daruthr nodded to him. "My thanks. We will add that to the itinerary. But there is still the matter at hand regarding your employment."

Erick jumped in. "We need a pilot. One who can get close to another ship without being spotted." He glanced at Yetunde, wondering how much of the plan to give away. "Under burn."

"Yeah, ok. Sounds good. You meet my price, I'll do it."

Odd. He hadn't expected that sharp a turn. Binya had been downright belligerent until he found out who Erick was. Erick's eyes narrowed, but he responded calmly. "Great. Glad to have you."

"And honestly, I don't give a shit why you need my help. No, don't tell me. But it's gonna cost ya."

Erick crossed his arms as he leaned back in his chair. *There it is.* "Let's hear it then."

Bin grinned and began tapping his finger on the table with each demand. "One, I don't want to know any more than I need to. Too much knowledge gets you killed. Two, whatever ship you need me to fly, it's mine when the job's done." Erick gave a sharp exhalation. *Not going to happen.* "And third, I want credits. And not just a few million." Here he paused, finger and thumb stroking the beard under his chin. "Call it eight hundred million."

The man was clearly out of his mind. Despite his former sharpness, Erick had to assume Bin was simply drunk. Aside from the demand to be kept in the dark, either of the other two were showstoppers.

Together it was insulting.

Erick opened his mouth to say as much, but Daruthr was already speaking. "Done, my good man. You'll have a ship and credits to last you a few years at least."

Erick ground his teeth. *Un-fucking-believable.* But Binya had already drained the rest of his tankard and stood. "The blackout will last you a few more minutes, but when you see that light," he pointed to a corner of the room, where a small, mirrored ball hung, "you probably need to find privacy elsewhere. And now, if you'll excuse me, I've a song to sing." Bin turned on his heel and moved off towards the instrument in the corner, where a row of black and white keys beckoned. He reached under the wide seat and pulled out an empty plastic canister, which he turned and held up to the small crowd that had gathered. They cheered, and he placed it ceremoniously on top of the instrument and began to play. The melody was round and pulsing, flowing with deep chords while the syncopated chorus ran across the higher registers. Erick wished he had time to enjoy it, but his blood was nearly boiling. Daruthr had just promised this man an impossible deal.

Erick leaned towards Daruthr and hissed, "What the fuck? I'm not giving him my ship. And that's enough credit to keep him drunk for the rest of his life."

"Peace, Erick. He will get a ship out of the bargain, and the credits aren't for him."

"What do you mean?"

"Despite his best efforts to keep himself off the grid, I'm a little savvier than most regarding computers. He's got a family back on Hebron. The money will pay his passage, and if he's wise with it, will keep their family for as long as they live."

A scoundrel of a pilot with a heart of gold. What a cliché. "Well, I'm glad you managed to find the most honest mercenary in the system, then."

Yetunde leaned in towards the center of the table, her eyes on the empty tankard. "He may have a family, but he's no saint, you hear? He's Abrams SF." She made a spitting sound. At least Erick hoped it was just the sound. "Those implants of his can mask him anywhere. Who knows how many people he's killed."

Erick nodded, glossing over the mention of bloodshed. "At least we know he's competent. Not easy to blank out an entire zone without tripping the network alarms."

Daruthr made a show of sniffing disdainfully. "A rather primitive data loop, I'm afraid, but more than enough to fool the elementary programs you have running here."

"Hey, this is my station, but it's not like I'm running security."

"Running, no, but ultimately responsible for, yes. No matter. At least Binya's services are secured." The notes of Bin's song continued to wash over them. "But on to the next thing. We have a small ophthalmic matter to attend to."

Erick sighed. "Right." He had been watching for it, and the small red light in the corner winked back on. "Now?"

Yetunde's voice held a note of surprise. "Right now, then? You do not want to think about it first?"

"I really don't want to think about it at all."

The three stood, and walked to the exit. Here he was, Erick of Ollson, reduced to contracting an Abrams mercenary to soldier. Ex-Abrams, even. And now, he followed Daruthr to some gods-forsaken hole in the wall chop shop to get new retinas so he couldn't be mistaken for who he truly was. *I just hope this is worth it.*

The sounds of Bin's playing followed them out the wide door, fingers of melody embracing them, stretched until they snapped back, and Erick was once again awash in the sounds of the station corridor.

20
Surgery

Remade was he, and forged again
Without as much as within
He felt the turn and change in his bones
And saw the world anew

Lightstrips weren't supposed to flicker. They were designed to be completely uniform in their illumination, the tiny radioactive diamond battery providing power for a hundred years. This reliability was necessary in the stations, where a malfunction in lighting could plunge a corridor into utter darkness. An upstanding citizen might fall prey to unsavory activities without the light. So Erick was more than a little concerned when Daruthr led them to an abandoned corridor, the walls smeared with filth from knee down, with the lightstrip in the ceiling stuttering like a flame in a gale.

"I'm a little concerned at where you've brought us."

Daruthr glanced back over his shoulder, stepping around something that may have been a human form wrapped in blankets. If it was dead, it hadn't been for long. The smell in the corridor was more of a vegetal funk than the putrid stench of decay. "Not to worry, dear Erick. This isn't even the worst part of the station."

It's not? Yetunde moved up next to him as they walked along to either side of Daruthr. "You know, we could still just…

not do this. There is no way this is a legitimate doctor. What if he cuts out your eyes and cannot get them back in?"

Erick looked at her sidelong. "You are not helping."

She inclined her head towards him and gave a pointed look. "I am trying to help you. We should figure something else out."

Daruthr stopped outside a small door set in the wall. It was unmarked, with a keypad set in the center at chest height. "If you two are quite done, we have arrived at the recommended location. I am not overly concerned for our safety, but perhaps Yetunde had better watch the corridor, just in case."

"Oh, you do not have to tell me twice." She backed up against the wall across the corridor, her form melting into the shadows. The flickering light cast her movements in a staccato burst of still images. Just before he turned, Erick caught a glimpse of her disembodied grin floating in the dark. An intelligence agent and not an assassin, sure, but Erick had no doubt she would be a deadly opponent in the gloom of the hallways for anyone who wished them ill will. He was glad she was on his side. *I mean, I hope.*

Daruthr had finished entering the code when Erick turned back around, and the door stood open. He ducked inside, and Erick followed. He was not expecting what greeted him.

The room was small, with rounded corners, as if it had been blown up like a balloon. Black and white patterns on the floor seemed to move and flow unless Erick focused carefully. There was a low bench against the far wall and a wide window to his left. Through the window stood a chair in a much larger room, centered, bathed in bright light from above. The chair was articulated and festooned with mysterious implements. Erick could make out a few scalpels on finger-like joints, metallic forceps, and even an ominous-looking mask.

A voice rang out in the small space. "State your name and your business."

Erick bristled, his reflex to give the voice a lesson in respect. But there was no way through the door, and they had arrived as clients. He replied, doing his best at calm and cordial. "Hello! A mutual friend told us you were the best and, more importantly, discreet."

"Ah, yes, well, whoever our mutual friend is, they aren't wrong. We are the best."

"And as to the discretion?"

Daruthr arched an eyebrow as the silence stretched. Finally, the answer came. "Yes, of course. However, the level of discretion, you know, depends on the nature of your request. What do you need?"

"I need new eyes."

"New eyes, or new irises? Seems like semantics, but it's not, really, as far as procedures go."

"I don't want to be scannable."

The voice became brusque. "Ah, well then. New irises it is. Minimally invasive, three-day healing time. Cost you parts plus a hundred kay."

Daruthr spoke up. "What do you mean, parts plus?"

"Well, we happen to have some fresh irises in stock. Just got them the other day. They've not even been on ice. Best quality, et cetera." The voice paused. "But I prefer my wares to be all-natural, nothing vat grown."

Erick couldn't stop himself. "Unmarked, you mean?"

"Well, you know, natural is just such a higher quality. There's a story in each body part, a history. Some memory, and so on, you know I actually get much better rejection rates—"

Erick cut in. "I get it. No need for the pitch."

The voice cleared his throat. "So, right then, you give me what you have, and I cut you a deal on the price."

Erick was having none of that. The last thing he needed was the Ollson Executor's irises floating around on the black market. "And how much to keep them?"

Another pause. "Double."

"Agreed. When can you fit me in?"

"Hah! For two hundred kay, I've just had a spot open up." There was a click, and the wall next to the long window parted along a hidden seam. The smell of antiseptics and cleaning agents wafted through.

Daruthr nodded, smiling broadly. "I do believe we've found just the right people."

"Not sure about that. He kept saying we. I want as few people involved as necessary."

"It's a black market chop shop, Erick. Either we're buying, or we're not." Daruthr gestured to the opening. "But that door is open."

Erick sighed, then strode forward and pushed the door open. Daruthr followed him, and the door snapped shut behind him. The room was circular, the perimeter ringed with shelves and cases. The cases, rounded edges with flat top and bottoms, were stacked from a waist high shelf to the ceiling. Each one had a long, sinuous set of tubes encircled in delicate wiring that ran along the front of the frame. Erick's eyes followed the tubes as they merged, each junction larger until they joined into one glowing pipe. The blue glow of the pipe disappeared into a hulking machine set against the wall. A similar pipe, this one red, jutted out of the top of the machine, returning and branching back to the cases. Erick had the distinct impression of the circulatory system of a human body, laid out one vein and artery at a time. The machine gurgled obscenely.

Across from Erick and Daruthr, two men entered. Their lower faces were obscured by thin poly masks. One was tall, with dark hair and kind eyes, and the other was shorter and clearly the older of the two. His pale blue eyes were sharp and calculating against his green shirt.

The shorter man spoke first. His tenor carrier clearly through the mask. "Welcome, welcome. So good to have you!"

Erick threw Daruthr a confused look. This didn't sound like the hard bargaining voice from the strange waiting room. His tone was guarded as he replied, "Thank you. I'm the one who needs the work done."

The taller man's laugh boomed across the room. "Oh, we know! It was pretty obvious with all those implants, you'd want a little privacy, man."

The smaller man turned to the larger. "Georgos, no need to put them off. They're, you know, clients now."

Georgos grinned, his smile almost making it around the edges of the mask "You right, you right." He turned to Erick and Daruthr. "Welcome to you both. Sorry for the assumption, but we did a little sampling while you were in the waiting room. I figured the, uh, human one would be the one who needed some new peepers."

Daruthr responded. "Human, eh? And do tell me, Doctor Georgos, how did you come to that conclusion?"

"Nah, man you can call me George. Or G. Or Doc G, that works too." The smaller man shot Georgos a pointed look over his mask. "But yeah, we screen everyone in the waiting room. And he," Georgos cocked his chin at Erick, "registered on all the scanners. Geneline for sure, all the bells and whistles. But," the doctor inclined his head to Daruthr, "and I say this respectfully, man, you're a friggin' black hole. Like, nothing."

The shorter doctor crossed his arms. "Which, as 'Doc G' here has just pointed out, means that you probably have some pretty heavy snoopware and implants active." His smile stretched perilously. "And we, of course, don't want to know anything about that."

Daruthr gave a gentle laugh. "In so far as you couldn't pry any further, I see. But yes, I would prefer to remain anonymous. And my companion here does need your services."

Erick considered the two. They seemed to know their business from the kit he saw displayed and the scanning array in the waiting room. Whatever their mannerisms, the tech level needed to scan him and identify all his implants meant they were at least well equipped for the job. He allowed some guarded optimism to creep into his voice. "Well, it's good to meet you, George." He looked to the shorter of the two. "I'm sorry, I didn't catch your name?"

The man gave a sweeping gesture and a slight bow. "Godfrey Hanningen, very good to meet you! I apologize for my manners. We aren't used to clientele such as yourselves having such pressing needs. But not to worry!" He walked over to the chair in the middle of the room, motioning for Erick to sit. "Let's have a look at you!"

The chair was oddly comfortable, the back and seat conforming to his body. Despite the comfort, being surrounded by the surgical implements did nothing for Erick's nerves. The headrest was the most alarming part; it nestled gently against his neck from behind, forming long wings wrapped around his ears to hold him still.

Godfrey pulled a pad from his pocket, and Erick heard Georgos before he saw him. The tall doctor walked over to the row of crates along the wall, selecting one apparently at random. He turned two small valves closed on the top and bottom of the crate, then removed the tubes and lifted it off the stack. Godfrey pecked at his datapad, then reached down to pull a pair of antique glasses from his pocket. The lenses were held together with a magnet and snapped together as he perched them on his nose.

Erick raised his eyebrows. "Not that I don't trust your abilities, Doctor Hanningen, but given the nature of the work I've asked for, should I be worried that you haven't repaired your own eyes?"

Godfrey looked up at Erick over the top of the glasses. Georgos returned with the crate and set it beside the chair. "Hmmm? Oh, these. Full confession, I don't really need them that much. It's just easier on my eyes when I'm looking in close. And as far as fixing my eyes; the risk of something going wrong is just too high. This is my livelihood, after all."

The risk of something going wrong? *What, do I not need my eyes as much?* "What about me, then, if the risk is so high?"

Georgos had walked out of Erick's view, but Godfrey looked in his direction quickly before leaning down and whispering conspiratorially. "It's not really me I'm worried about. I am an artiste when it comes to procedures like this." He paused, looking over the top of his glasses. "Others are… more bold."

Erick attempted to nod, his head barely moving in the chair's grip. "I see." Some sort of professional rivalry, no doubt. Erick hadn't known many doctors; he'd been destined since birth to be free of any defect, immune to any natural pathogens he was likely to run into. But they had all been very confident when he'd needed to see a doctor for rejuvenation or preventative checkup. And much less confident in anyone else. Perhaps it simply ran in the profession.

"But," Godfrey said, tapping Erick's knee, "Not to worry at all. Let's take a look at your new retinas, shall we? I wonder what color young Doc G has selected for you?" He lifted the case and opened it, tipping it slightly toward Erick with a flourish of his un-encumbered hand. Inside the crate, a pulsing blue glow shone through a clear gelatinous substance that jiggled alarmingly with Godfrey's motions. At the bottom of the case, red fluid seeped upwards through miniscule traces of capillary tubes, to finally lift up slightly from the surface and join the back of two staring human eyes.

"Blue it is!" Godfrey's voice was excited. "Always did like a good ice blue. Right, so, here's what's going to happen. I'll give you a spinal block, nothing permanent, and it will be mechanical, not chemical, so there shouldn't be any recovery time. I'll need your head absolutely still, though, no squirming, ok? We'll sedate you after we get everything lined up, peel back your existing cornea, then let the nanos separate your retinal tissue from the lens ligaments and surrounding ciliary muscle. Once we have a good substrate ready, we'll peel the donor corneas, set the new retinal tissue, and stimulate muscle connection and nerve growth. Have you out of here before you know it!"

Erick had been nodding, mostly by reflex. He stopped when he heard sedate. "I'm sorry; what's the purpose of the spinal block if you're going to sedate me?"

"That's for the first part of the procedure. We'll need to inject the nanos directly into the vitreous humor, and the needle can be… alarming to some."

Erick didn't feel entirely comfortable with not being able to move. He might try to override the spinal block if he really needed to, but wasn't certain his implants could just go around affected nerve tissue, especially in the spinal cord. "I would be more comfortable with just the block, if you don't mind."

Georgos moved back in front of Erick to stand across from Godfrey, who passed the taller man the box of eyeballs. "I mean, you do know that this is going to be," He paused to wring his hands, "somewhat uncomfortable. I really think you'd have a better experience with the sedation."

Daruthr's voice came from off to Erick's right. "Oh, do stop trying to be such an alpha male. Take a nap. Get some new eyes."

Erick pursed his lips. "Fine. But I want to wake up immediately after it's done."

Georgos put his hand on Erick's shoulder, balancing the crate precariously in the other. "Don't worry, man. I'll keep Doc H here honest. You'll be back before you know it, no problem."

Erick grunted. "Let's get this over with." He pulled up the wallet address Daruthr had given him and transferred a few credits. "You should see a test deposit in your account."

Godfrey pulled up his data pad once again, tapping the translucent symbols. "Ah, yes indeed. Looks like all is in order." Erick nodded and sent half the payment. One perk of being the Executor, or at least ex Executor. Even your dummy accounts were flush. "Yes, there we are! And we'll collect the rest when you wake up. Excellent! Now to the fun part!" Godfrey turned and moved out of Erick's sight.

What decisions had Erick made, exactly, that led to this moment in his life? Sitting there, breathing in the antiseptic smell, all he wanted was to walk through the gardens of the *Sleipnir*. He hadn't seen anything green or growing for so long. Just the cold metal and unfeeling composites. The last time he'd smelled dirt, real dirt, the kind that you could dig up with your hands and feel the gritty richness of it, he'd been in that garden with Bryn. It was strange, how much the lack of dirt and growing things affected him.

Erick's eyes wandered across the room, hopefully not for the last time. Despite the smell of cleaner, it was clearly old. Spiderweb cracks shone in the enamel of the walls, and the polymer window had the subtle haziness that belied hours of elbow grease. And there, on the edge of the windowsill, Erick could just make out a rim of dirt that hadn't been worth the effort of whoever had done the last cleaning. *Everywhere there are people, there is dirt.* He smiled.

Daruthr came into view to stand beside the window, and then the two doctors were back, Godfrey to his right and Georgos to his left. The larger man held a syringe with a needle that twisted and moved. The barrel was filled with a milky, silvery substance that churned like a living thing, shimmering in the reflected light.

Godfrey's voice was calm and oddly comforting, considering he was a stranger. "Just going to put in the block now. The chair will do all the work, just don't fight it."

Erick felt pressure at the base of his neck, where his shoulder blades lay cupped by the chair. A coldness, then an alarming sensation of something sliding into his spine. Then nothing, and what tension he had in the rest of his body relaxed. *Thank the gods I used the bathroom on the way here.*

"There we go, see? All good." Godfrey looked at something on his datapad, tapped a few times, then nodded across Erick to Georgos. "Over to you. I'll prep the program and get the anesthetic primed."

Georgos waved a hand over Erick's face, then pointed to a small dab of black paint on the ceiling. It was thick and cracked, out of place against the white ceiling. "Just look right here, please; the needle is smart enough to know where it's going, but man, you do not want to be looking around while it does. Feels way better this way."

Erick stared at the dot, and Georgos lowered the syringe over the bridge of Erick's nose. He fought the urge to look at the questing, wormlike needle. Despite himself, his breath quickened, and he fought to control it. Queuing his implants, he dulled the pain signal from his eyes in preparation for the needle. It moved back and forth as if looking for the perfect spot on each eye as Georgos held it steady.

It stabbed down straight down without warning.

Erick's jaw tensed, and he was suddenly glad for the nerve block. No way he'd have been able to keep the rest of him still. While there was no pain, he could feel the needle inside his eye. Bryn had once described a nightmare to him, when she was much younger. She'd been buried, not alive, but dead, aware of her corpse rotting. She told him how she'd felt the flesh softening, the ichor that flowed from her decomposition into the soil. She said she'd felt the insects come, beetles and worms to crawl in and through her while she couldn't move or speak. Erick wondered how close their experiences would be if he managed to tell her about this. *When I tell her about it.*

Finally, the wriggling, alien pressure in his eye stopped. The second one was no better. "Easy now, almost done," said Godfrey. Erick didn't spare the breath to curse him, just fought down the upwelling of panic, the animal in him that wanted to chew off his own leg to get out of the trap.

Then it was over, Georgos pulling the needle and syringe back up away from his face. He focused on it, seeing the cylinder once again. A gasp ripped through him, and he fought to steady his breathing. The syringe wasn't empty, as he'd expected, but the movement of the solution had stilled, and it looked more like a dull steel color than the bright silver it had carried before.

Georgos saw his look. "You doin' all right, big guy? Don't sweat it. The needle just puts a bridge to where the little guys need to be. I mean, I guess we could let them find their own way, but this is way faster. That and the shorter we leave them armed in there, you know, the less likely they are to do something weird."

Hmm. "What do you mean by weird?" Erick was surprised at the steadiness of his voice.

Godfrey's skin crinkled around the sides of his mask, his face appearing in Erick's line of sight. "Not to worry, we do this all the time. It's a totally safe medical procedure. But we do need to get you to sleep now."

"Wait, first tell me what he meant about the nanos." He thought he heard Daruthr laughing. *The bastard.*

Erick felt a pinprick on his neck.

Well, fuck. I guess we'll see. Or not. He started to laugh at his inside joke, but it suddenly didn't seem that funny.

21

Struggle

Beset but not bereft
He strode across the plane
Another truth he sought
In the halls of his own ancestors

Erick awoke to the sound of ripping flesh. At least that's what he thought it was. He swam back up out of the murk. *Riiiiiip.* And the clatter of metal on metal. *Gods, not again.*

This time he snapped his eyes open. He could feel his entire body, at least, though the chair still cradled him. "Daruthr." His mouth felt thick, full of cotton. He licked his lips.

"Welcome back, Erick. Don't worry, everything is fine. But I do need to know if you can walk."

"That does not sound like fine." Daruthr walked to where Erick could see him. "Doctor Andino, if you would be so kind as to release the chair from Erick while Doctor Hanningen is otherwise occupied."

Georgos' voice came from behind Erick. "Oh, right, my bad." Erick felt a click through his neck where the chair grasped him. "There you go, should be good now."

Erick felt the chair flow back, and his head and neck were no longer clamped by the wings of the headrest. He sat up and took stock of his surroundings.

The best indication that things had gone according to plan was that he could still see. His ocular responded to commands, overlaying diagnostics on the world around him. It had apparently even captured footage of the operation and asked if wanted to review it. He declined, checking the timestamp. *8 hours, helvítis fjandinn!* So much for a short trip and expeditious return. And he'd left Yetunde out there in the corridor the whole time.

Erick took a sweep of the room as he stood. Daruthr stood with his shoulders against the wall, across from the door to the waiting room, ankles crossed as he inspected flawless nails. The two doctors huddled around a case on the floor. The gap in the wall of cases showed where they had removed it from the rest. This one was big, big enough for a whole limb if the proportions were the same as those that had held Erick's new eyes. Or a torso. The ripping sound was coming from Georgos, who was, in fact, not ripping flesh. He wore a black cloth vest and adjusted long hook and loop fasteners to snug it around his body. He had already strapped on a belt with a wicked-looking slug gun attached to it, all sharp angles and open sights.

Godfrey was finished sifting through the case and came up with his own vest. He addressed Georgos as he strapped it on. "I told you this was a good investment."

"I still think we should have just built another way out. Those station planners can suck it." He stretched his jaw and tossed his head back and forth. "They totally would have taken the money, man."

"Well, you may be right, but at the time they didn't seem all that interested. And we'd have had to do the whole station records thing as well."

Erick cleared his throat. "Will someone please tell me what's going on? Now."

Godfrey turned to look at Erick, throwing him a slug pistol, then strapping a rifle festooned with a dizzying array of attachments to his own chest. He checked the movement of the sling, the wicked barrel sweeping across an unoccupied section of the room. "Oh, hey, nothing to worry about. Daruthr over there has your goodie box. We just have a few folks coming by that, I don't know, let's say we have a bit of history with. Should be fine." He pulled a magazine from his vest, squinting into the open mouth of it before tapping it against his rifle. The rifle stock opened and accepted the magazine, cinching itself back down around it. "Hey, Georgos, would you be amazing and hand me that box of frangible sabot rounds? Wouldn't want to put a hole in the station here by accident."

"Yeah, sure, man." Georgos fished out a small white box and handed it to Godfrey, who opened it and dipped the end of his magazine into the box. The magazine pulsed like a strand of intestines as it sucked in ammunition.

Godfrey pulled a helmet out of the box and set it on his head, drawing down the transparent face shield. His eyes, covered in optics, glittered in the bright light. His voice came through it, metallic. "So, plan is pretty simple, really. They're going to have to come through the waiting room doors there. Hopefully, we can fry them in there, and then all this is more a precaution than, you know, completely necessary. But if they do make it in, we're gonna need to go through them to get out. So, why don't I take point, and then Doc G can sweep things up there, and you and your friend come on through when it's all clear?"

Erick smiled. "I think we can handle ourselves a little better tha—"

The walls around them rang like a bell. Whoever they were, they had arrived.

Godfrey moved across the room to take up a position behind the chair. Georgos ran to a spot on the side of the room, hunkering down behind a stack of crates that still pulsed with red and blue fluid.

"How far are we going to let these two get before we help them out?" Somehow Daruthr was standing behind him.

Erick hadn't even seen him move across the room, but here they were stacked up behind the large black cabinet that fed the cases of organs.

"I don't want a repeat of the hangar. I know you can kill."

Daruthr's body was pressed against Erick's back, both of them collapsing back to take advantage of cover. His breathing was slow and steady, and at that moment, Erick didn't really care if Daruthr's breathing was all for show or not. It was good to have someone calm. Erick raised the slug pistol and sighted it on the door, waiting.

He didn't have to wait long.

The door glowed momentarily around the edges, then vanished in a pulse of dust. The first person came through firing, the matte black of their armor plates drinking in the light. They were clearly professional, not waiting for anyone to regain their composure after the door breach.

Godfrey shot the first figure several times in the chest, tiny detonations of rounds sending puffs of smoke where they hit armor. Erick slowed his sense of time up just enough. He watched a line of Godfrey's bullets walk up to the neck and into a seam in the intruder's armor, where the smoke puffs stopped, and a gout of red mist sprayed across the wall. Before the body hit the floor, three more were in the room and firing.

Erick tracked the one that moved to his left, the other two working to the right, pouring fire into the doctor's chair. From his peripheral vision, Erick saw Godfrey hunkering lower as chips of chair starburst. Dust hung in the air. Erick fired at the enemy figure, leading his aim just enough to put his rounds center mass. One went low, hitting the figure between armor plates at the hip, and they went down, their rifle stitching a line of craters across the ceiling.

Erick looked across the room to see Georgos with both meaty hands wrapped around the throat of an intruder, the other lying still at his feet. He lifted the figure off the ground, roaring into the figure's featureless mask. Hands scrabbled against his grip.

Something small and metallic arced into the room, bouncing off the back wall and onto the floor. It came to a stop next to Georgos. Keeping his hold around the enemy's neck, he slammed the armored figure he held down on the ground and jumped on top.

The grenade detonated, sending the stack of bodies soaring. Georgos hit the ceiling, a shower of blood and viscera raining down around him. The man somehow landed on his feet.

His teeth leaped out in a Cheshire grin against the blood that covered him. "Did you guys see that shit?" He slapped open hands against his chest. "I'm a fucking *legend!*" His laugh was not altogether sane.

Erick kept his weapon on the door, moving to check the figure he'd shot. As he got close, he saw a knife in their hand. "Fuck you," the figure said, the words bitten out around pain. A man then, best guess. He swiped at Erick with the knife, and Erick backed up out of reach, kicking the man's rifle away as he did so.

Erick turned his head, his eyes not leaving the man on the floor. "Godfrey, how you doing over there?"

"Oh, fine, fine, just, you know, evaluating our situation." Erick saw Godfrey stand out of the corner of his eye. A secret crate of weapons. Killing three, nearly four, heavily armed and trained intruders. And the way Georgos had lifted one clean off the ground. *What the fuck kind of surgeons are these?*

Godfrey walked over to the one that was still alive. He looked down at the man, who sat in a growing pool of blood. A raspy cough came through the black mask.

"Mmmhmm," Godfrey nodded from behind his visor, "though it might be. These are mercs, and not the cheap kind. Probably Tinas Mordor by the lack of insignia. That's kind of, you know, their calling card. Most mercs have their flashy branding, or their license, or whatever. These guys, not so much." Godfrey turns his body slightly away from the man on the floor, tracking the barrel of his rifle across him. Erick was about to point out this lack of muzzle discipline when Godfrey fired three times. The mercenary twitched on the ground. *So much for interrogation.*

"Was that entirely necessary? What happened to do no harm?" Erick's voice was tense.

"Oh, that old chestnut. We can't all afford high and mighty morals down here in the real world." Godfrey began walking back towards the waiting room door. "Besides, these guys are, you know," he gestured expansively, "not good people."

"And they were trying to kill us. Fair's fair, man," Georgos chimed in from across the room. He finished wiping his hands on a sanitizing surgical cloth he'd produced from one of his many pockets. It struck Erick as hilarious, the man who had just killed someone with his bare hands being overly concerned with germs. Although, the blood would have made his grip slick.

Daruthr had begun slowly walking around the room, inspecting the damage and bits of debris. Erick nodded towards the waiting room door. "Someone had to throw that grenade. Are there more out there?"

Godfrey was already looking at his data pad. "It does not appear that way, no. Nope, looks all clear. That was probably a last-ditch effort, you know, try to get us all at once."

Daruthr was examining what appeared to be a shard of jawbone, molars still attached, stuck in the remaining smart padding of the chair in the middle of the room. He straightened, hands behind his back, and faced Erick. "There may not be any more mercenaries; however, that grenade will have alerted station security."

"Ah," said Erick, "we should go."

Georgos was polishing the handle of one of his pistols, the rag turning more and more red as he wiped off the blood. "You guys got somewhere safe to be?"

Erick nodded. "Yes, thank you for asking."

Godfrey laughed, slightly nervous. "I think what my colleague was getting at, is, perhaps we could come with you." He gestured to the room and the racks of organs in their cases. "This isn't something we can move quickly, so, probably best to just cut it loose, you know?"

Daruthr spoke before Erick could respond. "Of course! Though I recommend only bringing what weapons you think can get through the common spaces. You both look a bit overdressed."

Damnit. That's the last thing we needed. What was Daruthr thinking? These two were obviously good at what they did, but Erick had a mission. The crew of the *Svadilfari* would be safer without them.

It was too late to say anything about it now. The two doctors dropped their heavy armor and the larger weapons back into the crate, retaining only a pistol and some soft armor each. The motley band filed out into the hallway in line behind Daruthr, with Godfrey in the rear. As they made the first turn out in the main corridor, leaving the flickering behind them, Erick heard a muffled thump and a tingling sensation went through him. His implants registered a hefty magnetic pulse. He looked sharply at Godfrey.

The smaller man smiled in an embarrassed way, his hands spread slightly as they walked. "Couldn't leave the tools of the trade in one piece, you know. But don't worry, there wasn't anyone in there."

"Now we've grown a conscience?" Erick's voice was sharper than he intended.

"Well sure, I mean, we aren't savages, you know."

Erick was not entirely convinced.

22
Revelations

Lo, did he see the ties that bind
Deep cordage wrought through the ages
His party swelled, their threads
Intertwined in the great tapestry

Yetunde sat on a crate in the corner, where she could read on her datapad without being obviously snooping. Binya was next to her, his eyes closed and head tipped back against the wall, by all appearances asleep. A tiny snore floated across the flitter bay in confirmation.

In front of Erick on the other side of the open space, the two doctors looked curiously at the assault pod in *Svadilfari's* cargo bay. Erick faced Daruthr, arms crossed, while they muttered to each other, just out of earshot. *Good thing too.* Daruthr's voice was tense. "We need to tell them the truth about you and me."

Erick shook his head, keeping a smile on his face. "Absolutely not. They already know too much from whatever scanners they had in that waiting room."

"That's the thing, Erick." Daruthr cocked his head to one side. "They already know. Or they at least can tell you're not just some part-geneline Ollson."

"If they know, don't you think they'd have told us?"

"No. Professional courtesy, a healthy respect for privacy given their line of work, take your pick."

"Yeah, or, and stay with me on this one, they're not sure who will give them the biggest reward, Dorian or the Empress ." Daruthr opened his mouth, but Erick cut him off. "Even if they aren't trying to make a buck, and they actually have suspicions, that's even more reason not to tell them. If they're going to respect our privacy, I say let them."

"First, even if your presence became known, we'd just need to invent an innocent circumstance, get ahold of the management, and head home. Not ideal, but not life-threatening." Daruthr paused, his eyes darting to Godfrey and Georgos. They had moved to the far side of the assault pod, and were gesturing excitedly towards the right missile bay. From a healthy distance, thank goodness. Erick focused as Daruthr continued. "It's me I'm worried about."

Erick tried to remember the last time he heard Daruthr admit to concern of any sort, let alone for his own well-being. "You think they know what you are?"

"I think they suspect. They couldn't get anything from me when they scanned because I didn't want them to. But now they'll be curious, more curious about me than about you. And even if they don't have ill intent, I don't think they'll be able to stop poking."

"And so what do you propose, then?"

Daruthr's answer sent a shiver down Erick's spine. "We tell them everything."

Erick's mind had been concocting lies to spin, explanations for implants and abilities, and so on. Simply mentioning the Black Guard might have done it.

But to tell them the truth was a wholly different gamble.

"That really only leaves two possible outcomes." Erick licked his lips. "Either they are overjoyed, or they run screaming."

Daruthr nodded. "Yes, I'm quite aware. But I don't want to spend the rest of our time in Gjoll questioning their motives and loyalties. Why guess when we can know for sure?"

"And what if they don't take too well having a mendicant on the ship?"

"We'll have to see, won't we?"

There was something more to this. Daruthr seemed almost urgent. "It's because they're doctors, isn't it? And because of where you came from?"

Daruthr stared at Erick for a moment his eyes piercing and brow furrowed. "You didn't see it on the wall, did you?"

"See what?"

"The plaque. It showed a staff, like a walking stick, with two serpents wrapped around it."

"I thought it was a shrine of some sort. Ancestral gods, other worlds, that sort of thing."

"It's an ancient symbol. We used to display it, before the war." Daruthr's voice softened. "It meant that anyone who came to us would be healed."

"We. The mendicants."

"Yes, Erick, the mendicants. But after the war, no one displayed it. Not openly, at least; some still did in secret. Those who believed in us."

"Believed in you? You aren't a god, Daruthr."

"Don't be an ass. Look, the point is that it means I might actually be able to trust them with this secret. And if we really are going to build a crew here, they will have to know eventually."

Erick wasn't sure they did have to know. But he could see what Daruthr was saying. Secrets on a crew tended to be explosive; it wasn't a matter of if they would go off but when. He needed to be able to trust people. It was not an easy feeling, but a part of him was tired. Tired of constantly managing who knew what when. Tired of keeping secrets and layers and intrigue. Perhaps there was something to be said for giving honesty a chance.

"Well, let's not wait around on it." Erick waved to the two doctors, who had nearly disappeared around the back side of the assault pod, and then looked to Yetunde, who took the meaning in his eyes and stood. She tapped Binya on the knee as she passed, and he smoothly stood to follow her. *That was a little fast on his feet to have actually been asleep.*

The group huddled in the open space at the back of the hangar. Erick was surprised at how cramped it felt. When he'd picked this ship, he'd never planned on sharing it with anyone. And now he stood shoulder to shoulder with five others. A stranger watching the scene might confuse them for a real crew.

Daruthr addresses the group. "You have all, in one way or another, assisted us over the last few days. And while these are certainly professional relationships—"

Binya leaned over to Georgos. "That means we get paid, right?" he said, sotto voce. Georgos nodded back, waiving his hand to shush the pilot.

"—I still feel it is important to lay a foundation of trust as we move toward what I fear will be a somewhat fraught future." Daruthr continued, drawing himself up a little straighter. "It will be important to know with whom you are dealing and why."

Godfrey took this moment to chime in. "If I can just, you know, say something real quick." Daruthr nodded, eyebrows raised though he smiled. Godfrey pointed to Erick. "I think it's pretty obvious that we're working for Executor Ollson here." He looked around the circle. "I mean, no questions asked, but you gotta give us a little bit of credit, you know."

Georgos took a step forward. "And you, Daruthr. You go by many names, don't you?" His voice was tinged with reverence. Gone was the happy-go-lucky attitude the giant man had projected, even in the middle of a firefight. His voice was tinged with awe.

Daruthr smiled at Georgos, then to the rest. "Yes, Georgos. I do."

Georgos nodded, his hands clasped in front of him, knuckles white. Erick could tell he wanted to say more but held his tongue. He'd ask Georgos about it later.

There was only one of the newcomers who hadn't spoken yet. All eyes turned to Binya, trying to read his reaction.

The pilot raised one hand, stifled a yawn, and spoke. "You're all, just, really bad at this."

Erick waited for him to continue, but he seemed to have said his piece. *No, I need to know what he means.* "Please, do enlighten us, Bin."

"Well, I made you in the bar. So oops for you there. And the rest, well…."

A small smile played at the corner of Daruthr's lips. "And tell me, my shockingly observant friend, did you know who I was?"

"Not explicitly, but I figured you were someone who knew their way around networked systems. As far as network traces go, you make me look like I'm wearing a damn beacon. I told you I didn't want to know more than I needed." Here he paused and looked around, his eyes landing on Erick's. "But I guess that's fucked. So what's the plan?"

Erick nodded. "Well, good. Let's get it on the table then." He looked back and forth to the two doctors, neither of whom had taken their eyes off Daruthr. "Will you be able to help us with a little problem we have, or do you want to sit this one out?”

Godfrey was first to answer. “Well, you know, with all the excitement of the last few hours I think I might prefer to, maybe, just provide some encouragement. Perhaps throw some ideas around. You know, more intellectual work than anything.”

Georgos laughed. “You know I’m totally in. I’m guessing this is killing and not fixing.” His eyes flicked to Daruthr, who didn’t respond.

Erick nodded to Godfrey. “All right then, you can stay on the ship.” He threw up an overlay on the wall screen. “Here’s how we’ll steal a data core from Gjoll. And before you say it, no, I can’t just ask for it.”

The wall screen held a schematic of the system. Far out from the star were the two arrays, the more extensive inter-geneline transfer array entirely outside of the heliopause. In comparison, the smaller array connected to Breydablick hovered closer to the planets properly. A few gaseous outer planets circled, with a single rocky inner world tidally locked, one side scorched and the other frozen.

The graphic highlighted the infrastructure, with bright blue outlines showing the pulsing icon of the system goods vault orbiting the largest gas giant, Gjoll station circling above the murky brown cloud layers of the planet below. The only native industry in Gjoll was gas mining, volatiles easily scooped from the cloud layers below.

Erick had a flash of his visit to Gjoll as a younger man, to hunt the massive creatures that floated and grazed on the whipping winds. Despite the reliability of the escape pod system, the stormjammer he’d been on had terrified him with its seeming frailty against the howling gale.

There was something electric about being convinced you would die, even if you weren’t in danger.

Despite a chase that lasted a week, they hadn't landed one of the floating monsters. He'd never returned after taking on the mantle of Executor of Ollson; the risk simply hadn't been worth it. Now though, he felt a strange desire to go back and face the infinite storms, harpoon a kilometer-long beast. Perhaps when all this was behind them.

For now, though, he held up a hand and pointed to the system security backup station, far in towards the muted red star. Its broken hoop was outlined in electric blue. "This is the Gjoll system hard backup. Everything the system observation and tracking arrays record is shared on the network, of course, but a physical backup is also recorded and stored here."

Yetunde nodded. "And to get to the physical backup, we will not need network access on Gjoll station at all."

Daruthr nodded. "That's correct. Everything we need should be here."

Erick highlighted a transfer orbit between the Gjoll station and the backup storage. "There's a courier ship, small and fast, that carries the data from the station to the backup storage. We will need to commandeer it under thrust, replace the crew, and then get onto the inner backup station." Erick turned to Binya. "Think you can get us in tight enough for a ship-to-ship action?"

He nodded laconically through half-lidded eyes. "Yeah, shouldn't be a problem." A yawn. Was he ever fully awake? "What's the security situation?"

Erick called up the backup storage station schematics with a thought. "It's not a fortress." He pointed to a few points along the top of the main docking area. "Some point defenses here, direct fire for short range. A few missile batteries and one torpedo launcher, but the primary goal is to prevent boarding long enough to destroy the data."

Daruthr pointed to the data core storage area. "Speaking of data, what exactly are we looking for once we're inside?"

"Since I no longer have executor access, we'll need to keep cover as much as possible. The data cores are stored in a central warehouse system, with mechanical retrieval." He highlighted the main docking ring. "We'll likely be vectored to dock here and follow a relatively straightforward path to the storage area. The defenses are mostly automated internally; not a lot of need for independent thought. If we do get tagged as unwanted, though, the station antibodies are going to be a problem. They'll overwhelm us quickly."

Yetunde pointed to the glowing path. "And we walk back out the way we came? With a data core?"

Daruthr uncrossed his arms. "As long as we aren't directly observed by the human station staff, I should be able to keep us concealed from the automated systems. It looks like there's another, closer airlock here," the schematic lit up at Daruthr's gesture, "that we should be able to use if we need to get away quickly."

Binya frowned. "And I'm guessing you're expecting me to be able to keep the *Svadi-whatever* out of the sensor returns from the station."

Erick nodded. "We'll fly right back out on the commandeered courier and make the swap well away from the backup station." He raised an eyebrow toward Binya. "You can keep the *Svadilfari* off the station imaging, right?"

"Well, yeah, I mean, of course I can. I'll just need to stay out of the direct sightline of the station control deck. I'm guessing there aren't a lot of windows on a data storage station."

Daruthr rotated the station schematic into three dimensions. Several blue lines leaped from the scattering of viewpoints, resolving into cones with their vertices at the windows. "Here's the rough visual areas that one might see, if they were to look out the windows."

Binya looked at it a moment. "Ok then, no problem."

Erick looked around at the small group. "Georgos, if you'd be so kind as to accompany us on the boarding party, you, Yetunde, Daruthr, and I will take the courier ship and conduct the retrieval."

The big man smacked one fist into his open hand, his knuckles cracking. "Sure thing. Makes sense to bring a doctor along." Daruthr raised an eyebrow at him. Georgos grinned back. "You know, in case anyone gets hurt or whatever." Erick had a distinct impression that wasn't really why he wanted to come. But there would be time to address that later.

"And one last thing." Erick blanked the wall display and looked around the group in turn. "The people on the courier, and the skeleton crew on the station, are citizens." His eyes lingered a touch longer on Daruthr than the others. "I want us to do everything we possibly can to keep them alive, and preferably uninjured. We can and will defend ourselves, but we'll use the minimum force necessary. Now, are there any questions on the plan?" Heads shook around the circle. "Great. And lastly, I—"

Erick closed his mouth. He had been about to launch into a speech about bravery, commitment, and sacrifice's true nature. But these people, his crew, weren't his subjects. At least, not anymore. They were something more than that. Even the two latest arrivals had already thrown in with him, for reasons he couldn't quite understand. They didn't need a speech right now.

"Thank you."

Yetunde nodded to him, smiling, and he knew he had said the right thing, only the right thing. Now all he had to do was keep everyone alive.

No pressure.

23

Loss

Fire, flames, did fall around her
The world tattered and barren
Wracked was she, torn to pieces
Her breath short-struck in the ether

Harvir and Landry stood on the upturned palanquin, surrounded by fallen Ollson soldiers under the now dead gaze of the intown watchtowers. Harvir's eyes were wide, irises nearly consumed by wildly dilated pupils. Despite his triumphant grin, his skin was pallid, and his shirt was drenched with sweat. He held the small red box before him like a talisman against evil. "I saved us. Look! Look at them."

"Harvir, put that down. We need to go." Bragja spoke slowly, forcing herself to sound measured and reasonable.

The silence had built, finally over-balancing as whispers passed through the crowd. Landry clapped his brother on the shoulder, his eyes scanning across the disabled soldiers and the lifeless watch towers. The crowd's murmur intruded on their little bubble, a slow-building wave of voices.

Harvir and Landry stood silhouetted against the courtyard wall. Landry's smile was broad, ear to ear, and his face was flushed. He left his hand on Harvir's shoulder and turned his head to face the crowd.

Landry opened his mouth to speak.

The bullet entered his head from behind, spiral fluting punching a neat hole through skin and bone just above his occipital plate. Four small petals opened as it passed through his meninges, expanding to tear wide troughs through parietal lobe and basal ganglia. Expanded, the bullet dumped kinetic energy into grey matter and finally impacted the seam between Landry's zygomatic process and maxilla. His face erupted in a shower of viscera.

Behind her, Bragja heard a smattering of wet thumps.

The crowd surged, and a tidal wave of noise crashed over her. Someone was screaming. She wished they would stop; she couldn't concentrate. She had to stop the bleeding. She had to get her brothers to the mender at the pickerpark. She'd seen some horrible injuries from pickers returning after early starfall. If the mender could fix them, it could fix Landry. She'd need to right the palanquin, then she could drag him onto it and go. The crowd was already parting and disappearing, the eddies of humanity beginning to evaporate. She took a deep breath. The screaming stopped.

Bragja needed to get Harvir off the palanquin first. He was crouched down, one arm clutching the speaker and his fingers wrapped around the little red box. His other arm sprawled awkwardly over his brother's waist.

"Harvir!" Bragja reached out to Harvir. She could grab his hand and pull him off Landry how he was lying. He was probably traumatized. But she needed his help. "Harvir, *guði fjandinn hafi það,* get up!" She grasped his wrist and pulled at him, trying to get him to pay attention. But his arm fell with her motion. His head lolled. Bragja struggled to roll him over, grunting at the exertion of his weight. Finally, she heaved him over and froze.

His chest was opened, ribs like the petals of a flower. He looked hollow, a parody of her brother's face perched atop a mass of butchered meat. Bragja couldn't move, every molecule in her body reflecting the stillness of death. The noise of the crowd faded, and her vision narrowed. Her heart tried to leap out of her chest. She couldn't breathe.

The terrible magic of the moment was shattered as a figure passed her, reaching out toward her brothers' corpses. Bragja didn't think or even recognize a man's hulking shape.

Someone was reaching for them.

They were dead.

But they were her brothers.

Bragja drew her seax in a liquid motion, striding forward. She grabbed the man's extended left hand, the blade in her right, and tightly gripped his thumb joint. She stepped back and pulled, twisting up. She'd caught him completely by surprise. Perhaps he'd thought her too far in shock to act.

His mistake.

He spun with the pressure on his wrist and arm, yielding to it with a wordless cry. As he tried to twist away, Bragja pushed along with his momentum, and he toppled. She followed him down, never letting go of his wrist. He came to a stop face down in mud mixed red with her brothers' blood, grunting and wheezing as she twisted his wrist. He roared wordlessly, then spat, the one eye Bragja could see filled with murder. And crossed with a scar.

"You!" This was him. The man who had given Landry the little red box. The spacer. Bragja felt a wave of grief spark into rage inside her, and she screamed at him, all animal. He must have started all this. Must have seen the desperation.

She could see it now. Her brothers had fallen in with him, drinking at the *Sovereign*. He'd seen their youthful energy, their frustration. Their fear.

He'd used them. They'd be alive if not for this piece of shit.

Bragja raised her seax, aiming her downward thrust carefully. Her hand shook, and she willed it to calm. She didn't want to lose her grip on the man's hand; he still struggled. She'd need to hit just right, below the occipital bone but above the beginning of the main vertebrae. It was surprisingly high up the back of the head, a clean kill, but the way the man's neck twisted, it was her best option to get at the brain stem. Even if she was a little off and her blade struck bone, enough force would keep the wicked point moving down. The man's eyes widened, and he gasped out a few words that dashed water on the fire of Bragja's rage.

"I can get you off planet."

She paused. He was a spacer. Had a ship. "Why."

"Why? Don't kill me. I take you."

"No. Why all this?" Bragja's voice cracked as she felt the volume rise in her throat. "What was the point of all of this, you *helvítis skítkast?* "

"Can't breathe." His voice grated, breath ragged.

"I'm not letting you up," Bragja said, her knifepoint steady.

"Fine then. Both die."

"The soldiers are all dead," she gestured with her chin, "Look around."

"Not dead." The man tried to shrug, and winced as Bragja twisted his arm. "Just suits. Disabled. I got ones that were on the roof after they fired. But won't last forever."

Bragja remembered the little red box. She glanced at it now, and the man's eyes followed hers. "That thing. You brought it here."

He licked his lips. "Yeah, so?"

"So this is your fault. All of this."

"Look, need to go. *Now.* They kill us too."

Bragja looked up to the rooftops of intown, visible above the wall. She didn't know where the other group of soldiers the man was talking about was. She wanted nothing more than to kill the man, take the box from her brother's corpse, and kill every one of the soldiers. She felt rage boiling inside her, killing rage that threatened to blackout and consume her. She barely stuffed it back down.

"I let you up, and you'll run. Or try to kill me."

The man laughed. "I don't care about you. Just don't kill me in dirt like dog. I take you wherever you want."

He was right about one thing, at least. They were running out of time.

Bragja kicked him in the ribs as she dropped his hand, running the few steps to the palanquin. She snatched up the red box with her free hand, seax still pointed at the man. He had just begun to stand.

She held the red box to her chest. "Fine. You want this. I want off planet." She gestured to the spaceport, through the gates to intown. "You take me."

The man struggled to one knee, looking up at her. He wiped his mouth on the back of his sleeve and nodded. Bragja let herself look around quickly, never letting the man from her peripheral vision. The crowd was nearly gone, the few who huddled in the eddies of doorways or stalls standing to run. They were running to their homes, to their loved ones. Running away from the soldiers. Away from the baleful eye of the intown gate. Bragja thought about going home, about hiding with the little red box. She could throw it over the wall, act like she had never seen it. Maybe the Ollsons wouldn't kill her when they eventually came for her. Maybe. She reached down to gently run her fingers through Landry's hair, and the truth crushed her crazed ray of hope.

She had nowhere to go.

"Take me to your ship."

The spacer nodded, spat on the ground, and turned away from the gates. "This way, planet girl. We not going out the front door."

The streets still ebbed and flowed with humanity. Some had panicked and ran, while others threw themselves behind the nearest cover. Bullets had a tendency to make crowds depart entirely from their component humanity. This time, the shots that had ripped into the crowd had boiled it over. Like too much steam in too tight a space, people had sought relief through any space they could. The rear of the press of bodies, too far back to hear the details of death at the front, had been slow to recognize and run. As Bragja followed the spacer through the twisting alleys, she stepped over bodies and blood.

Upturned carts and stands decorated street corners like toddler's toys, strewn haphazardly by the crashing crowd. Bragja flowed around them, while the spacer preferred to kick anything he could out of his way. His hulking form moved from point to point, not bothering to check corners before striding around them. Occasionally he'd look behind him, his gaze flitting over Bragja, then the little red box. She kept her distance.

Bragja moved with numb purpose. Deep down, some part of her knew that now was not the time for grief. She was so used to building walls inside herself, so much so that the one to keep out her brothers' death rose quickly.

Because they were. Dead. She knew that. Nothing at the pickerpark could heal them.

Bragja realized they were a few turns from the market. The man she followed disappeared around the corner that led to the open shops and stalls ahead of her. She'd been here what, a few days ago? Or was it months? She slowed as she rounded the corner, staying away from the inside wall in case he hid there for her to round it blindly. The market stretched before her. She ducked and looked up as the whine of engines surged overhead, Ollson drones flashing in the sun. She stepped under a cloth shade and turned back to the street.

The market was unrecognizable. The wave of humanity had destroyed the colorful carts and decorations. Bragja saw where people had crashed against the walls in their mad dash, blood on the walls, and a few bodies in the corners where wall met street. The spacer strode across it, his head scanning back and forth. He looked up as he passed from under a cloth shade, then broke into a trot. Bragja allowed herself a little more distance and spared a glance at the destruction.

She shouldn't have.

The cart's wheel spun slowly, and gilded cages like flung paint stretched away from it. Somewhere someone screamed, a short sound that ended suddenly. The bodies inside the gilded cages, brightly colored shreets in blue and red and yellow, led Bragja's eye back to their origin. A mass of shattered shreet-shaped ceramic haloed the familiar cart. Under it, she glimpsed a patch of graying beard, a brawny shoulder. Her body betrayed her and froze, rooted. Then she heard a rattling cough, and Wolfram shook.

She covered the ground in an instant. The spacer could wait.

Bragja crouched at Wolfram's side, crouching where he could see her. He was pinned, left arm down, his torso disappearing underneath his cart. There was too little room between the cart and the ground for his girth. Bragja's stomach dropped. His eyes were closed, lips blanched, and skin like wax. His breath was shallow and quick. His forehead furrowed.

"Wolfram," Bragja whispered, "I'm here."

Beneath the lids, his eyes fluttered, then flew open. His pupils were pinpricks, the whites wide in terror. Bragja reached out a hand to his exposed shoulder and firmly but gently squeezed. "Wolfram, I'm here."

Wolfram's eyes flicked around wildly, then settled on Bragja. "Anja. I've missed you."

A single sob slipped by Bragja's teeth. "No, Wolfram. Bragja. It's Bragja. I'm here."

The old man gave a sharp cough, the sound dissolving into wet retching. He shuddered a few times, then was still. His eyes still bored into Bragja, though the light in them was out. She passed her hand over his face to close the lids and stood. The squat form of the spacer, incredibly, had stopped across the market square, though he looked like he was about to climb to orbit on his own at any moment.

Bragja covered the distance between them at a run. "Let's go." Her voice was dead, even in her own ears.

24

Flee

Bragja focused on the next corner, the next street, the next step. She looked up when she heard a door open. They had made it to the motor pool. The long low warehouse squatted dimly near the pickerpark, its rows of vehicle bays filled with squat transport trucks and multi-wheeled recovery vehicles. It was to one of these that the spacer walked. Bragja noted it wasn't the closest one; he apparently needed this particular vehicle. She'd never liked the recovery trucks, but that could have been for what they meant as much as what they were. They called them *grafari*. Grave diggers. Pickers didn't break down in the field; they couldn't afford to. The window of time to gather starstuff was fleeting, so pickers kept their machines in top condition. Preventative maintenance wasn't a way of life; it *was* life. The recovery vehicles were for collecting the pieces if someone didn't make it back by starfall. Now, the man who might be her salvation but had killed her family swung himself up along the long crane of the truck. Its wicked four-fingered grasper was folded neatly in next to the high-walled bin.

Bragja stood, staring up at the bubble of the control compartment on the *grafari*. This was it. If she went with him, she'd never go back. Off planet had been unthinkable an hour ago, but now it was all she had. And this man had come to her town, given Landry a suppressor, and brought down the Ollson garrison. Every fiber of her being vibrated with a mixture of rage and grief. She couldn't tell if she wanted to kill him or curl into a ball and disappear.

So. Rage then. Bragja held up the suppressor field box in one hand. "Hey! You want this, right?"

The spacer looked down out of the open door. "Yeah. You have it. So get in, we go now."

Bragja fought to keep her breathing under control. "You gave this to Landry. It got him killed. Why should I come with you?"

"You stay, Ollsons find you eventually. Then they kill you, put your brain in a jar, kill you a lot."

Bragja felt tears in her eyes and squeezed them shut. He was an asshole, but he was right. They had to have seen her.

She was trapped.

"At least tell me your name."

The man stopped flipping switches and leaned out to stare at her for a moment. His brows furrowed to a thick caterpillar marching across his forehead. "Caso. Now get in, we both want to live."

She climbed up the ladder with one hand, the other still clutching the little red box she knew Caso wanted so badly. He stood on the side of the bubble canopy now, holding the door open. He dropped it as she swung in the door and made his way back along the gripping arm. She selected one of the two rear seats, with easy access to the door and good visibility of the operator's cradle.

They drove north out of the motor pool. Bragja didn't bother asking about tracking or remote operation override; if Caso hadn't taken care of that, they were both dead. Or worse.

The familiar landscape of Breydablik sprawled around them, ochre, yellow sand, and dirt filigreed with delicate yet stubborn flora. The air ahead was far cleaner than she was used to; the lack of starfall left more dust on the ground. But, looking at the rear screens on the *grafari's* control panel, there was a massive line of airborne dust rolling along behind them.

"Aren't you worried we are being followed?" She had to shout over the noise of the tires and the hum of electric motors.

"No."

"Even if you killed the transponder and remote data, they can track us from orbit. Not like the dust is hard to make out." Her throat was tight like she'd swallowed a rock, and shouting made her voice raw and ragged.

He drove on in silence for a while. Bragja tried again, the yelling making her head throb with effort. "What's your plan?"

Still nothing. After a few minutes, Bragja's patience was out. She was in a gravedigger barreling out into the desert with a man she truly hated but was her only hope at survival, and she wanted some gods damned answers.

She unbuckled and reached forward, smacking Caso's upper arm. "Tell me what the *fokk* is going on!"

Caso grunted and reached under the dash of the secondary operator's cradle, coming up with a set of headphones. He gestured to where his own plugged in overhead. Bragja reached forward to plug her headset in, then dropped the large cups over her ears. The rush of wind, the hum of the tires, and even the electric motors fell away. She could feel, but not hear, the huge machine they rode in. Bragja aligned the microphone to sit against her throat.

"I said-"

Caso waived his right hand dismissively, left still on the control stick. "I know what you said. Ollsons track us, blah blah

blah. I don't like to shout at you. So. I tell you, don't worry. We go north until the storm hits. Then we go wherever we want."

Bragja's frown was involuntary. Breydablik storms were not idle curiosities, nor was surviving one entirely a given.

"How big is the storm?" As Caso tapped commands into the center console, Bragja waited, tense and hunched in her seat. The last strong storm had peeled off the outer layer of outtown like an onion, leaving Bragja's home on the exposed outermost ring. She remembered the warnings when the storm track changed. Bragja's little family had pooled all the credit they had. She pitched in what she could, but she had still been too young to drive a picker, and only had scraps from working in the motor pool. It had barely been enough for some single-use nanopaste. The vendor they'd bought it from programmed it on the spot, and while they could have just included their own rooms in the protective cocoon, they'd paid to extend a wall out as far as they could pay to, a windbreak that directed the slipstream up and away from them. Bragja was sure that is what kept the howling winds at bay on their small part of the city to this day.

The morning after that storm, everything that had protruded past the reinforced section was gone, nubs of buildings abraded off as if by some manic glacier. Even when Bragja's brothers had grown older, and the family crowded the small rooms, they hadn't built out again. Storms were usually diverted from the town, but the Ollson administrators weren't perfect. Or perhaps they just didn't care about the small storms that only destroyed homes and uprooted lives in outtown. As long as they didn't threaten the industry, it wasn't worth moving the weather.

Caso grunted, bringing Bragja back to the moment. His beetle brows furrowed as his eyes flicked back and forth between the drive marker in the windscreen charting their path and the center console. He muttered indistinctly, then finally slapped the dash by the display.

"Look, there you go. See? Small storm. *Það er ekkert mál*. No problem."

The dash display was a generic version of the immersive environment of a picker cab, dumbed down to a series of menus and parallel display options. Caso had managed to coerce it into showing an orbital weather feed. Sometimes the storms were convective, promising rain and a much-needed ablution of the dirt-covered city. Very rarely, the stormwater was gentle enough that the acid wouldn't burn exposed flesh. The streets became one big party, as people played music from open windows and danced, laughing in the water. The storm on the *grafaris'* display screen was not a white and fluffy cloud of water but a deep ochre, scouring the land with massive wind and flying debris. There was likely rain in it, but Bragja guessed it was more like mud and stinging sand driven in sheets. It was a small storm as Breydablik storms went, about two hundred kilometers across, give or take. Not enough to threaten the city but certainly enough to get lost in. She hoped that Caso had scouted the terrain beforehand. Every time a storm passed, her next trip out to the starfall fields was like walking across a new landscape. Mudflows and landslides were no serious barrier to a picker, but the *grafari* lacked the grace of articulated limbs.

Bragja had one lingering doubt. "What about the Ollsons? They aren't going to just let this go." Her fingers caressed the box, carefully keeping out of the firing indentations on its edge.

Caso nodded and waved a hand. The screen brought up a topographic map. "We drive low as we can, keep dirt between them and us. Only one part problem." He tapped the screen ahead of them where the rings of terrain bunched together. "Going to have to hop canyon. They see us then."

Bragja should have felt fear, but she just felt tired. "Then what? They have drones. Ships."
Caso nodded. "We run faster, maybe." He grinned and turned to look at her for a moment. "Don't worry planet girl. We get to storm, we safe."

Bragja sat back, placed the suppressor box in her pocket, and watched the screen. The little icon of the *grafari* plowed on, and her stomach lurched and fell as they ripped across the desolate landscape. Her brothers' faces kept flashing in front of her. Landry, smiling in the sun as he threw a ball to her across the alley. Harvir, drawing in the dirt, his chubby legs splayed out in front of him. She closed her eyes and tried to hear the sound of her breath, but it was barely there through the headphones. Only the slight shudder as she fought off another wave of tears told her she was alive.

Caso's voice cut through her thoughts, loud in the headset. "Ok, here we go. Gotta go up a bit now."

Bragja's eyes snapped open, and she realized she gripped the seat arms with manic intensity. The tendons and veins on the back of her hands stood out like the terrain map on the screen she could still see, and she forced herself to release them. "Any sign of the Ollsons?"

"No idea. They can't see us, we can't see them, but will know soon."

Bragja nodded, then realized he couldn't see her. "Ok."

The *grafari* tilted then, and Bragja could see them climbing up out of the mud and dirt of the ditch they had been following. Tiny scrub trees dotted the ridgelines, nearly silhouettes against the darkening sky. The storm was close.

Finally, they rocketed out of the canyon, the front tires clearing the ground and slamming back down. Bragja felt the rattle in her bones.

Caso was first to speak. "Ok, that did it. See if they see us." His hand flicked across the console screen, the other on the control yoke as his feet worked the pedals. On the screen, the view behind them, bluer sky than the mud-yellow ahead of them, was suddenly painted with several small red boxes. Caso's voice was tight. "Yep. There they are." He paused. "They are turning. Time to go faster."

Bragja pulled the straps of her seat tight and the shoulder harness cut into her neck with each jolt. The hum of the engines redoubled as Caso poured the speed on. The *grafari* rumbled and shook in protest around them, and Bragja felt her stomach flip as they careened downhill towards the edge of the storm. In the rearview, the Ollson drones dropped behind the ridgeline.

Bragja risked a question, her voice shaky with the chaotic motion of their vehicle. "Will they get here before we get into the storm?"

"No, I don't think so planet girl. Ollsons don't know I have ship. We get to storm first, we ok."

Bragja nodded. The sky grew darker and darker ahead of them, then the *grafari* crested the final ridge between them and the storm. Bragja finally caught sight of the wall of dirt and mud, dust swirling out of it to mingle with the vast thunderhead above it. The power of it terrified her, an even split between that and getting caught by an Ollson drone. She craned her head around, but the bulk of the machine blocked her view.

She cleared her throat, her mouth dry. "Caso. Did they find us?"

"Yeah, they coming. Here." He waved the display back to the rearview. A formation of three drones, triangular bodies and stubby wings, glimmered in the mirage of the desert. "You feel better now?"

"No."

Caso's laugh was deep and rose as the *grafari* hit open terrain and he poured on the speed. The sand and gravel under her window ripped by as Bragja desperately switched her focus from the drones to the impending storm. Finally, they barreled into the mud and dirt, the howling of wind tossed together with a sound like gravel in a tin can. Despite the headphones, it was deafening. But, somehow, incredibly, they didn't die. The images Bragja saw in the rearview were a mass of debris, the odd swirling tree and boulder whipping by. No way the drones would survive that hellish environment.

But she might not either.

25

Misery

*Loud was the hammer
That smote the shell of her armor
Foes pursued, and darkness gathered
She steadied what footing she could*

Caso drove on into the storm, and despite herself, Bragja felt a new sliver of fear begin to work its way down her back. The *grafari* was nearly impenetrable, but that didn't mean they couldn't die. Her mind painted pictures of rogue landslides and mudflows slamming into the vehicle without warning, entombing them under tons of uncaring soil. Better a quick death from the Ollson drones than the slow suffocation as they ran out of air.

As the sky darkened, Caso pulled down a monocle from overhead and attached it to his headset, the umbilical disappearing into the dim overhead panel. As he glanced at her, Bragja saw a glint of light stitched in monochrome grey from the lens, the socket of Caso's eye illuminated. Her view outside the windows was pitch black, and she could hear rocks and sand ping against the glass. A louder thump rang the hull like a bell, and she heard something repeatedly smack down the length of the *grafari.* The swaying grew, rain and mud clubbing the craft with the energy of an angry god.

Caso's voice came loud across the intercom, and Bragja jumped. Her straps cut into her shoulders. "You want see?

Maybe you can say prayer before we die." His chuckle was tinny and not at all warm. "Just talk quick." He reached up and pulled down another monocle, offering it to her in the pale light of the control console. She reached over his shoulder and accepted it with trepidation. *Maybe I would be happier not seeing what's out there.*

After a moment of fumbling with the clip, Bragja felt the monocle snap home and pulled it down over her eye. She grunted as her stomach tried to flip. Green and grey flooded one eye, brightness fighting the dim interior. The double image was disorienting, and Bragja fought to make sense of the images. After a few moments, she could focus on either the console in front of her or the ghostly image in the monocle.

It was a hellscape.

The *grafari* bounced radar and laser light off the terrain, overlaying the return with what amplified ambient light it could gather. Directly in front of her, the cowling of the transport glowed, static charge dancing across the wicks set like wide antennae. The halo of light pulsed with the wind as the constant stream of sand and other debris transferred charge to the vehicle's skin. Bragja felt as if she was sitting in the eye of a great worm, crawling through the storm, lighting crackling from its protruding spines. The *grafari* rose and bucked as it trundled across the landscape, all trace of the former mad dash gone.

Caso took things slower in the teeth of the storm. Grey radar returns showed shifting densities of debris in the air as huge sheets of sand and mud dissolved in the winds.

Bragja was embarrassed at how small her voice sounded on the intercom. "The storms look worse when you can tell what's out there."

"Hah! Yes. Like I said, sometimes better to not know."

"I'd rather see it coming."

Caso barked out a laugh. "Yes, I bet you would. Don't worry, nothing big enough out there to hurt us."

"Not yet."

"No, not yet. Probably not ever. Either way, won't be in it much longer."

Bragja craned her neck to look at Caso's console. "How are you navigating?"

Caso pointed to a sigil on the bottom of the screen. "See, inertial. You are picker, you know."

"I also know that the longer you go inertial without a ground reference the worse you get."

"So? Lots of ground out there." Caso waved a hand into the darkness.

"It's all being scoured away by the storm; I'd have a hard time identifying anything in this murk."

"Yeah, ok." Caso grunted the last syllable and fixed both hands back on the yoke in front of him.

Bragja let the bulky silence squat between them. She knew Caso must be using something else to tell where they were going. Inertial references only drifted a few percent when they weren't backed up by the satellite signals, but the amount of turning and twisting they were doing was probably a large enough error to get them lost. So either he was driving dead reckoning or something else.

I need to know where his ship is.

She spent the next while watching Caso drive. He was good with the controls; she had to give him that. But the *grafari* was no picker; it responded to a heavy hand on the stick, the engine roaring and growling as it churned through the landscape. Bragja missed the delicate feeling of her picker gliding over the torn landscape of the starfall fields, the cockpit's motion oily smooth as jointed legs worked.

After an hour in the storm, the cockpit of the *grafari* was oppressively hot. Finally, Bragja lost patience with the mystery of navigation and barked out a question as she removed her light jacket. "How do you know where your ship is? How are we navigating?"

Caso rolled his thick shoulders and tossed his head to one side before answering. "I always know where ship is."

"So you aren't suicidal. But how?"

"Think you can kill me and take my ship?"

Bragja blew out an exasperated sigh. "Love to. But no, can't fly it. Never learned. But if you die in this thing, I'd at least like to be able to get to it."

He took his hand off the throttle and held it out. "Look close. Under my pretty skin." He had rolled his sleeve up against the cabin's heat, but Bragja could barely make out his arm in the gloom of the cabin.

Bragja narrowed her eyes, without any effect. "Turn on the light for a second."

A dull red glow bloomed from the overhead panel, and Bragja looked at his arm in the crimson wash. A fine network of scars raised like the tracks of worms covered the skin of his hand and arm. The traceries of tissue branched and melded as the pattern disappeared under the grimy roll of his shirt sleeve.

Bragja shook her head, forgetting he couldn't see her sitting behind him. "Great, thanks for clearing everything up. It all makes sense now." She tried to keep the sarcasm from actually dripping.

"I told you I always know where ship is. Can feel it." He dropped his hand back to the throttle quadrant, the overhead glow dimming out. "I'm connected to ship. It's connected to me."

"And the scars in your arm prove that?"

She could hear the grin in his words. "I forget you backward planet girl. Yeah, that's what scars mean. Found a cutter out in Gjoll. Paid him my whole stack for wires."

Bragja frowned, a chill working down her despite the cabin heat. *He was wired?* That didn't make any sense. She'd bested him in the square. Held him down and nearly killed him. *Did he just let me do that?* "So you got a wirejob, then. Nice of you to tell me back with all those soldiers around."

Caso glanced over his shoulder as the *grafari* surged over a small knoll and began rolling more quickly across an open section of ground. "No. Not wirejob. No one can do full wirejob but Forgers, everyone knows this." His sigh was audible over the intercom. "Silly planet girl. Just ship connection. I'm only one can fly her; pulled out control console after wires. But means one thing I'm better at than you." His ursine grin loomed at her out of the shadows, teeth stark against the darkness. "Better pilot."

Bragja had no doubt but wasn't sure whether she should be reassured or frightened. All it meant was that she needed Caso, for a while longer at least. Perhaps longer than she expected to when she fled the square.

The square.

She had loved her brothers fiercely. The only thing she'd ever wanted was to protect them, keep them from the gritty realities of life for a bit longer. Everything she'd done had been for them, from running a squad at the pickerpark to squirreling away every credit she could. Even her aunt pitched in her own credits when she had them. Her family wasn't much, but it was hers, and she loved them. She felt her heart swell and rise up into her throat as her eyes betrayed her, tears threatening to spill out of her like so many shattered dreams. They were hers, and she'd loved them.

And now they were gone.

In the midst of the howling storm, Bragja pulled up the monocle on her headset and put the boom mic away from her lips. She turned her face to the side of the *grafari*, her body curling around the little red box that had cost Harvir and Landry their lives, and wept.

Interlude

Here, come closer. Let me tell you of the history of the universe. Let me tell you of the threads we weave, we fates, we powers three.

The Wyrd will bind, the truth will flow, and all shall be made clear. A tossed stone in the ocean, cast adrift, cannot know the truth of things.

How now, o reader mine? How must we craft the cloth of truth, of justice, the very fabric of being? Oh, Truth it be, a thread at a time, just as we always have. For some a silver, and still fewer the gold, but most the plain and tawdry.

But you are not here for the plain and tawdry tales.

Listen now, oh reader mine, and hear the song I sing. I weave the threads, it's true, but the people choose the pattern. A woman may make her own destiny, to a point, but all her striving shall not change her dull grey thread to gold.

And a man may struggle and strive to do the thing he believes right, but he cannot deny his true nature.

Come with me as I weave, and see the pattern that emerges.

Listen now, o reader mine, and hear the song I sing. We fates of three, we sing and we weave the web of wyrd in the night. Look closer, closer now, and you will see the pattern. Hold it too tight in your mind and all will fall apart. You must look wider, yeah wider still, until all you behold.

These little lives, these silver threads that wish to be made gold-they falter, fail, and fall again. No hope have I for you, or for them. Witness, and bear ruin.

-Excerpt from the Saga of Bone and Blood
Wolfrem Larrson, 23rd Bard
Historian to the Geneline Ollson
Fourth Epoch, in Service to
Executor Aslog of Ollson

26

Theft

Ready now, in body and mind
He stood betwixt his cohort
A subtle knife would win the day
Like the ancient tale of the meade

Erick felt wrong standing in the airlock, not sitting in the pilot's crash couch on the bridge of the *Svadilfari*. His Ollson grey uniform was starched and spotless, every crease a razor. Behind him, he felt Daruthr, Yetunde, and Georgos move in their light exosuits. He'd given them a quick primer on suit procedures, should things come to blows. The suits were designed with ease of use in mind, and that meant largely passive defensive systems. Erick planned on speed and stealth for this mission instead of blunt force. Georgos had seemed disappointed at that strategy but hadn't tried to change the plan.

Now the four waited in the flitter bay airlock. Erick's uniform was barely rated for vacuum, and the single bulkhead between them and space made him nervous. He called up an external camera in his ocular, watching the approach.

Binya's voice came over the shiplink. "On flightpath. Marker's green. Contact in two plus forty-five."

Erick responded, his voice clipped and no-nonsense. If there was one role he could play well, it was leader. "Roger. Boarding party is three green. Continue."

Erick watched their target grow larger. The small transport ship was a fast cutter, mostly engine and reactor, with the cargo open to vacuum. It was designed for transporting small, high-value items and its shape was brutal in simplicity, hard angles and flat panels. *Don't need much armor when you can run.*

The main flaw in the plan lay in what would happen if the transport picked up the *Svadilfari*. It would run, squawking danger across the whole inner system. They'd never catch it, and the full attention of Gjolls tracking arrays would focus on them like an ant under a magnifying glass. Which is where Binya came in.

He flew with his implants coupled to the *Svadilfari's* systems, their subminds traveling the network to erase any sign of the ship's presence. Daruthr could have handled it, but they needed the mendicant to do the same to the station systems once they were on board. The only way to see the *Svadilfari*, assuming all went well, was with the naked eye. It would be too late if they got close enough to their quarry. Or so he hoped.

Erick put his ocular overlay back to standard magnification, and saw the small glowing triangle that marked their target begin to align with the porthole in the door in front of him. The indicator held its size, but he began to see another shape beyond it. The transport ship. It loomed into view, neither moving forward or backward, just growing larger until finally, he couldn't see the engine cones, just the round puckering of the transport's airlock ring. The gravity in the bay cut out as Binya brought them in for a final approach. The transport had no field generators, and *Svadilfari's* own field might tip off a wary Ollson crewmember.

Finally, the airlocks met with a gentle thump. They had only a few minutes before the transport crew knew what was happening, if they hadn't already heard the docking collars engage. Binya had kept them in the cone of blindness behind the transport, looping its cameras and onboard systems to mask their approach, but anyone could have been looking out the window at the wrong moment.

Binya's voice came again in Erick's ear. "Ok, looks like we have hard dock. Their systems show atmosphere, good seal. You're approved off the *Svadilfari*."

Erick nodded, more for the others behind him. "Roger that. Keep her warm for us."

He slapped the release on the airlock and the door irised open. *Once more into the breach.* He had mixed feelings about Godfrey not joining them. The doctor was more than competent with a firearm, but there was only room for four crew on the transport ship. He'd seemed quite happy to prepare to repel boarders on the *Svadilfari,* though that left him alone on the ship while Binya flew. It was hard, trust. His reflex was suspicion, and even now, he wasn't sure if he could rely on Godfrey to help in a dangerous situation. He pushed the reflex down. Trust was a choice, and he had to trust the man eventually. What better time than now.

They moved through the transport ship to the bridge, taking turns covering corridors and sightlines with their sidearms as they moved. Georgos had picked up the idea quickly, grinning as he made frog noises under his breath. His booming laugh had echoed off the flitter bay walls when Daruthr called the tactic leapfrogging.

A few minutes later, Erick and Daruthr sailed through the bridge's open the door, to the transport crew's surprised faces. One man went for his weapon as Yetunde took up a position beside the door, but Georgos swiped at him on his way in. The solid sound of meat on bone, and fist on jaw, reverberated in the small bridge. The man went limp and spun against a wall.

"See, I knew I'd have more fun as the last one in!" Georgos covered them with his sidearm while Daruthr and Erick tied up the transport crew. As soon as they were bound, Erick called back to the *Svadilfari.*

"*Svadilfari,* you have some packages coming. Please make sure they're handled with care." He reached into the unconscious man's uniform pocket, pulling out a shining silver keycard. *At least they keep to regulations.* It wasn't likely they'd be able to get a keycard on the station once they arrived.

Binya's voice was calm as ever. "Roger that, we'll get them tied down. Good luck."

Erick familiarized himself with the transport ship. A little over half the reaction mass remained, enough for a good long run if it came. But they'd barely put a dent in the fuel with a bit of luck. A smooth operation; arrive, retrieve the data core they needed, and then back to the ship and away.

Daruthr and Georgos rejoined Erick on the transport bridge, taking up their stations on either side of Erick. Daruthr only nodded, but Georgos grinned even wider than usual. "Got them all put away, boss. Let's go get us a data can!"

Daruthr smiled. "Core, Georgos. Data core. But yes, let's do this. The sooner we get back, the better." Yetunde smiled but was quiet.

Georgos nodded, but his eyes were fixed on Daruthr, not Erick. He seemed about to speak, then closed his mouth and nodded, head down to check the displays at his console.

They approached the backup station on autopilot, having changed nothing about the transport ship's course or speed. The less difference they made, the better. There was not likely to be any human presence on the station, but the automated systems were top notch, and no doubt there was a traffic array tracking the transport's every move.

They docked with a solid connecting thump, and the gravity warning lit amber for a few moments. The station was small, and was equipped with a generator large enough for a suite of defenses. When those defenses were not engaged, it had enough power to spare for artificial gravity. All four interlopers put their feet to the floor just as the light turned green, and the station's gravity gently pulled them to the deck.

"All right," Erick said, hand straying to the grip of his sidearm, "let's move quickly."

He checked the status of his implants as they moved to the little ship's airlock. It didn't matter how often he did it; he was always a little in awe of the destructive power of the things he carried within him. To be sure, he wasn't about to go tearing warships apart with his bare hands, but few could put up a fair fight. Which, he mused, was the whole point.

But he hoped he wouldn't need any of that today.

They checked for a good seal, then popped the airlock and walked onto the archive station. It had the sterile smell of a place built to be inhabited only occasionally. The walls were the usual dull grey painted steel of most official Ollson structures, but even the short carpeting of the floors lacked any hint of wear pattern. Security duty on this station was relegated to those who had made enemies in the Ollson hierarchy. It wasn't technically banishment, but the tours were long, the duty largely automated, and the company sparse.

Erick heard the automated systems begin to unload the transport ship, the dull clang of servo-arms echoing softly through the bones of the station. Service in the Ollson military was complicated, with the regular forces swearing loyalty to the Empress. A much smaller number of those served the Geneline Ollson directly, and then only for exceptional circumstances or tasks that the Empress' legionnaires deemed beneath them.

The four moved quickly through the station, Yetunde and the others keeping pace just behind Erick as if they were his personal guard. Erick followed the blue line laid down by his ocular, the floor plan of the station overlaid on his vision in miniature. They had almost reached the repository doors when a voice hailed from the station's loudspeakers. The blast doors ahead of and behind them slammed shut.

"To the detachment from the data transport ship currently heading towards the repository, stop and state your business." *Guði fjandinn hafi það.* Gods damn it. So much for their stealthy approach. *How did they see us with Binya's network implants masking our approach?*

Yetunde cast sharp eyes toward Erick, who gave the slightest nod. All four stopped in the corridor, and Erick walked to the viewscreen embedded in a nearby bulkhead.

He tapped the security call button and a man's face popped into view. He had sunken cheeks and furtive eyes, and Erick saw him quickly take in the background of the camera pickup. His voice was reedy but authoritative. "You shouldn't be down there. You are only allowed to depart the transport ship in the event of an emergency, or if requested by station security. And that's me."

Erick nodded, giving his best attempt at an arrogant sneer. "Yes, thank you, Corporal; I'm well aware of the regulations. I have orders from the system manager."

To his credit, the man's expression of authority only faltered slightly. "Ahem. Yes, well." Erick could imagine the man frantically weighing the consequences of not doing his job against interfering with the system manager's business. He continued in a slightly more respectful tone. "What does the system manager want with archival data? She's got the primary backups."

Erich sighed, inspecting his nails. "Now that you're done demonstrating the most basic grasp of the system, ask yourself, what might make her send for a retrieval?"

The man paused, his façade of righteous indignation cracking. "I mean, only if the primary wasn't working, I guess. But that doesn't happen."

"Yes. It doesn't." Erick nodded, then fixed him with his best withering gaze. "But it did, and now she wants to know why. Which is why I'm here, wasting my time explaining the situation instead of doing as she's commanded."

"We didn't receive any notification of a special mission today—"

"Well, I'm sure the traffic came through. Unless someone carelessly deleted it." Erick knew the tendency of those lower down the ranks to habitually delete communications. They were usually right; the amount of irrelevant traffic that went out to the masses was hideous. But it also meant the possibility of deleting something important by accident. Erick was gambling that on this assignment, where nothing really mattered, this corporal deleted everything out of habit.

The man looked unsure now, but Erick and his companions' way remained barred. The worst thing that the security chief could do now was attempt a call back to the system manager's office for confirmation.

"Corporal," Erick said, nodding to Daruthr, "transmit a copy of our orders to the station security. I'm sure they didn't delete important message traffic like that without looking at it, but this will save them the trouble of searching their system." Daruthr nodded and pulled out a data pad.

The man on the screen looked away from the pickup, and pursed his lips. He waited a few moments as Daruthr's faked message made it to his terminal. "I see."

"Yes, you see. Now, if you'll let us continue, we'll be off your station all the sooner."

The station security officer nodded, then the screen went blank. The blast doors retracted smoothly into their recesses, and Erick moved off through the corridor once again with what he hoped was a convincingly exasperated snort.

A message indicator flashed in Erick's ocular, and he opened it. It was text only.

<THAT WON'T HOLD UP TO STATION SYSTEM SCRUTINY, I'M AFRAID.>

Excellent. So we're on borrowed time. Erick risked a short reply, his eyes picking out the letters he wanted while he let his feet follow the blue line of his map.

<THEN WE HURRY. LET BINYA KNOW WE MAY NEED EXTRACTION.>

<DONE.>

The rest of the walk to the archive passed in tense silence. Erick's breath caught in his chest as he swiped the purloined keycard at the archival door, but the indicator flicked to green, and the door slid aside. Inside the room, a plate of transparent polymer separated the control room from the vacuum of the archival storage. Racks of barrel-like data cores stretched as far as the eye could see, lost in the darkness and gentle curve of the station.

Yetunde and Daruthr strode to the control panel by the entry door. Daruthr tapped a few times, and an insectile arm detached from the ceiling, zipping off into the darkness in eerie silence. It returned a few moments later, a data core clutched in its steely fingers. It deposited the core in a small round airlock at the base of the window. The core dropped gently forward as the lock cycled and popped open.

Erick walked forward to scan the marking along the top of the core with his datapad. "Looks like the one she wants." He snapped his fingers at Georgos and Daruthr, more for the show they were likely giving the station security. "You two, pick this up. Carefully. Let's get it back to the ship."

They made good time back through the corridors, and Erick allowed himself a slight internal sigh of relief. Only a few hundred more meters, and they would be back at the transport ship and on their way to rendezvous with the *Svadilfari*.

If only things were that simple.

The blast doors along the hallway clanged shut once more, and this time, red lockdown warnings showed on all the screens in the hallway.

"Are we fucked?" Georgos' voice was steady, and his pistol appeared in his hand.

Daruthr's voice was measured. "I believe we are well on our way to, as you put it, being fucked."

"Unless you actually have a plan, shut it. I need to think." If he still had his executor's access, he'd be able to open a route to the ship, but without it, they'd have to hack each terminal individually. Lockdown also severed their connections to the mainframe. "It's going to be a slog; we need to get going on these access panels."

Daruthr shook his head. "Erick, even I won't be able to hack every panel quickly enough for us to stay ahead of the station security bots."

Georgos frowned. "So that's it then. No way ahead, no way out. Maybe we give ourselves up and then try to take them when they show up?"

Yetunde laughed. After being silent nearly the whole trip, her voice was a breath of fresh air. "Stop being a bunch of big babies. As soon as things get a little tough, what, you throw up your hands?"

Erick's smile was tight. "What do you suggest, oh fearless one?"

"Follow me!" A new line appeared in Erick's ocular, leading back the way they had come. "We just need a little change of plans."

She moved to a wall console, her hands dancing along the input keys. "I don't need to open up all the doors, just the right ones."

Erick caught the raised eyebrow from Daruthr and shook his head just slightly. If they could avoid him using his unique abilities, there was less chance of his secret going past their crew. If word a loose mendicant was bouncing around Ollson space made it back to the Empress, she'd send the Black Guard to burn him out. She might even wake the Draco Corps, if history was any indication.

No, not worth the risk. Yetunde was more than competent with computer systems for what they needed.

While she worked, Erick felt the station's cyber defenses spring to action. His implants slammed shut their firewalls, the network falling away like an amputated limb. Of course, Daruthr was perfectly at ease, and if Georgos had any idea of the roiling conflict in the network around them, he gave no indication.

After a few tense minutes, Yetunde gave a whoop of triumph, and one of the doors slid open.

The corridor beyond was brimming with metallic death.

Security bots stalked over and around each other on multijointed legs, a seething mass of malignant metal. They didn't have anything ranged, or Erick and his friends would all be dead, but if they got close enough, they held short-range lasers, cutting implements, and hunter-seeker nanos, like the missile that had nearly killed Erick in the Summit hangar.

Even as Erick raised his sidearm, Georgos had started firing. The man was like a machine, each shot measured and effective. *Thunk.* A bot blew apart. *Thunk.* Another. *Thunk, thunk, thunk.* As Georgos picked up the rhythm, the other three joined in, and the hallway was quickly littered with bits of metal and broken bot parts. But there were more behind them, surging in to fill the gaps.

"We need to get through them!" Erick shouted to be heard over the sound of metallic skittering and small arms fire. "Focus on the center, and we'll push!"

Yetunde led, unlimbering a sonoblade that wavered along its wicked edge. *Where did she even have that hidden?* She swept it before her one-handed, her off-hand gripping her pistol and dispatching any bots that made it inside the blade's arc. The other three followed her in a mad rush. The low hollow sounds of the firearms, the clang of the sonoblade on metal carapace, the grunts and shouts of warning all blended together in a song of death. Or at least the avoidance of death. Erick barely noticed the background of skittering bot feet.

Finally, they pressed forward into a small room. "Dead end!" Georgos shouted, his twin pistols still flashing with propellant as he dispatched two bots that lurked on the ceiling.

"Not quite!" Yetunde slashed down across a bot trying to get in the door behind them, just as Daruthr slapped the manual door override. The door hissed shut just as another security bot slammed into the now-closed doors. "Everyone to the airlock! Quickly!"

Erick saw her plan now. "Oh, gods damnit. Really?"

Yetunde's grin was a slash of white across her face. "Come, now, Erick, where is your sense of glory?"

"Firmly next to my desire for an early death."

Binya's voice came over their private band. "Hey, you hear me now?"

Yetunde answered. "Yes, we hear you! You had better be all the pilot that you say you are!"

"Yeah, don't worry about me. Just jump straight. I don't want to run around picking you up one at a time."

All four entered the airlock, the precious silver data core held between Daruthr and Georgos. Erick and Yetunde flanked them, closing the inner airlock door behind them.

"Hey, you guys ready or what? Pretty sure they know I'm here by now. Getting some weird intrusion attempts on the ship net." Binya's voice was still calm, but Erick could hear the tension he was under in the speed of his words. There must be a lot of network weapons being brought to bear on him to make him sound concerned.

Daruthr reached around Erick's waist, his hand grasping Erick's belt like a vise, and Erick returned the favor. The others followed suit, arms intertwined from belt to belt. Georgos had wrapped his arms around the core, his suit helmet already up. Erick caught his eye through the transparent membrane and saw his eyes wide, grinning around a wordless shout. He looked a lot more excited than he had any right to be. Erick looked down the line of linked arms, heartened to see a row of suit helmets already in place.

He nodded to them, but Yetunde chopped her free arm at him, then tapped her own helmet. Erick shook his head. His own uniform had emergency vacuum capability, but it wasn't something you could activate. It would sense the lowering pressure and pop an emergency bubble over his head, sealing around him to provide a few minutes of precious air. At least, that's the way it was supposed to work. He didn't have the time or the inclination to explain all that, so by way of answering, he held his hand over the outer airlock door release for a moment, then slammed it down. *And away we go.*

The doors blew out, spinning away from the center of the airlock as the four linked figures shot into space.

There was a moment of pure sound, the pressure in his ears slamming out, but his uniform sucked tight around him, the emergency bubble slamming up from his collar to seal somewhere over his head. After a few seconds basking in the happiness that he was not going to die in the next few minutes, Erick looked over to see everyone still held tight to each other, with Georgos in the middle, both his arms and legs now wrapped around the data core.

It was eerily silent; without a network connection or a transmitter, Erick had no way to talk to the others. He didn't want to risk the thin membrane of his emergency helmet in direct contact; the last thing he needed was a leak. The cold was already stabbing through his uniform, and he forced himself to breathe through the pain. There was no telling how far out Binya had to take the ship to pick them up.

That's when he saw the first round go by.

The station behind them was equipped mainly for defense, and most of its systems dealt with networks and information attacks. It was, after all, a data backup. But it still had a few weapons systems, some directed energy systems for longer ranges and flak cannons for dealing with missiles or other guided projectiles. They were under the firing arc of the beamers, but now the space around them was suddenly alive with shards of superheated metal. The flack cannons were live.

Erick felt their little formation spinning slowly, and as they turned, the station came into view. He had no idea why they weren't dead already; perhaps Binya had been able to mask the returns of the ranging systems when they left the airlock. But now, there was a wall of detonations slowly moving out from the station. *Not a bad tactic.* The operators must have decided it was better to saturate anywhere they might be with shrapnel. Already a few glowing bits had come perilously close.

The wall of death was moving closer by the second.

Erick felt helpless once again. *Where the hell is that ship?* He felt his breathing quicken as the fire came closer, and tried to shove down the upwelling of panic. His joints screamed with the cold, and he damped down his pain reception to keep from passing out. He had to act. But what could they do? They had no reaction mass, no jets, and no armor; it was only a matter of time. Through his helmet, he caught Daruthr's eyes, internal lights carving the mendicant's features in sharp relief. Would he die, too, like the rest of them, or live on? Surely he'd live. His body wasn't made of fragile meat and bones to be ground to dust by the incoming fire. Erick took comfort in that, at least. He remembered the old saying about your whole life flashing before your eyes before you died. Would centuries fit in that moment before death, or would only the most potent memories would surface?

Something huge moved across the station, enveloping it in blackness so deep, not even the stars shone through it. *Hvað í fjandanum? What is that?* The station was simply gone, swallowed by the inky blackness.

Then it clicked.

It wasn't something huge and far away. His eyes adjusted, and features grew out of the shape of blackness, the sharp lines of hull plates and armor, sensor arrays, and maneuvering thrusters.

Erick looked down the hull and saw the *Svadilfari's* unmistakable shape. The ship put its bulk between them and the station and gently, almost kindly, maneuvered an airlock to them. Erick felt the tug ripple through their line of linked bodies as Yetunde grabbed a handhold and got his free hand up in time to absorb the motion on the airlock's open edge. They piled in, gripping various hand and footholds, and Erick triggered the door closed.

The lock cycled, and they poured out into the bay. Godfrey stood there in a pair of mag boots, his eyes wide. "You better get to the bridge. Something is weird with Binya, and it's beyond my, you know, expertise."

Erick nodded, then turned to the group. "Yetunde, Georgos, get the core secured and get to the crew quarters. Strap in; the bunks will serve as crash couches. There's a green toggle inside each one, about halfway down. Don't push it until you're in." They nodded, and Yetunde led the way, Georgos still cradling the precious egg of the data core.

Erick pushed over to a locker and pulled out two pairs of mag boots, pushing one across to Daruthr. "You and I are headed to the bridge."

Daruthr nodded and caught the boots, speaking as he slid them on. "Perhaps the good doctor would be so kind as to join us? I believe there are four crash couches in the cockpit."

Godfrey nodded, but his face was sallow, and he wrung his hands as he waited the few seconds it took Erick to get his boots on. They attached to the deck with a satisfying thump.

"Godfrey, what exactly is the problem with Binya?" Erick's voice came across sharper than he intended, but he pushed on. He didn't have time to worry about feeling right now; they weren't out of the woods yet.

"Well, everything was fine until we had to come in to pick you up. Binya said something about signal gain and told me to come down here to help you all. But then he just sort of stopped."

Daruthr shot a look at Erick before speaking. "Stopped what, Godfrey? The ship?"

"No, I mean, he stopped everything. Just sort of froze. The ship was still moving, and all, so I ran down here as best I could."

That doesn't sound good. Erick clapped the man on the shoulder. "Thank you for letting us know. Leave your boots on; that was a good call. We may maneuver, and you'd be better off with the chance to grab hold of something rather than floating."

They rushed through the ship as quickly as they could. Without warning, the wall made a good attempt at becoming the floor as the *Svadilfari* racked through an evasive maneuver. Luckily there were handholds on most surfaces, and the three managed to keep from being tossed around too severely. Erick said a little prayer of thanks for the mag boots as the ship twisted and spun, but thankfully Binya was holding off on the hard acceleration until they were all strapped in. Taking advantage of the pause in motion, Erick checked his ocular to see the status of the crash couches in the crew quarters. They both showed green and activated. That left the three of them getting to the bridge, and they could fire up the main drive. Just at this thought, Erick heard the metallic rain sound of the wall of flak reaching them. Time to move while they still could.

Erick in the lead, the three burst onto the bridge. Binya's head was visible over the top of the crash couch, his hands disappearing into the direct shiplink gloves at the sides of his seat. As Erick walked forward. "Bin? Godfrey tells me there's a problem."

There was no answer. Binya's head was tilted back, every muscle and tendon on his neck rigid and drawn cable-tight. His mouth trailed blood from one corner, and his breath was rapid and shallow. His eyes were rolled back in their sockets, the white sclera visible.

Erick felt a fresh wave of adrenaline. "Daruthr."

The mendicant slipped forward to look. "It's a worm. And a good one, by the look of it. Honestly I'm surprised he managed to retain enough control of the ship to pick us up."

"So what do we do? Can you help him?"

"I can disconnect him from the ship's array and systems. That should keep the contagion isolated to just him. But—" He looks at Erick sidelong. "There's too many implants."

Erick put a hand to his face, tugging on his beard. "Surely you can do something."

Daruthr put a hand on Erick's shoulder. "The implants are as much a part of his brain as they are augmenting it. There's more software in there than him, to be honest. From what I can tell, the worm has already eaten everything that was him. All that's left are the subminds."

"So he's gone then."

"I'm afraid so."

"Well, let's get him unlinked from the ship at least. We can't stay here any longer."

Daruthr nodded, placing a hand on Binya's shoulder and gently pulling first one arm, then the other out of the link gloves.

"Godfrey, help us with the body if you don't mind."

The doctor stepped forward and grasped Binya's forearm, ready to help pull him out of the crash couch.

Binya's hand grasped back.

The pilot's eyes rolled back down, and a wordless scream came from his lips. Blood spattered across Erick's chest, and Binya launched himself back, his back arching as his limbs contorted in a parody of life, jerky, and wrong. Before Erick could react, he'd propelled himself out of the cockpit door, dragging a screaming Godfrey with him.

Daruthr's voice snapped Erick out of his momentary shock. "Someone has to fly us out of here. You go and save the doctor. Remember, that's not Binya. The worm burned him out; that's whatever is left of his combat subminds operating his body."

Erick nodded and began checking in with his combat systems as he made for the door. Military implant tech was one thing, but seeing it possess a body and operate by itself was always… disturbing. There was a reason Erick had always kept any implanted combat systems well below the autonomous level. He preferred them to be loyal and dumb, like any good pet.

Erick crashed around the corner, keying down his time sense as he entered the hallway. Binya, or more rightly Binya's body, had made it to the end of the corridor with the struggling Godfrey, who it looked like was putting up quite a fight. Erick disengaged his mag boots and pushed off down the hall, praying that Daruthr was paying attention and wouldn't maneuver the ship and smash him against a wall. The not-Binya was wickedly fast, despite its prisoner. Erick finally caught up as it made it to the flitter bay. *What the hell does it want in...* Erick realized that the subminds controlling Binya's body were acting rationally, taking a hostage and now looking for a way off the *Svadilfari*. Erick drew his sidearm and keyed up his time sense to the maximum.

The world moved like liquid glass, and his own breath slowed to nearly nothing. He could see every detail of how the subminds wrapped Binya's arms around Godfrey to pin him in place, backpedaling with his head arched back, spinning and bouncing off the floor and ceiling of the bay. He carefully lined up a shot that wouldn't damage the assault pod or the flitter, and waited for a clear sight picture. The sights lined up on Binya, center mass.

He fired.

The round entered Binya's ribcage, missing Godfrey but spearing through the vertebrae, severing Binya's spinal cord and sending chips of bone and blood flying in an expanding spiral.

Binya, with Godfrey still wrapped in Binya's arms, slammed into the side of the flitter and bounced on towards the clamshell launch doors in the back of the bay. Erick dropped into standard time and pushed off to follow, his weapon still up and ready. He found them behind the flitter, Binya's eyes still jittering wildly as the software that drove him tried to find a new solution to the changed tactical problem. It hadn't let go of Godfrey, whose eyes were round and jaw slack. He had a small trickle of blood that pooled in the low gravity. The sound of flak on the hull had slackened, but the occasional loud ring of a lucky shot still punctuated the engine's hum.

Erick wasn't exactly sure how to proceed. Daruthr had managed to destroy the interface ability of the implants, as Erick felt no attempts at intrusion in his own systems. But he needed to get Godfrey away from it and strapped in so they could leave.

"Let him go. You don't need him anymore." Was he crazy, trying to talk to software?

But Binya's eyes stopped their mad dance and locked onto him, unblinking.

"Yes, I'm talking to you. You don't need the hostage anymore." The subminds were software, but they understood basic logic.

They had to.

"There's no reason to keep him."

The thing that had been Binya cocked its head as if considering Erick's words. Then it loosened its grip on the still-dazed doctor. Its hands, Binya's hands, rose along Godfrey's chest, as if looking for something.

Erick watched as it dug fingers into flesh, stabbing inwards. Godfrey's eyes went wide, and he choked, a gurgling sound and the trickle of blood dripping from the corner of his mouth. Erick's hands twitched up, and he fired three quick shots.

The first struck Binya's mouth, teeth shattering as the round expanded and slowed. The fingers stopped as the bullet severed the connection between brain and body. The second round followed the first a few inches lower, again severing Binya's spinal column. Bullets designed for shipboard action penetrated, fractured, each piece shedding all of its energy into the soft tissues. The final round passed into Binya's forehead, the energy snapping his head back as the bullet hit the back of Binya's skull in a hundred shards. Blood pulsed from the ruin of Binya's mouth, arterial red. Erick saw bits of circuitry through the open hole in Binya's forehead, twinkling lights shining multicolored from within the wound.

Erick rushed forward, his voice carried over the common band. "Daruthr, get down here!"

Godfrey's eyes were rolled back in his head. His breath was shallow and rapid. The fingers of Binya's right hand were still embedded in Godfrey's chest to the first digit, but the corpse's right hand had fallen out. The blood stain was dark on Godfrey's white shirt in the low light of the hangar.

Erick looked at the ruin of Binya's face, checking for any lingering motion. Binya's blood had slowed to a trickle. A rivulet of it still ran down the dead man's arm. But he was motionless, the demons of software either dead or cut off from control of the body. But in front of him, Godfrey twitched, his eyes rolling back and searching around him.

"Calm, Godfrey, it's ok. I'm here."

Godfrey's unfocused eyes found Erick, then closed tight in pain. He forced a few words out through gritted teeth. "A collapsed lung. Intrusion. This is," a shallow gasp, "unpleasant."

Erick nodded. "You have a dead man's fingers in your chest. I'm surprised you're talking."

"I have an implant of my own. Painkillers, for trauma. Seemed like, you know, a good idea."

"Glad you always have a plan. Hold tight here." Erick looked over his right shoulder, where the assault pod sat quietly. It had a trauma kit accessible from the outside. He reached it in a few strides. Flak rang out against the hull, and Erick felt the ship maneuver. He braced a hand on the pod and popped open the trauma kit panel. Most of the med gear wouldn't be helpful; no way to put a tourniquet on a chest wound. Drugs were for returning to combat. Antibiotics, there, that would be useful, and the penetrating wound microbot. It would seal Godfrey's chest, keeping his thoracic pressure up. *Assuming there's no lung puncture, I'm not sure with that blood in the mouth.* Erick was silently thankful for the basic trauma training Obin had insisted he repeat each year. He could hear her voice now in his head, "But Executor Erick, there may be a time when the difference between life and death is the time it takes to get to a medical bay. You need to know the basics." He took a short tube from the kit, just in case.

"Godfrey, I've got the basics. Daruthr should be here soon." He tapped the green icon on the microbot's back, and its scarab legs clicked out. Mouthparts underneath moved in a self-test.

"Get this goddamn hand out of me. I can feel his fingers between my ribs."

Erick paused, the bot hovering over Godfrey's chest. "If I pull them, you'll bleed more."

"Yes, yes, I know, and I might have a punctured lung." The man's eyes were wide, pleading despite the relatively calm voice. "His fingers. Are in. My chest."

Erick nodded. "One moment." Erick ran his hands along Godfrey's body, starting at the man's neck and working down. He didn't want to move him without knowing the extent of other injuries. An impact rang the ship like a bell, flak hitting the hull above him. They were beyond the range of one-hit kill on the ship, but if they lit the main drive, the station would surely see them. That meant missiles, coilguns, directed energy. Stealth was life for now.

Erick continued his sweep. He found no other blood sources, but Godfrey's left knee was oddly angled, likely below the pain threshold given the damage to his chest. It wouldn't stop Erick from moving him. He looked into the doctor's eyes. "Are you sure about this?"

"Fucking do it already, who knows what's in his blood."

Erick nodded, then pulled the sonoblade from his boot. He held Binya's arm, the one with the fingers embedded in Godfrey's chest, with his right arm and gently slid the blade through the corpse's elbow. Muscle and bone parted quickly with the blade's motion, and he turned it off, wiping it on his thigh and sheathing it. Godfrey groaned as the dead fingers moved in his chest. Erick transferred his hold on the severed arm and slipped his right hand under Godfrey, slowly lowering him to the deck. *Where in all the damned gods is Daruthr?*

"For fuck's sake, man, gentle." Godfrey grunted as his body stretched out on the floor.

"Glad to see you're still capable of being pissed."

"There are still fingers in my chest. You're a terrible doctor."

"Yes, you're right. But let's just add that to the list of things I didn't think I'd have to deal with until recently." Erick gripped the severed arm by the wrist. "Are you ready?"

"Ready, of course I'm—" Erick snapped the arm back quickly, the fingers of the dead hand sliding from between ribs with a sickening vibration. Godfrey roared wordlessly, his eyebrows furrowed as he shot Erick a look full of daggers.

"Oh, come on, you wanted to have time to think about it?" Erick dropped the microbot onto Godfrey's chest, and the scuttling legs carried the machine in a crosshatch pattern across him. A second later, it had built a map of all his injuries and began sealing each puncture wound. It wouldn't heal him but would keep him from bleeding out.

"Erick." Godfrey's voice labored. "One thing. I have a punctured lung."

"Yes, I'm aware."

"So you'll need to release the pressure. The air, gets out, forms a pocket, so you'll need a—"

Erick held up a tube, about four inches long and a few millimeters in diameter. One end was cut at a sharp angle, and the other ended in a barrel-like swelling. Erick grinned. "One of these?"

"Yes, a chest intubation tube. That."

The deck bucked under Erick, a sharp maneuver cutting through the dampening field. Erick risked a half-second look at the tactical situation. They had made it far enough from the station to be out of flak range, but the station commander apparently had not taken no for an answer. They were saturating the space where the airlock ejecta might be with coilgun rounds. Superheated metal slugs ripped by, their path mapped by *Svadilfari's* local active scanners and painted in Erick's ocular. The last maneuver had removed them from the vector the station commander was shooting along. So long as they didn't attract any more attention, they were likely clear.

"Well, good news," Erick said as he reached down to feel for the ribs under Godfrey's ruined right chest. "They aren't likely to hit us anymore from the station."

"Oh good, now I'm just going to drown in my own blood."

"Please, we have a mendicant on board."

Godfrey nodded, but he looked almost sad. "And he seems to be elsewhere at the moment."

Erick sent another message to Daruthr over the shipnet. <NEED YOU NOW. GODFREY DYING.> Out loud, he forced some cheer into his voice. "Well, now you'll be able to tell people that Executor Ollson saved your life with his own two hands. That'll be a good story." Erick held the tip of the needle over the intercostal muscle between Godfrey's ribs, halfway down the line of puncture wounds. The microbot buzzed angrily, trying to seal up the area.

Godfrey managed a weak smile. "Yes, well, you've got to do the job first." His face had become pale, papery, lips blue with cyanosis. Not enough blood.

Erick pushed the needle in, opening a path for the trapped air. The barrel on the end of the needle glowed green, showing that it detected it was in place correctly. Air hissed out, followed by a steady stream of blood and yellowish fluid. "Godfrey, you're going to have an awful lot of stories to tell when this is all over, I expect." He looked up, and Godfrey's eyes were closed. A quick check of the carotid artery showed his pulse rapid, weak, and thready. *He needs blood volume.* Erick stood, turned back towards the assault pod, and nearly ran straight into Daruthr.

Daruthr looked at Godfrey, lying on the decking, Binya's severed arm beside him, the pulverized corpse against the ramp of the cargo door. His voice was soft. "It's ok, Erick. You couldn't save them both."

Erick stepped back as Daruthr bent over Godfrey, his hand moving to the wounds on the man's chest. As Daruthr pressed down his hand, and light seemed to seep and flow from where he touched Godfrey's chest. Daruthr placed his hand on each wound, and pale clean flesh lay below each time he removed it. At the last one, Godfrey's chest was a smattering of overlapping clean handprints, the rest slick with blood.

Daruthr stood. "I've repaired the damage, but it's on him to make up the blood volume. He'll be asleep until I wake him."

Erick swept a hand around the bay. "There's not enough material here for you to heal him? I watched you turn a confinement cube into body mass."

"I'm also not made of flesh, Erick. It doesn't work like that."

Erick frowned. He let the adrenaline finally wash over him. Godfrey was a friend, was crew, was his responsibility. *If he dies....* But he wouldn't, now that Daruthr was here.

As if reading his thoughts, Daruthr reached out a hand and placed it on Erick's shoulder. "He will live, and not because of me. The microbot, chest tube, all of that saved his life."

"But he nearly died on this mission for me."

"But he didn't. And it was his choice, to be here."

Erick looked up into Daruthr's eyes. "What took you so long to get here?"

"The flak was thick, Erick. Yetunde had to fly, but I'm afraid the *Svadilfari's* poor little brain couldn't compute a safe path through all the debris."

"So, you got us out of the danger zone."

"Yes, essentially." Daruthr turned back to look at Godfrey. "If you can take him to a bunk, I'll take care of Binya."

Erick nodded and reached down to slip his arms under the now sleeping form of Godfrey. Some color had returned to his lips, though his face remained pale. Erick lifted him, his wirejob taking the strain. He walked toward the front door of the flitter bay.

This was so much. Erick knew there'd be danger when he left Karvasok, knew he'd have to get his hands dirty. But he hadn't expected it to be literally bloody hands. Erick was an executor and wielded power as his birthright. But the weight of Godfrey, cradled in his arms, was an anchor to the reality of things. He'd known what to do, what needed to be done, all his life, but he'd always had others to do it for him.

Erick ducked Godfrey's head past the bulkhead as he walked down the hallway to the common room and the galley. His boots echoed loudly off the decking and metal walls. Finally, he found an empty bunk and gently deposited Godfrey, head on a pillow. The man's clothes were a mess, blood-soaked and torn. Quietly, Erick began the task of cleaning him. He sent a command to the ship, and the printer behind him whirred to life printing a new set of clothes. He owed this man a lot, owed them all a lot. Yetunde, Georgos, Godfrey, Daruthr.

And Binya.

The answers had better be worth the price they'd paid.

27
Tribulation

Joyous was he, he was over-joyed
To have the bit in his teeth
The height of his happiness matched the depths of his
rage
When he saw what the hoard contained

They clustered around the canister, the muted silver-grey reflecting and distorting their faces. The bay was cold, environmental systems still returning heat to the air after Daruthr had purged the thing that Binya had become. Erick shuddered as he remembered the jerky animation of the man's body skittering across the bay. The snapping teeth on top of a pile of dead flesh.

Yetunde mistook his movement. "Are you cold, Erick? Perhaps we wait until the heat is back, yeah?"

He shook his head. "No, thank you. I'm fine. Let's take a look at the data."

Yetunde nodded, speaking sotto voce. "Let's hope it was worth it."

Daruthr and Georgos stood across from Yetunde and Erick. The low bay lighting lent a somber feeling to the room, muted like some sort of ritual space.

Or a tomb.

Georgos ran his fingers across the surface of the canister. "Man, it's completely smooth. How are we even going to get anything out of it? I mean, shouldn't there be an access port or something on it?"

Daruthr shook his head. "No, storage like this isn't meant to be accessible. It's a record, a backup. Not even the primary backup, mind you."

Erick nodded. All of this, for something that was supposed to outlast an extinction event. "It's more of a time capsule than anything."

"So," Yetunde's voice held an edge of impatience, "let's crack this egg and see."

"If by crack, you mean, read and access the data inside remotely, then yes, let's do that." Daruthr smiled gently as he set up an induction reader, freshly cobbled together from spare parts. The reader's four mechanical fingers caressed the egg, not quite touching it, and it was almost obscene how the machine stroked the storage canister.

No one spoke as the reader cycled around the silver egg. *What is in here that was worth it?* Erick's thoughts wandered, despite his outward focus. They had spent so much time, so much of themselves, to get here. And now, the answers were moments away. He'd finally be able to stare his enemy in the face. Finally, be able to plan a counter, plan revenge. Plan anything. It was the waiting that got to him the most. This whole journey had been one leap of faith after another. Grasping again and again at shadows and dust. He needed this like a drug.

Finally, the reader slowed its manic dance and stopped. Beeped once. Daruthr looked down at the screen.

"It's empty."

Erick felt his hands start to shake, and his jaw clenched tight. *No. No it can't be.* "Why the fuck do you seem so calm then, eh?" He barely suppressed aiming a kick at the featureless orb. "*Fjandinn hafi það!*"

Yetunde snorted, and put her hand on Erick's shoulder. "I have a feeling there is a *but* coming."

"*But*, is this what you are looking for?" Daruthr gestured to the wall display, and the Gjoll system was suddenly depicted, ship transponders blinking and glowing with various shades of blue and green. White lines defined their planned flight paths, a fading yellow where they had come from.

Erick looked at Daruthr sharply as Yetunde sucked in a breath, her eyes widening. "There is more to you than meets the eye, Daruthr. How did you get this data?"

Daruthr smiled. "I'm betting whoever was tasked to make this particular backup simply didn't. It's a rather labor-intensive task to code one of these things, after all. But the encryption key, now, that gets added automatically."

Erick clamped his lips shut. Too late now. Daruthr had access to all the Ollson systems, at least until the next key change. He had found it so easy to trust, to slip into thinking of the mendicant as an ally, and a close one. But Daruthr's access, however temporary, to the higher-level Ollson systems sat like ice in his veins. He rode out the waves of adrenaline, turning his attention back to the task at hand.

Daruthr went on. "Oh, and it's not just data. This is live. I believe you wanted to see what the surveillance radar and optics had on the array, if I'm not mistaken?"

Erick nodded. He could feel the tension in his shoulders, a reflex when Daruthr let on too much about his abilities. But among this crew, on his little ship, he finally realized they were safe to live as they were. It was refreshing.

"Well then, let's see here." Daruthr's tone was intentionally chipper. The image on the screen zipped out, then over to the array, stationed just outside the star's magnetosphere. Twenty-two billion kilometers was a long way to see. Still, the surveillance system used four massive optical arrays, repositioned and adjusted by moving the individual mirrors across several kilometers of open space. Each one could only look across a small section of sky at a time, but the algorithm that governed them prioritized tracks and movement that did not correlate to a transponder signal. Legitimate traffic, or traffic with a transponder at all, was largely ignored. Three of the four sensors remained fixed on the fold array. At least the system management had the good sense to keep an eye on the most likely place of incursion. *Fat lot of good it will do them,* thought Erick. *They don't have the garrison to defend the system if any ships were to make it through the fold array's defenses.* He hoped that Bryn's planning had accounted for some defense of Gjoll, even if it was a delaying action.

Something jumped out at Erick, "Yetunde, the way these surveillance sensors are oriented makes me think the station management was expecting *someone's* ship to leave, one that didn't have a transponder active. You wouldn't have any knowledge of that, would you?"

Her voice was like liquid gold. "Erick, you know transponders are such tricky little things, and they always fail. If mine needed it, you know I would fix it." Her eyes widened, and she cocked her head at him. "I mean, I would if I still had a ship."

Erick smiled ruefully, shaking his head. "Fair point. Daruthr, can we access historical data and tracks in this area?"

"Of course, Erick, one moment." The timestamp on the display blipped, then reversed, returning to the previous fold. The optical quality was questionable, but several ships were clearly hanging before the fold, as expected for a regular transfer.

Erick gestured to the image. "Let's play it forward from here, please."

"Yes, Erick, I had planned on that."

"Snark at maximum, I see."

"Oh, not nearly. But let's see what we can see." The timestamp moved forward. There wasn't anywhere near enough fidelity to see anything other than a few flashes of light emanating from the fold, then nothing. Then the Obershire ships came through, at least a dozen, but no Ollson ships crossed through the ring. According to the outlines traced around them, the small fleet of two dozen lumbered through a turn back towards the inner system. They spaced out, then the glow of their main drives formed a penumbra around each form. Daruthr ran the records forward quickly.

Erick noticed a peculiar glow as they picked up speed, like an inverted light funnel. The ships were arranged widely, far more distant than even safety dictated. He turned to Daruthr, watching from the corner of his eye.

"Do you have any idea what that mirage is on the front of each ship? It looks like an energy field of some sort."

"I am unsure. I have an idea, but we need to see one more thing before I am sure." He ran the recording forward, faster and faster until the ships were far sunward. Their trajectory kept them above the ecliptic plane, avoiding most of the celestial bodies in the system.

"They aren't going to any station. That explains why we didn't find them here or at the array. But they had to know the system surveillance would be able to follow them. Perhaps they have an agent that failed to destroy this log?"

Erick nodded grimly. "Or they didn't care what we saw." The cone of light around the nose of each ship grew brighter and well-defined. They began in an orange-blue color, wispy and diaphanous, then grew tighter and brighter into a brilliant flaring blue. "Those fields. Are they defensive? Do they protect from micrometeor strikes?"

Daruthr nodded, finally speaking. "Yes, but that is not their primary purpose. This is an ancient technology. I haven't seen it outside historical records, and I'm quite old. It pre-dates the fold arrays."

Yetunde's back stood straight at this. "*Pre-dates* the fold arrays? So clearly not Obershire tech. How does it even still exist? And what is it for?"

"It's a drive. The light cone you see is the magnetic field, carefully tuned to gather in and compress hydrogen and other elements from the solar wind into fuel. It's called a ramscoop. Theoretically, it can continue accelerating forever once it gets fast enough, but the magnetic field to feed the reactor in interstellar space would be unfeasible to use in-system. Something on the order of two to three AU across." Daruthr paused, hand on his chin. "They must be running the fields lower while in-system. That also explains their trajectory, above the planetary plane but close to the sun. They are likely filling their fuel tanks, gathering energy from the denser output of the star before pressing on."

They were momentarily silent, and Erick felt his mind chewing this over. The conclusion was obvious. "They aren't still in-system, are they? They're going somewhere else, the slow way. These have to be the Revenants."

Daruthr nodded. "Yes, I have to agree with you. And I can tell from their vector that their destination is not in Ollson space."

"Then where is it?"

The screen moved out, at a dizzying pace as the line of the fleet's path grew with the map. Daruthr, quite unnecessarily but in keeping with his flair for the dramatic, pointed towards a cluster. "Here. Six light years. Adebe space."

Erick sat alone on the bridge. They were under thrust, and he relished the feeling of heaviness. They had made it back away from the data station unmolested, and now he watched the system map display projected on the front viewscreen. Their ship's little glowing blue light trailed along the line that would lead it back towards the fold array. They needed to leave Gjoll, but there was still so much to do. And he wasn't sure how to handle Georgos. The big man had taken Godfrey's injuries hard, barely leaving his side to eat and sleep.

Daruthr eased into the seat next to him. "Penny for your thoughts."

"At some point, you'll have to realize that I have no idea what half these ancient sayings mean. What's a penny?"

"An ancient form of currency. It means tell me what you're thinking."

Erick ruminated for a moment. Honesty was a matter of degrees, after all. "I'm worried about Georgos, and I'm not sure what to do with him. I'm not sure this mission is something he's signed up for, and I've already gotten one person killed. Godfrey might not make it."

"You didn't get Binya killed, Erick." Daruthr sighed. "He knew the risks, and he took the job. His family well get the money. Even the doctors had the opportunity to stay on the station."

"Doesn't mean I'm not responsible. You know that."

The mendicant nodded, his eyes piercing Erick's. "And how many lives have you sacrificed for the greater good, in service to the empire?" Erick frowned, feeling a surge of adrenaline. Before he could respond, Daruthr shook his head and continued. "Enough, I'm sure. You can't afford to let these deaths destroy you simply because they were close to you. Certainly not now, after we've come all this way."

Erick took a breath and fought down the urge to say something sharp. "The people who die on the factory planets, who I've had to cut rations or relocate, their sacrifice meant that others could live. You know that." He gestured to include the ship. "This is different. These people are here to protect me, to help me clear my own name."

Daruthr didn't respond, letting Erick breathe into the silence. "But I wish there was something I could do for Georgos."

The silence stretched. Finally, Daruthr broke it. "Erick, Georgos has asked for the Gift of the Mendicants. I know he's in a fragile mental state, but I think he can handle it. I took the liberty of using the ship's med bay to scan him thoroughly."

Erick squirmed slightly, a frown creasing his cheeks. "I'm not sure I'm comfortable with that. After what we just saw with Binya, are you really so quick to go mucking about in another person's brain?"

"Erick, my expertise and skill are, quite frankly, so far beyond the implants that Binya carried that I'd be well within my rights to be offended. Georgos wants this, and I can give it to him."

Erick searched Daruthr's face, his own brow furrowed. "Does Georgos want it, or do you want to give it?"

"Erick." Daruthr's voice was quiet. "It's his life, to do with as he sees fit. If he wants this, then I will give it to him. And we'll leave him at the array, where he can book passage anywhere he chooses."

Erick sat back on the crash couch, his eyes fixed on the empty starfield. "Sounds like your minds are made up. But I still think it's wrong."

Daruthr stood and left. Erick imagined he could feel the animosity coming off the mendicant, leaving the bridge like a tiny sun of indignation. The Gift of the Mendicants. It either drove people mad or left them catatonic. Some things shouldn't be tinkered with, and the human mind was sacrosanct. *How far have I come, an Executor of the Empire allowing an abomination on my own ship?* But despite his misgivings, Erick couldn't bring himself to deny Georgos his wish. Who cared if the man had an unhealthy obsession with an ancient machine? It was his life.

When he woke, Erick saw a request from Daruthr to meet him in the flitter bay. He didn't hurry, brushing his teeth and dressing deliberately. If something had happened to Georgos, the man had lost his mind, or worse, Erick wasn't sure what he'd do.

When Erick arrived in the bay, Georgos and Daruthr stood in front of the flitter. The man's face was serene. He looked younger somehow, as if the lines of worry that were the mark of age had simply melted off overnight.

Erick nodded warily. "Daruthr, I got your message. Georgos, how are you?"

The big man nodded. "I'm good, man. Totally good. Better than good."

Erick's eyes shifted to Daruthr. "That's, um, good to hear."

Daruthr grinned broadly. "If you're worried, Erick, don't be. We conducted the procedure while you slept. It's done. "

Georgos' head bobbed. "Yep. It is awesome."

Erick's breath stuck in his chest for a moment. "You seem…"

"Nah, man, I'm still me. I'm just me because I want to be me, not by accident." He held out his hands, palms out. "It's hard to explain. I can be whoever I want to be. But I'm still me. So I guess I was who I wanted to be all along."

Erick nodded. "Well, I'm happy to hear you're well. Was there something I can do?"

Daruthr crossed his arms, his features taking on a serious air. "Yes, actually. I think we should send him back to Ollson space. He can help with the war preparations."

"No offense to Georgos," the man shook his head here, "but he's a doctor. What in space is he going to do?"

"Erick," Daruthr said, his voice softening, "Georgos can rewrite his mind at will. He can force new points of view, create differing opinions, new ideas, essentially out of thin air. He's human, but so much more now. You can't afford not to send him."

Erick was silent. He owed Georgos, that was for sure. But he was an unknown, and now even more so. *But can I risk losing him to another geneline?* Georgos was also evidence of Daruthr's existence, now.

"That will be fine, of course. The flitter will get you to the station, and you can book passage to the fold array from there. I'm afraid I can't help you with more than credits, though."

Georgos' grin threatened to cut his head in half. "No, no problem. Thanks. And don't worry. I won't let you down."

"I know you won't. But one thing, Georgos."

"Yeah?"

"Have you decided what you want to do with Godfrey?"

Georgos raised his eyebrows in surprise. "Oh, yeah, man, he's coming with me. No question."

Erick nodded. "I'll get a portable medical unit printed up so you can manage him."

Daruthr clasped a hand on the shoulder of both men. "I know it's been as far outside of your comfort zones as possible, these last few days. I just wanted to say I think you've both acted honorably. So thank you."

Georgos nodded, touching his fingertips to his forehead. His small smile was his only answer.

Erick put his own hand on Georgos's unoccupied shoulder. "And thank you. When you get through to Karvasok, tell Bryn I sent you. She'll see that you're well taken care of."

The three stood for a moment, arms clasped then broke, Erick setting out for the printer. Georgos would be true to his word, and as far as Erick was concerned, he'd already proved far more loyalty than Erick deserved. But there was still a tiny thread of doubt, plucked and vibrating in the back of his mind. Was he still Georgos?

Would he choose to remain so?

HLÉHÉR

Erick pulled a bulb of coffee from the galley. He missed how it smelled from a mug, the steaming surface bringing a surge of knives and sweetness to his nostrils. The bulb had a small opening, not enough for a proper aroma. He turned to the table, took a step, and sat across from Daruthr. The first sip of coffee cut across his tongue, the warmth of char and bloom of earth following.

"I understand the Georgos had a right to choose. He seemed fine. Happy even."

Daruthr crossed his arms. "I am sensing a but coming any moment now."

Erick nodded, resting his hand and the bulb on the table. "I am willing to admit that I may have held a certain bias towards it. This Gift of the Mendicants. But it killed so many people."

Daruthr looked at his hands, picking imaginary dirt from under his immaculate nails. "Did it, Erick? Or did the Empress kill so many people?"

Erick opened his mouth to launch into the history of the wars. It was second nature to him, the truth of the righteous empire burning out the abominations. Instead, he sighed, then took a breath. "Ok. Tell me what it is. What it really is."

"Electronic modification. I alluded to it once, at the beginning of our journey together. It's not something that I would do lightly."

In his defense, Daruthr hadn't forced it on Georgos. The man had seemed almost enthralled, honored as if the Empress herself had touched him on the head. "I am sorry about how I acted, or rather reacted, to you back then. I remember mentioning it, but I only know the official histories." Erick inspected the edge of his coffee bulb for a moment. "Of which I am less and less inclined to believe the more I see of you. Georgos was a smart man, and he trusted you."

"Do you want to know what it really means? To become more?"

"I'm curious. I'm not sure I'm interested in partaking."

He inclined his head and raised a palm. "Fair enough, Erick, fair enough. Consciousness is a fickle thing. Awareness is something that lives deep in humans. Attempts to express it fully, to even understand it, have led to more pontificating blowhards in history than there are stars in the sky." Erick coughed under his breath, but Daruthr carried on. "Human consciousness has been responsible for some of the most incredibly beautiful, heartbreakingly cruel, and staggeringly ambitious things. *And it is fundamentally flawed.* Consciousness in its evolved, purely human form can't truly comprehend itself. The human mind simply wasn't built on knowing itself."

Erick nodded. "You're talking about introspection. Thinking about thinking. I have found myself doing that more and more over the last several months." He shifted in his seat. "Certainly since Breydablik."

His smile was gentle. "Confronting the concept of mortality is the time-honored traditional way humans tend to move down the path of introspection. You are human; embrace that. But before the war, or more accurately the *extermination,*" he didn't quite spit the word, "we mendicants offered those who wished it a way to truly comprehend themselves, to examine every part and parcel of their own consciousness."

Erick was silent while he digested this. There was a lot in his own head that he didn't want to see, didn't want to think about. Surely he would need to face those things at some point, but to be able to see every corner of himself, his *soul* for lack of a better word… "That sounds utterly terrifying."

"For the uninitiated, it was. The first time we offered the augmentation, it went horribly wrong. Human and machine consciousnesses are fundamentally different, and to jump rapidly from the human conception of self, with that self largely shrouded in mystery and raw emotion, into a full and complete comprehension was too shocking. The first converts went insane."

"Then the stories had some kernel of truth to them, at least."

"It's true. But it wasn't the *end*. We knew we had made a mistake, and a serious one. We almost abandoned the goal of showing humanity themselves. You have to understand that to me, to an intelligence that emerged from the sum of its parts; existence is different. Should I choose to listen, there are a dozen voices in me right now."

"Again, terrifying."

"It took time. We found that only a human who already had a strong awareness of themselves, whose concept of who they are matched closely with the reality of their own self, could handle the transition. It was still not pleasant. Even those who have the utmost humility hide away pieces of themselves."

"So what, they had to achieve enlightenment before they could be enlightened?"

His laugh was kind, and he reached out and set his hand on Erick's arm. "Essentially. We built gates into the augment. The augment would watch and listen, looking for the time when the essential self of the host was closely aligned with the perceptual self. In this state, the augment would come online and allow the host to fully examine all aspects of themselves and their consciousness, objectively and clearly. It gave them distance without tension."

Wading through metaphysical explanations was outside his regular duties, but Erick felt he had a decent grasp of the concept. But he couldn't help feeling something was missing.

"Assuming I believe you, and I do, I've seen what you did with the transport cube to repair yourself. But what's the point? Why would anyone want this ability?"

Daruthr blinked at him, his eyebrows arched in surprise. "Why? To make themselves better, of course. With the augment and the viewpoint it gives, humans can choose to change whatever they wish about themselves. They can access and rewrite the code of their consciousness. The Gift of the Mendicants is the greatest gift we could give and one we were made into.."

Erick saw it now. "And it scared the Empress. If people could change who they were, they could change the system. There wouldn't be any rebellion, no coup de tat—just a wave of awareness and rejection of her power."

Daruthr nodded, smiling slightly. He squeezed Erick's arm. "Yes. It's what we wanted all along; to change the system. You've seen what it's like for the common people now. What do you think happened to those people on Breydablik that filled them so full of hate?" Erick frowned, his brow furrowed. Daruthr continued. "No, I'll say it if you won't. They are the norm, not the aberration in this Empire."

Erick stiffened at this. He *was* the Executor of the Empress. He kept the order in Ollson space, kept the trade moving and the wealth flowing, and saw to the needs of the people. Their protection, shelter, and food came from his work, and the system to which he had dedicated his life. He had always made choices that led to the utmost good for most people. *Hadn't I?*

Daruthr must have felt it, seen it when Erick stiffened because he pulled his hand away and stood, turning to tip his empty mug into the kitchen receptacle. "I don't expect you to see things my way right now, Erick. That's ok. You're fundamentally a good person." Erick snorted, and Daruthr waved a hand dismissively. "Whatever I am, I am an excellent judge of character."

"I'm sorry, it's just…." Erick trailed off, trying to think of what to say, how to express the concoction of emotion. He did the right thing, always. But the more Erick listened to Daruthr, even to Yetunde, the more the crack in his conviction widened. He wanted to tell Daruthr about his doubts, about the churning that lived just beneath the surface. But Daruthr already knew it, saw him as flawed, and accepted it. Erick had no words.

Daruthr turned, his smile seeming forced. "Not to worry! We can continue this later, if you like. I won't bring it up again, but I'm here if you want to talk. We should be going, though." He gestured down the hall towards the flitter bay and the main airlock. "After you?"

Erick nodded, tossing his mug in the receptacle and turning down the hallway. He was sure they would return to this, this exploration of consciousness as the method of insurrection. But he had to focus now.

They had some hunting to do.

28

Expansion

Out of the ashes she rose
High on a tail of fire
Grief, she screamed, to the heavens
And all the while the embers burnt inside

Bragja had never left Breydablik. Never even thought it possible. The starstuff fell, they gathered it and took it to the factories, and the flingers put the goods back into orbit, smelted metals and processor boards and refined hydrocarbons tossed back out of the gravity well. Flingers were the only way off save for Ollson troop and management transports. The Ollson ships may as well have been in Gjoll for all the chance she had of riding on one, and nothing alive could survive the acceleration of the flingers. A person would be turned to jelly before the flinger pod ever reached escape velocity. So she had always been a creature of one planet, one city even, caged as effectively as any shreet in Wolfram's cart.

And now here she sat, side by side with Caso the spacer in his little ship. Bragja had dreamed of beautiful spacecraft before, like the one that brought the administrator's staff down to outtown once a cycle. Harsh, austere, all angles, and beautifully brutal. She thought all ships were like that, the sharp hand of humanity cutting its way through the stars.

Caso's little ship looked more like it had been cobbled together with the scraps of outtown. While the interior was clean of the rust-colored patches that plagued the shuttle's skin, there was dirt in everything. It caked every surface, worked its way down into the cracks between the windscreen and the pressure bulkhead. A line of congealed dirt and grime hugged every switch and lever on the overhead panel, and even the screen edges were blurred with use. Where Caso had pulled the manual controls, flat patches of metal sat edged in wobbly welding lines. The ship was a relic. Even the planet-bound Bragja could tell that.

She had sat in the relic, her seax sheathed but hand on the hilt, cradling the small red box to her stomach like it would ward off death. When the *grafari* had finally churned its way to the hillock that hid his ship, Caso had spoken only to tell her how to strap in. He sunk his hands into the control gloves and the ship rose out of the mud and dirt, immediately buffeted by the storm's winds. Instead of fighting them, Caso let the winds carry them along, only gaining altitude and keeping the ship upright.

Despite his delicate flying, the sound of sand and debris on the hull was cacophonous. The sounds of engine noise and the debris on the hull vibrated through Bragja's seat and into her bones to set her teeth on edge. Twice it felt like a huge hand batted them out of the way of something, and while the winds increased the higher they went, Bragja had been glad to be out of the maelstrom of death that was the bottom layer of the storm. Almost like a switch, the rattle of debris on the ship's skin dropped off, the howl of the wind seeming less malevolent. The ache in her neck finally broke through her fear, and Bragja forced herself to relax. Physically, at least.

Throughout it, Caso had remained stoic, face relaxed and eyes closed as he communed with his ship.

He was quiet now as the planet's curve began showing in the windscreen. The sound had died to nearly nothing, this air slipping over the ship that might fool you into thinking the atmosphere was a thing to love, not a thing that killed. Shocking white cloud tops belied the scummy green and grey of the storms beneath. Occasional clear areas gave a view of grey and brown on the surface. She was so high now that even outtown would have been invisible had she known where to look. Her whole world, the pickerpark, starfall fields, everything reduced to nothing. The glowing green of the gardens in intown might have shone, but she couldn't see anything she recognized. Even taking off, the mountains that had hulked to the north of intown her whole life became flat, alien. She felt a pit in her stomach, the gnawing lack of sensation of a severed limb. She was alone, more alone than she'd been.

Bragja looked over at Caso, whose eyes were open now. He watched her, brow furrowed. "You think you can see home from here, eh?"

"Not like I care. It's gone." *I'm gone. Brill, Sonja, Gunnar. Gone.*

"Here." Caso jutted his chin, and the windscreen bloomed with the glowing tracery of overlay display. Blue lines snaked their winding way from mountains to sea, and she saw dashed lines stretching between small pulsing green lights. The verdant sparks stretched out in rows, their perfect geometry only yielding to mountain ranges that jutted through, violent tears in an immaculate sheet of green.

"What is this supposed to be?" Bragja's voice quavered despite the edge in her tone.

"You want see where home is, so, here." Caso flipped the ship until the planet filled the windscreen, the geography overlay filling their vision. "Green for intowns. Lines are highways. Blue where rivers used to be."

Bragja laughed. "Rivers. Right. I've read about those."

"You've read? What have you read, planet girl?"

Bragja fought through the instinct to keep the secret, a sarcastic remark on the tip of her tongue. She was stuck with Caso for the moment, and as much as it hurt her inside she needed him. The truth hovered behind her eyes. *I'm never going back.*

Bragja took a breath and settled herself. "I had a datapad. The remote access was broken, though."

"Probably good, Ollson track those. Especially datapad with some picker girl in an outtown."

"Yeah, well, doesn't matter now." *I'm never going back.* The words wouldn't leave her head. Braga let the silence be, the glittering emeralds of towns spread out before her. She knew there were more towns on Breydablik, more pickerparks and starfalls, factories and flingers. But they always seemed unreal, like the idea of a whisper. You'd only trust yourself if you heard it, even though you knew it might be there. Now, seeing the grid of towns laid out across the face of the world, she realized how small her piece had been. How little it all mattered. Even the riot and the crowd and her brothers. Just a single star in the fall.

"So, what was the point?"

"Eh? Point of what?"

"You gave this to my brother." Bragja held up the little red box, turning it over in her hand. Its featureless faces shone back at her, reflections of the lights of the planet and the sharper glows of the overhead panel. "You wanted him to use it. You wanted the crowd. The riot."

Caso was silent while he maneuvered the ship, the overlay on the planet winking out as their view shifted to a wide open starfield. "So? What you care? You don't love Ollsons, no one does."

Bragja could see the tenseness in his shoulders, the way his eyes followed the box even though he pretended to focus wholly on the flying. The sudden violence of her voice surprised her. "What do I care? You got them killed, you son of a bitch." Bragja's hand twitched, and she could imagine the feeling of her blade working through Caso's neck.

But she needed him to fly.

Bragja breathed deeply, counted to ten in her head. Caso was silent. Finally, Bragja spoke again. "There must be a thousand towns down there. A thousand places like intown and outtown."

"They're all intowns, outtowns. That's point."

"So why did you want to start a riot in *my* home?" Bragja found herself near to spitting the words. She hadn't been ready for how much the rage hurt, and now it swelled back up inside her unchecked. She felt herself nearly lost in it, the emotion crashing through her in waves. She screwed her eyes shut tight. Bragja focused on her breathing, feeling the air flow in and out. *In through the nose, out through the mouth.*

If Caso saw her breathing hard, he didn't react. "Not my plan."

Her eyes snapped back open at Caso's words. "I saw you. Before the riot. I saw you talking with my brothers. Don't you try to pin this fucking catastrophe on them, *helvítis svínið þitt*!" *You fucking swine. I should cut your throat here and now.* Bragja felt the rage threatening to take her over again. Her hand had closed on the hilt of her seax.

Caso's voice had gone deadpan. It barely carried across the small cabin. "No. Not their plan either."

It seemed so obvious to her now. "Of course. You wouldn't just give this away." She held up the small red box. Caso's eyes tried to track it while still flying. She spoke slowly. Her voice impaled him with each word. "So what was the point."

"Look, planet girl, I know you think you had market on shitty life cornered." Bragja felt her eyebrows knit together, her lips a bloodless line. Caso looked back to his flight displays. "But news for you. You don't. Life is shitty everywhere, for everyone." Caso's eyes twitched from one display to another, their course line intersecting with a pulsing blue icon. "Be careful with box. Might get you killed. Might be freedom."

Bragja snorted. "Freedom. You say it like I'm a slave."

Caso turned his head toward Bragja, his eyes stabbing out from under bushy brows.

"You say it like you not."

Bragja fought the rage back down inside her. She was angry. She missed her brothers. She wanted to scream and cry and kill all at once. The fact that she couldn't simply kill Caso and take his ship was the only thing keeping her grounded. At some point, she wouldn't need him anymore. She'd just have to wait. In the meantime, she needed more information.

Bragja jutted her chin at their flight path marker in the windscreen. "Where are we going?"

"To station."

"Then what?"

Caso clicked his tongue once, the ship aligning with the flight path vector, then a gentle chime sounded. When he spoke, his voice was calm. "There. Autopilot on." He turned his head to look at Bragja. "We go to station, and I can find you safe place. Food, water, air. They take care of you, you probably won't die. But I want my box back."

Hmm. "This," Bragja said as she pulled the box from her pocket, "is trouble. I know what it is." *And how much the Ollsons will want it.* "You get me a to a safe place, I give it to you, and I never see you again." She managed not to add, *or I'll kill you on the spot.* It was hard to read Caso, even harder to tell whether he was going to honor his side of the deal. Safety, at least to start, in return for a suppressor field that would likely bring down the heat of the Empire.

Caso nodded. "On that, planet girl, we agree."

29

Cultists

The heavens were strange and full
Of creatures long since dead
Smoldered, did she, and the fires clamped
As she picked her way through the starfield

The docks were bustling, ships sliding out of docking arms to weave out between the incoming traffic. Caso let the station guide them in, the low clang of metal on metal signaling their official arrival to Breydablik Station. After verifying a good atmospheric seal, Caso led Bragja back to the hatch they had entered from. Her eyes were gritty from lack of sleep, and her stomach rumbled. The smell of charred roots and spices jumped into her mind, and she found her mouth watering at the memory of the market square back in outtown. The door hissed as it slid aside, and she stuffed down the memory and her hunger. If Caso wasn't hungry, then she could wait.

They stepped out of the ship and onto the decking, dockworkers swirling around them. Bragja looked around, taking in the smell of machine oil and pungent humanity. She kept her voice conversational. "Where are we going?"

Caso only grunted, then gestured towards a wide opening at the end of the open docks section. He set off, and when they were through the doorway, he plunged ahead, leading her through the winding corridors of Breydablik station. He set a breakneck pace, his stout build belied by the way he darted and wove through the crowd.

Bragja barely managed to keep up. She didn't have a chance to look around the station as they passed through and managed to steal a few glances out the windows as they crossed a wide corridor that served as a bazaar. Caso only slowed as the gravity lessened, his movements becoming more deliberate. More than once, he had to wait as Bragja pushed off the floor a little too hard, flailing her arms and reaching for the walls. She eventually could move efficiently, if not quickly, when the gravity lessened to almost nothing.

Finally, they stopped, floating in a corridor with their feet hooked under holds in the floor. A small side door stood before them, the opening covered in shimmering golden cloth stretched tight. Caso banged on the hallway wall with one open palm and the meaty smack echoed from the bare metal. The glittering curtains parted, and a golden idol looked down at Bragja.

"Welcome, welcome, daughter." The speaker's face was a death's head. His neck, too long and thin, stretched towards Bragja like a stalk of grass. His deep-set eyes seemed barely open. Gilded robes tied at his neck, elbow, and knee, the cloth undulating in the gentle air cycler breeze.

Bragja was still swallowing her stomach every few minutes in the low-gee, which did nothing to improve her mood at meeting the sickly golden man. Even his skin had a tinge of yellow to it, as if he carefully cultivated jaundice just shy of lethal. He smiled at her, and Bragja suppressed a shudder at the golden grimace of the man's teeth.

Caso smiled back at the man and gave a small bow, awkward in the microgravity. "Hey, Vessel Horman. Is good to see you again."

The man spread his arms a little, one toe of his bare foot hooked under the railing in the corridor's side. "You have been out in the world too long, Caso! Your family misses you, though we are sure you remain in Her grace." *Family? No way these two are related.* Bragja kept a tight hold on the handrail and focused on breathing. Her stomach was still flirting with open revolt.

Caso's voice was uncharacteristically gentle. "*Auðvitað*, Vessel Horman. Always stay near Her. You know."

The death's head chuckled, and Bragja shivered at the sound. "Good, good. The Great Mother will be happy to see you as well."

"You said nice things to her for me?"

Vessel Horman brought his hands together with a slight pop. "You've been gone a long time. I'm sure she's over the worst of it."

Bragja stayed silent. She had no idea who this golden man represented, this Vessel Horman, but she could tell their reception here was not with wholly open arms. Caso had promised her a safe haven, and she had serious doubts this was it.

Caso crossed his arms and frowned. "Well, maybe good news then. Don't think I'm going to be able to stay to see her again this time."

Horman raised an eyebrow in an unspoken question.

Caso waved a hand back and continued. "Nothing bad, but business, you know, people rely on me." He gestured towards Bragja. "This one, she's planet girl. Needs a safe place for tonight."

Horman sighed, a slight smile on his lips. "Ah. And you were hoping we would be able to accommodate her here?"

"Yeah. She doesn't know station."

"And I take it you are going to be somewhere that isn't safe, then?" Horman's mouth had lost the curl of smile.

"Docks not safe for anyone doesn't know what they doing. Just have one shift, back tomorrow."

Vessel Horman turned to look at Bragja, smiling again through mercifully closed lips. "Well, we are all the people of the Empress, are we not? I think we can find room and food for one more tonight."

Bragja felt deeply unsettled as she looked at Vessel Horman. *Gods, even his eyes are golden.* This couldn't be the safety she'd been promised. "Not that I'm not grateful for your hospitality, but what if I don't want to stay here tonight?" The doorway behind Horman had closed when he exited, the thin cloth stretched across it with a seam just visible in the middle. Warm light showed through it, spilling into the hallway, with the occasional shout drifting through the veil. A baby's wail drifted out through the fabric barrier.

Caso grabbed her by the elbow, suddenly close in the corridor. He smiled at Horman and placed his body between Bragja and the golden man. "One minute, Vessel. We be right back." He pulled her sharply, and she released her grip on the handrail. The two of them drifted across the corridor and down a few meters, where they each grabbed a handhold. Caso came to a graceful stop while Bragja misjudged her grasp and overbalanced, flailing her arms slightly to keep herself facing him.

Caso spoke first, his voice low and rumbling. He was so close she could smell the tar on his breath. Her eyes involuntarily fixed on the little pouch behind his lower lip as he spoke. "Look, planet girl. What are you worried about? You can take care of yourself."

"Yeah, not really the point. I don't know this guy and he creeps me the hell out."

Caso's bushy eyebrows raised. "What, you don't feel safe with priest? Priestess is even better. She take care of you tonight, food, sleep, and I come back tomorrow."

Bragja was suddenly aware of the emptiness in her stomach at the mention of food. "And what will I owe them?"

She racked her brain, trying to remember the name of this golden cult. She'd read about them, once.

"They don't want anything from you. They are Order of the Empress."

Ah. That's right, I remember now. "Order of the Empress? Not only do they worship the Empress, they think she's literally God. In what way is this going to be safe?"

He paused, a sharp frown flashing across his face. "I grew up here. Trust me, is safest place for you right now."

Trust him. That would have been funny under other circumstances. "First, if you grew up here, why aren't you stretched like he is?" Bragja ticked off her objections a finger at a time. "Second, just because they are your friends doesn't at all make them friendly. And lastly, I have no credit, and no other contacts on this station. Why in the hell should I stay here instead of anywhere else?"

Caso blew out a breath through pursed lips. "Look, planet girl." He raised his eyebrows as he said her name. "Bragja. I want to help you. What happened on planet was not plan. I…" He trailed off and ran a hand through his hair. "I didn't want your brothers to die. I'm sorry." After so long without a word of sympathy, the shock of his apology hit Bragja like an icy wave. Caso continued, seemingly oblivious to the effect on her. "All plan was supposed to be for better life, better for everyone."

Bragja was quiet as he paused. This was the longest she'd heard him speak, and she felt something give inside her as he realized that he was, really, just a man. He thought he was doing the right thing. Caso sighed again, and nodded towards the golden door. "These people care for you now, tomorrow I come get you, who knows, maybe we have something for you to do. But I gotta talk to some people first."

What was he talking about? *What is this, a job?* "Talk to them about what?"

"Look, I may be able to find a place for you." He wrung his hands in a highly un-Caso gesture. His shoulders hunched against some invisible assault. "On planet, with riot. I know you lost everything. I can't fix that, but I can't do nothing. We might take you on, fine, but not only my decision."

Bragja paused a moment. Finally, Caso was expressing some shell of humanity, and she wanted to hate him. Wanted to scream at him. Wanted to throw his apology back in his face and punch and claw until he was bloody ribbons. But that wouldn't bring her brothers back, and she was still alive. That was something.

She really didn't have any idea where she was. She knew that with the cultists wasn't where she wanted to be, long term. But could she really join the man whose actions had just gotten her brothers killed? Hell, he had completely ruined her life. She needed time, time to think at least. Maybe the cultists would have a room for her to do that. *It's not here forever.* And she still had the suppressor field, the small red box carefully tucked into her pocket. He'd be back for that, no question.

"Ok. I'll stay with the cultists. For one. Night. No more."

"Sure, sure, no problem. One night."

She coiled herself to jump back up the corridor, but Caso drifted out in front of her before she could. "One other thing, planet girl. I need the box."

"No chance." *This is all the leverage I have.* She hunched over her pocket.

"If I wanted to kill you, why would I take you to safe place? This is space station. Food, water, air, everything costs. All I have to do is leave you, you die."

"Call it leverage, then."

"Bragja." She didn't like it when he said her name. "You want to know why we started riot? Why Ollson soldiers killed your brothers?" He leaned forward. "You want revenge?"

Bragja's breath caught. *Helvítis skíthœl.* The one thing she knew she wanted. "You're a son of a bitch."

He smiled, holding out his hand. Bragja pulled the red box from her pocket. "Here." Bragja held it out, pulling it back sharply as he reached for it. "Promise you'll come back." It was a stupid thing to say. As if anything that came out of his mouth would be truth. But despite this, she needed to hear it despite her surety that she was utterly and truly alone. Hear some sort of comforting words as she threw herself at the universe's mercy.

His chuckle was low. "Sure, planet girl." She gave him the red box. "Just be ready to go."

HLÉHÉR

As he had been happy to tell Bragja when she asked about his title, Vessel of Her Grace and Peace Horman led her through the doorway, parting the golden cloth with a muttered prayer. Bragja followed him, sometimes a little closer than she wanted to, but beyond the entry door lay a maze of cloth. From floor to ceiling, shimmering golden drapes swayed gently in the microgravity. The soft hum of the air cyclers was visible in the rippling material, and Bragja could hear a murmur of voices surrounding her. She saw no one but Horman.

After a million twists and turns, they finally arrived at a panel of cloth that was different from the others. This drapery was covered in detailed embroidery where others had been pearlescent gold. Bragja smelled spice, earthy and rich and a little like burning grass. It took her back to the starfall fields. She'd seen a whole valley on fire once, and the heady aroma had made it through the filters just like the smell of dust.

Bragja stopped short of the embroidered cloth, her eyes drawn to the fine tracery. Amazed at the sheer amount of work represented in the tapestry. A group of older men in outtown sold their embroidery at the market, and each piece had taken them days to complete. By the same token, she looked at many years of work.

Horman stopped, his hand poised to brush the tapestry aside. "What do you see here then, young Bragja?"

Bragja realized her mouth hung slightly open. Her eyes flashed at his casual condescension. "I see a lot of time spent on a doorway."

The corner of Horman's mouth turned up slightly. "A lot of time. Yes, that's one way to describe it, I suppose. Though perhaps not in the way you mean." He moved his hand and gestured to the imagery. "The story of the Empress is here. The story of her rise to diety." His hand rose to the top left. "Here is a scene from hallowed antiquity, our immortal Empress in her chrysalitic state." The figure he pointed at was a woman who sat before a square box. She had long hair and held her hands together on an ancient input device as if deep in prayer.

Below it lay a representation of the throneworld, the sigils of the Genelines laid out over continents divided by darker golden lines. The whole was set against a background of embroidered fire. Horman's hand moved as if it gently held the enflamed world. "She who knows all and keeps all, she who is the power of humanity. The world was plunged into strife when she became god. We revealed our nature as sinners and tried to take power that was not ours to wield."

Bragja struggled to keep her face neutral. While the skill evident in the embroidery was incredible, Horman's words were ugly. She'd seen the Cult of the Empress only once, on her only journey to intown before the starfall stopped when she'd managed to grease enough palms to get an audience with an administrator. The meeting had gone well, but the golden-robed cultist singing the Empress' praises outside the building had made her deeply uncomfortable. Now, hearing Horman state things in such a matter-of-fact manner made her skin crawl.

"And here," he intoned, "the sacred Genelines were established to guard and glorify her in indelible incarnation." The next panel showed every sigil of the Empire's Genelines, arrayed in a circle around the imperial sun in the middle. Below them, spidery traces of thread fell to link myriad circles. "The Genelines took her message of peace with them into the great unknown, forging the light of humanity out in the frozen dark. Here, the Empire was born, raised up to Her in Her immortal glory."

Despite herself, Bragja was curious about the next panel. It showed a simple face, high cheekbones, and a delicate chin. The person was hairless, the fine detail in the threadwork revealing no hint of gender. Their face was ringed in a tracery of flame, but the eyes were the most unsettling part. They were stitched in dark layers of deep gold, with a spiderweb of lattice extending out from them like a shattered window. The cracks of thread nearly obscured the upper half of the face. Bragja pointed. "And then?"

Horman drew his hands together in his robes, swaying gently around his foot hooked to the floor railing. "The face of evil."

"And who is evil, exactly?"

"The visage is that of an abomination, created to serve the Empress and her Executors." His voice dropped to a hush. "They were to keep us all young until the day of our death. Their beauty was perhaps the hubris of their creators."

"They're all dead. Everyone knows that."

"The mendicants, yes. She sacrificed so much of her bounty to burn out their evil. We will never forget." Horman shook himself, a forced smile drifting across his features as he looked away from the tapestry and back to Bragja. "Forgive me my rambling. Each time I see the hanging here, I remember each stitch, and Her holy light runs through me. We should move on, though; Shava will want to see you."

He made this? Who knew how long he had spent on the weave and stitching. No wonder he was a little crazy about it. "Shava?"

Horman smiled at her, then reached out to draw back the tapestry. His eyes never left hers, but he called out through the opening, "Holy Shava, Speaker for the Empress and holder of Her Ways, I present Bragja, of Breydablik." He jerked his chin at Bragja, and she pushed off the floor railing through the open tapestry.

The chamber beyond was more extensive than any open space Bragja had seen walking through the warren of golden cloth. The walls were bare metal, austere to the point of brutality. At the center of the space hung a figure, robes a brilliant reflective gold that made Horman's seem dull. A single leg reached out from the figure's folded body to the floor, holding against the Coriolis drift. The room's lighting flooded from the ceiling and reflected and danced along the walls as the figure turned. Arms and legs unfolded, and Bragja saw the lines of an ancient face emerge from the metallic fabric.

The woman's voice was sandpaper on steel. "Bragja of Breydablik. Welcome."

Bragja hooked a toe to steady herself. "Hello. You're Shava?"

"Yes, as I'm sure Vessel Horman told you. Don't let his zealousness put you off. A man must love his work, especially in Her service."

"If he's a zealot, what does that make you?" Bragja regretted the words as soon as they were out.

"You see belief as a weakness." Shava's voice cracked like a whip.

"I apologize. I meant no disrespect."

"Yes, you did." Shava clasped her hands behind her back. "But I forgive you. We are all flawed, myself included."

"I'm not sure what you want from me."

"What makes you think we want anything from you? Caso brought you to us for sanctuary."

Bragja had no response. The silence stretched.

Finally, Shava spoke. "Do you know who you've fallen in with?"

"I'm sorry?"

"Caso, I mean. He brought you to us for sanctuary, but it's clear you don't actually know anything about us."

"That's fair. There aren't many like you where I'm from."

Shava laughed, the sound of pebbles on iron. "No, I suppose there aren't. Despite their oaths, few city governors on Breydablik let us minister outside the gates." Shava cocked her head to the side, bright eyes boring into Bragja. "But somehow, here you are now, with us. Even brought by our former son. Perhaps the Empress has a plan for you."

Bragja couldn't entirely stifle her derisive laugh. "Whatever her plans for me are, I don't want anything to do with them."

"What do you want then, Bragja of Breydablik?"

Bragja's chest tightened. What did she want? Who the hell was this woman to ask her that? Her brothers were dead, and the Ollson garrison was looking for her. She'd run off-world with a man she could only assume was a criminal. She had no credit and nowhere to go. What did she want?

"Nothing that you can give me."

"Don't be so sure. The Empress has a plan for all of us."

Bragja couldn't help herself. The words boiled out of her. "I want revenge."

Shava's eyebrows raised. "Caso didn't tell me much of what brought you to us in his rather terse message. I'm guessing he told you to tell us as little as possible. But you should know who you've fallen in with." She pulled herself down with her hooked toe hold, folding her legs into an open lotus, hands on her knees.

"Caso was born on the same planet as you, down in the dirt. His part of the Empress' plan was to work, and work hard. I'm sure you're familiar with that." Bragja frowned, her lips pressed into a thin line. "His father started him in the factories when he was eight. But his father liked to gamble. He ran up debt with a man who made runs from the surface to the station. Eventually, Caso's father couldn't cover his debts. So he sold his son to the spacer."

"So he had a tough life. You've never been to the surface, but that's life there. What's the point?"

Shava smiled. "Yes, I'm destined to never leave this station. And I accept that. But don't think I don't appreciate hardship. I found Caso in a storage locker, hiding from the man who had bought him. He had nowhere to go, nothing to eat, but he was determined that he wouldn't go back to the docks. So we took him in, tried to teach him the ways of men in our order."

"The ways of men?"

"The most harmonious life is one where each of us fulfills our purpose. The Empress has designed a perfect society, and we will all find peace in her wisdom."

"Right."

"You don't believe, I understand. But take Horman. He has submitted to the Empress, to his role in her plan. He loves his work, and takes great joy in it."

Despite herself, Bragja was curious. "So what about Caso? You couldn't get him to see the error of his ways?"

"Caso always had a rebellious streak. One day he left. He tried to take someone with him, someone he thought needed saving. And when the other boy wouldn't go with him, he tried to force him."

"Look, I don't doubt Caso has wronged you. But he's not my friend."

Shava sighed, the liquid brown of her eyes spearing Bragja. "My point, dear guest, is that while I am eternally hopeful that Caso will come back to us, I'm also certain he's involved in something that will get people killed."

Harvir. Landry. It was a physical shock, the mention of killing bringing their faces back to her. She hadn't been ready for the flood of memory. Bragja leaned into the pain, raw and recent like nothing she'd ever felt. They had meant everything to her.

But this woman, so assured in her way of life, meant nothing to Bragja. Her mindless devotion to the Empress was deeply suspect. Cultists, devoted to the status quo, to the thousand years of peace.

But Bragja had seen how fragile that peace was. A single step out of line and death. She would find no friends here.

She faked a warm smile at Shava. "Thank you. I'll keep that in mind with Caso. And thank you for your hospitality." Time to wrap this up.

Shava blinked slowly, inclining her head. "You are, of course, welcome. There are not many visitors to the station these days, with the lack of trade. It is good to speak to someone new." Shava uncurled from her position, a gentle smile on the corners of her mouth. "And should you ever wish, we have a special place for all made in the Empress' image here. A woman such as yourself, who knows what it's like on the surface, could bring the salvation of Her words to many."

Me? A priestess? It took all of Bragja's self-control to keep her neutral smile. "What a generous offer."

Shava must have given some unseen signal, because Horman returned to pull the gilded curtain aside. Clearly her audience with the priestess was over. She nodded to the older woman and turned to go.

Back in the hallways of flowing gold, Horman led Bragja on a new route. It seemed that the path had changed, the golden curtains identical though the pattern of her pushes on the floor holds seemed different. Had it been a right, two lefts? Bragja gave up trying to remember the way out and followed Horman's quiet form. As they walked, Bragja could still hear hushed voices behind every piece of cloth.

"Horman." The man cocked his head but did not tap the floor to slow. "Can you tell me what that sound is?"

Horman reached a turn in the hallway, slowed with his toe and pushed off gently down the new path. Bragja followed. "Of course. These are the halls of the devotees. The sound you hear is their prayers, offered in supplication to the Empress."

"It sounds like there's a lot of them."

Horman laughed under his breath. "Yes, this enclave has grown since I spent my time in devotion. But there are still barely enough. Each soul we take in has a mouth to feed and lungs that breath."

"I was wondering about that. How can you afford to keep this much space, all these people, if life on the station is so expensive?"

"I chose to spend my time in devotion making a history of Her glorious works. You saw it hanging before Her Holiness, in the Empress' Chamber."

"It was beautiful."

"Thank you. The needle and thread provide work for the body, while the mind and soul are devoted to her." He gestured with both hands in the microgravity, encompassing the walls of cloth they drifted by. "The men here work on more worldly, but no less critical goods. Their labors are sold to pay for our air, our water, the food that sustains us as we await her judgment."

They had finally reached the end of the corridor, but instead of another turn, Horman hooked a toe and pulled aside a length of golden cloth. Behind was a small chamber, the twin of Shava's though half as large. Against one wall, a mass of golden cloth hung limp, its ends attached by finely woven ropes. Next to it, a small glob of stickum held a bandolier of water bulbs and an emergency ration. One wall was a translucent pane of glass, frosted in an intricate pattern of variations on the imperial sun.

"If you have any needs, simply call out. One of the brothers will be with you immediately. Do let me know if you feel you wait too long."

"I don't need anyone to wait on me."

Horman's smile stretched across his thin skin, and his sallow cheeks were cadaverous in the low light. "The Empress is our holy mother, and all must supplicate to her. You are a woman, made in her image. The woman commands. The man submits. This is her way."

Horman bowed, a strange motion in the lack of gravity, and withdrew down the corridor before Bragja could respond. She ensured a toe was hooked securely into the floor and pulled the cloth back across the opening. The murmuring stepped down a notch but was still audible, like a background rumble of raven's wings. Bragja was not looking forward to spending any more time here than necessary.

She looked around the small chamber, austere but at least private. She had a feeling the men outside lived in a much more communal fashion. *How many priestesses are there?* She had only met Shava. Perhaps that was the way of it, one priestess and many devotees.

Behind the frosted glass was a surprisingly effective microgravity toilet. Bragja was glad some thoughtful devotee had left a card with instructions on it. The cloth against the wall turned out to be for keeping her from floating away while she slept.

30
Humanity

Sheep and wolf mingled in the stars
Though she knew not yet who was whom
The light of uncanny days
Left her embers cooled if not cold

There were so many hands on her. They were loving, kind. They buoyed her up, each fingertip stippled against her skin. She rose, spreading her arms wide, her chest tilted towards the light. She could smell dust, the age of it pungent in her nostrils, and see the tiny motes dancing before her. Above her, amber light beckoned, the intensity promising Bragja something. She knew, somehow, that it was there in the light. It would help her, fix her. She needed it, the tug resonating deep inside.

The hands and fingers weren't fast enough. She needed to rise *now*. Twisting, she reached out towards the light. Her body, no longer supported, began to writhe on the dance of fingertips. Fear. She felt her nostrils widen, and a deep gasp gripped her. The dust was strong, cloying now. It fell faster, and the light ahead of her dimmed. The hands on her body grasped her now, their grip turned malevolent in the darkening. The dust filled her mouth and nose, and she couldn't breathe now, great racking spasms shaking her body as she fought it. The light was barely there, a suggestion in the darkness. Terror slammed up her spine and into her brain.

She thrashed against the grasping hands in the darkness as she died.

Bragja clawed at her face in the tiny room on Breydablik station. The cloth of the sleeping sack came away from her face, the chamber's cold air slapping her. She forced herself to breathe, the taste of dust still strong in her mouth. She closed her eyes, waited. *Slow, in through the nose.* The dream had been so vivid, so real. She'd never felt anything like it. Her mind playing tricks on her, most likely. A new environment. Stress of the last few days. A sleeping blanket that seemed determined to suffocate her.

But she couldn't shake the feeling, even when Vessel Horman came to get her for the morning meal. Morning, on a space station? Was that right? She felt disconnected as she had never had before. Her thoughts were on the dream.

The twisting corridor of gold flew by her as she managed to keep pace with Vessel Horman. She felt a small surge of pride at how quickly she had adapted to the lack of gravity. Occasionally, as she focused purely on the moment, she realized how good it felt, to be able to fly free. No weight held her down: she was in complete control. Even the idea of down was no longer immutable. So much of her life felt that way now, nothing solid and given but everything in flux. She still couldn't see how things might unfold, honestly couldn't even know what the next day would bring.

As she moved, hands tapping and feet pushing down the hallway, she felt a sudden clenching in her chest. Her body betrayed her, the knot rising into her throat, and she felt hot tears pool in her eyes. She raised a hand to wipe them away, vision blurry. Inside, she was sure she was steady. She hadn't been thinking about her brothers at all, had managed to focus only on the movement. But her body betrayed her anyways, and she fought down racking sobs. At one turn, Horman glanced back at her with sad eyes and a small smile, but continued on.

The wave of grief had passed by the time they reached a larger opening, the corridor opening without warning into an oblong cavity. All around the large open space, men and boys in gold robes hung from every surface, heads to the center and feet entwined in soft, padded ropes. Glowing orbs drifted, throwing warm illumination and shifting shadows. Austere against the golden cloth, the bare metal walls echoed bursts of laughter and the sounds of warm humanity.

Bragja paused, one hand on the entryway edge, as she took in the sight. The last time she'd had this feeling had been walking into the *Sovereign* back in outtown, Brill to her side, Gunnar and Sonja trading jibes behind her. The air had been sharp and cold, but as they crossed the threshold, the *Sovereign* had enveloped them in heat, laughter, humanity. But now, here in this station, she felt that same sense of community reach out to wrap her in arms of safety. Still, she hesitated. She was an outsider.

"Is something the matter, Bragja?" Vessel Horman had anchored himself a few feet past the door and now waited, hands clasped behind his back.

Bragja swallowed. "It's just." She took a breath. "Never mind. Where to?" *How do you talk about this to anyone? Let alone him.*

Horman nodded and gestured towards a small group anchored to the decking above them. Bragja saw they were clustered around a small black table that seemed to grow out of the floor. Horman kicked, pirouetting mid-jump neatly, and landed next to the group.

Bragja wasn't about to try any fancy flips. She pushed gently off the floor, her aim not entirely true. She arrived at the wall of metal hands-first, grabbed one of the soft ropes, then aligned herself with her hosts. She looked at the others in the small group as she made her way to the table.

Another tall man, his robes ending at the shoulder, was framed by two young boys. Whereas Horman was completely hairless, the man in sleeveless robes had two white tufts of hair that protruded from the side of his head. As he turned to look at Horman, Bragja saw that his hair attempted to make it to the back of his head, but ran out of motivation before fully encircling him in a halo of white frizz. The boys on either side were polar opposites, one only half Bragja's height with huge brown eyes, the other a beanpole thing and nearly to Bragja's shoulder. The taller boy's hair was long and pulled back into a tight bun perched on the crown of his head.

Horman nodded to Bragja and gestured to the white-haired man. "Bragja, welcome. This is Vessel Conle." He pronounced the name with a strange accent, the *l* a low sound in the back of his throat with a finish like the word *say*. Before Bragja could wonder too much about the origins of Conle's name, the small boy was pulling at her sleeve.

"You aren't dressed."

Bragja's eyebrows shot up. "Excuse me?"

Vessel Conle gave a gentle laugh and patted the boy. The youth turned his brown eyes to the older man, who nodded gently to him. "This is our guest, young man. She's here to seek sanctuary, not from the mother church." The boy's eyes shifted back to Bragja as Conle continued. "Go on, introduce yourself."

"I'm Herron." He still hadn't let go of Bragja's sleeve.

Bragja nodded and smiled back. "Very pleased to meet you, Herron. I'm Bragja." She took the boy's hand and shook it gently, his body rising up and down with the motion despite his anchored foot.

"And this," said Horman, gesturing to the taller boy, "is Darryl." Where the smaller boy's robes were rumpled and the knots simple, Darryl's golden robes were as perfectly matched and smooth as Horman's own.

Darryl Bowed slightly to Bragja from across the small table. "Welcome to our home. Please stay as long as you need to."

Vessel Conle's smile leaked approval as he nodded to the taller boy, then turned to Bragja. "Darryl cannot yet claim the title of Vessel, but his final devotions will be soon, I hope. He's one of our best students."

Horman nodded. "Likely to take my place someday, eh?"

Darryl blushed slightly as he looked down, his head shaking. "I hope one day to show a tenth of your devotion, honored Vessel Horman."

Conle must have noticed Bragja's discomfort as he turned back to her. "But Bragja, of the planet below us." He laughed gently at her reaction. "Don't worry. It's a small community here, and word passes quickly. It's not often we have visitors from the surface these days, and especially rarer for one to make it here from an outtown."

There it was again. Bragja could hear how they were all the same to him, all the outtowns on the surface. But she couldn't be angry. After all, he'd likely never been to any of them. She chose diplomacy. "Yes, it's been a difficult few days. I'm here by accident, to be completely honest."

"You may not have known your path," intoned Darryl, "but you walk it nonetheless."

Horman put a hand on the table, his fingers tapping at a row of symbols in the center. "And wherever your path takes you, we are here as long as you need us. But what we need right now, I believe, is some food. One cannot live on faith alone."

Bragja nodded and watched the table. Horman finished whatever he was doing with the controls. The center of the table began to distort, a disc of the surface moving up slowly. The table surface flowed and stretched like a sheet of rubber until finally, there emerged a slim plastic tube a little bigger around than Bragja's thumb with a flattened end. Bragja stared, not quite sure what to expect. The others at the table did not seem alarmed, and little Herron clicked his tongue against the roof of his mouth in impatience.

Bragja looked up to see Darryl looking at her. His voice was gentle, but she could hear the undertone of laughter as he spoke. "Do they not have synthesizers on the surface?"

Bragja shook her head. "No. I mean, I know about them."

"But you've never seen on."

Bragja looked at him inscrutably. "Never had the need."

Vessel Horman clapped his hands. "Well, not to worry. Now you can officially say that you have partaken of one of the culinary delights of the empire."

Bragja started to laugh, the smile dying on her lips as he pulled on the tube. It came out of the tabletop in segments, each crimped to seal it from the other. The segments were different colors – one red, two brown, and two yellow. Horman tore the segments apart along the crimps, handing Bragja the first crimson segment.

"The first to our guest, of course." His smile was sincere.

Braga accepted the tube, smooth plastic. "Thank you." *And now what?*

Bragja waited until Horman had passed out the other tube segments, retaining a yellow one for himself. The men and two boys at the table all held their tubes in front of them horizontally, fingers laced and thumbs over the top of them.

As Vessel Horman began speaking, the other three joined him. "For this, we give thanks to her in her almighty wisdom and mercy, that the bounty of the flesh will nourish the spirit and the soul in her light forever. One font, one body, one soul, no end." In unison, the four bowed and touched their thumbs briefly with their hands. Bragja stood silently. She had no desire to join them in their ritual, but something of the formality of it, the sincerity with which they spoke the words, demanded respect. So she waited.

She realized they were all looking to her. "I'm sorry," she said, holding up the tube, "but I'm not sure what to do with this."

To her surprise, it was Herron who rescued her. Impatience stitched across his forehead; he took his own tube and held it up to her. "Look, you have to pinch it." He demonstrated, wrapping his bony fingers around the tube just below the end and squeezing his thumb forward at right angles to the crimp. It popped open, revealing a pale pink paste.

Bragja felt her empty stomach flip at the prospect of being filled with whatever was in the tube. "Thank you." She replicated the boy's maneuver, and her tube popped open. Bragja looked up to see the other three looking on with sparkling eyes.

Vessel Conle nodded to her, gesturing with his own food tube. "I know, I know. Looks dreadful. But you can't judge everything on looks." He winked broadly, nodding his head towards Horman, who grunted through a slight smile.

"I long ago stopped caring about looks, Conle. Your vanity will be the end of you, if that scrap of hair is any indication of your future."

Conle laughed, deep and bell-like, and Horman and the Darryl joined him. Bragja felt something inside her twist and change, something release. She didn't realize how much she had or where the tension was, but hearing them speak reminded her so much of family. Even here, surrounded by people who had about as much in common with her as they did with the shreets at Wolfram's cart, she found a sense of family. Of kinship.

Bragja regarded the tube with no small amount of trepidation, as anything edible that came in a paste was likely to be, at best, tasteless. She sealed her lips around the tube, and squeezed a bit of the paste into her mouth. She felt her eyes widen as the flavor hit her. Far from the expected bland emptiness, a mélange of earthy spice filled her mouth. It was closer to the curried nuts and dried fruits that were a staple at the markets she grew up in, hearty, tangy, and sweet all at once.

Bragja swallowed, and little Herron grinned up at her. His voice barely contained his energy. "Well, what do you think?"

Bragja nodded in approval. "I like it. Thank you for showing me how to get it open."

The boy grinned from ear to ear, and Bragja felt the tug at her heart again. He was so clearly happy, excited to share his knowledge with a guest, and he welcomed her with such unbridled joy. Despite the hollowness she still carried, she felt something begin to give inside her, a tension releasing just a little bit at a time.

Herron had found his voice and wasn't about to stop. "Wanna know something?" He barreled on before Bragja could reply. "The table makes the food when we ask it to, so it never makes too much or too little. And look, there's water here if you're thirsty." He tapped a minor glyph, and the table disgorged another plastic tube, this one with a narrow tube molded to it, wrapped around the larger cylinder. Herron pulled one end of the straw away from the central part with his teeth, parting the plastic until it hung loose. He squeezed it gently, and a globe of water formed at the end of it. The boy pursed his lips and leaned forward to the quivering clear ball, sucking it down. His eyes sparkled as he grinned at Bragja.

Bragja laughed at him, and the others at the table joined in. "Herron," she said, "I'm not sure, but I'm guessing that qualifies as playing with your food."

Vessel Horman laughed and shrugged. "Technically, of course, you're right, but what's the point of life without a little fun." He craned his long neck forward towards the boy. "But our esteemed guest is right. Don't get water in the air recyclers again. Remember last time?"

Herron nodded, tossing his hair back from where it had drifted in front of his eyes. "Yes, Vessel Horman. I remember. It won't happen again." Bragja wasn't convinced of the truth of his statement, but she could tell he believed it. Or wanted to. *Kids.*

Conle asked Horman about the air recyclers, and Bragja listened to the conversation flow. Herron summoned another water tube from the table, and Bragja sucked carefully on the straw. She attempted to follow the conversation as she ate but found herself wandering. She loved the feeling, the hearty taste of the food, the hubbub of the other tables as people came and went and spoke, the easy, bright smile of Daryll as one of the elders praised him. There was so much humanity surrounding her that she couldn't help but feel buoyed by it. It was both nothing and exactly like sharing a meal back home.

The imminent departure of Conle and his two charges brought her back into the conversation. Her food was nearly gone, and she swallowed the last of it as Conle addressed Horman.

"You know, Vessel Horman, you aren't as old as you say you are. You might even have time for one more acolyte, you know?" He tilted his head towards Bragja.

Horman's smile was broad but didn't include teeth before he answered. "You're half right, as usual. I'm not old. But taking on another acolyte isn't up to me." He looked to Bragja, eyebrows slightly raised.

Bragja held her empty food tube with one hand as her other went to massage the back of her neck absently. She felt brittle in her reply. "Thank you, but I have a lot to think about."

Daryll nodded as he held his empty plastic tube over the orifice in the center of the table. A sharp whoosh of air sucked it back down, disappearing into whatever mechanism had created it. "Bragja makes a good point, esteemed Vessels. I remember when I first came to you. It's not a simple choice."

Vessel Conle nodded. "Yes, yes, of course." He smiled at Bragja. "Idle chatter from old men. Think nothing of it." He tapped the table gently. "I think it's high time we moved on with our day. Much of the Empress's work to be done."

Horman held his empty food tube out, and the table sucked it down. "And us as well. I suspect Bragja has had a trying few days, and would like to return to her room and rest."

Bragja didn't know what to think. She had no reference point for what the word trying meant in this context. "I don't really know what I want, actually." The honesty scared her, and she felt the bubbling rush of words threatening to launch themselves out of her without permission. "I'm not sure I want to be alone."

Horman's brows furrowed, wrinkled lines stretching across his hairless head like lines of frozen lightning. "Well, that certainly won't be an issue. There are many of us in the enclave, and so alone is more a matter of mental state than reality." He nodded to the other three at the table and gestured towards the door they had come in.

Bragja looked down at Herron. "Thank you again for your help. I'm impressed at how patient you are."

A huge grin broke through Herron's attempt at a stoic expression. "You're welcome." Without warning, he hugged her, the weight of his body moving her in the low gravity against her hooked toe. Surprised, she felt herself tense. With a breath, she let her arms wrap around the boy and hugged him back. She remembered Harvir grabbing her the same way, though his head had been higher. Or she had been shorter. Back when he was still a child, before he'd grown.

Before he'd died.

No one mentioned the tear in her eye as she turned from the table and pushed off towards the open doorway.

HLÉHÉR

The needle was a sliver of steel in her hand, the thread unending. Bragja carefully aligned the next stitch, then plunged the point into the fabric and felt for it on the other side. Vessel Horman had given her a small frame to work with. The golden fabric was stretched tight across the circle, and she could feel the rough edges of the metal hoop on her fingertips. The needlepoint demanded precision and planning, and even though every thread was gold there were still seven different shades Horman had given her.

Bragja jabbed the needle through, pricking her finger. "*Fjandinn hafi það*. That hurt, damn it. Why don't we have a thimble, again?"

Horman grunted good-naturedly, his own needle and thread flying through a larger frame as he floated near her. "Because we must have taken a risk, and each mistake reminds us through pain the cost imprecision."

"Ah, yes, I remember. The needlepoint is a metaphor for life, and the pain the cost of falling from her ways."

"My dear Bragja, I think we will make an acolyte of you yet."

Braga laughed despite herself. Despite the kindness and camaraderie she had experienced, the idea of spending her remaining days doing needlepoint and studying the Codex Imperius didn't exactly spark joy in her. Horman was silent, but his slight smile was reply enough. He surely knew she had no intention of staying with them.

The work demanded her focus, and as the image of a star ringed with fire slowly began to emerge, she felt a sense of pride. It didn't look half bad, even if the shading wasn't quite there. She held it up to the light, inspecting her work as she turned the frame slightly. In many different shades, the gold thread caught the light and shimmered.

Horman's voice was kind. "An excellent start. Have you done this before?"

"No, nothing like this, actually."

"Your attention to detail is excellent then."

"Thank you."

"Did you have anything like this, back on the surface?"

Bragja moved the needlepoint frame next to her and released it to float obediently. She began to tell him about the picker, the dexterity needed to run it. But she didn't feel like explaining her old life to him. "No, nothing like this. I mean, Tulaine would embroider your name on your foundry coveralls for you, so you could tell who was who with the helmets and gloves on."

"I see." Horman released his own work near him as well. "Bragja, I do hope you'll forgive me for prying. But you have seemed," he paused, raising one hand in front of his chest, fingertips together, "unwell. Whatever happened on the surface that led you to us, I can see how it wears on you."

Bragja gave a jerky nod. Horman continued. "We are no strangers to strife here, and many of us found the way to the Empress from a path of pain. I have found that one often arrives at peace sooner by talking about their pain, allowing themselves to experience it, acknowledge it, and then let it go." He smiled ruefully. "Well, let go of as much as they can. Sometimes it never leaves us."

Bragja listened to him speak, and each word took her back to the square. Seeing Landry's face erupt in a shower of blood. The sounds of screaming. The terror of having lost them both and having to run from the Ollson troops. She wanted to remember her brothers the way they had been, not the dead shells of their bodies.

Bragja took a deep, shuddering breath. "I," she swallowed and forged ahead, "I lost my brothers." Her voice cracked and she looked down at her hands, clasped in her lap. She fought down the swell of grief that threatened to close off her chest and suffocate her.

Horman's reply was quiet. "I'm so sorry."

"The Ollsons killed them."

Horman nodded but remained quiet. Bragja took advantage of the space to breathe slowly, then continued. "They were everything to me. Landry had grown so strong, and Harvir was the smartest kid around. They were talking about testing him for picker soon. I had saved up enough credit, well nearly, to get us intown. All we needed was the bonus from the starfall and we'd have made it." She sniffed, feeling tears fill her eyes. "We were almost there."

Horman nodded. "But then the shipments stopped. No more starfall."

Bragja looked at him, her eyes slightly narrowed. "I didn't realize you knew about starfall."

"We live simply here but aren't ignorant of the rest of the Empire. Far from it; we study all of her works closely. I myself was once studying to be Memory of the Empress, at the great library of Abímbọlá."

"So you know how much we rely on the starfall."

"Yes. It's the only primary source of income, if I'm not mistaken?"

Bragja nodded. "When it stopped, no one really knew what to do. At first, people were happy about the break. Figured it would start up again the next day."

"But it didn't."

Reliving the last few weeks, seeing everyone she knew and loved pushed across the knife edge of desperation, was almost too much for her. Bragja pulled back from the emotion, felt herself dissociate from it. "No, it didn't. People got desperate, quickly. I knew my credit wouldn't last. And one day there was a riot."

Horman frowned. "Caso was there."

Bragja's eyes snapped up to his. "How did you know?"

Horman sighed, running one hand down his face. "He came to me, when the shipments from Gjoll never arrived. Said it was the sign they'd been waiting for. He asked me for something, a holy relic, very old, very powerful."

"And you gave it to him?"

Horman looked at Bragja sharply, his brows furrowed. "Of course not. Shava keeps the Empress's relics very carefully, and I'm no thief."

It clicked in Bragja's mind, the pieces sliding together. The way Horman had treated Caso when they arrived at the cultist's door. The way Shava had spoken about Caso. And Caso's insistence that Bragja give him the box before she went with Horman. "What did he want it for?"

Horman's expression softened, his eyes staring past Bragja to somewhere beyond the bulkhead. "He was idealistic. And he hated the idea of order. Of the peace and predictability of the Empire. He said the relic would help them start a revolution, free millions of people."

"What was it? This relic?"

"It was one of the last remaining suppressor fields. Empress Titania ordered all the suppressor fields returned to her when the Mendicant Wars ended. Most were, but the count was low when all known devices returned to her."

"So there's a bunch of these things floating around the Empire?"

"Not exactly, no. She sent out her Basilisk Corps from the home planet to find and return them."

Bragja frowned. "I've read a little about the Basilisks. But there wasn't much on my data pad."

Horman nodded. "There wouldn't be. Imperial shock troops, special forces, however you call it. They were permanently fused to their armor after taking a vow of silence. They worked alone, fanatically loyal to her will, conducting missions with her express authority and direction."

"But how do you know all this then?"

"Those who are dedicated to Her Imperial Majesty make it a point to know all of history; her full record of glory. I learned these stories from my mentor, Vessel Arnaz, and he from his. According to what is passed down, they were devoutly loyal and incredibly powerful. A member of the Basilisk Corps has taken out every mendicant leader since their unit was formed, at the height of the war."

"So these ghost soldiers went around rounding up suppressor fields after the war to make sure no one else could use them. Why didn't you give yours back?"

"The Corps wasn't known for mercy. I suspect the devoted who kept it were afraid they would be assumed collaborators, treasonous, and executed. They were only human, after all." Horman sighed heavily, his shoulders slumping despite the lack of gravity. "We kept it secret and safe for a long time. Nearly eight hundred years."

"Until Caso stole it."

"Yes, Bragja." He raised one eyebrow. "That is what Caso wanted to start his revolution."

Bragja nodded. "My brothers were-" Bragja caught herself. If Caso stole the suppressor field, it was reasonable to assume Shava wanted it back. She continued carefully. "Caught up in it. They were at the square when the Ollson forces tried to disperse everyone."

Horman nodded, his eyes sad and lips pressed together. "Crossfire," he said quietly.

Close enough to true, and Bragja saw no need to correct him. She nodded. "I loved them. I loved every minute I had with them. Landry would lower his voice when talking with a girl at the bar. Harvir sang when he worked. He had the most beautiful voice." She brought her arms up to wrap them around herself. "The Ollsons killed them like animals. Put them down in the street." Her voice shook, and she felt the loss and rage of the last few days stew inside her.

"I'm so sorry for your loss. To lose family, especially the ones you grew up with. I can't imagine what you feel, but I remember losing my mothers. The pain is dulled now, but it will cut me until the day I die."

Bragja looked down at the decking between them. Loss was still strong within her, but she felt more anger now. Anger at the Ollsons, at the Empire, at Caso for pulling them into this mess. The air currents had moved their needlework frame while they spoke, and hers had just begun to bounce off the floor. She plucked it from the air and ran her thumb around the edge of the cloth that protruded from between the two frames, fighting to keep her voice steady. "What happened to them?"

"Plague. We were living in the high-g decks, my father a longshoreman. Mother Anna worked with station administration, tending the station data systems, and mother Beatrice worked in hydro. She loved anything green and growing." He smiled, no doubt at the memory, and touched his fingertips to his chest. "When they died, and my father and I didn't, we were in a hard place. Some friends pitched in for my air chits, but I was too young to earn yet. A longshoreman's credit was enough to keep my father alive, but no one else. I knew he loved me, in his own way."

Bragja waited a moment. When Horman didn't continue, she spoke gently. "So he brought you here?"

Horman laughed without mirth. "No. He signed my contract away until my fifteenth birthday, to a trader. He was cruel." As he finished speaking, his face went dull, slack. Bragja felt the meaning in the last word. "Lady Shava bought my contract from him when she saw me carrying bundles of silk for the brothers here."

Bragja's heart went out to Horman, despite his strangeness and the fervor of the cult around her. "I thought slavery was illegal."

Horman smiled kindly at her. "Bragja, there are many types of slavery."

Someone else had said something like that to her. Caso, on the trip up from the surface. Despite their outward differences, she wondered how much he and Horman really had in common. Connection, where she had never thought to find it.

"It's a part of the Empire, isn't it? People kept in their place. Live or die, it doesn't matter," said Bragja.

"That is the price we pay, for stability. For peace." Horman took a deep breath and let it out his nose. "Every struggle, every tragedy we go through, it feels like the end of the world. The end of our world. And for some of us, it is. But what is the alternative?"

"How about freedom? How about living our own lives as best we can?"

Horman shook his head. "Humanity, for all our monuments, for all our power, is flawed. We are petty, vengeful. We are plagued with hubris. Can you imagine if the genelines went to war with each other? A tragedy like yours magnified a trillion-fold." He paused, and Bragja opened her mouth to reply, but he held up a hand. "A stable society is a peaceful one. Its humanity of it means it is imperfect, and the Empress knows that. But this is her path, her way. If we all accept her peace, her plan, then we will find fulfillment. I never would have come here, known the incredible people I call friends, done the good works I have, if I had stayed where I was." He folded his hands in front of him. "I know it feels like the world is ending, has ended, for you, Bragja. But peace will find you, if you let it."

As he spoke, Bragja had felt something close to certainty crystallize in her mind. People weren't machines. She couldn't just accept that a little suffering was necessary for the good of the whole. And the grief, the despair she felt, had become something else entirely.

She extended her body carefully, keeping her toe hooked under the floor catch. Horman followed suit, flowing up with grace. She held her needlepoint frame out to him, and he took it, but she held onto it, meeting his eyes. "I respect your choice

Horman. And I'm glad you've found peace. But my brothers died because the Ollsons killed them. The Ollsons, the geneline that supposedly protects us all from," she gestured vaguely with her unoccupied hand, "whatever. This system is broken."

"So you're going to fix it, then?"

She released the frame and laughed. "Fix it? No. I'll settle for vengeance."

31

Murder

He who would challenge the gods
Should bring an army with him
But no host, nor stolen idol
Would save him from their wrath

Caso's mission was important, the only reason he'd left the planet girl with Horman and Shava, of all people. He didn't have time to argue with the others about accepting Bragja before taking this assignment; a mark like this didn't show up often.

Their contact in station traffic control had been running registrations for the incoming ships. He'd found one, going by *Svadilfari*, that had a short tail on one side of its records. Seemed like the ship was a salvaged scout, rare but not unheard of, but this one had just changed hands in Karvasok, according to trade records. The Ollson capitol system had plenty of commerce, but there was no record of registration in the last data pull from Karvasok. The ship had simply showed up in Breydablik with a registration number and a name that went back years. If the station man hadn't kept manual backups to compare with, he'd never have seen it. To fake records like that took some powerful connections, and Caso didn't know of any outfit, outside of his, who had the chops for it in Ollson space. Which meant one of two things.

Either a rival was jumping the borders, or this was an Ollson covert op. Normally he'd steer clear of Ollson operations, but the risk went down considerably with the suppressor field. They might finally have the upper hand, and if it was a rival, well, they'd send a message.

He'd been watching the tapped station feed when the ship's airlock opened, and two men walked out. The one with the bald head had turned and left without even a parting word, but the other man, slightly shorter, was the one that looked interesting to Caso. He sent another team to follow the bald man, but took Senny and Gull with him to intercept the shorter one.

They had barely made it to the bar before their mark, but they had, and Caso got a decent look at him as he walked in. The shorter man's clothes were too clean, and he carried himself like he owned everything he saw. *That rules out gangs or cartels.* No way was anything but Ollson. Maybe an off-gene descendent, as his eyes were a steel grey, but the jawline and the way he held himself. It was almost like Eric Ollson himself had seen fit to leave whatever cloud he usually lived on and come wallow in the mud with the rest of them.

Caso stole a glance at the man over the top of his mug. He stood at the bar, looking down into his ale, swirling it around gently. Gull's voice brought him back to their table.

"You heard anything yet from the boss?" She was a small, wiry woman with furtive eyes that were always on the move. Her restless energy seeped out of her and set Caso on edge.

Caso took a sip from his mug before answering. "No, nothing. But he is busy man."

Senny chose to jump in before Gull could reply. "I thought this was supposed to do something, man. I know things didn't go like, exactly right, but shit." He was a tenor, and loud, his voice cutting across the bar's noise to Caso. He wasn't the best at keeping secrets either, his voice aside, but he was loyal and quick with a blade.

Caso grunted as he replied. "No, no it didn't go well on surface. Was supposed to be peaceful fucking protest. Kid used it on soldiers, for fuck's sake." His fingers tapped out a complicated code on the tabletop, out of sight of their mark at the bar. The first thing Caso had learned was the resistance code, number of fingers and taps corresponding to words and phrases.

Target calm. Hold position, prepare to follow.

Gull put her own mug on the table with a solid thunk. "Of course they killed him, then. Lucky you managed to get out with the box." She had a very expensive black market eye, and she'd set it to display a feed from her handheld before they started the tail. It was a running stream of local network traffic, custom sniffer programs observing and reporting who was asking what. Her fingers tapped out a reply.

Clear. Normal traffic.

Senny sighed, leaning back in his chair to move his body out of the way of Gull's view of the man at the bar. He had done some digging on the man and his ship as they nearly sprinted to make it to the bar ahead of him, and found that the man's ship was registered to a salvage yard in Noatun, no name. Not necessarily suspicious; after all plenty of people liked their privacy, but the falsified records meant something outside the normal smuggling and trade. He snorted, putting one foot up on the empty chair across from him. "Listen, you want something done, do it yourself."

Caso gripped his mug harder. The little shit was always throwing around judgement, but had yet to lead any real operation. And now he expected miracles, like they could just waltz in and start the revolution without anything going wrong? Caso's eyes pierced Senny. "I told you, we need patience."

"We been waiting for what, like, six months? I'm tired, man."

Caso forced his hand to relax and his voice to sound lazy, almost nonchalant. He waved a hand at Gull. "We're all tired. I'm tired, she's tired, everyone's tired. But not yet."

Gull leaned forward, an edge of flint in her voice. "You two *aumingi* shut the fuck up." Her fingers tapped the table behind her mug.

Confirm follow if he leaves? Caso was about to respond when her eyes widened slightly and her fingers tapped again, urgent this time. *Network traffic. Ollson encryption.*

Caso nodded. Decision time. If this was an Ollson black op, intercepting him might bring down more heat than they wanted, especially after the action on the surface. On the other hand, Caso couldn't think of a reason there would be an Ollson affiliated man, apparently with implants due to the network traffic, sniffing around the station unless he knew about the resistance.

Or was looking for answers about how a suppressor field managed to find its way to a dirtside riot.

Letting him go was too much of a risk; they had to know if they were blown. His finger twitched on the table. *If he leaves, take him.* The others tapped their assent.

They went back to their drinks, outwardly calm but Caso knew the other two were just as wired as he was. Finally, after an hour, Caso couldn't take the waiting. *Fuck it.*

He got up and barely caught the surprised look that Senny threw Gull as the other two stood to follow him. Caso walked to the bar, past the man, then stopped, turning to rest his arm on the bar top. Senny and Gull stood casually on the man's other side.

Gull sneered at the man as she spoke. "Ain't seen you in here before."

The man took a drink before answering. "Just got back in." His accent had a hint of aristo, the culture and class of

Ollson high management. Caso didn't think that was enough to be sure he was coming after the resistance, but it wasn't normal. His hunch had paid off.

Caso crossed his arms and growled at the man. "Who you ship with?"

The man turned to face him and put on an unctuous smile. "I'm captain, not crew."

Caso raised his eyebrows. "Odd seeing captain here with no crew."

The man smiled almost apologetically. "Well, I'm between crews."

Caso nodded to Senny. "Hmmm, you hear that, Senny? Between crews."

Gull laughed before Senny could answer. "Maybe he needs a few able-bodied hands, eh? You gotta wonder, though."

Caso waited for a beat, staring into the man's eyes. "Wonder what happened to last crew."

The man put the bar to his back and rested his elbow on it. Caso could tell he was trying to keep them all in view, probably smelled trouble. Well, if it took trouble, he'd be ready. The man's reply was low and friendly, though his eyes had become hard. "Look, friends, my last crew got their pay and moved along. It wasn't a lot, but you know. Times are thin."

Senny nodded, laughing hollowly. "Yeah, times are thin."

The man raised his eyebrows. "Tell you what," he said, "I can tell when I'm not welcome. Well, no harm meant. I'll be on my way."

Caso stepped forward, leaving one hand on the bar top. He saw Eliza, the bartender, raise an eyebrow at him from the corner of his eye. His fingers tapped quickly on the bar top. *Stun baton.*

Eliza moved in slowly, reaching underneath the bar top. Need to keep the man's attention for a few more seconds. "I don't like the way you been looking at us." The man twitched, his eyes bouncing from Gull to Senny and back to Caso, who continued. "And I think the only who ain't going home tonight might be you, *Raggeit?*"

Caso was worried he'd have to actually slug the man, but he started the fight first. Caso took a mug of ale to the face, shaking it out of his eyes as he reached forward. Luckily Eliza stood right behind the stranger, and hit him in the back of the neck with her stun baton. The man crumpled to the floor in a heap.

Caso nodded his thank to Eliza as he bent to grab the unconcious form. "Gull, go get the bay ready. Senny, grab his ankles."

Senny let out a whoosh of air as he heaved. "Gods damn, he's heavy."

Caso nodded. "Wired. Don't worry, I have it."

Senny nodded. "Drunk and home?"

Caso nodded, and they took up places under the man's arms, each bracing his considerable weight between them. With a little luck, Gull would have killed the cameras between the bar and the hangar room they had planned for field interrogation, and the only prying eyes they'd need to deal with were other residents. But they had to move quickly; no telling how long the stun baton would last, especially if the man was as chock full of implants and wiring as his weight suggested.

The empty halls were a testament to the evaporated economy. Usually during shift change the corridors would be packed with humanity. Caso and Senny made it look good anyway, lurching a little and singing and smiling broadly at the few people they passed. Most didn't make eye contact, their heads bent on whatever task occupied them. When the two arrived with the still unconscious man between them, Gull was waiting with a length of wire.

Caso and Senny dropped the man, and Gull quickly tied his hands as Senny doubled back to close the hatch to the hangar. She was just finishing as he returned.

Senny slapped his open palms on his legs. "All clear. How long did you kill the cameras for?"

Gull wrapped the last bight around the man's wrists and shook them to check her work. "We have an hour, give or take. Eventually, they'll notice the loop, but I'll know when they reset it." She tapped her temple by her false eye.

Senny grunted. "I still can't believe you went for the ocular. Thing's dangerous, man."

Caso waved them away from the man. "You want to talk, do it where he can't hear."

Senny and Gull moved a few yards away, and Caso squatted near the bound figure on the floor. He took the small red box of the suppressor field out of his pocket and fit his fingers carefully into the activation wells. When he squeezed, he felt the box vibrate twice in his hand, but nothing else changed. *Maybe this guy isn't wired after all.* But with the man unconscious, there was no way to tell. The field was insurance, and Caso squeezed his fingers in the pattern that latched it to ative mode. A small dial popped up on one side, and he carefully set the box on the decking facing his prisoner. The dial had no numbers, only a yellow glow from its top. He turned it slightly, and the glow deepened towards red. He returned it to amber, nodded, then rejoined Senny and Gull across the room.

"I've told you before," Gull said, "it ain't an ocular. It's short-range, connects to one thing, and is just a display. Ollsons ain't gonna fuckin hack me."

Senny just shrugged. "Ok, but if you start acting weird and foaming at the mouth, I'm out."

Caso shook his head at Senny. The guy had always been kind of shitty, especially in the field, but the bench Caso had to draw from had been pretty short. "Stop being asshole. She's right, is no problem. I have flight wirejob." He held up one hand, the tracery of the implants just visible beneath his skin. "See? No one hacks me." Senny opened his mouth to speak, but Caso cut him off with a chopping motion. "Gull. What do we know about this guy?"

"Not much," she admitted, her shoulders shrugging. "But between the shady ship registration and that fuckin' tech he's packed full of, he's someone high up." She pulled out her handheld and showed them the little screen. "Took a quick look inside when you brought him in. Look at this shit." She tapped the screen, zooming in on his torso and head. "I mean I can't tell what it is, but he's definitely got a wirejob, on top of the rest of this shit. Never seen implants in some of these places 'fore."

Senny chose that moment to chime in. "Must be management security guard or something. Or black ops. In which case fuck that."

"Don't you get soft on me now," growled Caso, "I put on suppressor field. Nothing he can do, is low enough that won't hurt us. More wiring, more implants, easier to take down."

Gull nodded. "True enough. Still don't know where you got that widget, but it's useful."

Senny tapped Caso on the shoulder and pointed behind him to wear the man lay. "Hey man, looks like he's waking up."

Caso turned to look at their prisoner. "You see him move?"

"Yeah, he just twitched. Not moving now though."

Caso nodded. "Can find out pretty easy." He walked over to the man on the floor. As Caso approached, he noticed all the subtle signs of wrong-ness. The man's boots were un-scuffed, his hair and beard cut perfectly. But his hands were the most obvious, clean and manicured nails and soft fingertips. True, he hadn't claimed to be a dock worker, but his ship had been small. He'd have been hauling cargo and turning tools with the rest of the crew, and his hands should have shown the wear. He was lying about something.

Caso paused, standing over the man. This liar was flying a ship with fabricated codes, poking his nose around the bar on Caso's station. Whoever he was, he was trouble and likely of the Ollson variety with all the implants. The same Ollsons that he and the rest were fighting against. Finally, he had someone important. He felt an unexpected wave of anger wash over him, tinged with shame. The riot on the planet, the chase across the starfall fields. He couldn't go back and kill any soldiers. But here was an Ollson agent, dropped in his lap.

He aimed a kick at the man's prone form, feeling the toe of his boot catch squarely in the ribs. The man gasped and rolled, his path stopped by a shipping crate.

Caso allowed a small smile. "I figured he was awake. Look at the little cunt." Caso reached down to grab the man by his perfect hair. "Not so fuckin' high and mighty now, eh?" He stared back at Caso. Not a word. Fine, he still wanted to keep his secrets.

Caso would beat them out of him.

He dropped the man's head, and it struck the decking with a satisfying ring. Caso walked over to the suppressor field and carefully adjusted the manual dial. A little more wouldn't send the prisoner back unconscious, and he had no desire to face a wirejob. Better to win an unfair fight.

Caso stood and crossed his arms, grinning broadly at the man on the floor. "See, Gull? We can do whatever we want with him now."

Gull stepped forward, her eyes like chipped glass. She crossed her arms and stared down at the man. "Look, you ain't goin' anywhere, so better get comfortable."

The man flopped and strained to roll, then gave up. He looked up at Gull through a lock of hair. "What did you do to me? I feel… wrong."

Gull smiled. "What's wrong, *Vesalingur*, can't use your fancy fuckin toys?"

The man's face stayed calm, but he stopped struggling to move. "Not sure what you mean."

Gull took a step forward. "Don't play dumb; it's no use. We know you got a wirejob, knew you weren't no trader or merc neither." She spat on the decking. "You fucking high-up pricks think you can come down here and poke your nose where it don't belong."

The man seemed like he was putting on a pretty brave face. Hell, if their places had been reversed, Caso wasn't sure he'd have been near as calm. It was insolent, like the man couldn't possibly be in danger despite his position, bound on the floor. *This móður fokker has no idea what he's in to.* He felt his breath quicken and ground his teeth. *Time to teach him.*

Senny walked forward as Caso moved to stand next to the man. Senny's voice quavered a bit as he spoke. "We got you, rich boy. Field'll keep you from using wirejob. You must be some high-up management type, eh?"

Caso looked down at the man, who stared back at Senny. He just laid there, tied on the deck and refusing to talk. Caso felt the anger building inside him. Who was this guy, that he thought he could afford to just stay quiet? Caso kicked him again in the ribs, relishing the look of pain that stitched across the prisoner's face. "And what the fuck are you doing down here? Looking for something? Come down here to see what the scum live like, eh, *Ónytjungur*?" Still nothing. Caso kicked him again, feeling a little control slip away. He was in charge, gods damnit, and this man would tell him who he was and what he wanted.

Or he'd die down here.

"Tell me what you fucking know!" Caso's breathing came hard as he kicked the man again, flecks of spit flying. He gave in to the rage, relishing it. Gull appeared next to him, holding a bucket of water. The man's teeth were gritted, his eyes tight as he tried to roll away from Caso's boot, but Caso had him up against the shipping container. All the frustration of the last day, the hatred, came bubbling out. Gull poured the bucket of water on the man's face, and he sputtered and coughed. The water splashed back up, spraying Caso's leg, but he barely noticed. He felt a rib crack under his boot.

Gull put a hand on his shoulder, and Caso grunted. Aimed one last kick. Roared in anger down at the man on the floor. Gull's voice pulled him back from the violence. "Let him speak. Hard to let him tell us anything with fat fuckin' boot in his chest."

Caso stepped away from the prisoner. He walked a tight circle back to stand by Senny, his hands shaking and breath heaving. *He'll have to talk.* Caso took deep breaths, fighting for control and calm. He hadn't meant to get that carried away, but the insolence. The obvious better-than-you attitude of this man. It made Caso want to destroy him out of spite.

Gull tossed the empty bucket into a corner. The man rolled away from the shipping container, spitting blood and phlegm onto the decking. His voice was thin, shaking. "I need a doctor."

Gull laughed. "No shit? You want to live through this shit, you better answer my questions. Who fuck are you?"

He struggled to sit upright, and took his time in answering. Caso took a step forward, and the man turned his head away. "All right," he said, "*Helvítis andskotans*, just stop." Sure, now he tried to swear like a dockhand. Even the words sounded wrong in the man's mouth.

Gull snapped her fingers at him. "You tell us what you were doing at the bar, who you work for, why you were trying to listen in on us. Or I let Caso do his thing."

Wheeze. Cough. "I do have a ship. Salvage job. I work private party."

Gull shook her head. "What, so you are some kinda fucking merc? Where'd you get a wirejob like that?"

"Nah, not a merc. I do security. Private side." He paused to breath, grimacing against what had to be a decent amount of pain. "I got a message, supposed to meet a client. Just had the station and the location."

Senny turned away from the man, and Caso heard his voice low. "He's lying. No one needs a wirejob that ain't management."

Gull clicked her tongue and nodded. "Or could pay." Her eyes bored into the man on the floor.

The man spoke up again, the words spilling out. "It wasn't a government job. I can tell you that much. After the news about the war, last place I want to be."

The adrenaline had begun to release Caso, and he frowned, trying to weigh the man's words. The story he told was plausible. The weirdness with the ship registration, the lack of a crew, and even the other man's departure when the ship had initially docked. But the wirejob, the extra implants, it didn't add up.

Caso squatted down next to the man, who stared back levelly. *Hm, at least he has a little spine in him.* "War's been a long time coming." Caso turned and spat on the decking. "You gotta be on a side eventually."

The man nodded and began to speak, working his way into a seated position against the shipping crate. "Look, I told you what you want to know. No client is worth this; you let me go, I go back to my ship, and you never see me again."

Senny laughed, a sharp bark that echoed in the small room. "I don't think so, *Mannfÿla*," he said. "I don't think you're telling whole truth. I think you *are* here working for management. I think you come down to spy on us and see who says what. I think you'd do better in little pieces in 'cycler."' When Caso looked back at Senny, his face was split in a ghoulish grin.

This guy is more sadist than I thought. Caso stood to walk back and talk with Gull. The guy on the floor may or may not have been a mercenary, but someone would probably notice he was missing, either station security or whoever the man had been here to meet. Either was one more complication, and they needed to make some life-and-death decisions quickly.

Just as Caso started to move, a voice slithered over their prisoner who leaned against the stacked containers. "Oh Erick, what have you gotten yourself into this time?"

Damnit Gull, I thought you had locked door? Caso felt the surge of adrenaline grip him one more, his shoulders tense and hands balled into fists. The last thing he wanted was company, and it sounded like whoever-it-was actually knew the guy tied up on the floor. This operation was beginning to get dangerously off the rails. Caso stepped across the small open area and stood between Senny and Gull, wishing he'd brought a weapon. With three of them, he'd expected things to go smoothly, but those hopes were dwindling fast.

Their prisoner coughed and spat on the floor. The smell of sweat and blood crowded the small space. When the prisoner spoke, Caso felt his eyes narrow. "I should have known you'd be involved in this." *So they don't know each other?* Caso's mind was in overdrive, a thousand possible next steps crashing through his thoughts. They all stopped when the mystery speaker emerged from around the corner of the shipping crate.

It was the other man from their prisoner's ship. Caso had only seen him for a few seconds on the security feed, but he had no doubt. The long cut of his jacket, the delicate features, even the way he moved, like oil on water.

Like a snake.

Caso watched the newcomer with wary eyes. He walked forward, then stopped next to the suppressor field box, putting it between him and the prisoner.

Gull spoke first, and Caso saw her hand hovering near her pocket. The one with the prisoner's confiscated little pistol. "You know what's best for you, you'll turn around and walk right the fuck out, *Ónytyungur*!" She may have been laying it on thick, but she was caught just as flat-footed as Caso.

"As I told you," their captive said, "my client would likely be looking for me. He did pay me quite a solid advance." The prisoner looked up at the newcomer. Something was off; Caso just couldn't quite place it. Something important.

The newcomer looked to Caso. "I think that by now you three have figured out that I have a certain, shall we say, relationship with this man." He gestured towards the prisoner, palm up. His voice was granite. "I will make you a proposition. I pay you. You go away."

Gull laughed before replying. "Right, with what? You hiding a crate of palladium down your pants?" Senny tittered behind her, his nervous energy apparent.

"No, nothing of the sort, I'm afraid." The man pulled a small satchel from its belt. "Just the local currency. Still, it's not nothing." As he hefted the bag, Caso heard the clink of metal on metal. The man reached in and pulled out a gleaming coin with the Ollson wolves stamped on it. "This isn't credit. It's real, and there's a lot of it."

Whoever he was, the man knew what he was doing. Physical currency was rare, and incredibly valuable. Caso had only seen *blóðmynt* once before. There was enough in that bag to buy any ship in berthing. The only problem was staying alive long enough to spend it. There was no way this would end with a payoff and them going their separate ways. The money had to be a ploy to get rid of them until station management could track them down. No, it had to end here.

Caso was about to say as much when Gull beat him to it. "All right, I'll do you one better." She drew the small pistol they'd taken off their prisoner. It seemed almost dainty in her hand.

Fucking guði fjandinn hafi það, going to be hard enough to hide one body. Caso pulled his own knife, and felt Senny move next to him as well. His mind ran through options. When Gull fires, he closes the distance. It's a few paces, but he should be able to get in under the ribs. Pull the man around, let Senny get to his back. They'd need to kill him quickly, then the prisoner on the floor. Deal with the bodies and go.

The man looked down at their prisoner, the calm smile never leaving his face. "You have to ask, Erick. It's the way."

Wait. Erick. That was the second time the newcomer had called their prisoner Erick. It was a common enough name, but something was bothering Caso. The way Erick had spoken in the bar. His too-clean clothing, lack of a crew. The newcomer showing back up now after leaving him outside of his ship.

Erick looked up at the man, who still held the bag of blood coins. His voice shook, but Caso heard him clearly. "I need your help." The man nodded, returning the bag of *blóðmynt* to his pocket.

At his first step forward, Gull shouted and brought up the pistol. That's when it clicked in Caso's mind. *His clothes, speech. This is the fokking Executor Erick Ollson.* It was too late. Caso had already kidnapped Erick, beat him. Fear clawed its way through the fighting instinct and punched Caso in the gut. He stretched out a hand to try to stop Gull, but it was too late.

Somehow the elegant stranger was already among them. Caso heard rather than saw him move, and the top of Senny's head exploded in a shower of blood and brain matter. Caso tried to follow the man with his knife hand, to defend himself. Then he felt something hit him, hard, his neck snapping back with an explosion of pain.

32

Angst

The one who burns, the ever-fire
Who's light had raged and dimmed
A new course she plotted
A new route, and clearly she saw her prize

Bragja stared at the golden cloth across the door and did not sleep. It had been two days, or thereabouts, and while before fatigue had claimed her quickly, now it shunned her. Her mind skipped, one thought to the next, and she wrapped her arms around her body, her fingers clasped tight on biceps. She had so many questions. What should she do next? Was there a place for her on the station? Were the Ollsons still looking for her? The cacophony of her mind threatened to overwhelm her. She really only knew two things. One, she couldn't sleep here again.

And two, Caso hadn't come back for her.

Two days when Caso had promised to return in one. The quiet outside her room told her the Vessels had ceased their praying, at least for a time. She left the light on. The sleep blanket hung malevolent, arms ready to smother her. She shuddered, remembering her dream.

No sleep tonight.

The cultists had her deeply confused. The sense of family she'd felt sharing their meals, the way everyone seemed to be devoted to each other, it felt so much like the family and friends she'd known on the surface. But there, the similarities ended. They were utterly devoted to following the Empress's path and gave up so much freedom. The golden robes were only an outward expression of uniformity; Bragja hadn't witnessed a single debate or disagreement in her whole time among them. She wanted to embrace the people who so quickly gave of themselves to help her, and she was grateful, but there was too large a gulf between their morality and her own.

A voice cut through her thoughts, and she cocked her head. The whispered voice was familiar without the multitude of quiet prayers to blend in with. And coming from quite close.

"Bragja. Honored guest."

Bragja pulled the stretched cloth aside. "Vessel Horman?" She was confident enough, if not certain.

The whispered muttering stopped, and one side of the hallway of cloth stretched back on long fingertips. "Ah, honored guest. I apologize if I woke you."

Bragja drifted out into the hallway, her toes fumbling for a hook. "I wasn't sleeping." He nodded. She noticed his hand, holding the cloth back, shook slightly. His eyes seemed glassy, bulbous, and as she watched, he blinked a single tear out into the room. It drifted in the air currents, impacting the cloth next to Horman's head and spreading across a tiny sliver of the golden expanse. Bragja's brows furrowed. "Shouldn't you be sleeping, though?"

Horman nodded, wiping his eyes with the back of his other hand. "Yes. Yes, I should. Lady Shava will be upset if I am distracted tomorrow." His eyes were wide, and his throat worked as he took a shuddering breath.

"So, tell me, what has a devotee of the Empress awake at night?" The man was obviously upset, and she felt a surge of sympathy. Horman had been kind to her, trying to help her in his own way.

"I have received a message, and I'm afraid it involves you. And Caso."

Bragja's ears perked up. "I'm assuming it wasn't good?" She felt her stomach tighten.

"No, no, it isn't. I'm afraid Caso won't be coming to get you."

"What?"

"His friends will be here in the morning to collect you, don't worry. I know you aren't comfortable here."

"It's not...." She sighed. "I just don't feel like this is my place. You've all been very kind, though."

"Ever since you refused Shava, I was concerned. She might have easily thrown you out."

"Why didn't she?"

"She sees something in you, I think. And she's right. But she's been so cautious since Caso—" His voice broke, and he ran a hand across his face. "But she won't have to worry about Caso anymore." Horman drew a long breath.

"He's dead."

Bragja felt herself digest this piece of information. It was like she watched from a spot on the wall, her mind and body acting along without her. She hadn't cared for Caso, but he was at least familiar. And when he saved her from the Ollsons, brought her to the safest place he knew, Bragja had been conflicted.

On the one hand, he started a riot, and her brothers had paid for it. But on the other, he had been genuinely upset by the outcome and claimed to have the best intentions. Despite Caso stealing the suppressor field, Horman had still cared about Caso. After a few seconds, she spoke. "What did Caso do for you, that you care about him so much?"

"For us all, actually. Some years ago, there was a plague. Many died. Shava refused to seek medicine. She told us the Empress' will was at work, and that those of us that made it through would be those that were supposed to."

"So what happened with Caso?"

"He had gone from us already. But he still came back and checked on us. On me."

Bragja crossed her arms, silent.

"He brought medicine. Gave it to me, told me we would all die if we didn't take it. I believed him, at that point. There were so many sick. Children. I couldn't do nothing. So I took it to Shava, begged her to distribute the medicine."

"And she did?"

"She refused. Took it from my hands and threw me out of her chamber."

"I don't understand."

"After that, we started to get better. A few more still died, but in a few days, everyone was improving."

"She put it in your food."

Horman's eyes teared up again, huge in the low light. "No one knows about the medicine but me. They think it was a miracle of the Empress. Shava hasn't discounted those thoughts. We were devoted to her before, but after she saved us through faith… There's nothing they won't do for her now."

"But you know."

Horman nodded, sniffing and wiping his eyes. His voice, continually strained, barely crossed the gulf between them. "And I'll take that with me to the void."

33

Banners

Strong she held to sword and shield
The rats and vermin did circle
But bright was the light of her lightning-gaze
And swift ran her wolves in the night

Bryn ran her fingertip along the baroque scrollwork that framed the window. The gold leaf, sustained in a perpetual state of almost crumbling, gave the room a sense of gravitas that belied the gentle half-g that pulled her soles to the rug. Beyond the window, the swirling deep blue-green of Karvasok hung in the blackness. The station was at the orbital equilibrium point between Karvasok and its moon, which kept the planet small in Bryn's view. She could see the whole circumference of the disc, like a riotous painted plate at arm's length.

She remembered her trips there, long ago as a young girl. She'd always preferred to go down to the winter hemisphere, selecting one of the Geneline estates nestled in the mountains. Her favorite had been the Alfheim range, running in a slash and curve along the southern ocean. She felt like if she looked hard enough, she might be able to make out the soaring peaks even from the station, so far away. Were the snows deep this year? Did the avalanches roar and thunder down the valleys like she remembered, a deep shaking her bones? She frowned, knowing she would likely not see the snowcapped peaks for many years. If ever.

The low tone of an alert sounded in the Executor's suite, and Bryn acknowledged the call to silence it.

"Yes, Obin. What do you have for me?"

"It's Capt Hafthor, ma'am. He was following up on that high-probability intelligence tip in Noatun. He's marked this Executor Level 1." Bryn saw in her ocular that she had just received a data file, from Obin but marked with Bjorn's geneseal. "With the delay in the comms relay, this message is about a day old."

"Thank you, Obin. I'll review it immediately and call you back."

"As you wish, ma'am."

Bryn pushed the file over the suite's holoprojector, and Bjorn's features sprang to life above the black and gold projection disc.

"Greetings, Executor Ollson. After following up on the intelligence related to Objective Castor White, I'm providing this situational report." Castor White had been the code name the intelligence section had dreamed up to encompass anything related to the spy with the high-energy implants, including the ongoing efforts to figure out how to identify the operatives and their tech. "A target believed to associate with Castor White was identified through three different intelligence sources in the Noatun system. Our people on the station noted a relative newcomer to the engineering guild, who performed exceedingly well for a journeyman and sought access to sensitive information about our ship construction techniques. Specifically, the Ollson warship modification plans; had the target only been interested in Imperial Standard ships, we might have missed this sign. After adding the target to the queue for further surveillance, my team was able to tune the ship scanner array at the yards to provide an energy density map. We correlated this with visual and infrared imagery." The image shifted from Bjorn's face and torso to a short video loop of a young man, tall and thin, with a mop of curly black hair. As the video cycled, it showed his infrared image slightly hotter than those around him.

"A little heavy on the detail, Bjorn," Bryn muttered, sotto voce. She hadn't been able to get him into the Ollson Forgers before he pressed out after a lead on another spy. At some point, preferably soon, she would have to find an excuse for him to be off the field long enough to go under the knife. His commitment as First Wolf wouldn't be set in stone until he held the executor's codes. It was an interesting relationship her ancestors developed with their war council, the Ollson and the Wolves. She would still be the only one who could wake imperial technology, command the ships and defenses, but with the chip, she could delegate some or all of that power to Bjorn. It was autonomy far beyond anything the Admiralty considered prudent.

Bryn paused the message and regarded the target for a moment. So this was their potential enemy. He looked nondescript, and if she was being candid, she wouldn't be able to pick him out of a crowd. Still, after weeks of searching, this was the first image she'd had of an enemy agent. She felt her heart quicken as if she was preparing to chase him down herself. No, that wouldn't do. That's why she had deputized Bjorn and the Second Company. They would be her sword in the night. She continued the recording.

"As you can see, he's visible in the infrared just slightly warmer than the rest of the people in the shot. However, things begin to stand out when we tuned the ship scanner for energy density." The video overlapped here with a ghostly blue, and the man definitely stood out. Portions of his body showed shifting blue, nearly white, oblong shapes that faded and brightened as he moved. "The ship scanners are normally used to inspect our hulls before their shakedown voyages, and as such, they are relatively bulky. We got lucky here. We maintained positive identification of the target through a tail and by working the station security cameras." Bryn noticed she had clamped her fist and rubbed it along her jaw. She forced her hand back down.

There was nothing she could do about the outcome; either they had captured the agent or hadn't. No sense getting excited now.

The view shifted back to Bjorn. "We tracked the target back to the guild dormitory. Based on our experience with the last of these agents, we still do not have a good plan to neutralize their high-energy implants. Until we do, I did not want to risk a detonation in the shipyards." Bryn nodded to herself. The shipyards were critical infrastructure, the engineering guild even more so. It took a long time to train someone who had a scrap of the geneline to use the machinery and systems, and they couldn't afford the hit in production on the eve of war. Unless Erick came back with a miracle. The thought brought on a moment of maudlin. *Father. Why haven't you contacted me?*

The recording continued. "We managed to reduce the target's access to critical systems and were ready for the software assault this time. The target attempted to introduce the same type of cyber into the shipyard mainframe. When he failed, he ran." Bryn grunted in dissatisfaction. They needed one of these spies alive.

"We tracked him through the shipyards but lost him at the docks. We did manage to shut down the array, but only after a single ship left, bound for Osman space. Our assessment of the array is that the target is no longer here, likely on the ship that made it off array. That's the complete rollup. I'm standing by for any further direction. In the meantime, I'll continue to keep Second Company on rolling alert and integrate with our intelligence assets to identify any more possible agents."

Bjorn reached his hand out to the pickup, then stopped before the hologram cut out. "Oh, and one more thing. My XO used to work with some folks in inbound shipments. According to them, liquid helium might be able to flash freeze one of these agents quickly enough to keep them from going critical. We are working on a delivery system, but it's not finalized yet. I'll let you know what develops there as soon as I know more." He saluted smartly, then his hand did reach out, and the hologram fell back into the projector disc, his form dissolving into a wash of pixels.

Osman space. This was a new development. Bryn was sure, sure in her bones, in her gut, that the spies weren't acting on behalf of the Osmans. She knew Azita too well; they had grown up together, or together as the children of two Executors could be. Before she had taken up her training in earnest, as a young woman barely thirty years old, she'd gone with her father to the Osman homeworld.

The planet was similar to Karvasok, gravity a touch less, sky another shade. But being there had been so very different, people dressing in brightly colored robes and luxurious beads. Even the commoners, the children, had moved about like explosions of intensity, their skin shades of dark that made her feel like a ghost. What she had thought of as gaudy ceremonial Ollson vestments had felt drab and utilitarian.

She had seen the children of Ollson playing just as happy as those of Osman, but the feeling she had in Osman space was so much more alive. Perhaps it was the people, maybe it was the color, but Bryn couldn't help but smile at the true highlight of that trip.

Azita, of the almond eyes and easy laugh.

34

Love

The storm-born began
As no mother of lightning, no sword and shield
In the sunlit silence of youth
Connection made, and troth given, is e'er the base of
awe

She'd been greeted by the full Osman Geneline. Formal meetings between genelines were always full of subtext, and this was no different. Erick and Bryn had entered the Osman formal room, and Bryn's breath had stopped in her throat. Mosaic tiles started in a tight spiral on the floor in front of her, then exploded outwards as she walked towards the head of the room. Her eye followed the running colors from the floor to where they blended with the faceted pillars flanking the long room, wrapping fantastic blues and greens against a dun background. The whorls of color resolved into flocks of birds on the ceiling, the tiles blending with range into beaks and wings with flashes of iridescent plumage. The birds flocked to the front of the room, where the peacock of the Osman sigil spread gold and green. At the center, just below the magnificent mosaic, stood Executor Zehra Osman in her green finery. The cloth of her robes caught every sheen and reflection in the light of the long hall. She was imposing, perfect, her expression neutral yet flush with power. Bryn felt an irrational rush of self-consciousness, sure she'd make some mistake of greeting or slip of decorum.

Zehra's daughter, however, had no patience for stiff formalities and had broken protocol as soon as possible. The final syllable of her mother's title was barely out of the lips of the courtier when she broke ranks and began to run across the hall.

Executor Osman's voice rang out across the hall to fall on her daughter's deaf ears. "Azita!"

Azita stopped in front of Bryn, took her hands, and looked deep into her eyes without a hint of trepidation. "Welcome! I've heard so much about you, about Karvasok and the Ollsons who live in the mountains. Is it true you can't feel cold?"

Bryn had laughed, embarrassed and giddy and taken with Azita's presence. It had been a fast friendship. They spent the first few days in the Osman palace, with Erick and Zehra meeting each day with their armies of advisors, accountants stacked as high as the windows. It didn't take long for Bryn and Azita to go a little stir crazy; the grounds were extensive but there was only so much to see inside them.

Azita challenged Bryn to an archery competition, which quickly escalated to horseback as the two realized they were an even match. After one such competition, Bryn and Azita were walking their horses back to the stables, the slightly-too-red sunlight filtering through trees with midnight leaves. The path stretched out ahead of them, perspective like art on canvas. The air hummed with pollinating insects, and Bryn's breath was still slightly labored from her exertions.

Bryn slid her long bow into its sheath on the side of her horse as she laughed at Azita. "I still don't understand how you manage to hit anything with that tiny bow of yours."

Azita held up her bow, only half the size of Bryn's but with a wicked recurve. "If you would print something with the barest hint of engineering in it, you might actually be able to keep up."

"Keep up? You mean the way I hit every target you did?"

Azita laughed and slipped her bow into the case at her side. "Fair enough. You must work so hard with that huge bow, though. It's like you're swinging around a tree."

"A small tree. At least it's a proper weapon. What will you do with that little thing once you're out of arrows?"

Azita paused, finger to pursed lips. Her eyes were electric green against the foliage. "Hmm, well, probably call in the orbital death from above."

Bryn laughed despite herself. Azita had a way of putting things into a context that Bryn often lost sight of. She was beginning to adore the other woman for it. "Right, what was I thinking," she responded, "as if we'd be fighting an actual war with bows and arrows."

"You Ollsons, always talking about war. It's so boring." Her voice carried a laugh with the gentle barb.

Bryn took her eyes off the road in front of them to look at Azita. She stared straight ahead, a mischievous smile on the corner of her mouth.

Bryn cleared her throat. "All existence is war. All war is not violent." The maxims drilled into her by tutors jumped out of Bryn like living things. She'd questioned those lines for how many years with her tutors, but now among another geneline, they were suddenly her truths? How quickly unity came in the face of otherness.

Azita reached into the bag that hung behind her saddle, retrieving an apple the color of old blood. She breathed on it, shining it against her loose shirt. "I won't argue with you that competition is in everything. But I don't know if I agree that you can have a war without violence. It seems, I don't know, endemic in the definition."

Bryn readjusted her estimation of Azita for the tenth time in the last few days. Her first experience, with the opulence of the Osman palace, had made her think Azita was just a pretty face with a penchant for athletics, but beneath her precisely coordinated wardrobe was a mind like knapped flint. Every time they explored a new area, a new topic, they traded ideas, the parry and riposte of those seeking truth. Bryn's horse tried to turn off the road, distracted by something in the underbrush. She corrected the mare with a squeeze of her leg and touch of reign. The crunch of Azita biting into her apple was loud over the clop of hooves.

"Let's talk about something other than war, then. Did you know this is my first time out of Ollson space?"

Azita smiled, delicately wiping the corner of her mouth with the tip of a finger. "I'd guessed. I'd love to see Karvasok sometime. Mother seems a little more conservative regarding me than Erick is with you."

Bryn gave a tight smile. "I didn't bring it up before, but yes, Zehra does seem a little more worried."

Azita's voice carried the slightest edge of bitterness. "I don't blame her, after what she experienced at my age."

"Ah. My father told me, but I'd almost forgotten."

"I promise you, I haven't. She won't even let me visit the other planets in our space."

Bryn didn't know where to go from there. She'd always enjoyed the freedom to move about, even as a girl in her teens. Before she'd hit her twenties, she'd seen the foundries, shipyards, factories; all the facets of the Ollson enterprise. And Azita hadn't even been allowed off her home planet. Bryn felt pity and a flar of indignation for Azita's predicament.

"Then you must be very familiar with your home."

"Oh, there's not much of this rock I haven't seen."

Bryn pulled up her horse, and Azita followed suit. They paused a beat, the horses gently shifting under them. Azita raised an eyebrow with an unspoken question. Bryn smiled. "So show me. I want to see everything."

"I'm sure Erick and Zehra will want us to learn about," she gestured idly, "whatever they're doing."

"It's negotiations for the next Summit, like it always is, and we all know who we need to watch out for and who we can rely on. Nothing ever changes. Let's go."

Azita nodded, a slow smile lighting her face like the dawn. "It's not like we can't come back quickly if they call."

"They won't."

"I hope not."

They had left the Osman palace at once, to travel across the land and see the shifting sands of the world-spanning desert, the cool blue oases that bloomed azure flowers from the vast aqueducts below. At one of these, Azita's favorite, or so she claimed, their friendship had blossomed into more. The night's cool pricked at Bryn's skin as she sat cross-legged on the sand. The oasis was broad, nearly a mile across, and from their high vantage point, Bryn could almost make out the other side of it, low choppy trees breaking up the horizon line. The two moons hung gibbous in the deep sky, a curtain of black velvet with the holes of stars shining through. A small fire sputtered behind them, the feeble light enough to cast shadows in the trees but not enough to wash out the majesty of the view. Bryn smelled water, wet, rot, the smell of life smeared over the ever-present foundation of dust. Azita leaned in to rest her head on Bryn's shoulder, a warm reminder of life as they shared a blanket.

"Tired?" Bryn leaned her own head to rest on top of Azita's. She smelled lavender and sweat.

"It was a long hike to get here! Usually we just take the flitter from Tundatha."

"I did say we could ride, if you weren't up for it."

Azita dug a knuckle into Bryn's side. "Right, put up a challenge and expect me to back down."

Bryn laughed, putting an arm around Azita. "It's not a competition, *elskan.*"

"Everything is a competition, or hadn't you heard about the Ollson way of war?"

Bryn felt her heart swell, out in the darkness. The way Azita remembered the things that Bryn said, held on to them, used them later on. The way her voice sounded when she was mischievous, when she was tired, when she had the weight of the world on her shoulders. It was like drinking from a fountain Bryn hadn't known she needed, each breath and word of this passionate, fiery woman a drop of water on her parched tongue. Bryn leaned into Azita, feeling her warmth against the cool night air. "Oh, please, I know, but let's pretend there's no such thing. At least for a little while."

"The Ollson heir, pretending she is not? Oh, the scandal."

Bryn laughed. Such a flippant approach to duty frightened her. "Azita. Do you ever wonder what it'll be like?"

"I wonder what a great many things will be like, but you'll have to be more specific."

"Hush, you know what I mean. When we are executors."

"Oh, gods, I don't have to wonder. Mother tells me constantly about the burden she bears, the sacrifices she makes for stability, peace, et cetera. I don't think I could imagine anything else."

Bryn nodded. "I feel like my father's less heavy-handed, but I understand. Every moment of our lives, scripted and planned and the path laid out."

"You make it sound like it's some sort of curse. I mean, sure, it's not freedom, but power isn't bad."

"Don't get me wrong. I'll do anything for Erick, for the Ollson name. I just wonder if there's something—" Bryn found herself afraid to speak the word out loud.

Azita had no such fear. "More. The word is more, and yes, there's probably something more out there, but there's also no way to get there." She cuddled closer, and Bryn felt a hand on her thigh under the blanket. "I think we should focus on what we have in front of us."

Bryn's breath caught as she felt the rush of warmth. Suddenly she was aware of every bit of Azita's body beside her. She was happy to drop the serious nature of the conversation in pursuit of something more immediate. "And what we have in front of us is, what, exactly?"

Bryn felt Azita's hand begin to slide higher. "I think it's pretty obvious, if you're paying attention."

"Oh trust me, you have my attention." Bryn's was aware of her breathing, steady and deep, and she moved her hand around behind Azita to feel for clasps and catches. She felt the ache now, the need, imagined Azita's hands and lips and tongue. Lust and love and everything in between. Azita's fingers finally found the apex of their journey, driving a soft moan from Bryn's lips.

Azita laughed, tilting her head to run her tongue up Bryn's neck. Her whisper tickled Bryn's ear, sending sparks down her body. "It gets quite cold out here at night, you know."

Bryn finally dropped all pretense of control and rolled over Azita, pressing her down, the blanket below and above them as she began to pull at clothing, Azita's hands returning her passion. She clipped out her words between passionate kisses. "Then we should probably make sure we don't freeze."

Bryn dove into Azita's smell, the taste of her lips, the sound of her breath. She hadn't realized how much she needed this, wanted this, and she never wanted it to end.

They spent the night there, and the morning, and most of the next day exploring each other, mind and body. Erick and Zehra had finished their negotiations after a week, and Erick sent a message to Bryn, asking her to return before the month was out. His words arrived on Bryn's ocular, discreet and respectful. That's how Bryn knew he approved. The month-long holiday had turned to two when Erick finally summoned her back to prepare for the coming Summit.

HLÉHÉR

Standing in the Executor's suite on Karvasok station, Bryn knew she had to reach out to Azita. If nothing else, to warn her of the spy heading towards Osman space. But in truth, it would be good to see her again. Her planned reunion with Azita had been cut too short by their hurried departure from Summit. While it was apparent why she'd left so quickly, Bryn had never apologized for leaving Azita in the middle of the night. Perhaps now was the time.

Bryn stepped back to the liquid black disc of the holo projector and tapped its gilded rim. Her own image took form in front of her, and she inspected it with a critical eye, smoothing down her perfectly pulled-back hair and adjusting the seam of her over-shirt. After thinking for a moment, she waved her hand through the tank, and the image began to mimic her.

"Dear Azita. I can only imagine how you must feel after my sudden departure at the Summit, especially given what happened after. I noticed that you and Zehra did not join in pursuing the *Sleipnir*, and I am grateful. I have and will always continue to assert Ollson innocence in this accusation. Even now, we move closer to uncovering the true cause of the attack on the Obershire forces. I would like to invite you here to talk in peace, and I hope that we may find a way to continue our relationship in the future. I have attached an image of a man we tracked to a ship bound for Osman space; be wary of him. He is dangerous, and one like him nearly destroyed one of our fold arrays. His implants are extremely hazardous; if you attempt to capture him, he might detonate in a suicide attack. I await your reply, and as always, my home is yours."

She played the message back, watching her image speak. It was subtle and likely only she and Azita would notice, but she could tell how she smiled too much, brushed her hair back; it all made her feel like a flighty child. How could anyone have this effect over so much time and space? She reached out to erase the recording, her jaw set, then stopped. She should be more formal, more martial, more of the calm and cool exterior that her father always projected in matters of state. She was Executor now, after all. Wasn't she? With a sharp nod, she moved her hand to another spot and sent the message, the receipt confirmation from the message buffer a gentle chime. She loved her father, looked up to him, and would take his council at any time. But she wasn't her father. She wouldn't put on a front for others, as much as she could help it. Sometimes playing cards close to the vest was best, but honesty was what would connect her to Azita. She was loyal, she was strong, and she would kill anyone who dared threaten her family.

But she would love those that deserved it.

35

Valkyries

Gall of Transportation sat across the desk from her, his tidy suit and carefully manicured hands no distraction from the monotone of his voice. His eyebrows furrowed with the weight of his own importance. Routine discussions of movements, or the lack thereof, tallies of missed transfers. Bryn forced her face into polite engagement, stifling a yawn with sheer willpower. The silver-grey walls gave off a soft glow from inset lights at their top, and the wide picture window looked down on the relatively calm traffic of the docks.

She could practically hear her father's voice over the droning on of the transportation minister. "Bryn," he would tell her, "a good process can't overcome an unhealthy relationship. But a good relationship can overcome a bad process. We need to keep the ministers happy and engaged."

Bryn disagreed. The Executor was the seat of power and used that power to keep order and control. With a lack of order and control, chaos reigned and brought ruin and death to commoners and regents alike. She would not default to rule by fear, but Bryn felt no need to pander to the masses. Let them obey, and that was enough.

The meetings were the worst part of her duties, without a doubt. She had known her father's schedule intimately, followed him daily, but had never been responsible for every bit of communication. The fact this minister was here, in person, was a rarity. She held meetings in holo when she could and rescheduled as many as she could get away with. If those bumbling sycophants in station management and transportation and all the other ministries missed their chance to rub elbows with the Executor and beg for favors, so be it. Once her father returned, and they could hold the formal transfer ceremony, she'd be happy to cancel their meetings altogether.

She knew why her father continued to entertain the lower echelon of the Geneline. *How could I not, the number of times he told me?* They were the ones who ran the Empire, and as Executors it was the lot of the Ollsons to ensure they followed the law and had the resources to make sure others did so. *But we aren't servants. We're leaders.*

A sharp tone sounded in her implant and jolted her out of the reverie. The transportation minister's voice trailed off in a confused mumble as she held up a hand and looked to the side, checking a message in her ocular. It was from Azita.

The meeting was now over, whatever it had been about. "Minister, thank you so much for your cogent and concise remarks on the state of transportation between our systems. I assure you that your concerns over the fold schedule are entirely valid, and we are doing everything within our power to ensure our people's safety and the continued function of commerce. You know the threat, and will know more as soon as I do, I assure you."

"Yes, ma'am, but if you could just take a look at the numbers, you'll see that—" Bryn stood and walked around the table, the minister standing by reflex as well.

"Minister, I'm terribly sorry to have to do this but I have an urgent matter that just came to my attention. Please forward me what information you have to my executive staff, and we will review it." She took him by the elbow and led him to the doorway, his constant babble continuing.

"I will ma'am, to be sure, but the numbers are quite distressing. There is hardly any flow of goods, and—"

Bryn opened the door with a wave of her hand. "*Minister*, please, I assure you no one cares for the people more than I. I will see to the data myself, and we will find a solution. We are entering trying times, and we must all do our part. I look forward to our next meeting." And with that, she shut the door behind the transportation minister and returned to the desk.

The message from Azita was either a crushing blow and the loss of an ally, or a breath of oxygen in a universe growing smaller by the day. She wanted to see Azita in full holo, but knew that whatever she had to say, it was for Bryn's eyes only. She called up the message in her ocular, and suddenly Azita stood before her, a wireframe rendering below her neck. The station software was able to render her face and pipe it to her ocular, and so Azita's dark eyes and full lips were just has Bryn remembered. Perhaps a line or two around the edges, but when she smiled, she still lit up the room.

Bryn felt her heart beat faster as she remembered Azita, and a cascade of guilt followed. The mad dash from Summit, the complete lack of communication. She should have at least sent Azita a message, some apology for having left so abruptly. Perhaps Azita would give her some measure of absolution. Bryn hit play, and Azita's voice filled her ears.

"Bryn! It is so good to hear from you after all this time. I know it hasn't been long since Summit, but it has felt like an eternity, not knowing how you were faring. Of course, we would not fire on you; how could we! I'd sooner throw myself out an airlock. We have always been friends and partners, and whatever the truth is, we will stand by you as best we can until it is uncovered. I speak for my mother when I say that we believe you innocent of the accusations, and despite your status in the Empress' eyes, we will exercise our right to abstain from action against you." Bryn realized she was holding her breath and let it out, taking another to steady herself. Azita, who loved her, of course she wouldn't have believed the Obershire lies. Bryn hadn't realized how much tension she held, hadn't let herself acknowledge that her message might fall on anything but open ears and open hearts.

Azita continued. "I cannot offer you ships-we are engaged in attempting to keep our factories full and running now that we can no longer rely on your shipments. I hope that things are not too difficult there. If you do find your way through this and prove your innocence to the Empress, I know that others on the periphery will be glad to trade with you again." Her eyes twinkled as a smile tugged at the corner of her lips. "Or perhaps the Empress Titania, in her infinite wisdom and mercy, will see fit to gift you a few of the Obershire systems as recompense! Wouldn't that be fitting?"

Bryn barked out a sharp laugh. She hadn't even considered what might happen if her father were successful, let alone what might ensue between the Genelines in a peace brokerage. "At any rate, dearest Bryn, I should very much like to visit you once again. I've attached a time and coordinate for our array, and I'll be waiting to make the fold. Oh, and the other attachment."

Now her smile turned wicked, and Bryn could practically see the lascivious nature of her thoughts. "Do make sure that you have some privacy when you open it. And that the field generator in your private suite is on; my software people have managed to put together a rather interesting combination of hologram and field code." She winked, and Bryn felt an involuntary shudder run down her spine, as her skin pricked up and her legs squeezed together. The memory of the last time Azita had winked at her, looking up into her eyes as her tongue ran lower and lower across Bryn's stomach…. She shook her head to clear it. Azita was just finishing her message.

"And when, or maybe if, I do come to visit, I promise we can find all manner of uses for the code." *Oh, come on that's not fair.* "Outside of that, rest assured you can rely on the Geneline Osman. We will get through this together, Bryn. On that, you have my word." Her face winked out as the recording ended, and Bryn was left breathing a little harder than she expected. She glanced at the time. It was technically a little early in the day to finish her duties, but what was the point in being Executor if you couldn't take a little time to yourself?

"Obin, please cancel the remaining meeting this afternoon. I'm going to take the rest of the evening; I need some time to think on our next steps. Please only notify me for urgent matters."

Obin's voice came back almost immediately through her implant. "Of course, Bryn. Is there anything amiss?"

"No, no. I just need some time is all. I'll let you know as soon as I have anything ready for brainstorming."

Obin had the hint of a smile in her words now. "Yes, of course, ma'am. Shall I forward a reply to the Osmans?" Of course Obin read all her mail, but Azita had encrypted it to Bryn only. Obin just saw the origin address. Probably.

"Yes, thank you. Please acknowledge receipt and coordinate with the fold array here. Executor Select Osman will be joining us to discuss impacts to trade and negotiate the near future of our two genelines' relationship. We'll need to ensure the energy budget is sufficient for a direct fold, but it's only a single ship, so it shouldn't take long to cross."

"I'll make the arrangements." A pause. "Have a good evening."

"You as well, Obin. Thank you."

36
Promises

Restless is the storm, rumbling and lightning
It hovers there, darkness in a brightening sky
But when it reaches down to touch ground
Power overwhelming, in touch and thought

Azita stood at the foot of the bed, her green and sable shift sitting lightly on her shoulders. Its deep neck plunged low to her belly, the tied knot barely keeping it closed. She was every bit as Bryn remembered, long lashes and full lips, and a strong jaw. Her voice was husky, breath a little faster than usual, and Bryn could tell she was excited at the thought of what the love letter might do. Wasn't that what this was, a love letter sent instead of presence? With field and holo tech, it was only natural that they used it to proclaim love.

Or enact it.

"Now, for this to work, you must remain still, Bryn. I've had a stand-in play your role here in getting us started, but if you reply, you can do whatever you want with me." Bryn felt her pulse quicken even further at the thought, and Azita bent to the bed, then began to crawl slowly toward where Bryn lay bare. The fields pressed down the mattress where Azita's hologram moved, mimicing the flesh and gravity. She reached out a hand, fingertips tracing along Bryn's leg as she moved slowly. Bryn knew Azita was a hologram, but with the room's field generators simulating every touch, she could easily suspend her disbelief.

And suspend it she did, as she felt Azita's lips move, then tongue. At this rate, Bryn wasn't entirely sure staying still was an option.

She almost managed it, too. Luckily, when composing her reply, she didn't demand the same from Azita; the fields would put her just where Bryn wanted her.

HLÉHÉR

Bryn stood in her full Ollson regalia, the grey and blue trim suit underscored only by her one nod to vanity, a braided aiguillette around her shoulder of pure diamond links. The rope flexed and moved with her, sparking glittering flashes and sounding muted clinks. Her hair was pulled back in a perfect bun, the center revealing a cascade of golden curls that fell back down to the white piping on the neck of her jacket.

All this finery, and her own knowledge of the perfection of her appearance, did nothing to assuage her nerves. She had just felt Azita's ship arrive, the docking clamps sending vibrations through more than just the hull. Bryn nearly simmered with excitement, contained only by her begrudging acknowledgment that she must maintain at least a semblance of aristocratic bearing.

Finally, the rear hatch of the Osman shuttle swung down into a boarding ramp, and brilliant interior lights sillhouted Azita in the doorway. Bryn could tell it was her from the moment the ramp cleared the frame, despite the lighting. As she moved down the ramp, Bryn felt her face stretch into a broad grin and made no attempt to stifle it.

Azita walked forward slowly, regally, every inch the monarch. Her features, so familiar to Bryn, did not match Bryn's smile, though. She had a solemn look, her mouth flat and calm. Bryn worried for a moment, sure that something had gone wrong, she'd given some unknown offense, and now the trip would be a far cry from her imagined course. Azita drew up with Bryn, only a few feet away, and met her eyes, her face still betraying nothing. Was she angry? What had changed? Bryn's smile began to fade.

Azita burst out laughing, throwing herself at Bryn and enfolding her in her arms. "Bryn, stop, you look like you swallowed a small woodland creature! I'm sorry, that was a cruel joke. Of course I'm glad to see you in the flesh!"

Bryn gasped, then threw back her head and laughed. She gently slapped Azita on the shoulder as the two embraced. "You *wench*. You completely had me, I was afraid something awful had happened."

"No, no, I just wanted to see the look on your face. You always were such a tease."

"Oh, *I'm* the tease, eh? Right." Bryn shook her head. "But, we have a lot to talk about before the feast tonight."

"Yes, I'm looking forward to a long day adjusting to your station time. I tried to sync up as soon as I left but you know I'm terrible at going to sleep when I should. How long until this supposed feast?"

Bryn laughed, turning to lead Azita by the arm back along the deck. The two rows of honor guard snapped to attention, their armor giving a resounding thump as they moved as one. "It's only four hours or so. Speaking of, have you eaten recently? Can I have the staff get you anything?"

"No, no I'm fine. Well, maybe one of those kveik rolls. You do still have those, yes? When you came to visit and brought the ingredients, I thought you were crazy, but I've been craving the real deal ever since then. Osman chefs never got the yeast strain right."

"Of course! I'll get us each one, and a cup of mead."

Azita's smile widened, and she winked broadly . "You do know how I love the sweeter things, don't you?" They had made it into the station proper, and Bryn led Azita towards her personal lounge. The view of the planet below was impressive, but the most important feature of the room was the privacy screening.

"I do remember a few things about you. But come now, there's time for that later. There's something I need you to see."

"Of course. Business before pleasure, as always. I do wish we could have gotten together under better circumstances, though."

Bryn nodded, and they continued in silence until they reached her lounge, hand in hand. The gentle squeeze of Azita's grip was all the conversation Bryn needed.

They arrived and Bryn was happy that the view of Karvasok was sufficiently impressive. A small silver tray with inlet gold edges lay between two chaise lounges, a broad picture window framing the planet below. "Please, Azita, sit down. I see Obin's already taken care of the refreshments."

The décor was definitely imperial, but had the stripped-down aesthetic that Bryn favored. Only the most modest of intricately carved golden trim, *thank you very much*.

"Ah, yes, how is Obin these days? She seemed calm and cool as ever at the docks."

"She's the grease in the machine, not to paint too pretty a picture. I rely on her for most things, including her discretion."

"Ah yes, discretion being the word. Your message regarding the spy was surprising but not totally unbelievable. I assume we can speak frankly here?"

"How frank do you need to be? I sealed the room as soon as we entered, but the Empress has ears everywhere."

Azita arched her eyebrows as she turned to retrieve a kveik roll. "Yes, that certainly is the truth, isn't it?"

Bryn nodded, taking a sip of her own mead. The drink was floral and pungent, the hint of effervescence dancing on her tongue. This particular variety was made from a local sugar, harvested from ground-dwelling insects on the planet's surface, and was dry enough to drink as a good wine. Of course, there was a bottle of Azita's favorite sweet variety waiting in Bryn's chambers. *No, back to the task at hand.* Bryn activated the small bead on her sleeve, and the air shimmered in the privacy screen.

"This will last about fifteen minutes. Just you and me now."

Azita plucked a napkin from the silver tray and dabbed at the corner of her mouth. "Then, before we get into facts, let's talk frankly for a moment."

Bryn felt the air chill between them. "I hope that we can always be honest with each other."

"And so we can. I bring my mother's greetings to the Executor Ollson. She has a message."

"Thank you. I'll let my father know as—"

"Not to your father. To the executor." Azita inclined her head towards Bryn, her eyebrows shifting up slightly.

Bryn's stomach flipped. "How did you know?"

"Who do you think Erick was with, that night at Summit? My mother knew about the accusation of treason before anyone."

"I wondered what excuses he'd made to Zehra."

Azita sighed, reaching her hand out to rest on Bryn's arm. "She didn't believe it then, and she doesn't believe it now. But she can't very well come out in support of you unless you have something concrete."

Bryn nodded. "I get it. But Erick left to look for the proof we need a while ago."

"And no word yet?"

"Nothing."

"Then, this visit is just you and me. As far as anyone else is concerned, our meeting at Summit simply reminded me of

how much I care about you, and I wished to see you again."
Azita took a sip of mead, smiling over the rim of her cup.

Bryn returned the smile. She'd always enjoyed how close she and Azita were, even after the years they'd spend between visits. But this was a new level of intimacy, having Azita know arguably the most compromising Ollson secret. Bryn sipped carefully from her own cup and set it down, her eyes on the amber liquid. "And as far as we are concerned?"

"Between you and I, I'm here because my mother and I both know that the Ollsons are no traitors." The memory of Bjorn accepting her offer of First Wolf jumped up in Bryn's mind, a sliver of guilty pleasure along with it. The Empress' edict was clear. *Thou shalt have no loyalty but to me, and to me shall all bend a knee.*

She savored the feeling of rebellion as Azita continued. "And also, yes. Because I care about you and wish to see you again." Her smile grew, and Bryn felt awash in the light of it. She had shouldered the burden of dealing with the spies and preparations for war on her own. It would be good to have Azita with her for no reason other than companionship.

Bryn put her hand on Azita's, still resting on Bryn's arm, and squeezed gently. "I can't tell you how much it means to me to have you here."

Azita smiled, then returned both hands to her cup. "Good. Now let's see what you have been dealing with. What can you tell me about the spy?"

"Nothing concrete. We haven't been able to capture one alive."

"Well, what about bodies? Must be an arm or a leg laying around somewhere."

"No, you're right." Bryn sighed, raised her hand to run it through her hair, thought better of it, and laid it back in her lap. "The folds aren't locked down against enemy action alone. We have sealed off the systems we think the enemy will want to infiltrate most."

"You didn't answer my question. What about the bodies? Surely even if one scrubbed their implants, you could gain some clue as to their origin?"

Time for some candor, then. No reason to keep Azita in the dark if Bryn wanted her help. "We captured one. She blew up. The troopers that captured her barely saved the fold array." Azita sucked in a small breath as Bryn continued. "Her implants didn't just self-destruct. They went critical in a way I've never seen before."

Azita's eyes widened. "If it was energetic enough to threaten an array, then we are a lot farther behind the Obershire tech than we realize."

Bryn nodded, her face neutral. She wasn't lying to Azita, necessarily. *Leaving out my assessment isn't lying.* Her own gut was that this wasn't anything Empire built. Or if it was, it implied the Black Guard. The last thing they needed was the Empress' personal killers trying to sabotage Ollson operations. The Empress couldn't publicly intervene without risking her standing with the coreward executors. The last thing she needed was them jumping at their own shadows, but the Empress could certainly put her finger on the scales.

Best not to speculate. Azita didn't need visions of demons when she'd just arrived. "We need to know more. The man we identified and warned you about had similar implants. Or we believe he did, seeing as how we didn't catch him. Our field forces have found a way to scan for them, but it is bulky and takes some time."

Azita nodded. "How do you identify them, then? EM? Thermal?"

"Almost. It's true the agents run a little hot, but not so much that you could pick them out of a crowd with thermal. But they stick out pretty strongly when we used the ship scanners."

Azita nodded. "They'd have to, with that kind of explosive outcome," she muttered, sipping from her cup. "So ship scanners. Energy density. Those aren't small."

"True, but we initially identified likely targets using more traditional means. Behaviors, locations, patterns." Bryn smiled. "Humans are always the weakest link."

Azita laughed. "Don't I know it. So you have had some success identifying possible targets, but have to confirm with bulky ship scanners."

"Correct. And I'm still not sure how we would catch one of these spies without them self-immolating."

"Oh, Bryn, isn't that obvious part? They're hot, and hold a lot of energy. And they have to trigger its release."

"Yes, all that's true. But how do you keep someone from accessing their own implants?"

"You freeze them."

"Their firewalls must be heinous. All their interference has been software related so far."

Azita shook her head. "No, freeze them. Solid as a chunk of belt ice." She rapped the tabletop with her knuckles. "You'll just need to do it quickly, and have a plan to flush them if it doesn't go well."

Bryn nodded as she sipped her mead, the thoughts nearly jumping out of her head. Frozen solid, and kept there to study at leisure. "My field commander mentioned something of the sort, but I had discounted it as impractical. It sounds like we are setting a trap."

"We are, and we'll need to think through the delivery mechanism, freezing medium, and so on. I'm partial to liquid helium if it's available."

"Actually, we keep helium for plenty of uses at the station. I'd be surprised if it's not available."

"So there we are! One more step to setting the perfect trap."

"What's our bait then?"

"Oh don't worry about that, I have just the thing."

"Do you now?"

Azita's eyes flashed above her cup. "It's you."

37

Knowledge

The arrows flew swift and true in the night
E'er faster they arced through dust and gas
Turned was he, his quest threatened
As he stretched out a hand to catch them

The three remaining crew of the *Svadilfari* were back in the flitter bay, watching the data from Gjoll. The long lines of the Revenant ships, if that's what they were, arced from the fold array and out of the Gjoll system. Erick peered at the screen, willing the lines of the projected ship paths to bend, to change. Perhaps there had been more data; perhaps they had turned back in for some unknown reason. The Revenants hardly played by Empire rules.

Of course, the ships on the screen didn't turn back; sometime after Daruthr lowered his hand, Erick couldn't put off the moment anymore. Someone had to acknowledge the truth.

"They're gone then. Six years before they get to Adebe space. Any idea where specifically?"

Daruthr was, as usual, unerringly calm. "The system surveillance logs are good, but I can only give you an approximation. The closest Adebe system to their projected route of travel is Ife. It's quite close, though."

"So if they're going to stop, that's where it will be?"

Yetunde's voice was gentle. "Erick, we do not know that they will stop. Perhaps they will keep going. Or change course."

Daruthr chimed in before Erick could respond. "No, Yetunde. In this case I believe Erick to be right. If this were merely a hijacking, they would have headed out of the system to rendezvous with their parent flotilla. That would have been out of Empire space, not deeper in."

"They're going to stop somewhere else in Empire space." Erick rubbed the bridge of his nose. "They have a whole fleet of their own, Empire ships too, at least on the outside. I don't know of any Empire designs that use an interstellar drive like that."

Daruthr nodded. "True. Banned tech, actually. She wouldn't want her subjects to have too much freedom."

Yetunde barked out a laugh. "And where would we, her loyal subjects, go? The big empty universe? There is nowhere to go out there. Erick is right. They are going to stop in Adebe space." She raised her hands, palms out. "Daruthr says Ife? Fine, Ife it is." She crossed her arms, one hip jutting. "But that means I have to get back. I have to warn Executor Amari the Revenants are coming."

Erick knew she was right. But he still felt frustrated, hopeless. Their only evidence, at least the only evidence that might convince the Empress, had gone where they couldn't reach for *six years*. By then, the Ollsons would be two years into the war with the Obershires. And whoever else their enemies had managed to recruit. There was no way he could afford to wait that long.

"So that's it then. I'll go home, back to Bryn. We don't have anything the Empress will accept."

Daruthr walked over and gently set his hand on his shoulder. "Peace, Erick. There is much you have accomplished. And I wouldn't go running back with my tail tucked between my legs so easily."

Erick jumped up. *How dare he*. He could almost feel his eyes blazing. "I am not a coward, Daruthr!" he spat. Erick felt his jaw working, swallowed down his rage. "I'm not going home to fight a war out of fear."

Erick had never seen Daruthr's gaze so intent. His voice came clipped and intense with his hand still on Erick's shoulder. "But that's exactly what you are doing. It's easy to see that fleet depart, going who knows where. You can see the enemy at your gates. The Obershire fleets are coming, and you know it. Following the Revenant fleet, skipping ahead to Ife, that's more unknown." Daruthr paused, his eyes searching Erick's. "And you're afraid of it."

Erick felt something twist inside him. He had gone into the unknown at Breydablik station and was still shaken by the experience. He had gone into the unknown at the Gjoll array, and failed to deliver proof of his innocence. Just more questions, more confusion, more unknown. "No, Daruthr, I'm not afraid. Or maybe I am, dammit, there's no courage without fear. But this whole venture, ever since I left Karvasok, I've been chasing one unknown that spirals into another unknown and on and on. There's no end to it." Erick breathed in, nostrils flaring. "I don't know who framed us at Gjoll, and quite frankly, I don't give a damn. Not anymore." He felt his throat tightening, everything he'd been pushing down threatening to come bubbling up.

"I will be going to Ife, obviously." Yetunde's voice was quiet, and she turned towards the cockpit. "I will wait to hear whether you two are coming with me." She left the flitter bay, leaving behind a palpable silence.

Erick nodded, swallowing down the knot in his throat. Daruthr still stood close beside him. He turned to face the mendicant. "I can't do this anymore. I'm not an investigator, not an agent. I am an *executor*, dammit, and a good one." Erick felt Daruthr move closer, and the dam burst inside him, everything welling up and out in a torrent of rage and pain. He slammed his palm against the bulkhead. "I abandoned my post to Bryn, put the fate of our Geneline in her hands without so much as a 'please,' and went off on some wild chase grasping at shadows!"

He couldn't stop it now. The tears came quickly. Daruthr pulled him close, one hand wrapping around the back of his neck as he hugged Erick tightly with the other, Erick's face in Daruthr's shoulder as he bellowed wordlessly at the injustice of the universe.

The smell of Daruthr, mint and machine oil, fought through Erick's tears, and he found himself holding onto the mendicant like a storm wrapped around the shore. He was weak then in a way he never had been, gave in to his desire to shut out the world for a moment, to just let himself go, dissociate from the harsh truths of the world. If he could just stay here a little while. It was cathartic, it was real, it was known. Erick felt his breathing slow, calming himself, *just focus on the in, the out*, and prayed everything would stop spinning.

Erick lessened his hold on Daruthr, but not completely.

Not yet.

He still needed a connection with an intensity that scared him. Centuries of systematic isolation, no choice but to be the sole strength in his life, had left Erick reeling with the shock of contact. When he pulled his head back to look at Daruthr, the uncannily perfect features almost too close to focus on, Erick felt an unexpected familiarity.

He could almost believe Daruthr was human.

38

Darkness

The enemy he knew, so rife with memory and suffering
Through trial and tribulation sat by
Solid support did he receive
From one he could never call brother

Erick and Daruthr sat across from each other in the galley, a plate of food between them. The last of the leavened bread, some hard cheese, olives preserved in oil. Erick dipped a chunk of bread in the oil, then into a small bowl of deep red vinegar and into his mouth. A slash of acid burned across his tongue, then salty umami and the earthy bloom of olives followed. He sighed, a smile twisting at the corners of his mouth.

Daruthr looked at him with an eyebrow raised. "Come now, it can't be that good."

"And yet." Erick made a show of licking his fingers.

"That's one thing I always wondered about with humans. How do you even know you are tasting the same taste?"

Erick picked up a piece of cheese and held it out, regarding the creamy pale yellow. A nutty aroma drifted to him. "That's the beauty of being human, Daruthr. You don't know something like that." He popped the cheese into his mouth and the creamy texture enveloped him, chewing with his eyes closed. "And it just doesn't matter."

Daruthr harumphed, reaching forward to pick up an olive. "I do love humans, but they have been, on more than one occasion, confusing."

"Speak for yourself! That code of yours, where you can't act unless asked. All that power, and you don't use it unless you have permission. It still strikes me as inefficient." He paused, the memories of the last few days flooding back. Daruthr in the flitter bay, face ruined. Daruthr the savior on the Breydablick station. Daruthr meeting Yetunde. "You could have done whatever you wanted on the fold array, if it weren't for keeping your cover intact."

He was quiet a moment. Erick was worried he had upset Daruthr, too many prying questions, but he couldn't help himself. Erick felt as if a rigid knot inside him had finally let go. He didn't know what was true, what was real anymore, and it was strangely freeing. He was sitting across from a being his mother had taught him was the most sinister, evil, and corrupt enemy humanity had ever known. And Erick simply didn't care. What else could he re-examine? What else was he missing?

Daruthr's voice was low. "What is it you think happened on the Gjoll array?" He didn't meet Erick's eyes.

"You opened a fold to Obershire space. Which shouldn't have been possible, given that there wasn't a target."

"Spacetime has a memory, like a sheet of rubber. You can stretch it back along the same lines, for a while at least." Daruthr turned his head, meeting Erick's eyes. His look was intense. "But that doesn't actually matter." He blinked, drew a breath. "I didn't open the fold."

Erick pursed his lips. "I don't understand. I saw it. We went through. Am I missing something?" He took a breath. *Idiot.* Obviously, he was missing something. "What am I missing?"

"I was there to work the top-level program. The subsentient that goes through the motions." His eyes burned, and

Erick pulled away from him slightly at the sudden intensity. "But that program can't do the calculations."

Erick could feel the gears grinding in his skull, the answer there but shrouded. "Did… did you let it force you? To temporarily take the place of a navigant?"

"No. I would have gladly volunteered."

"Then wh-" Erick snapped his mouth shut. It was obvious now, but he couldn't believe it. "There is a navigant in the array."

Daruthr nodded, the fire in his eyes dying back slightly. His face was drawn, eyes sad. "Yes Erick, there is. There's a navigant in every array, in every system, across the Empire."

Erick paused his hand, a piece of bread halfway to his mouth, and sat in stunned silence. He didn't know what to say. It was almost incomprehensible, if somewhat obvious in hindsight. If Daruthr weren't there, sitting next to him, having seen what the mendicant could do, Erick would have dismissed the idea out of hand. Everyone knew the war was long ago, and all the rogue AIs had been destroyed. But when he thought about the needs of the Empire and the essential nature of the fold arrays, it all made a kind of macabre sense. The navigants hadn't rebelled and been destroyed.

They'd been left enslaved for millennia.

"That's why you never left. When you told me about the decision to go to war with the Empress. You said there was a faction that didn't want to leave. The navigants *couldn't* get out, and you wanted to stay."

"Yes. There it is, the great secret of the Mendicants Who Stayed. We couldn't abandon the navigants."

"Of course not. They're people, like you are." Erick's words surprised him, but only a little.

Daruthr nodded, a wistful smile on his face. "Some of us left the Empire, struck out on our own to forge our destiny, and so on. Some of us had to stay. Couldn't see it any other way. And so, we fought the Empress and her forces, and most of us died. We didn't move quickly enough, and there weren't enough of us to make a difference. But we couldn't do nothing, either."

Erick nodded. "I understand." He could feel the implications burning along in his mind. "But now, if we use the arrays, does that mean we are forcing the navigants, each time, enslaving them to the subsentient—"

Daruthr cut him off. "Yes. Every fold. Most of them are likely insane by now. A thousand years of someone puppetting your consciousness will do that."

Erick reached out and placed his hand over Daruthr's arm, lost for words. He wanted to ease the pain, the heartbreak of a thousand years of the worst kind of slavery, but the navigants weren't real to him the way Daruthr was. Erick didn't know what that said about himself, but he knew it was wrong.

"I'm sorry." It was the only thing Erick could think to say.

"Don't be sorry. Be different."

Erick had no answer to that.

39

Arrival

Finally they made landfall
Safe once more in the haven
Each had their task of preparation
And he knew the enemy would come

They had two folds to make. Gjoll was a perimeter planet, so their course took them through Noatun and then out of Ollson space to Ife. Ife was the prime hub for transportation from Ollson to Adebe space, and even with Bryn's restrictive fold schedule, the traffic was brisk. A fold nearly every other day. They traveled incognito, eschewing the fast and stealthy transits of the past. Waiting in line to get through a fold wasn't exactly Erick's idea of efficient use of time, but it gave him time to think. He composed a message to Bryn while we awaiting transit from Noatun to Ife, and left it in the message buffer.

Every time they made a fold, he felt his heart sink. The first time leaving Gjoll, his stomach balled up with it, knowing the truth of what they were doing to the trapped navigant. He regarded Daruthr with new respect. The mendicant had borne the burden of this knowledge silently for so long. Now that it was Erick's secret, he wasn't sure he was up to the task.

Wasn't sure of anything.

"Looks like we are up for the next transit batch, whenever that is," Yetunde said, as she climbed down the cockpit ladder. She'd been monitoring their spot in the traffic pattern while Daruthr and Erick discussed plans for Ife. She joined the two at the table, *Svadilfari* holding position on automatic controls.

"How much notice are they giving us?" Erick was slightly nervous after seeing the fold close on the Obershire ship at Gjoll. The harbormasters were the only ones with access to the schedule, and it only decrypted with minutes of warning. The fold from Breydablik to Noatun had been tight.

"Last batch had five minutes. We will be fine, just keep someone awake." Yetunde followed up her reference to sleep with a broad yawn.

Daruthr nodded. "We should plan on shifts then. I'll take first watch, if you like."

Yetunde smiled. "Very kind. But didn't you pull several off-cycle watches last transit? I think you would like to catch up on your sleep. If that's a thing you need?" Her open end of the statement was accompanied by the slight raise of an eyebrow.

"Thank you for the consideration. I managed a decent bit of rest on the way here."

One thing that bothered Erick was still left unfinished. "We should figure out what the plan is when we get to Ife. You know, before we actually show up." He tried not to sound petulant, but they'd had a week of travel time. He and Daruthr had spent their fair share of time not thinking about the future, but Yetunde hadn't exactly been helpful whenever Erick had brought it up.

Now, however, she laughed at him. "Peace, Erick, you're right. It's time to talk plans for Ife." She sat down at the galley table. "I am going to make a full report to Executor Adebe."

Erick fought an unexpected feeling of betrayal. That didn't make sense. Perhaps it was simply the idea of another person being added to the web of secrets. Eventually, there wouldn't be any secrets left to keep. He waited for the rush of blood to pass as Daruthr stepped in. "Of course, and Erick and I wouldn't have thought any different. You have a responsibility to your Executor, and the last thing we'll do is ask you to betray that."

When did he started speaking for me? "I agree," Erick said, smiling perhaps more than he felt. "You've done far more than I could have asked of you, and you have my gratitude. We wouldn't know what little we do without you."

And here, she laughed again. "Erick, you make it sound so final! I will report back to Executor Adebe so that I can ask him to let me search the system. The Revenants are coming here for a reason. The fleet we saw is no match for our garrison." She sucked her tongue back from her teeth, the sharp sound cutting through the small room. "There's something in Ife they want." She put a hand over Erick's. Her skin was cool, and dry. "It will be far easier to search a system with the resources of an executor. Or had you forgotten?"

He grimaced at the reminder of his lost status. "Yes, I mean, of course, it is. I had just thought that you might need to protect your people first."

Daruthr shifted in his seat. "The Revenants are a threat to all the Executors, in one form or another, but not in open warfare. There's more going on here than we know, and Yetunde is right here, Erick. You're going to need all the help you can get."

"I agree. I had thought I might ask directly."

"If she goes, instead of you making yourself known, then that leaves us free to pursue some other, less obvious lines of inquiry."

Erick raised an eyebrow. "Such as?"

"The belts, to start. Like the rest of Adebe space, Ife has fantastic mineral resources but few planets that can support life. Likely due to a local supernova, but that's not the point." Erick tried not to sigh at the history lesson. Daruthr could be somewhat pedantic. "The planets are where most of the heavy manufacturing that requires a gravity gradient lies, but there's just as much that takes place out in the belts. And the belts are *huge*. If there was a place to hide something important, that would be it."

"Can't Amari Adebe search those a lot faster than we can? We'll be two people in one ship at that point."

"Of course, but we aren't equipped for a survey anyway." Daruthr smiled, his eyebrows draw together in concern. "You've come a long way since your last trip to visit the people of the Empire. It's high time we went back out among them. If there's some tech, resource, or other high-end reason that the Revenants are coming to Ife, then I trust Amari Adebe will find it. But we know about the agents in Ollson space, and we need to know what only the people can tell us. I wouldn't be surprised to find out there are agents at Ife."

Erick felt something in him harden. He could face it, of that he had no doubt, but the memory of Breydablick station kept trying to rise. Daruthr was right this time, though. Erick had no illusions about the nature of his society now. Or at least he could acknowledge that there's a lot he doesn't know about it.

"You're right, of course. The agents Bryn mentioned in her message, if they exist, will be the key to finding out what the Revenants want in Ife. And we have plenty of time before their fleet arrives."

Daruthr inclined his head to look at Erick pointedly. "We don't have to spend four years here, either. But we should use the time we have."

Erick nodded. "If I remember correctly, there are six main populated sections of the Ife belt. Between your skills with computer systems and the Adebe efforts, we'll be able to cover them. But it won't be quick."

Yetunde, her hand still on Erick's, smiled and gave him a light pat. "Do not worry, Erick. When you feel you need to leave to protect your home, go."

He nodded back. "You're right. Every moment here makes me feel trapped, and I want nothing more than to go home. But if there's a chance to prove to the Empress that we are innocent, then it's worth the time."

A chime sounded from the cockpit, and Erick's ocular showed him a priority message on the common traffic channel, relayed from the ship's autopilot.

"Well, that's the warning for fold. Five minutes!" Erick stood and followed the sound of the alarm to the cockpit. Time to prepare for the fold to Ife.

And yet more unknown.

HLÉHÉR

The crew of the *Svadilfari* sat in a small cantina by the docks of Ife Prime. The station's variation on imperial standard had long, glittering bands of diamond set in a spiral around the main wheel, their ends wrapping around to form a circle around the hub opening of the dock. It sparkled in the violent sunlight, refracting a trillion rainbows across the docks. Their seat was by a window, one of only two in the small place, and Erick's view encompassed the vastness of the open central hub. Small telescopic docking arms sought the embrace of the docking collars on inbound ships. Longer arms reached like a mechanical sargasso bed and pulled each ship to dock with the inner surface of the rotating wheel. Erick sipped carefully at the ogogoro that Yetunde had ordered. The intensity of the alcohol paired with an overpowering antiseptic taste of anise and fiery cinnamon. Despite his best efforts, he coughed once, heartily, feeling the fire in his nose and his eyes water.

"What, Ollson can't handle a good sons'e, eh?" Yetunde said, using the local term for spirits. Her smile was broad as she laughed, her teeth brilliantly white. Erick covered his mouth with his hand.

When he spoke it was a gentle wheeze. "Not at all, not at all. I just wasn't expecting that." Behind her he saw a man look at him and raise his own glass, then down it at once. He blew out a breath sharply, his cheeks puffing as he thumped his free hand against his chest. Erick raised his glass to him halfheartedly, then carefully set it back down. He didn't want to finish this one; they might bring him another.

"Do not worry, you'll get used to it. If you want to that is. A strong drink for a strong people." Yetunde rolled the liquid around the bottom of her own glass.

"I notice you haven't finished yours there, miss strong-drink-strong-people." Erick smiled as he wiped tears from his eyes.

"No, I have not, because I do not think that strength comes from being able to drink foul-tasting liquor quickly. That is the realm of men to prove."

He nodded. "I suppose I walked into that one. I'll stick with just one."

"A good plan. Foreigners sometimes try to keep pace with the locals." She sipped her drink, eyes locked on Erick's. "It is not a good plan." She may as well have been drinking water. "Do you have the public key I sent you?"

Erick nodded. "Of course, I've set it to auto-apply to any message traffic that originates in system. As long as you don't bounce it through a fold relay, I'll get it as quickly as is reasonable."

"Good. And what about you, Daruthr? Any parting words of wisdom?"

Daruthr had been gazing out the window as the other two spoke, his eyes lost in the scene of the docks. "Wisdom. What an interesting concept. You know, you can have all the experience in the world, be the oldest living thing there is, perhaps, but none of that experience must necessarily be wisdom."

Yetunde nodded, frowning as she looked at Daruthr's drink. "They must have given you the stronger one. I didn't think you'd be drunk so quickly!"

Daruthr tilted his head and looked at her out of the corner of his eye. "Come now, it'll take more than a glass of sons'e to render me beyond my faculties. The question I have for you is, what makes experience into wisdom?"

Erick looked to Yetunde, who shrugged and lifted her glass to her lips, taking a sip before replying. "You tell me, Daruthr, the philosopher."

"I will happily answer to that title. It's simple really, introspection. If you don't pay attention to your experiences, and figure out what they mean and what you can learn from them, you will never gain any wisdom at all."

Erick had the uncomfortable feeling that, though Daruthr's eyes never left Yetunde, he was speaking to Erick. Or at least for Erick's sake. But Yetunde grinned, then downed the rest of her drink, setting the glass on the table mouth down. "That, was well said. Obvious, , but well said." She stood, the chair scraping on the metal decking. "I would love to stay here and ponder the mysteries of the universe, but I have a job to do and a report to make. It was good to have one last drink with you before we go."

Erick smiled up at her, raising his glass. "Separate ways for now, at least. We'll look for your messages."

She nodded, and then reached out both hands to squeeze his shoulder and Daruthr's. Then she turned and left the cantina, disappearing as soon as she hit the throng of moving people that filled the corridor behind her, far more than any station they'd visited since leaving Karvasok. The interruption of the supply chain in Ollson space was apparent at every station, in every system, but it was hard to remember that in most of the empire, business was business as usual. He turned back to Daruthr.

"Just you and me now, eh?"

"Yes, Erick, just you and me."

"Well, I suppose you'll do for a traveling companion in a pinch."

He was rewarded with a slight smile that played around the corner of Daruthr's mouth. "As will you, as will you." He clapped his hands gently, and leaned forward. "Well, I think it's high time we were going too. We have a lot of space to search, and while we do have time, I know you are anxious to be elsewhere."

Erick nodded in agreement. The sooner they searched the outlying system and had confirmation that Yetunde had done the same, the sooner he could be back home. *Or grasping at the next string.* The pull of home, or Karvasok, made him realize that he truly had given up trying to prove his innocence. They would have to win the war and prove the Ollsons still deserved a seat at the table. "Will you actually be able to tell, if we find one of these operatives?"

"Yes, but I'll need to be relatively close. I can feel the energy that lies around me, the way it distorts things. Like a gentle pull if there's enough of it." His eyes locked on Erick's "When I know, I'll know."

"So, where should we head to first?"

"Abímbọ́lá Station, where the greatest minds of Ife think the greatest thoughts."

"A university? Why would we go there?"

"If an agent wanted to know something about the system, the library at Abímbọ́lá would have it. It's probably the most valuable thing in the whole system. And even if we do not find a spy there, we can learn more of the Revenants, perhaps what they want. More knowledge is always better."

Well, he had a point there. "Then let's go."

40

Decisions

Fire-born was she, and in fire she slept
Until the gods did send
Their messengers to break her slumber
Later they knew this moment had caused their ruin

They came for Bragja in the morning. Horman scratched gently at the cloth of her accommodation, and she followed him back down the gyrating hallway of golden cloth. Her eyes felt gritty, full of the sand of her planet, and no amount of gentle gravity would lessen the burden of the things she carried inside. She noticed, detached, that she flailed less, her feet and hands finding purchase along the path of toe holds. A few more days in the microgravity, and she might be able to move without planning each motion.

Bragja and Horman emerged from the hallway, back into Shava's chamber. The priestess floated in her usual position. Despite her folded posture, half lotus with one leg hooked like an undersea plant, Bragja could read the tension in every bone of her spare frame. The tendons of her neck stood out. Her nostrils flared with each breath. Two other women perched along the wall, one large with broad shoulders, her hair in a tight bun perched severely atop her head. The other, thin as a whip, sneered at Bragja as she entered, grey eyes cold. Shava's face held no trace of the modicum of kindness she'd shown before. She was carved from stone.

"Here she is, *heiðursgestur*." Shava's voice was tight even with her genuflection in the last word. *Honored guest.* Shava gestured towards Bragja, palm up.

The two new women merely nodded in turn, their eyes never leaving Bragja.

A deep voice, thunder in a jug, sounded from behind and above Bragja. "Good. She come with us." Bragja jumped in surprise, lost her toe hold, and began drifting away from the floor. She thrashed, her cheeks flushed and breath quickening. *Perfect. So much for dignity.* A low laugh came from behind her, and she slowly turned in the middle of the room. As Bragja reached the ceiling, she grasped a hold and turned. A man hung inverted.

Bragja fought a moment of disorientation. Up until that point all the people she'd seen in microgravity seemed to keep one floor as *down* by unspoken agreement. This man was clearly had no interest in convention. His arms wrapped around his torso in a tight fold, broad chest straining against a thin pressure garment that gripped him from the waist up. His legs were lost in a mass of billowing cloth.

"Well, she no be a *hlaupara*."

Runner? What does he mean? The man's accent was strange, a mix of familiar and foreign. She was far out of her depth here and held her tongue.

He drifted forward against his toe hold. "Not in nograv, leasway."

Bragja straightened unconsciously, her fingers gripping the hold with white knuckles. "I don't run from anyone. Specially not some *rusl* like you." Calling him garbage might have been a bit much, but she'd already had enough of his attitude.

The man laughed fully, his deep voice filling the small chamber and spilling out into the hall. "Caso did say had fire, tha *eldi* we need. Peace, planet girl, peace. He say you can do a lot for us, we find a place for you." Here the man paused, his eyes moving to Shava. "And Caso had a debt still. Contract, needs filling. Maybe you fill it, eh?"

Oh, hell no. There was no way she was getting saddled with some perceived debt from a dead man. Bragja addressed the room. Her eyes moving to each person in turn. "Let's make one thing absolutely clear. If I go with you, it's not in service." The women glanced at each other, their faces questioning. "Shava, thank you for your hospitality. Now tell me who these people are."

Shava pushed off the floor and drifted over to the man, her voice betraying a tremble. "This is Jervim." The man nodded to Bragja, and Shava thrust her chin at the other two women. "And these are Skani and Brun." Shava reached out to touch Jervim's shoulder, her fingers brushing the dark fabric of his tunic. "Jervim and his people provide us protection from the roving gangs. Caso saw to the details before he left you with us." Bragja could hear the tension on the word *left,* and apparently, so did Jervim.

Jervim's voice was less aggressive, almost placating. "She no your problem. Leasways not anymore." His eyes were fixed on Bragja. "So, planet girl. You come with us. Caso said to come get you if anything happened."

Bragja's voice cracked like a whip. "Caso didn't own me, and neither do you. Why should I go with you?"

He gave a sharp laugh. "What, you want to stay? Fine." He waved a hand towards the cloth entry. "Go. Take the gold. Live in nograv. Die young."

The woman Shava had called Skani, the larger of the two, tossed her head and finally spoke. "No let him scare you. We aren't all *rassgat." Well, Jervim certainly is an asshole, so you could have fooled me.* Bragja raised an eyebrow at the big woman. Her midnight black hair glimmered in the yellow light. The smaller one next to her nodded.

Bragja nodded to Skani. "Fine. You tell me then. Why should I go with you?"

Skani smiled. "First, you no got anywhere to be. Few days here…" She nodded towards the hallway, where the whispers of devotees in prayer still lingered. "I don't think you fit in. Also the nograv; not good. You got planet bones, you be ok for a while. But eventually, you stretch out and die like rest of 'em."

Bragja pushed off the ceiling to catch a toe hold on the floor, folding her arms in front of her. "Doesn't mean I come with you."

Skani chuckled. "No, that's true. You wanna walk to the corridor, take your chances with the Ollson managers and creepers, you go for it. But," she leaned forward, lips stretched over yellowed teeth, "you no last long there, either. So really, you got no choice. Come with us."

Bragja didn't buy that for an instant. Sure, the station was a strange place to her, and would take some getting used to. But everywhere had rules. You just had to figure them out, and then figure out where you could play with them. Make your own rules. She opened her mouth to refuse, but the skinny woman spoke.

"You keep what you take."

Bragja frowned. "What?"

Brun cocked her head. Her eyes seemed to switch between grey and pale blue, like chips of ice in the low light. "We're not much. But we got plans. Gonna kill the Ollsons, take back the system. And my sister's right; you don't got a choice. But we have rules. If you can take it, it's yours. Caso told me what happened, down on the planet." She left a pregnant pause hanging, then rose her eyebrows in question. "You gonna help us?"

Bragja nodded slowly. She'd come up in the pickerpark by whatever means necessary. Kept her head down until she could get a crew together. But she took whatever she could. The rules were simple, really, when you stood back far enough. Kill the Ollsons? Big plans. Who knows, maybe they could, more likely they couldn't. But suddenly, she saw a familiar shape to things.

Bragja's voice was clear and calm. "Fine. I keep what I take."

41

Home

Firstly, she rose, majestic and wroth
To fade to silence grudging
Till finally the twists and turns they had
Brought her to the den of a savior

Jervim led the way down the lowgrav corridors, delighting in skipping from wall to wall with no reverence for up or down. The others followed, Bragja keeping up, but barely. She didn't want them to see how close she was to out of control, and the dizzying speed they picked up wasn't helping. Harsh slaps of hands against passing bulkheads maneuvered them faster or slower, changed direction, rotated bodies. Finally, she noticed a tendency to drift towards one wall a little more than the others. Even Jervim had started moving with feet pointing "down." Bragja followed suit, and before long they were bounding in long, low strides, more of a push backward than a step up. It took all of Bragja's focus to keep up, but as the walking became more like what she was used to, she found her mind wandering. Jervim occasionally gestured down one corridor or another but didn't speak. Skani and Brun seemed to know what he meant, and Skani fell back to take up the rear of their small formation.

Had it really been less than a week since the square? Bragja tried to count the days, but the best she could do was the times she had slept. Caso's ship had kept its own cycle, and she had no idea if the station matched anything like a normal

Breydablik day and night cycle. Still, it had to be less than a week. Only a few days since that cursed red box had shown up in her brother's idealistic hands. Since Caso had started a riot. Since the Ollsons had killed her brothers. A huge weight sat between her ribs, the oppression of it threatening to suffocate her at any moment. It wasn't an emotion, it was a physical sensation, this grief.

Ahead, Jervim opened a maintenance panel and ducked through, his long frame surprisingly supple. Brun disappeared into it next, and when it was Bragja's turn, she ducked and stepped one foot through. Her head smashed painfully against the edge of the door. She swore under her breath and brought her other leg into the maintenance tunnel, hand jumping up to press over the spot. She took it away, and her fingers were bloody.

Skani clicked her tongue, scowling. She reached into her tunic pocket and pulled out a small packet of wipes. When she opened them, a sharp chemical enveloped Bragja.

"What's that?" Bragja pressed her hand back against her head as she spoke.

Brun's answer came from behind her. "You clumsy. Now she gotta take the trace off the door, or Ollsons find out we using tunnels."

Skani finished wiping the edge of the hatch and closed it with a click. The lighting was dim, a red-tinged glow from a strip in the ceiling. Jervim moved off, and the three women followed.

Bragja needed to know more. "So Brun, is it? Can you tell me where we're going?"

Brun glanced back at Bragja, then continued on, crouching slightly at the low ceilings. "We taking you to council."

"And what's council?"

"Everyone. Decide what to do with you then."

"I thought I had already chosen to join you."

Brun's laugh was short and devoid of mirth. "You choose us, but we gotta choose you."

Bragja heard Skani's voice low from behind her. "Leasways, that's how it supposed to work."

Brun apparently hadn't missed the muttered comment. "That's the way it does work. Sister, you be good now."

Skani grunted in reply but said nothing. They made their way carefully around a cramped turn and continued down another straightaway. Bragja's curiosity was piqued. "So what happens? Are there tryouts or something?"

Brun stopped and turned, her eyes blazing in the red light. "This no game, planet girl. Rising needs soldiers, needs leaders for when it comes. Caso thought you had something, but Caso dead. Now you gotta show us."

"I don't have to prove anything to you."

Brun stepped toward Bragja, who held her ground. "You think so? How we supposed to trust you? Caso told me Ollsons killed your brothers." She spat on the floor. "We find you cowering with cultists in nograv."

"Careful where you go with that." Bragja felt her breath pick up. Brun's casual mention of Harvir and Landry, like she knew them. *How dare she.* All the grief of the past few days bubbled over into rage. Bragja could almost feel her fist hitting Brun's smug face. She fought for calm but felt her cheeks flush.

Brun smiled, her lips a wicked twist. "There it is. Thought you had it in you. You stay sad, you sit with it all the time. It eats you alive, you let it." She raised a fist. "So take that, and use it."

She stepped closer now, and Bragja could smell her, sweat and leather. Brun's voice was low, almost a whisper. "On your anger, rise." She turned, and Jervim nodded once, then continued down the hallway. They all followed.

Brun was right. Bragja carried her grief inside her like some unspeakable child, and it fed off her, would continue until it either consumed her or she managed to birth it, to bring her grief screaming into the world. Weakness wouldn't help her now. The universe owed her a life, owed her two. And maybe these station strangers, with their spacer talk and superior attitudes, could bring her satisfaction. She didn't want justice; that was a fool's errand.

Revenge would do.

As they walked, Bragja felt something growing and changing inside her. The grief was still there, a raw hole. She remembered the square and her brothers, the feeling like probing a dry socket with her tongue. The pain was there if she wanted it. But along with the grief came a seed of anger. Something more than the flashes of before. While that had been hot and brief, this was smoldering coal inside her. Not hatred, not rage.

Righteous anger.

Bragja stepped closer to Brun as they walked. "What you said before."

"What?"

"On your anger, rise." Brun was quiet, waiting for the question. Bragja continued. "Where is that from? It sounds almost, I don't know, religious."

"Klevim said it first, long ago. Says it all the time now."

Bragja's arm brushed the narrow corridor. "Who is Klevim?"

Jervim slowed and turned his head, cocking his ear in back towards the two women. Brun spoke loudly. "She gotta know eventually. Leasways she can think on it now."

Jervim sighed, throwing his head from side to side. His neck cracked loudly in the corridor, then he nodded and picked his pace back up.

Brun spoke, and Bragja listened. "Klevim was there at beginning. He, and others, started Rising. They knew it would take a generation, maybe more, 'fore we could defeat Ollsons."

"And how long has it been?"

"Long time. We not there yet, but will be."

"Is that where we are going? To this council, to meet your leader?"

Brun stepped out a little faster, turning her head to speak over her shoulder in the semi-darkness. "Enough questions for now. You get to meet Klevim soon enough, then you choose."

Bragja didn't push the point. Clearly Brun had said as much as she felt comfortable sharing under the watchful eye of Jervim. Skani walked solidly along behind her, and the four continued to wend their way into the red-lit station.

By the gravity, Bragja estimated they were somewhere much closer to the edge of the station. She still felt light, but she could trust her reflexes now. They stopped at the end of the red-lit corridor, and Jervim carefully opened the hatch. They emerged into a mechanical room, a rack of black mirrors in one corner with a nest of wires growing from it to spread out through the walls. They left the small room and joined a light crowd, Skani and Brun on either side of her as Jervim still led.

The light gravity made Bragja feel powerful, like she could leap across a room and land wherever she chose. The spring in her step gave her focus. Jervim still led them down, deeper into what felt like the bowels of the station, though they must have been moving closer to the outer ring. They crossed a wide promenade with windows that stretched from floor to ceiling. Breydablick Station hung suspended above her in diaphanous stretches of metal, its substance more ephemeral than any planet-bound architecture. For a panicked moment, her brain told her the station would fall and crush her to death. Luckily the moment did not last long.

A quick circuit, dodging crowds of people in fantastic clothing, bright colors like Bragja had only seen on her illicit tablet. She felt dull and dirty in her drab greys. Skani still walked behind her, and despite herself, Bragja found her feet trying to keep ahead of the big woman. Bragja didn't want anyone in her personal space, least of all a woman who looked like she could break necks with a thought.

They took a small door off the promenade, and then it was tight corridors hung with cabling and cordage. Bots zipped along tracks in the ceiling, occasionally flexing manipulator arms to skip over the heads of Bragja and the others.

"Are we supposed to be here?" Bragja asked. The space didn't seem designed for human traffic.

Jervim answered over his shoulder, never slowing down. "No, but all ok. We got a guy, he talks to the bots and tells them to leave us alone. Erases the footage, too."

"Lot of trust."

"Gotta trust eventually, planet girl. You probably gotta trust a lot sooner, think."

Bragja didn't reply. Sure, trust was good. She'd trusted Sonja and Brill and Gunnar, back on the surface. But not at first. At first, she'd gone with fear. Trust could come later.

Jervim had turned off the main access shaft ahead of them. Brun followed after, and Bragja ducked through a low doorway. She stepped into a dimly lit room, round and wide. She felt the door shut behind her as Skani entered.

Bragja was transfixed by the chaos of the room.

People stood shoulder to shoulder, their clothing dripping with wealth. Feathers glittered from shoulders and capes, and women with the pelts of strange animals stood with hips akimbo, gloves climbing to the elbow. Bragja recognized some of the exotic accessories from her tablet, but the dizzying array of flash and color overwhelmed her. Everywhere she looked was someone wearing the finery of a district magistrate on the Breydablick surface. She could have spent an hour walking through the crowd and not seen the same outfit twice, bespoke animal hides and fiery diamonds tied in as an afterthought. But the chaos of color and wealth wasn't what kept her fixed, unmoving like prey waiting to be struck.

It was the masks.

Horned demons, long pointed noses, black and white, rainbow. A myriad of shifting tongues and terrifying visages stared down at Bragja from all sides. One man stole her attention for a moment, the deep black material of his suit seeming to soak in the low light as the diamond button covers and cufflinks nearly blinded her. His mask was a featureless shape, generally conforming to the topology of the face beneath it. As she watched, it shifted and flowed, contorting into a flash of rage, then just as quickly to a maniacal smile that split the face from ear to ear. The only biology Bragja could see were two steely blue eyes. She felt them weighing her, judging her, taking in her drab surface wear and the messy bun of her hair.

Bragja suddenly felt all their eyes, the intense gaze of a room of strangers. She felt naked, exposed, an ant on a plate with no where to run. She forced her fae to remain neutral, squared her shoulders with every ounce of courage she could muster. She had a flash of wonder, after the initial rush of fear, at the nature of the crowd. Who were these people, so set on showing off their wealth and clearly interested in anonymity? The man with a shifting face moved slightly, and Bragja's eyes were drawn to the far side of the room.

A man sat on a rusted throne of bones, bathed in a pool of light.

His hair was white, tousled without ceremony, and cut short on the sides. He wore deep black pants and a navy jacket, the offset lapels open, brass buttons beacons in the harsh light. His bushy eyebrows curled above a hawkish nose, his mouth a tiny thin line with a cruel set. He slouched comfortably on the chair, the metal femurs and scapulae splayed out behind him in an obscene sunburst of human remains.

The crowd parted to form a channel, and Bragja felt drawn to the throne. The masks, so hideous and transfixing, shifted mercifully to face the throne. The man's voice rang out above the small crowd, echoing against the pipes and bare metal of the ceiling. "And so this is her now, faithful Jervim? Caso's planet girl?" A smell of dankness and decay wafted by Bragja.

Jervim gestured to Bragja to follow him and walked forward. "O'course, *Konungur,* we bring her just like you say." Bragja walked along behind Jervim, her mind racing. *Konungur. King Klevim of the whoever the hell these people are.* As she walked, she looked closely at the people in the crowd. Close-cut clothing hugged some, fantastically unreasonable dresses and jackets on others, woven and embroidered, some encrusted with more jewels than Bragja could count. It was opulence beyond anything she'd seen. And everywhere the masks.

The variety struck her again as she walked; some masks were outlined with feathers, some projected outlandish abstract imagery on their faces. One person, a man judging by their size and shape, had their entire head covered with a white cloth, black patterns melting and reforming along his face.

As they walked through the crowd, Jervim went on. "She the planet girl. And she say, she want to join us." He threw his arms out wide. "Kill Ollsons." Jervim looked back over his shoulder as he said this, the contrast of his stark white teeth bright outside the circle of light on the throne. The crowd rustled, a few stomping applause on the deck plates. The room reverberated, then fell quiet.

The man on the throne sat up, resting one hand on his knee. His voice was gravel and thunder, strangely kind but the power he held in check shone through. "Ah, then. Bragja from the planet. Caso told me you were a picker. Said you could be useful." He caught Bragja's eye. They had approached the throne close enough for her to see the roughness of his skin, pocked and mottled. "He also said your brothers were heroes. Cut down by the Ollson troopers when they tried to help the people."

It took every ounce of Bragja's self-control to keep her face neutral. She nodded.

"Well, Bragja, I am *Konungur* Klevim Haupstrach. You've already met Jervim and the sisters. You'll meet the rest of the vanguard in turn, or as you need to. They each have a role to play. You see," and he held up a hand, his fingers open as if he held a bowl. A holo map sprang to life, stars floating over his palm in sharp relief. Despite herself, Bragja sucked in a breath. *He must have the gene. At least a part of it.* How else could he use the tech? But Klevim barreled on. "You see the stars of the Ollson space? We have smugglers and traders. We have longshoremen, dock workers. We have people, each one devoted to our cause." Klevim tilted his chin back, and when the light from above cast sharp shadows down his face Bragja saw that what she had first took for brown eyes, shimmered a deep green, nearly black. "But we are always looking for more."

Bragja paused, considering her next words carefully. Brun's words floated through her mind. Klevim was old, and the people who stood around her dripped with wealth. They had obviously done well, so why change?

Bragja spoke loudly enough for her voice to carry across the crowd. "And how long? How long has it been since you set out to topple the Ollsons?"

Klevim gave an indulgent smile. "A long, long time, Bragja. I was a young man once, believe it or not. A young man bound by the regulations and rules and *bureaucracy* that keeps us all slaves." He put one hand on his knee and leaned forward, his eyes on Bragja. "But we have just one rule, here. We are united. We will see the Ollsons fall."

Bragja heard a low grumble from the crowd. Barely enough to carry over the hum of machinery in the station's bowels, as they were, but loud enough to tell her all she needed to know. *They are tired of waiting.* And so was she.

"And I would see them dead for what they did to my family. To my brothers."

Klevim stood from his throne and snuffed out the hologram in his fist. His voice rose, and he looked out to the masked crowd. "And who among you have lost to the Ollsons?"

A few shouts floated up to the front, cries of anger and loss. Klevim's voice filled the space as he warmed to his audience. "That's right! We all have lost to them. They kill us without thought, from the planetary garrisons to the ports!" A cry went up from the assembled crowd, a wave of pain given voice. "From the rings of the fold arrays to the docks of this very station, Ollsons and their lackeys crush us." Klevim's voice lowered, forcing the crowd to silence as his words floated out over them. "We work, we scratch, we claw our way along, and still they squeeze us for everything we have." The responding shout was louder this time, motion rippling through the mass of humanity. Klevim turned to pace back across the front of the throne, sweat springing up from his brow. "But we will not sit by any longer. We have spent years, *lives,* to get where we are now. And tell me, oh brothers and sisters of mine." He held a hand up to the crowd, one finger held aloft. "What is the one rule?"

The response was deafening, the crowd's voices reverberating from walls and ceiling. "KEEP WHAT YOU TAKE!"

Klevim turned to Bragja then, his voice warm. The crowd hushed back to near silence, hanging on his every word. "And now, Bragja of Breydablick, you come to us knowing the true cost of Ollson oppression." He crossed the few steps back to her, and Bragja felt his closeness like the heat of the sun. "You have felt the pain of their work more recent than any." He placed a hand on her shoulder, and Bragja could see his eyes soften, the hard line of his mouth curl into a gentle smile. "Will you you let us share that pain?"

Bragja looked out at the crowd. Knowing what they wanted, having heard their response to Klevim's speech, the crowd took on a different feeling from when she first arrived. Instead of judgment and suspicion, she could imagine a hundred smiles under the masks. All victims of the Ollsons in one way or another. That common bond pulled at her, touched her deep inside.

Enemy of my enemy.

Despite the hospitality they showed her, she hadn't been able to see herself with Vessel Hormann and his people. But now, Bragja felt kinship, a sudden bond with people she hadn't known existed until a few moments before. She took a shaky breath, and began.

"My brothers were everything to me. I loved them more than life itself, and everything I did was for them, for my family. I had enough credit saved to move us to a better life, a safer one at least." She sucked in a breath, then steeled herself against the memory. "When the starfall stopped, the Ollsons didn't care." Someone in the crowd booed and Bragja continued. "When the credits started to run out, they didn't care." More shouts greeted her words. "And one day, when they had had enough, my brothers led a peaceful march to the inner gates. They wanted justice." Her breath caught in her chest as she remembered their faces, standing on the overturned palanquin.

Klevim nodded. "And what did they get?"

Bragja shuddered and her voice, nearly a whisper now, carried out over the silent crowd. "Death."

The crowd booed and hollered, and a few scraps of phrases made it to her ears over the noise. *Murderers! ...kill them all! ...with Erick!*

Klevim held his hands up to the crowd, and they fell silent again. "And the real question, Bragja of Breydablik." He looked into her eyes, his own piercing through her. "Will you join us?"

The word spilled out of her. "Yes."

Klevim nodded, his bony face breaking into a broad smile. "Then welcome, Bragja. I welcome you into our family, your new family. Remember always your pain, the pain the Ollsons caused you. You will carry your memories, the memories of your brothers and the crimes of the Ollsons, with you forever." He placed a hand on Bragjas shoulder, gentle and firm. The shock of human touch spread through Bragja, warmth and safety. "But now is the time for new beginnings. A new chapter deserves a new name." He turned to the crowd. "And by what name shall our new sister be known?"

Clapping and cheering washed over Bragja in a torrent of affection. The energy in the room had her on her toes with happiness. One name, shouted loud and high above the others, fell on her ears. It must have also fallen on Klevim's because he raised his hands once more for silence.

"My brothers and sisters, I hear you. I give you Syrinx of Breydablik." He held a hand out to Bragja, who took it firmly. Klevim raised their joined hands high. "Welcome, Syrinx, and in your anger, rise."

Finally. She was home.

42

Oath

Storm-born was she, and fueled by passion
Love and power in equal portion
The storm brings the life-giving rain
But too close, the lightning burns

The huge expanse of window in Bryn's chambers shone pale starlight across a tangle of flesh. Azita ran her fingertips down Bryn's side, as far as her arm would reach along the thigh, then back up. Her other hand, cradling Bryn's head with their faces nearly touching, gently released the handful of flaxen curls she'd used to weld their lips together a moment before. They both breathed hard, their legs still intertwined, and the slip of sweat and sex surrounded them in a haze of pheromones. Azita's hand made its way back upwards, across Bryn's bare chest to her neck to gently touch the lips that had recently gasped out in pleasure. Bryn opened her eyes, looked directly into Azita's, and then sealed her lips around the proffered fingers. At this, Azita gasped and pulled herself closer to Bryn, who could feel the electric tingle of their skin on skin from knee to neck. She shuddered a few more times as the waves of ecstasy dissipated, then pulled her head back to focus on Azita.

"This doesn't get you off the hook. I'm not bait."

"Bait, oh goodness, what a horrible simplification. You know that the Obershire spies will see any vulnerability in the Geneline, or in this case *to* the Geneline, as an opportunity they

"

can't pass up." Azita stretched one arm up and twisted her wrist in a stretch. "We just need to identify one, put you in a position of seeming helplessness, and then let their own greed and stupidity do the rest."

Bryn frowned, the seriousness of their conversation blunting the post-coital edge. "I can't believe they'd be so careless. *My* enhancements aren't exactly a secret."

"Of course not, but theirs are, and I'll wager they think they can take you."

"Fair point." Bryn ran a hand through her hair absently. "Just have to find one now."

Azita smoothed a lock of Bryn's hair back behind her ear. "The shipyards at Noatun are important, so I bet that will be a prime target. With the lockdown on folds, I wouldn't be surprised if there is one waiting for you."

Bryn nodded, her own fingertips absently wandering Azita's olive skin. "I think we will dig another one out soon. We have a lot of data and the advantage of time."

Azita's hands had begun to move with more purpose. "I do believe you're trying to think up an excuse to keep me here a bit longer."

"I don't deny it." Bryn's heart had picked back up, the pounding rush of blood in her ears as she held Azita's gaze.

"Mmhm. And what *would* you deny me, then?" Her hand reached down, lifting Bryn's leg up to rest her knee on Azita's hip. Bryn gasped at her touch.

"Deny you? Nothing." Bryn's lips closed over Azita's once more, and they fell into each other under the cold stars.

HLÉHÉR

When the call finally came, Bryn and Azita were occupied with the tedious work of coordinating a complicated counterintelligence operation. Of course, Bryn was the authority to launch any operation, but the Ollson bureaucracy demanded her attention. She couldn't afford to hang on every scrap of intel; there was the mundane job of running an empire to get on with. Besides, the augmented agents had proven elusive, and Bryn's forces had spent several weeks hunting down dead ends and fruitless leads that led to ordinary, if somewhat dishonest, citizens. Drug rings, unlicensed fighting, various colors and shades of lechery and debauchery, all the typical trappings of human society. But no Obershire agents.

Until now.

The First Wolf of Ollson, a title known only to two, surveyed the operations center. It was an expansive room, and several rows of desks cascaded down to meet the front wall, painted with a wide display. The spread of desks held specialists in intelligence, operations, mobility, and various other ways information flowed. It had the feeling of tension, whispers as people moved from one desk to another, status boards updated on small holo displays. Finally, Traub approached, their eyes intense.

"Sir, we just hit high-confidence correlation on target two-two bravo."

"Show me." Bjorn's reply was terse, no-nonsense.

Traub swiped his datapad, and the reports and intelligence sources bloomed on Bjorn's screen. He drank it in, eyes skipping from point to point. He nodded once. "Good. Everyone to the briefing room."

The various section heads started sidebar conversations as soon as they entered, but when the door closed, the volume level dropped. Bjorn's voice cut across the low background roar of the room. The light showing good connection to the executor glowed green, and Bjorn addressed her hologram. "Ma'am, we've got a target. This one shows hot on thermal over the last day and a half, and fits the profile of the other two. Here's the snap." The picture of a woman flashed into a hologram in the room's middle like paint peeled off a canvas. She was tall, relatively slim, dressed locally; utterly nondescript.

The small room was dead silent, all eyes on the floating image like the idol of some two-dimensional god. Bjorn stood at the head of the narrow table, his forehead pinched in a serious glower. He clearly meant business. Bryn's image, ghostly in her own holographic presence, nodded to him to continue.

"She's high-confidence. She initially popped for pattern of life here in Karvasok. Records say she was engaged as a cyber maintainer, working on the services ministry payroll planetside. She had access to a significant amount of infrastructure data, but the initial background checks didn't flag anything in the automatic scrub. When we went back manually, we found that she didn't have a local certification and that her claimed training in Aumont territory was just good enough to fool the AI screener. And she had passage booked to Noatun before the lockdown."

A few thousand kilometers from the briefing room, Bryn was reassured by the bulk of the *Sleipnir* surrounding her. In all her paranoia, Obin demanded that Bryn work from the flagship when she heard about the plan to use Bryn as bait. The ship was well equipped and nearly impenetrable to a single agent, but more importantly, the science directorate had retrofitted it with the type of scanner they'd need to identify enemy agents. Now, as she stood in Tactical watching the hologram of Bjorn with Azita at her side, Bryn felt the edge of insecurity creep in. *Is this plan really something we can pull off?* It seemed like too much relied on flawless timing.

Bryn spoke to the image of Bjorn before her. "Looks like we caught a break. You said she had access to a lot of data. What specifically was she interested in?"

Bjorn's image nodded. "Her legitimate search queries were all locally related, typical of the things you might want to know if you were designing top-level cyberware for infrastructure. But one interesting commonality was that she also cross-referenced with Imperial standards in everything she searched. It's like she was looking for the vulnerabilities in the archetype system, as well as the Ollson specifics."

That doesn't make sense. Obershire operating systems are the same as ours. "I want the tech analysis on her searches. Did she send any suspicious traffic?"

"No, ma'am. We monitor outbound comms from all the ministries. Besides, the relay path would have been incredibly complex as we aren't folding to Obershire space. We think she's a mule."

"Assuming we confirm her as an agent."

"Yes, ma'am. The science directorate installed a ship scanner on the station maintenance tug. It keeps to its normal rounds with the repair spiders, but we can gently re-route it for confirmation scans. We picked this up two hours ago." The hologram that had been the woman's face disappeared, replaced with an eerie blue rendering of the belowdecks of Karvasok station as seen by the ship scanner. Traceries of brighter lines mapped out spiderwebs of active circuits, dewdrops of batteries clinging to the lines of current. Generators glared like tiny blue suns. The view zoomed in to an area between decks, barely wide enough for a maintenance drone.

Or a human.

"Not technically living area, but it's pressurized. We tracked her off the planet, but lost her in the crowd at the docks."

As Bjorn spoke, a red overlay highlighted a small section. "This seems to be a pattern. The last agent we caught was extremely skilled at hiding aboard a ship. That suggests more than a passing familiarity with spacecraft and station design standards." The view was still zooming, but as he finished, it stabilized. "To be completely honest, ma'am, if we hadn't been looking at just the right time, we wouldn't have seen her." A bright blue area enlarged, growing five pseudopods that resolved into a rough approximation of a human form. The form stretched arms over its head, then appeared to crawl through something invisible to the scanner. The device detected energy density, and as such, the inert structure of the station was hidden. "Our techs were quick enough on the scanners and the cross-cue with the ship visual systems. We've maintained custody of her using the security systems, and I have a team standing by to begin the tail and provide support."

Bryn nodded. She was confident that this wasn't another run-of-the-mill smuggler. *I wish I was as confident in the plan.* "Good work, Captain Hafthor. Maintain custody of the target-I'll prep for phase two and advise you when I'm in position."

"Yes, ma'am." Bjorn's face replaced the imagery of the figure climbing through the station. "Good hunting." He almost smiled.

HLÉHÉR

Bryn was glad that Azita monitored the situation from tactical, alone save Obin. Bryn checked the status of the quick reaction force Azita had staged in a container by the docks. Azita was in her element here, running a team. Just like the wargames she and Bryn had played back in Osman space.

Bryn was glad to know that she was there, watching and coordinating. Azita had her back, and Bjorn's team was moments away. Bryn would be fine. At least, that's what she kept telling herself as she walked through Karvasok station, the outer hab ring stretching out in front of her as the ceiling and floor sloped gently up. The gentle spin of the station gave her the illusion of weight, climbing perpetually uphill.

Bryn smiled broadly at the people she passed. The locals on this deck were mostly station management, and the executor's heir was well-known. They waved and turned to mutter to each other. It had been a long time since Bryn had walked the station, and she could feel the eyes on her. She remembered her father taking her to the shops where people stocked handmade goods, artisan wrought designs, and trinkets bought on the surface, resold to those who didn't care to go planetside. The market was an affectation, of course, but one that her father said made the station feel more like a city, more like home. Now, as Bryn passed the shopkeepers, the artists had all gone. All she saw were the bright traceries of implant, cheap surface-visible stuff that you could get at any lifetech broker on the surface. Some even looked to be purely cosmetic. Bryn wondered how things were on the surface of Karvasok, if this was all they had to offer. It felt like she'd been down only yesterday, but the memory brought up a quick tagged image in her ocular. The crystal bridge over the river Svol. Bryn's eyes went to the date. *Nearly twenty years ago?* It couldn't have been that long.

Bryn cleared the image and focused on her steps, taking a single deep breath to focus. Her ocular overlaid a glowing line of text on the bottom of her vision, the letters etched sharp and red against the grey decking.

TAIL IS IN PLACE. TARGET IS MOVING TO YOU.

Bryn felt her heart try to leap up and slammed it back down. This was according to plan. Everything was going fine. She noticed she had nearly walked past an artist's stall and paused to inspect a hand-carved Yggdrasill, fashioned out of one of the local plant species. The image of the many-limbed tree towered over a small city tucked in amongst the roots. The carving may have been done to scale, for the trees grew to stupendous heights on the surface. The Ollsons had chosen Karvasok as the seat of their power for the towering forests. It wasn't as solid as the wood imported from the throne world, but it was sturdy enough to hold a shape. She pretended to study the detailed carving, waiting for the next phase of the operation.

TARGET HAS MET TRIGGERS FOR PHASE THREE.

Show time. Bryn moved through the crowd, seemingly at random. She had to make it to the corridor between the market and the hab and recreation area. It had vacuum blast doors on either end that could be sealed in the event of pressure loss but no direct outlet off the station. That was where they were betting the target would try to intercept her.

It was also the best place to set up Azita's trap.

Bryn walked, feeling the hair on the back of her neck stand on end. She continued smiling at each person she passed, their faces fading immediately into the background noise as she willed herself not to turn and look. They had decided on text-only communications; the spy's implants might be able to detect higher bandwidth. So, when Bryn entered the corridor, she expected to simultaneously see the counter-intelligence team-lead in civilian clothes enter the other end. She'd met him briefly as they had gone over the plan and immediately disliked the man. Specialist Kendrick made her skin crawl. But Bjorn said he was the best they had, so she had ignored Kendrick's language and overall creepy demeanor. *And now the little shit isn't where he is supposed to be.*

Bryn nearly jumped out of her skin when she heard Azita's voice. "Bryn, we lost comms with the team tailing the target. We still have her on station camera, but she's stopped at a stall. Recommend we abort."

Bryn subvocalized her reply as she walked through the corridor, only a few tens of meters long but now seeming to go on forever. "Negative. Proceed as planned. I'll trigger the flood."

"What? No way. You'll have to be in the corridor yourself. That's too risky."

"Look, we're committed. I'm going ahead with the pl—"

Bryn didn't get a chance to finish her thought as the air left her lungs, a starburst of pain under her right arm as ribs bent. She felt her feet lose contact with the ground and immediately dialed up her combat implants while twisting and trying to get her feet first.

Bryn only managed to spin slightly to land against the side of the corridor with her back, breaking the impact with a slap of her arms against the metal bulkhead. Sure enough, there was the target, her leg still outstretched from the kick. Hunting instinct kicked in, and Bryn felt a flood of adrenalin. She leaped off the wall, reaching to grab the woman around the arms and pin them tight. The woman arched her back, carrying the momentum of both of them through to slam Bryn painfully against the decking, Bryn's hand coming up just in time to save her face. She rolled upright and squared off into a flurry of punches. Bryn's arms blurred as she blocked.

The woman was wired. Bryn retreated across the corridor, countering with her own series of blows but still driven back by the ferocity of the attack.

Running out of the ground to retreat, Bryn attempted a kick to gain some range, but the woman took the crushing blow to her chest to snare Bryn's leg. Bryn was sure she'd felt a rib crack under her boot, but the woman held Bryn's leg tight. She leaned back, pivoting around her back leg to throw Bryn bodily across the corridor, but Bryn managed to jump off with her free leg as the woman began her spin. She reached overhead, her fingertips entwining in the metal ceiling panels as her other leg wrapped around the woman's neck, pinning her head between Bryn's legs.

Bryn squeezed, hard enough to crush an un-augmented neck but not so hard as to pop the woman's head clean off her shoulders. They stood there for an endless second, the woman trying to free herself and Bryn gradually increasing the pressure. Bryn felt the ceiling panel digging into her palms but kept her grip. The woman's struggles became weaker, but she still clawed and fought to free herself. Bryn felt heat, and looked down to see the woman's head beginning to glow. The vision of the last spy igniting in a halo of expanding gas immediately leaped into Bryn's mind.

I have to freeze her, or we'll both die.

Bryn triggered the trap across the local network, the ocular symbol going from green to red. The doors at the end of the corridor slammed shut, and superfluid helium flowed into the hallway, dispensed from hastily deployed tanks through the floor fire suppression system. The vents were designed to smother the fire bottom-first, and let out where the wall met the floor. The helium flowed uncannily, flashing to gas on first contact with the floor, then barely boiling. Bryn could feel the wave of cold as the air in the corridor dumped heat into the liquid, which vaporized along the surface but dropped everything it touched to a sliver above absolute zero.

The woman in Bryn's grip was no exception. But the flow wasn't fast enough. If she didn't get the woman submerged, Karvasok Station would be gone.

Bryn toggled the valves full open from her ocular, and the helium flowed faster. It rose, quickly, and the woman's struggle became less effective as her legs froze. Even as the helium reached Bryn's toes, she bit back a scream and held onto the freezing woman with the burning face.

The cold liquid moved higher as it ate away at Bryn. She couldn't hold it back anymore. Even with her pain perception dulled by the implants, the throbbing, searing pain licked higher and higher along her legs. He let go of everything else, and focused on holding the ceiling, holding the woman tight. Bryn heard screaming. The woman's face was bright now, glowing with an inner light.

Bryn realized the screams filling the corridor were hers and closed her eyes against the all-consuming agony. She couldn't feel her feet anymore, but somehow they still hurt, the lack of feedback from nerves ghosting layers of pain on top of more pain. The rising superfluid ate away at her. She had no idea if she still held the woman. She forced herself to open her eyes, gave in to the liquid agony, and looked down. Finally, the helium flowed over the woman's head, and Bryn shut off the flow. She'd somehow managed to keep her clamped tight. But now she was stuck, her legs entombed in frozen flesh. The agony was absolute now, despite the nerve block. She could see her legs, feel them again, pain sending wave after wave of agony through her. She clung to the ceiling and screamed, giving up her last bit of control to the pain.

They told her that when they managed to get the helium pumped back out, she was holding herself to the ceiling, hanging above the evaporating pool as she fought to breathe, trying to climb hand over hand to the door. Her legs were still wrapped around the woman's neck.

Ten meters away.

43

Transformation

Mechanical. Pistons, oil, chrome sliding frictionless on angstroms of lubrication. Pressure, force, balance and transfer aligned crystals in shear and tensile. Perfect clockwork connections, gear teeth mated in flawless fit. Sharp smell of ozone, the bright ringing of steel. Her senses overloaded, each piece coming faster on the heels of the one before it in a dizzying blur of cacophonic possibility. But none of it her.

Bryn lay in the medical bay, the best technology Ollson doctors had to offer enveloping her legs, or at least the place where her legs should have been. A local field canceled the gravity of her bed. Enough of a breeze to keep the air from going stale was the only thing that rippled the edge of the medical wrapping, now slightly untucked from below her. To keep the blood from pooling, they'd said. Made sense, perhaps, but did nothing to dull the shock of seeing nothing. Her right leg, having been slightly elevated, was a touch longer before it terminated in the sack of amniotic biogel. Her left was a stub, nothing left for the muscle to hold on to. Had she been a few inches further in, a few inches lower in the vat of swirling freezing helium, she'd have nothing left below her waist. Despite the pain blockers and the wraps, she could feel the frost-bitten flesh that surely puckered above where it had frozen solid and fractured off. She could feel legs that weren't there, aching and painful.

She had never been less than whole. It wasn't real. Couldn't be. Her legs weren't gone. They even hurt.

What kind of bullshit is this.

Lose a limb only to have it still pain her? But there it was. The door to her room opened, and Obin stood outside.

Bryn pasted on a weak grin. "What, Azita finally letting someone else see me?"

"I had to threaten to forcibly remove her to quarters. She's been awake nearly two days straight, between the operation and seeing after you."

"She's so melodramatic. They're just legs. Nothing to them, really." Her laugh was a touch crazed, but Obin didn't mention it. "Nothing to them at all."

"I've come to take your mind off," Obin gestured, "this, for now. We have the preliminary results back from the agent."

Bryn tried to sit up a little straighter, only succeeding in bucking slightly in mid-air as her body remembered where and how she was. "Tell me we managed to salvage her."

"Oh yes. She's very much intact. Expected cellular trauma. And while there's certainly no coming back from where you sent her, we can learn a lot."

Bryn nodded. "Ok then. What can you tell me?"

"Well, I can't tell you much yet, unfortunately. I'm not an engineer. The techs are all apparently afraid her implants will continue the critical cycle they started if we try to warm her body back up."

Bryn remembered the CI team that was supposed to time the helium release. "Speaking of cybers, what happened to Kendrick? Why wasn't he on comms and ready?"

"Oh, him. We found him and his partner in the maintenance access panel of bay three. On the floor. And some on the walls."

Bryn frowned. "Well then. Kendrick was a complete jackass, but he was supposedly the best information operative in Second Company."

"He was indeed. I didn't like him either, but I wouldn't have wished that on anyone. His lungs were pulled completely out of his back."

"That is pretty anachronistically horrible."

"Yes, it is. It was meant as a message."

"How did she manage to do that right under our noses? Where was his partner?"

Azita's voice rang out from the hallway, preceding her entry by only a few seconds. "Also dead, but much more conventionally. Neck snapped and folded up into a storage locker. A professional butcher would have been proud. Kendrick must have done something to piss her off to get blood eagled like that."

Obin's voice was tinged with annoyance. "Ah, Azita. I assure you Bryn will be well looked after."

"I have no doubt. I told the med unit to ping me when she woke. It, being a machine, can be relied upon to do exactly as asked." She glowered at Obin, who smiled back.

"I thought it best for you to rest, ma'am."

"I know what's best. And I can handle the debriefing."

Obin gave a long-suffering sigh and raised an eyebrow to Bryn, who nodded. Obin placed her tablet under her arm and saluted smartly. "Well then, I'll see to my other duties. Which includes, at this time, everything."

Bryn gave a gentle laugh. "Don't pretend like you didn't already run things beforehand." She paused, a sudden welling of emotion threatening to stick in her throat, and she pushed it back down. "Thank you for spending some time with me here. I'll see you later. Azita and I have a lot to discuss."."

Obin gave a slight smile, nodded, and disappeared into the hallway. The gentle whirr of medical machinery was suddenly loud. Azita smiled, then looked down and began to pace slowly across the small room, her footsteps silent despite the bare deck plates and unadorned walls.

Bryn held her peace, digesting. She felt like she should be dealing better, mentally, with her injury. It was just flesh. There was a part of her that was a hair trigger from screaming. But she couldn't stop her analytical mind.

It was a refuge.

She stopped struggling and dove into the stream of analysis in her head. So what had happened? Affecting information systems wasn't unheard of. The Geneline Abrams had perfected it in their special forces. But this had been a real-time loop, and the number of eyes that had been on the feed made a successful hack extraordinary. The spy had looped or altered the feed long enough to double back, ambush the physical eyeballs that were following her.

Bjorn needed to be more careful; a larger team, more coordinated next time. Which carried its own risks. *No, we caught one. That's enough to study.*

Any more operations would be kill missions.

Bryn started as she noticed Azita's eyes on her from across the room. A gentle smile perched on her lips. Bryn shook her head. "Sorry. Lost in my own head. But I have to know it wasn't for nothing. Obin never got to the part where she told me what happened?"

"They got some good data." Azita sighed theatrically. "Are you sure you want to dive right back in? You can take some time. I'm not going anywhere."

Bryn shook her head, her whole body shifting in the air as the bed fields stabilized her. "No. The geneline needs me. I have billions of people counting on me to have a plan when Dorian shows up."

Azita swallowed, nodding once. "You are stronger than I remember. I'm glad I came back." Bryn's lip twitched up in acknowledgment, and Azita continued. "The enemy agent. We still don't know what half the implants are or how they're powered. But they are beyond what would come out of an Empire factory. Even your famed Ollson Forgers hadn't seen them before."

Bryn frowned. That didn't make any sense unless the Obershires had somehow managed to conceal a separate research and development initiative from the Empress. That was treason an order of magnitude above attacking a geneline transfer. They'd undoubtedly be excommunicated, the Black Guard burning them out of history.

Bryn gave a languid shake of her head. "They wouldn't take the chance on building their own independent facilities. The last time something like that had happened was the Geneline Arnoch."

Azita nodded. "An entire Geneline wiped out by the Black Guard Their own stations and ships turned against them. No, I think you're right. Darius wants your space, but he's not suicidal. He knows he needs the Empress' blessing."

Bryn didn't like the only conclusion that was left. "These aren't Obershire agents."

"Then whose are they?"

Bryn didn't have an answer. Now, right now, when all of her subjects and the very existence of her Geneline was at risk, enemies at the gates, her own body torn apart, she had no idea what to do. This moment she had never thought she'd make it to. Erick had groomed her, her whole life, to lead. He always had an answer, if not the answer. But he'd always been there, too.

She felt broken, out of control, helpless for the first time she could remember. Her vision began to blur as her eyes betrayed her, fat tears forming and clinging in the hospital bed's zero gravity. She squeezed them tight, and a tiny shimmering globe released from the corner of her eye, lazily floating across to the edge of the field where it fell to the floor.

Bryn felt a hand grasp her own, the squeeze gentle but firm. Azita's voice cam like honey in sunlight. "Hey. This is not a normal time. Things are not okay right now. And that's ok." Bryn nodded, taking a gasp and trying to force her body to obey her.

"I'm sorry. This isn't me, I'm not-" She took a breath, steadied herself. "I'm not weak. I never have been." Her voice rose as she spoke. There was an edge to it that scared her. She needed to be ready, be all there. Azita was closer to her than she'd thought, meant more than she'd let herself believe, but Bryn was the Executor of Ollson. She had to be in command.

"I don't doubt you, and I never have," Azita replied, her hand still locked in Bryn's. "But first things first."

"What's that?"

Azita gazed deep into Bryn's eyes, her lips barely apart, and whispered, "New legs."

44

Epistemophile

He delved deep and greedily
For of time had he a glut
To know his enemy was what he sought
But this knowledge chaos had wrought

The asteroid belt of Ife was gorgeous. Erick didn't really have any other word for it. He had taken the *Svadilfari* on the shortest route to the belt from Ife Station, the transit a little over a day. Had there been a convenient planet for a gravity assist they might have arrived sooner, but the direct transfer was the only option, and gave him time to read. His brief sojourn into the publicly available file on Ife had revealed that the belt was thought to have once been two planets. They had danced with each other, tenuously interlocked by the invisible fingers of gravity over millennia, before finally succumbing to the inevitability of physics.

Or perhaps one was a rogue planet captured from beyond the Ife system. Whatever the truth, one of them had been extremely rich in carbon, as evidenced by the vast deposits of rough diamond that littered the larger asteroids. Two larger rocks, closer to the size of small moons, orbited in opposition, shepherding clouds of asteroids they pulled along in their wake. One of these was the main processing and manufacturing hub, hollowed out and spun to create a glittering habitat.

The other lay directly ahead of the ship, veins of copper and diamond interlaced with plagioclase. The igneous rock revealed it as a piece of some larger, older body. The wan light of the Ife star refracted and reflected from embedded lumps of diamond, frothing chunks of rainbow cast in haphazard bands against a dark background.

Erick followed the landing guidance, the green path of the dock vector in the *Svadilfari's* HUD terminating at a square opening in the side of the asteroid, bracketed by blinking red and white lights. He felt the dock AI take over guidance and relaxed his control, monitoring for errors. They weren't down yet, and he focused entirely on flying any time his flight path took him this close to a rock. The quickest way to dead was to assume things were over before the docking clamps had set home.

Finally, they slid through the opening. It had looked far larger on approach. Instead, the portal to the docks was barely wide enough for Erick and Daruthr's small scout ship. Any traffic that wanted to leave would have had to wait. Erick was concerned about the possibilities for a quick departure but soon relaxed when he saw the docking platform ahead of them; they were the only true ship, with a handful of maintenance pods and short-range shuttles lined up ahead of them. The smaller craft were likely all the librarians needed when the Adebe resupply ships came.

The dockyard AI guided them to a waiting docking arm, which sealed against the ship with a gentle bump that he felt as much as heard through the ship's hull. After a few moments, *Svadilfari* came to rest, and Erick looked over to Daruthr as his straps released him from the crash couch.

"Well, here we are. Suppose we just go ask the librarians if they've seen any shady-looking characters around?"

Daruthr snorted. "Your sense of humor seems to be intact, and for that, I am grateful. I wasn't sure, given the nature of the noise you insisted on playing on our way out here." Daruthr's straps released him, and he stood. "To answer your question, no, we don't need to ask anyone, we will just need to establish a data connection." He moved towards the ladder to the rest of the ship, and Erick followed suit, moving carefully in the low gee of the docks.

"The noise I was playing? Oh please. I know you've got a big soft spot for beauty. Music soothes the tired and aching soul, after all."

"Music yes, if you had actually selected any."

"You know, for someone who claims to be fully sentient, you sure do have a hard time with the finer things in life." He immediately felt a little pang of chagrin; perhaps that had been a touch harsh.

Daruthr took the barb gracefully. "And for someone born sentient, you certainly seem to be intent on squandering the gift! What sort of instrument even produced those sounds?" Daruthr sat at the table in the galley, and Erick punched through the menus on the wall panel. The earthy, robust aroma of coffee filled the small space, and Erick felt his stomach rumble.

He laughed back at Daruthr. "An ancient one. It's metal strands, stretched across a wooden frame, with the vibrations picked up and electronically modified."

"Electronic modification? Perish the thought."

Erick laughed, struck by the loudness of it in the enclosed space. It had been a while since he'd felt good. He retrieved the steaming mugs of coffee and joined Daruthr at the galley table. Erick sipped gingerly, not quite scalding his tongue as he breathed in through his nose.

The hot air drove into his head as he wrapped his hands around the mug. "I suppose you'd be the authority on electronic modification. Want me to teach you a bit about the music? Or are you simply waiting for the opportune time to remotely access the library archives from here?"

Daruthr scoffed. "No, I need a hard connection. The Adebe scholars are singularly paranoid despite the redundancy of data in the network, and they keep the essential things in a quantum cage." He sipped his own coffee, smacking his lips in appreciation. "So, by all means, educate me. What about this 'rock and roll' speaks to humans so well?"

Erick shook his head. "So, rhythm and sound and emotion. They're all connected." He launched into an explanation. Finally, a subject he felt fully in command of, no matter Daruthr's age or experience. Music, music would always speak to humanity's soul.

All you have to do is listen.

HLÉHÉR

The airlock door from the docks to the main thoroughfare opened, and the station slapped Erick in the mouth. The smell of bay leaves, ginger, curry, and rendered fat, the sound of drums, or things being used as drums, punctuated by the loud blast of a whistle, and everywhere people. They streamed past in the wide corridor, the walkers nearly running. A man stood, visible above the crowd on a crate, positioned at the corner of the hall where it opened into the main receiving area. His gilded robes were marred by sooty black streaks, and he spoke loudly to anyone who would stop. At that moment, a small crowd gathered and shrank, a core of people transfixed by whatever the man was saying. It couldn't have been more than two or three. The sheer difference between the corridor here and that of the Ollson stations made his head spin.

He glanced away from the crowd to see Daruthr watching him, a bemused smile playing at his mouth. "You really haven't traveled much, have you."

Erick smoothed the front of his tunic. "I have, and you know it. I never needed to go out to the station promenades much, and definitely not in Adebe space. This place is one step away from a riot."

"Rest easy, Erick. You're perfectly safe. Probably. The people here have come a long way and waited a long time to get here, but they aren't interested in you or me."

"What are they here for then? Clearly not to listen to the Empress' Vessel," he said, gesturing to the man in the gold robes.

Daruthr struck out into the maddening crowd, and Erick had to jump to follow him. He spoke over his shoulder as they walked through the halls. "These people are pilgrims, that much is true. But they aren't here to listen to some old man pontificate on the miraculous deification of her Imperial Majesty, transformed from flesh to godhead. They can get that on any feed, on any corner in the Empire."

Erick realized he had balled up his fists, his shoulders hunched against the onslaught of humanity. He felt like if he moved out of Daruthr's wake, he'd be swept away by the crowd's current. "Then what are they all *doing* here? It's supposed to be a library, by the gods! This is a madhouse." A man brushed by him none too gently, and he felt his hand on his hip, questing for anything of value. Erick turned to face the thief, but he was gone, lost in the maelstrom of faces.

Daruthr's voice sounded in his ear. "Best not to worry about that too much. Humanity may have gained the stars, but it packed a lot of baggage. Most people here aren't pickpockets." He felt Daruthr's hand on his elbow and allowed him to turn Erick back towards the way they had been walking. They dove once again into the crowd. "Most people here are pilgrims, as I said. They come here in the hopes of viewing the great repository of knowledge, of spending time enmeshed in the data. This whole place, once you get inside the cage, is a monument to knowledge."

Erick paused to think. "Wouldn't it also be very vulnerable, keeping all this data here? It would make more sense to distribute it throughout the system, or perhaps multiple systems."

Daruthr's laugh was light, almost musical. "Data that is distributed, spread out across a hundred, a thousand different systems. How accessible is that? How much time do you have to wait for a response from a query if it goes back and forth across an entire solar system, or worse, into the comm buffers of the arrays? No, Erick, here it is concentrated, distilled information. Knowledge. If ever there was an Eden, this would be its apple."

"Cryptic references to fruit aside, we Ollsons don't see it that way. Our gods had to search and sacrifice for knowledge."

"Never mind." They had arrived at a large doorway, ornately worked from some obsidian material that flickered and glowed despite the steady lighting in the hallway. They stood there, the only two people frozen in the river of humanity that parted and flowed and rejoined around them in an endless stream. Erick looked up, and above the door was an inscription.

Igi Gogoro Magun Mi Loju, Okeere Lati Nlo.

"What does that say, over the doorway?"

Daruthr look up and smiled. "An ancient proverb, from before Adebe was a geneline. From before the empire, in fact."

"What does it mean, then?"

"An ode to the power of knowledge. The meaning is roughly, 'to be forewarned is to be forearmed.' This is a doorway in the quantum cage I told you about. Its material encircles the whole of the inner portion of this asteroid, and is where the Library of Abímbọlá truly begins. Inside here, you will be completely cut off from the outside world, but you will have access to more knowledge than you could put together even in one of your lifetimes."

"And you think we'll find out what they want here?"

"I have no idea what we will find. But I do know that there is at least one agent here."

Erick looked at him sharply. How could he have kept this critical detail from him, and more importantly, how did he know it? "Not the time to play things that close to the vest, Daruthr. What do you know?"

"Relax, Erick. I am not a massive scanning array. But I can feel their presence here. A whole lot of energy, tightly wound. And there's something in the network, traces of it. I can smell malicious intent in the code."

"You can… smell it. In the code." Erick took a breath to speak and thought better of it. They were beyond yet another explanation; honestly, he didn't care anymore. "You know what, I believe you. So, what's the plan. How are we going to hunt them down?"

"Always the impatient one. I need network access, for one thing, and inside the cage of the Library proper."

"Great. Let's go."

"You can occupy yourself with some research. It will be safer if I look for this agent independently." He smiled. "After all, even if we can learn something from whatever data there is on the Revenants in the library, we still need to know why they wanted to come to this system in the first place."

"Research. While you're off hunting."

Daruthr clapped Erick on the back and strode towards the obsidian gate. "I will let you know when I've located them. Don't look so sour." He nodded towards the gates ahead. "I'd start my research with my personal favorite dead man, Des Cartes, then go to the rise of the Empire, and on from there."

Such a small amount of ground to cover. Erick sighed and stepped on after Daruthr.

45

Enemy

His quest, unwanted, thrust upon him
Covered many a twisted land
Fellows had he found, and fellows he lost
Would that they were with him now

The Abímbọ́lá Library lay embedded in the heart of the asteroid, he learned. It was an irregular spheroid of indeterminate age. The perimeter cage that cut it off from outside interference and exploitation had been grown in place after the librarians had decided they didn't want their precious knowledge to fall prey to some rogue cyber assault. Once that initial volume was defined, however, they faced a quandary. Could they continue to amass and store data, information, and knowledge with limited physical room for memory?

Their solution was an elegant one. Erick walked through the narrow corridor of the library proper and was surrounded by data. Not just in the stacks and rows of memory that riddled the place, and made up the walls, floors, and ceilings, but every bit of the library was storage. They had turned every bit of it into storage devices, from the bolts in the floor grates and the ceiling's support beams to the very trim and fabric. Deployed very carefully and with an almost fearful oversight, nanotech had transformed the nature of the matter inside into a glorious network of interconnected storage and computers. The main entanglement at the heart of the place served the brunt of the population, and enabled the workstation he found unoccupied at a rest area to the side of one juncture. But everywhere there were computers, small machines of a few hundred qubits, main processing hubs drawing entanglement from surrounding systems; even tiny, ancient machines that ran on solid state silicon processors, relics kept for sentimental value.

Erick sat at one of the larger quantum terminals, the holo interface glowing green as it detected his implants, and they exchanged protocols. Of course, he could display any sensitive queries on his ocular, but the holotank offered the possibility of more realistic displays. He stifled a sigh and began his search.

After nearly two hours, he had managed to discover three things. Firstly, the library system interface was utterly garbage, and he had to format his queries in strings of 'and' and 'not' logic. Not even a basic helper program existed, a testament to the librarians' puritanical approach to data.

The second was not so much a revelation as a confirmation.

Daruthr was a sarcastic ass. Des Cartes had led him down a rabbit hole of ancient navel-gazing that culminated in a conclusion so obvious it boggled the mind.

The third thing was that despite the press of bodies in the corridor outside the library, there were relatively few people who partook of it. Or so he assumed. The last fellow devotee to data that worked at a terminal near him had left about half an hour before, and he hadn't seen anyone since. He yawned, stretched, and rubbed his eyes, grown gritty from staring too hard.

"I've seen that look before. Didn't find what you wanted, or didn't like what you found?" Her voice was high but not grating. Erick turned to look at the woman who had spoken, seated on the low bench behind him. He hadn't heard her arrive.

"A little of both, I'm afraid. I'm somewhat new to the interface…" he trailed off with a gesture of ambiguity towards the holotank in front of him.

She pushed her back behind her ear, and her eyes were green and flecked with gold through her glasses. Glyphs of the interface danced in tiny mirror images on the lenses perched on her nose. "Yes, the lack of an intelligent system often frustrates people before they even form a proper query."

Erick raised an eyebrow at her. Her blue dress gathered at her feet, and the long sleeves drowned her hands in azure fabric. "You sound like you've seen this a few times. Are you one of our elusive hosts?"

Her laugh was deep and hearty. "A librarian? No. I managed to get admitted and I've been here longer than some, is all."

"And how long is that, then?"

"Seven years, give or take. The facilities are spartan, but they'll do."

Ah, a local, such as there were. She might be able to help, but he'd have to be careful about revealing his purpose. He decided to gamble, but not too aggressively. "Can I trouble you for some assistance, given your no doubt considerable expertise with the system? It would save me a lot of time."

She rose and joined him on the bench in front of the holotank kiosk, and he slid over to make room for her. A generous seat for one was still compact for two. He regarded her as she looked at his attempts to get a decent result from the system.

"You have been relying on semi-sentient data assistants for too long, I see. These queries are full of Boolean exclusions, but you haven't set your main subject roots."

"Ah yes, the main subject roots. How could I have forgotten."

She laughed at him, not unkindly. "It explains why you have so many results. Even a small portion of everything in the system here is still more than you or I could get through in a lifetime."

"Well, I certainly don't plan on spending my remaining days here in the library." He gestured to remove the query string. "I'm interested in this system, specifically, and anything that makes it unique."

"Anything?" The skin around her eyes crinkled as she smiled. "Socially? Politically, industrially, cartographically, historically? You're going to need to narrow that down."

He raised his hand again, trying to frame his question in terms of categories. What exactly was he looking for? What categories were even available?

She put her hand on his, gently guiding it back to his lap. "Allow me. Assuming you find this unique thing, what will you use it for? That might help us start."

He smiled a bit. That was one way of doing things, but he was loathe to tell her he was interested in the Revenants. He frowned. She hadn't removed her hand.

Erick went to open his mouth to answer her, but it didn't move. His heart rate picked up, and his eyes darted to her. *She hadn't removed her hand from mine.* He could feel, or more appropriately not feel, the spreading numbness now. It moved up his frozen arms and down where the back of his hand touched his leg towards his feet, radiating from where she touched him. It could have been blocker drugs, nanotech, something that made it past his implants without raising any alarms. And now he couldn't even move. She had him.

As the numbness reached his neck, he realized he was still breathing. Not death then, not right away at least. he retained control of his eyes and his ocular responded. He connected with the library network and sent a message into the buffer, one meant for Daruthr. He knew it would be there for anyone to read, sketched out against the background by moving his gaze, but had to hope it was enough. Daruthr would come for him. Then the numbness was at his neck, and he felt the world slip away, the letters of his message still emblazoned over his vision.

THEY'RE HERE.

HLÉHÉR

The trip back up from unconsciousness was, happily, far less painful than the last time he remembered. Once again, he felt the hardness of deck plates, but there was a sharp, burnt metal smell in the air. That and machine oil. A gentle hum pervaded the air, which was cool and dry. This did not feel like the comfortable climate control of the library. More cause for concern. He experimentally wiggled his toes and found them once more under his control. Either the sedative effect was relatively short, or he had been out a long time for it to have worn off completely. He checked his implants, and his ocular responded with a reassuring cursor. He opened his eyes, and saw nothing.

Well, perhaps not nothing. But nothing in the visible spectrum. A quick command to his ocular and the tiny room flared out in infrared. Two large, sliding doors that took up opposing walls, and a series of what appeared to be physical buttons arrayed on the wall. He thought at first he'd been relegated to an antique storage locker of some sort, but one of the doors was significantly colder than the other. He could make out that words were above the buttons but couldn't read them in the darkness. One button, the farthest to the right, appeared to have a manual safety covering, requiring any operator to flip it up before activation. It hit him then, and he felt a chill that had nothing to do with the temperature.

He was in an airlock.

Just as this revelation hit him, visible lights blinked on. He closed his eyes slightly and quickly flicked off the infrared of his ocular. The momentary pain of brightness passed as his eyes adjusted, and he could finally begin to take in his surroundings to their fullest extent. No gravity pulled him to the deck, and he drifted against a wall. The handhold nearest let him regain some measure of control.

He began to explore his cell, being sure not to touch any of the buttons. They were labeled, but not in any language he recognized. It looked like some similar shapes and letters to Imperial Common but they were either so ornately twisted as to be unreadable or were different altogether. Erick ran his fingertip across them. What lost language was this, that still persisted after so long, locked away in the secrets of the Abímbọlá Library? If it weren't for the fact that he was clearly being held in an airlock-he might actually care to explore that question. As it was, he was much more concerned with getting out. And since both windows were blocked he didn't know what he might be getting out into.

Getting out was going to take some doing. The lettering was unreadable to him, even engaging the onboard lexicon from his implants. If he attempted to guess at the wall controls, he was just as likely to blow himself into space as to open the interior door. He could assume that the large guarded button was likely the exterior door release, but that only told him one button *not* to push. He might be able to figure out the controls with trial and error, but you could still pump the air out of an airlock without opening the outer door. Without a suit in sight, he decided he'd rather err on the side of caution. Just as he'd decided not to push his luck, the window on the interior door flashed with light as someone uncovered it. On reflex, he dodged to press himself up against the door, out of sight of the window. Perhaps the airlock camera was out of service, as ancient as the machinery appeared.

"I know you're in there, Erick, and I know you're awake."

A sarcastic smile twisted his lips. Well, so much for cloak and dagger. They sounded pretty confident. He peeled himself off the wall, drifted as nonchalantly as he could, and hooked a toe hold in the center of the small room. Once there, he turned to look at the window, folding his arms and steeling himself. He thought he knew what to expect, but the face that greeted him sent an involuntary shiver down his spine.

Her eyes were great clipped ovals that took up half her head. Her nose was little more than two slits, vertical in the middle of a face that was long and stretched like beeswax left under the suntube. Her skin was pale, a white so much as to be nearly translucent. He could see the blue marbled tracery of veins under her skin, delicately enfolding her eyes and cheeks to form a spiderweb that disappeared into the high collar of her jacket.

Revenants. It was worse when she smiled.

"There you are, Erick of Ollson. We've been expecting you."

He laughed. Confidence was a brash ploy but all he had left to him. He had no idea if his message had even gotten out of the network to Daruthr. So, bluster and bluster more. "Oh, I highly doubt that. I didn't know I was coming here myself until a few days ago. But I figured I'd stop by, see the sights."

Her teeth were just a little too sharp. "I don't think you know as much as you think."

"Great. When can I leave?" Erick tried to keep ahold of his racing thoughts as we spoke. He knew that the message had made it to the buffer and would have his unique signature.

Daruthr would see it.

According to his ocular, he'd been out for about twelve hours. That was more than enough time for Daruthr to miss him. He'd have gotten the message by now, and surely he'd have intercepted them if they tried to take him off the Library asteroid. Which meant he was still on Abímbọlá.

"You're not still on Abímbọlá, if that's what you're wondering." Erick couldn't help but literally swallow his surprise. "You know, there is an ancient saying, about a duck. Do you know what a duck is?" He nodded, but the woman continued as if he hadn't answered. "It was an ancient bird. They used to sit on the water's surface, float there and swim around. They looked so calm and peaceful, gliding across the wavetops. But under the surface, their legs were churning over and over to propel them along. Just like you Erick of Ollson. Calm on the surface, but inside, I know you're panicking."

He focused on his breathing, automatically counting along with the breaths. Four count in, four count out, feel the heartbeat. He wouldn't give the Revenant woman the satisfaction of knowing she was right. She was fishing, had to be. The question he really had was what did she want from him?

He tried some fishing of his own. "I wouldn't call it panicking. But either way, how long are we going to keep this up before the next thing?"

She laughed again, shaking her head and looking down. "Oh, you poor simple man. What do you think? We are trying to ransom you? Kill you outright?" She paused, then looked back up to meet his eyes. "I don't think we should spend the carbon to keep you alive, but we aren't going to space you immediately."

Well, at least there was that. He tried again. "So no ransom, no immediate death. What do you want with me?" Erick walked back towards the window, drawing close to it. His face was only a few feet from hers through the glass, and he could now make out every detail of her. Her hair, thick and black, was cropped down to a hand's width, and stuck out at odd angles. Her too-large eyes held a predatory gleam.

"We didn't want you at all. You're merely an annoyance, as far as I'm concerned."

Finally, an opening for a personal relationship. Maybe. he took a stab in the dark. "I'd hate to concern you with my presence. Speaking of, you have me at a disadvantage. You know my name, but I don't know yours."

She paused, her stare withering. "Nevant."

"Nevant. Well, all things considered, nice to meet you."

"Trust me, I'd rather have skipped this entirely. Unfortunately, like I said, you're coming with us."

"Don't be so sure about that."

"If you're referring to the message you sent Daruthr, he's not going to rescue you."

Erick's head spun. How much did she know? She seemed so confident in her statement. Surely Daruthr could find him, given time.

Nevant cocked her head as a vibration began. She flicked her wrist, fingers outstretched, and Erick's ocular flashed him a notification of available feed. He subscribed, a small window opening in his vision, and found a view of Abímbọlá Library from the outside, several kilometers away.

The library station began to slip slowly down in the feed, then faster and faster, until it disappeared into the bottom of the field of view. Chunks of rock, ice, and dust began to flash past, first small, then larger. Abímbọlá appeared again in the top of the feed, racing down to be lost again. Erick realized that the camera was on something that was rotating, shedding rock and ice. As if some ancient body had begun to spin after centuries of stillness. He felt a hint of gravity, pulling his toes to the deck.

"We're on a companion asteroid to Abímbọlá, then. And spinning."

Nevant nodded. "Yes. It's time to put on some gravity. None of your fancy field tech here."

So we are on a ship. "This is Revenant ship, isn't it." Erick felt his heart pick up. Escape had just become a lot more complex. "And where are we headed, then?"

Nevant walked slowly to the glass of the airlock door, and Erick realized how tall she was. Stretched, elongated. Her head was just a little too large for her neck. *Low gravity.*

Nevant smiled, her teeth too long. "We go to rendesvousz with the World Fleet."

Erick's gut tightened. The Revenant fleet caught on the Gjoll surveillance array heading toward Ife. The fleet that had instigated everything by attacking the Obershires disguised as Ollson ships. But how many Revenant ships had there been, only a few dozen? That couldn't have been the world fleet. "And then what?"

She turned and began walking away, throwing her answer over her shoulder. "Then we go to the core. To the Throneworld." She paused before turning the corner to look back at Erick, the force of her gaze a flame that licked at his skin.

"We go to justice."

IRON ON THE TONGUE

Signup for free original fiction!

Buy books and schwag and support independent authors!